Reap the Whirlwind

ABOUT THE AUTHOR . . .

BERNICE M. CHAPPEL was associated with the field of education in Michigan for twenty-nine years. During this time she was a classroom teacher for nineteen years, followed by ten years as a school social worker. She holds a Bachelor of Science degree from Eastern Michigan University and a Master's degree in Education from the University of Michigan.

Since her retirement, Bernice M. Chappel has visited nearly every country in North and Central America, several in South America, most of the Asian countries and a few European nations.

REAP THE
WHIRLWIND

A Documentary
of Early Michigan

Bernice M. Chappel

WILDERNESS ADVENTURE BOOKS

Copyright © 1987 by Bernice M. Chappel

Library of Congress
Catalog Card Number: 87-50674

ISBN: 0-9611596-8-5

Typesetting by
LaserText Typesetting Services
3886 Sheldrake Avenue
Okemos, Michigan 48864

Published by
Wilderness Adventure Books
320 Garden Lane
Box 968
Fowlerville, Michigan 48836

Manufactured in the United States of America

CONTENTS

Also by Bernice M. Chappel

_____

In the Palm of the Mitten

Bittersweet Trail

Lure of the Arctic

Cover Design by Marjorie Nash Klein

Typography by Thomas Boufford

PREFACE

Reap the Whirlwind is a documented account of the Territory and State of Michigan covering the years between 1795 and 1866. Historical events, involving nearly one hundred real people of the time, are shown as they are experienced by members of the Parker family. (The historical characters mentioned in the book are listed on page 411.)

The plot revolves around injustices which were inflicted upon American Indian and Negro peoples and the way in which the Parker family and their Quaker friends attempt to improve conditions.

Actual accounts of punishment of crime at public whipping posts and death on the gallows, the heart-wrenching banishment of Indian tribes from the state, daring Underground Railroad Negro escapes to Canada, and the terrible experiences of Union and Confederate soldiers in the Civil War, all give an accurate picture of the early years of life in Michigan.

Bernice M. Chappel
1987

Chapter One
1795 — 1815

THE ORPHAN

1795

1

LUCRETIA WAKENED WITH A START. Had she been dreaming again? Ed breathed softly beside her. She sighed. If it was God's will, she must accept the fact that she would be childless.

There it was again. A shiver ran up her back. "Ed! Ed!" she called as she seized her husband's shoulder. "Are thee awake? I hear a baby crying!"

Ed sighed. "Go to sleep. 'Tis cats fighting."

She sprang from bed and felt her way toward the door. The wailing continued. A prayer raced through her mind. "Please, God, let it be a baby." In her haste she stubbed her toe on a chair. Oblivious to the pain, she yanked the door open. In the darkness something light-colored writhed on the porch floor as the high-pitched wails continued.

Cautiously she reached toward the squirming thing.

Her hand touched something soft—something knitted. A knitted blanket!

Seizing the screaming, wriggling bundle, she rushed inside. "Ed!" she shouted. "Thee must get up! 'Tis a baby! Light the candle! Hurry! Hurry!"

Muttering under his breath, Ed groped about on the table until he found the candlestick which he held to a faint glow of dying coals in the fireplace. Lucretia rushed to the table to unwrap the screaming, kicking baby.

"Hm-m-m," Ed said softly. "Thee was right. Thee did hear a baby." He held the candle so the flickering light fell on the wailing infant's face. "Homely little mite, ain't it?"

Lucretia bristled. "How can thee say such a thing? 'Tis a beautiful baby." She gazed adoringly at the newborn child as she clasped it to her breast. "Would thee make a fire so we can heat milk?" She dragged a straight chair to the fireplace. Her husband hastily pulled on his knee-length black trousers and draped a shawl about her shoulders.

"Thee will catch thy death of cold in thy night clothes," Ed remarked. The wailing continued.

Going to the fireplace he laid kindling on the dying coals and waited for it to catch fire. "Who does thee think left the little tyke here?"

"I don't know, but surely 'twas the hand of God that sent this baby to us." Lucretia slowly unwrapped the child from the cream-colored knitted blanket. "Someone must have loved this baby," she commented, "to have wrapped it in this nice blanket." She unfastened the infant's diaper. "Wet," she murmured as the child's screams continued.

"Ed! 'Tis a boy!"

He rushed to her side. "So it is. Angry little bugger, ain't he? He's screamed 'til his face is blue."

Lucretia hastily covered the tiny body. "Thee would be angry, too, if thee were newborn and someone had left thee on a cold porch in November. Ed, he can't be but a few hours old. The cord looks like it had just been cut."

Ed shook his head. "'Tis strange. Some young girl must have been in the family way and she couldn't keep him. But why did she leave him here?"

Lucretia slowly rocked the baby in her arms. "'Twas the hand of God guiding her," she murmured. "God has answered my prayers." Suddenly the wailing stopped and the baby opened his eyes. Lucretia smiled. "See? He knows I love him and that I need him." She brushed the dark fuzz on the child's head with her lips. "Would thee heat a little milk for him?"

Ed threw wood on the fire and hung a small container of milk from the crane. Slowly he said, "Thee knows this baby likely was conceived in sin. Does it matter to thee?"

Lucretia's voice was low but forceful. "However he was conceived, he had nothing to do with how it happened. Thee and me will raise him as our son—the son we've prayed for for ten years." She studied the infant's features. "Dark hair, blue eyes—Ed, methinks he resembles us."

Ed laughed. "Come now. That is wishful thinking. But his coloring is like ours, ain't it? He looks better when he's not crying."

"Thee will love him, Ed. But we have to feed him and put a dry diaper on him. What can we use?"

Ed removed the milk container from the crane. "If thee will tell me what thee need, I'll get it."

"Get a hand towel. That will do for a diaper. And one of my new handkerchiefs from the top bureau drawer—and he has to have clothes. There's so much to do."

Ten minutes later the baby, wrapped in his blanket and in a dry diaper, ravenously sucked on a milk-soaked nipple made from one of Lucretia's choice handkerchiefs. As she cuddled the child she nodded when Ed remarked, "Now I know why thee was saving those handkerchiefs. Thee has said for five years, 'They're too nice to blow my nose on.' "

Warm, dry, and with a full stomach, the baby slept in Lucretia's arms. Ed sat nearby. Finally he said, "Can't we make him a bed in a bureau drawer? 'Tis late and thee needs sleep."

"Thee go to bed. I couldn't sleep. I'm too happy and thankful." He didn't answer. Soon she continued. "What would thee like to name our son?"

"I'd like a good English name. I'd like to name him for my father."

"Henry. Henry Oliver Parker. That's nice, Ed."

Young Henry Oliver Parker sighed with contentment as he sucked vigorously on his cloth nipple.

1802

2 ———————————————————

Lucretia bustled about laying out clean clothes for her seven-year-old son. "Come, Henry," she said. " 'Tis time for thee to get dressed for First Day Meeting."

The boy ignored his mother's request and continued playing on the floor. She went to the bedroom and soon returned dressed in the typical dark clothing of the Quaker women of the time.

"Son, put the top away. Father has gone to get Polly and she's already hitched to the buggy. Thee must get dressed for Meeting."

The boy smiled at his mother, a smile that never failed to melt her heart. "Son wants to play with the top. See how good I can spin it?"

"Thee does well, but thee must stop now."

" 'Tis hard to make it spin good. Now that I know how, I want to keep trying until it goes right every time."

"I know thee likes to do things right, and that's good. But thee can play again after Meeting. Now Henry, give me the top and get dressed."

The boy's face flushed. "No!" he shouted throwing the top against the wall with such force that it bounced halfway across the room. He jumped up. "I'm not going to Meeting! I won't sit there doing nothing!"

The door opened. "Are thee ready?" Ed shouted. "We're going to be late!" He glanced from Henry to Lucretia. "What's wrong?"

The boy stamped his foot. "I ain't going to Meeting!"

Ed removed his flat, broad-brimmed black hat. He stroked his dark beard. Finally he said firmly, "This family goes to Meeting together, Son. Either thee will get dressed or I will dress thee like a baby."

The child's blue eyes flashed as he stamped into the bedroom to put on a smaller version of clothing identical in style and color to that worn by his father. He emerged from the room and went to the buggy in sullen silence.

" 'Tis sunny but cold," Ed remarked. "Soon now we'll have snow. This year, Henry, thee will build big snow men."

"I can't make them good like thee. And I can't spin the top good like thee. I can't do anything as good as thee can!"

Ed clucked to the sleek bay mare. "Get up, Polly. We're late." He put his hand on Henry's knee. "When I was seven years old I couldn't do the things thee can. I couldn't read or figger until I was nine years old. But I learned how to do other things by watching and by helping my father."

"Was that Henry Oliver Parker, like me?"

Ed nodded. "Thee are still a child and God does not expect children to do things perfectly. They learn by doing things over and over. Thee are too hard on thyself."

Henry smiled the dazzling smile which signified to his parents that an apology was coming. "I'm sorry I was rude."

Lucretia's heart melted. "All is forgiven," she murmured. In a moment she continued. "At Meeting today thee should pray that God will help thee to control thy temper. Thee are like two boys—one polite and loving and the other angry and wanting to hurt people. Ask God to help thee to hold thy tongue when it wants to say rude things."

"Yes, Mama, I will."

They rode in silence for several minutes before Lucretia said, "Methinks I'll invite the Hoyles for First Day Dinner." Ed nodded his agreement.

Soon they pulled up at the plain Meeting House. Boys and bearded men tied the horses in the shed while white-capped women and girls in dark shawls and dresses went inside.

Lucretia loved First Day worship. She was thankful this day that harmony had been restored to her family. She had looked forward all week to the hour of silence in the Meeting House. There, in the general silence, all worry was cleared from her mind. She believed it was an experiencing of the presence of God. At times, when because of illness or extremely bad weather, she was unable to attend First Day Meeting, she felt empty and deprived.

The Meeting House was nearly filled, men and boys on one side, women and girls on the other. The Elders sat on benches at the front. The plain, straight, hard pews, the plain white walls, the drab clothing of the people, and the worn Bibles, all were pleasing to Lucretia.

Silence was not continuous for the hour of worship. Out of it came testimonies, questions, prayers and exhortations from worshipers who felt moved to speak. A few people were exhorters who told in detail what God had revealed to them when they had sought Him.

After a few minutes of silence for worship, John Becket rose to his feet. "Friends," he said, "I cannot delay my strong convictions about the issue of slavery. As thee all know, the Society of Friends in England started an anti-slavery movement many years ago—back in 1671. We American Quakers took up the fight that began more than a hundred years ago." [1, 2]

John Becket's voice was soft, but forceful, not the voice of a man easily angered, or of a man who readily backed down. He did not speak often in Meeting. Everyone listened attentively.

He continued. "But we are not doing enough to stop the evil system of slavery, and though our state of New York abolished slavery a few years ago, we all know it flourishes in the South. Since the Fugitive Slave Law was passed in 1793 the United States government allows slave owners to claim escaped slaves if the owners give proof of ownership before a magistrate." He paused. "Friends, our duty is first to God and humanity, and second to the government. We all know of the heavy penalties given to persons who aid a slave's escape or who interfere with the owner's recovery.

"The Bible warns us. It says, 'They have sown the wind and they shall reap the whirlwind.' God will punish this country if we don't stop the buying and selling of humans.

"I'm speaking only for myself," Becket said softly, "but if slave catching is what is required of me by my government, I shall turn my back on my government. I cannot help the government to continue the practice of enslaving human beings." He sat down and wiped his brow.

Charles Hoyle rose as John Becket sat down. "There is much sin in the world," he said, "and many people suffer. It is unjust, but this meeting is for worship. We are not here to discuss what is right or wrong with our government."

Lucretia rose. Her voice trembled. "We worship God by our actions. In aiding slaves as in helping other unfortunate people, we worship God." She sat down aware that Henry was listening intently.

After the service the women chatted with neighbors while the men brought the buggies from the shed. Lucretia spoke to Mary Becket. "I agree completely with thy husband on the slavery problem," she said quietly. "I wish we could do more."

Mary nodded and whispered, "Perhaps thee can—sooner than thee might think."

Sarah Hoyle came outside and Lucretia hurried to speak to her. "We'd like Charles and Sam and thee to take First Day dinner with us," she said.

"Thank you, Lucretia. We'd like that. We'll drive along behind you."

As Polly trotted on through the bright November sunshine, Ed and Lucretia discussed the evils of slavery. "Can thee imagine if we were slaves that our owner might sell Henry to one plantation, me to another miles away and thee, Ed, to still another? We might never see one another again."

Henry asked, "Do they do that, Papa?"

Ed nodded. "Just like we sell cows and horses. If I have chances I will help every slave to escape that I can." He looked into Henry's troubled eyes. "But Son, anything thee hears thy mother or me say about helping slaves to escape is not to be repeated. Thee must not talk to others about it."

"Yes, Papa, I'd like to help them too."

At the Parker home the men unhitched the horses and put them in the barn. The women went inside where Lucretia placed more wood on the smoldering fire. Taking Sarah's shawl she said, "The chicken should be 'most done. It was simmering when we left for Meeting." They visited about the children and housekeeping as they worked.

Sam and Henry had followed the men to the barn. Henry showed his friend the calf his father had given him for his seventh birthday. The family dog was at the boys' heels, his plume-like tail waving happily.

"Yellow Boy likes the calf," Henry said. "Has thee noticed dogs like little animals?"

Sam stared at the calf. "I'd like a calf of my own, but Pa won't give me one. He says I have to earn it. Did thee have to earn this one?"

"No." He rubbed the calf's ears. "What does thee have to do to earn a calf?"

Sam hesitated. "I have to do better in school."

Henry nodded. "Thee doesn't read and spell very well," he agreed.

The barn door slammed as Ed and Charles went to the house. Henry continued. "Why doesn't thee work harder at school? Thee just sits and don't do anything. I like learning new things."

Sam's fair complexion grew red. "I have other things to think about, like why does thee have a calf and I can't have one? Why am I punished—spanked—for everything I do wrong and thee ain't?"

"I don't know. Our parents ain't alike."

Sam stopped in front of Henry, his face flaming red as he stared into Henry's eyes. "Thee is right! I am a Hoyle but thee ain't a Parker. The Parkers ain't your parents! I heard Pa and Ma talking. They said your own mother didn't want you and she left you on Parker's porch. Everybody knows about you!"

Henry's fist met Sam's chin with a resounding *thwack*. As he fell Sam's hat sailed under the calf's feet. By this time both boys were rolling and punching one another on the floor of the calf pen. Yellow Boy barked wildly and pulled on Sam's jacket.

"Thee lies!" Henry yelled as he again landed a punch on Sam's nose. Blood spurted.

Sam raked fingernails across Henry's face. "I didn't lie! Thee's an orphan! Thy mother didn't want thee! She left thee like we drop kittens at somebody's farm!"

Henry's fists flailed wildly. Sam was no match for the enraged boy. Finally, spitting out two front teeth, he gasped, "I've had enough."

"I ain't! Thee are going to take back what thee said!" Henry continued punching and pounding Sam as they rolled on the manure-covered straw. "Take it back! Say it's a lie!"

Yellow Boy's barks became frantic high-pitched yips. The barn doors opened. "Boys!" Ed called. "Come to dinner!" He hurried toward the calf pen where Yellow Boy barked wildly. "Henry! What are thee doing? Let Sam up!" He grabbed the boy by the collar and lifted him off the floor before setting him on his feet. He helped Sam up as he inspected the children. "Thy mothers will be indignant! Two Quaker boys fighting like street urchins!"

Sam, bent over, coughed and spat. A trickle of blood ran from both nostrils.

Ed repeated, "Thy mothers will be indignant when they see your best First Day clothes all torn and covered with calf manure. Whatever ails thee?"

Henry wiped his scratched face on the back of his hand as he glared at the spitting, coughing, disheveled figure leaning against the gate of the calf pen. "He lied, Pa! He's telling lies about us! He's going to take back what he said or I'll—I'll—" Suddenly great sobs broke from the boy's throat. His shoulders shook.

Sam stopped spitting long enough to shout, "I didn't lie! Ask your Pa!" He searched in his pocket for a handkerchief.

"What does thee want to ask me, Henry?"

The boy continued sobbing. Ed turned to Sam. "What did thee say to Henry?"

Sam wiped his nose gently. "I told him he ain't a Parker and that his mother left him on your porch. 'Tis no lie!"

Suddenly the barn was very still. The only sound was that of the calf nuzzling her hay in the manger. Henry's blue eyes were fixed on his father's face. "Tell him he's lying, Pa," the boy begged.

Ed put his arms about his son. "He's not lying. 'Tis the truth." His voice was sad.

Without a word or a backward look Henry dashed outside and ran pell mell into the thick maple woods behind the barn.

3   *1812*

THE COLD APRIL RAIN PATTERED on the roof of the Parker cabin. Inside the candle-lighted home was warm and cozy. The fire in the fireplace threw flickering shadows on the wall and on Ed's and Henry's backs as they sat reading. Lucretia, on the opposite side of the table, knitted rapidly, occasionally glancing up at her men.

Ed muttered, " 'Tis going to come to war. I don't favor war but President Madison and Congress won't take much more from Great Britain."

Henry stared at the flickering candle. "The country ain't ready for war with Great Britain. We only have a small army and a few seagoing ships, while Great Britain has more than a hundred battleships. From what I read, much of the country don't want war."

Ed nodded. "Yet I can see how the president and Congress feel. We can't allow Great Britain to board our ships, take our men by force and compel them to serve in the British Navy. I gather that many of the men that are seized are American citizens, though Great Britain claims she only takes former British seamen."

Lucretia put her knitting away and went to the water-pail on the kitchen table. She drank from the long-handled dipper which was used by the entire family. Talk of war disturbed her. Quakers, when they felt strongly about an issue, would defend their belief even if it meant war, but she hoped Ed and Henry were not ready to commit themselves to favoring war with Great Britain.

Outside old Yellow Boy set up a din with his furious barking. Lucretia opened the door as a dark figure came up the steps.

"Evening, Lucretia," the man said as he tipped his flat black hat.

John Becket. Her heart pounded. She knew what he wanted. "Come in, John," she said softly. "Are there others with thee?" He nodded. "Bring them in."

Henry and Ed hurried to the door. "How many has thee?" Ed inquired.

"Two. A man and his wife. Can thee take them to the next station tonight?"

"I'll take them," Henry volunteered. For several years he had known about his parents' involvement with escaping slaves. Occasionally in the night he had been wakened by whispered conversations followed by the hushed voices of his mother as she fed the frightened people in preparation for the trip to the next station.

"Are thee sure thee wants to get involved? Thee are young, only seventeen, and if thee are caught it means jail," Ed warned.

John Becket went to the buggy and spoke quietly to the occupants who followed him up the path toward the porch.

Henry already had his jacket on and his hat in hand. " 'Tis time I do my part. I'll hitch Polly up and have the buggy here by the time they've had a lunch. Where do I take them?"

Ed said, "I'll go with thee to the barn and give thee directions." He took his jacket from the hook beside the door as John escorted two frightened-appearing Negroes into the house.

"This is Cindy and Joe," John said. "I'll leave now. Henry here will drive thee. Thee are in good hands."

"Thank you. Thank you," they murmured.

Lucretia closed the door as Ed and Henry went toward the barn. "I'll have something for thee to eat in a minute. Sit at the table."

The woman looked to be about twenty-five, Lucretia thought as she observed the worn wrinkled clothing. The man might be a little older. "Don't be frightened. Thee will soon be on thy way." The man nodded. They sat without speaking.

Quickly Lucretia sliced bread and cold ham which she placed on the table with a pitcher of milk. "Go ahead—eat. Don't wait." She set plates, cups and silverware before them.

Five minutes later Henry was at the door. After murmured thanks the Negroes were hurried to the buggy. As they pulled onto the narrow deserted road Henry spread a blanket across their knees. " 'Twill help keep thee dry," he said. " 'Tis a miserable wet night. We should be to the next station by nine o'clock." They didn't answer.

"Been on the road long?" Henry asked.

"Four nights," Joe replied. "People is been good to us. We don't know who they is, but they is good to us."

Henry explained, "We don't tell our last names. It's safer that way for thee and for us."

No one spoke for several minutes. The horse trotted along splashing through mud puddles. "Does thee have children?" Henry asked.

"We's had two. They's dead," Cindy replied.

"I'm sorry."

Joe's controlled voice revealed anger as he said, "Massa whipped them so bad they died."

A chill ran up Henry's back followed by a flash of

anger. When he had his emotions under control he said calmly, "How old were thy children?"

"Four. They was twin boys," Joe replied.

"What did they do to be whipped so bad?"

For a moment neither parent answered. Then Cindy said softly, "I worked in Massa's house. He told the boys not to come there. I was working in the kitchen and didn't know they was in the dining room looking at the purty things—purty dishes. Massa catched them there and yelled, 'Git out!' They was so scared they bumped into a dish cabinet. It tipped over and broke many dishes."

"He whipped them so bad they died because they broke those dishes?" Henry asked.

"Yes sir," Joe answered. "He hit their haids."

"Did he have a doctor?"

"No sir. He says he's got lots a little nigger boys. When our boys died, Cindy and me run away. We is goin' to Canada." Joe spoke in a flat tone of voice.

They were silent for some time. Finally Henry said, "I figger we should be there soon. My father said the house is just beyond a white church on the left. Someone there will take thee to the next station."

Fifteen minutes later they passed the church. Just beyond a house showed through the mist. "They've gone to bed," Henry said. "Wait here." He ran up to the front door and knocked—three slow raps followed by four fast ones. He waited a few moments and repeated the signal. Suddenly the door opened.

"I have some merchandise for thee," Henry said to the figure in the darkened doorway.

"Fine. Fine. How many?"

"Two."

"Bring them in."

When Henry returned with his passengers a young man held the door open. "I'm John," he said cordially.

Henry replied, "I'm Henry and this is Cindy and Joe."

A door opened and a young girl appeared. "Do the people need a lunch?" she asked.

"Thank you," Joe replied. "We ain't hungry."

The girl threw wood on the smoldering fireplace coals. John said, "This is my sister, Susan. There's no need for our parents to get up. I'll take Cindy and Joe to the next station."

Five minutes later the passengers were loaded and John drove onto the deserted road.

" 'Tis a good night for our business," Henry observed with a smile.

"You didn't meet anyone?" Susan asked.

"No, 'twas smooth sailing all the way." He grinned. "And there's 'most enough water in the road to sail."

"Sit down, Henry. It's a long drive back and Mother made a custard pie for supper. Would you like a piece?"

"Thanks, I would." He watched Susan with an appreciative eye. She was slender, of medium height with sparkling blue eyes, golden hair and a lovely complexion. Her light-colored flowered dress was dainty and attractive.

"Sit anywhere at the table," she called. "I'll only be a minute."

Soon she was back with two pieces of pie and a pitcher of milk. "You've never been here before," she said as she sat across the table from Henry.

"No. My father has though. He's Ed—Ed Parker."

"I know him. Then you're Henry Parker."

"That's right. And you're Susan—?"

"Susan Thompson, the daughter of Rev. Richard Thompson, Methodist minister. There—you know all about me except that my mother is named Josephine."

"Mrs. Thompson makes very good pie," Henry said with appreciation. "Can thee bake pie?"

"Of course, though it's not as good as Mother's. You're

of the Quaker faith, aren't you?"

Henry laughed. "My 'thees' and 'thous' gave thee a clue. Yes, we are Quakers."

"They're good people Father says."

A sudden knock ended the pleasant conversation. Susan went to the door.

"Can I come in?" A swarthy man pushed his way past Susan. "I'm Sheriff Calkins from the County Seat. I hear you have guests."

"We have no guests, Sheriff, except my friend Henry Parker. He's just about to leave."

"Where's the minister?"

"In bed. I'll call him." She went to an adjoining door and called, "Father, we have company."

"Where's your brother?" the sheriff asked.

"I really don't know. Sometimes he visits Sally Holmes. He'll likely be home soon, if you care to wait."

The sheriff directed his attention to Henry. "You're Henry Parker?"

"Yes."

"Where are you from?"

"About fifteen miles west of here."

"Why are you here?"

"I'm calling on my lady friend, Miss Thompson."

"You come here often?"

"Not as often as I'd like, but as often as Miss Thompson allows."

Rev. Thompson, a tall man with white hair, came through the bedroom door. "I heard the conversation," he said. "Did you wish to see me?"

The sheriff shook his head. "I understood you were to have guests tonight. I'd like to inquire as to the where-abouts of your son."

Susan hastened to add, "I've already told him, Father, that John may be calling on Sally."

Rev. Thompson nodded. "Yes, yes. A young man of twenty is expected to go courting, even on such a night as this. Have you forgotten, Sheriff?"

The sheriff snorted. "Reverend, will you say on your honor that you have no other guests than Henry Parker?"

"We have no other guests than Henry Parker."

The sheriff turned. "You're known to be an honorable, honest man. Your word is good enough for me. I'm sorry to have disturbed you. Good night." The door closed.

Susan collapsed into her chair. "That was close. If Cindy and Joe had waited for a lunch, he'd have caught all of us red-handed."

Rev. Thompson said thoughtfully, "We're going to have to find other stations. They're watching us, and Henry, you'd better tell your father they'll be checking on your family. The sheriff is smart. He'll sniff out every clue. Those rewards paid by slave owners are tempting to some people."

Susan worried, "I hope John will make it back safely."

Rev. Thompson nodded. "He will unless an officer is waiting for him at the next station. We take chances, but we go into this work with our eyes open. I consider that helping the slaves escape from bondage to be a part of God's work." He turned toward the bedroom. "Nice meeting you, Henry," he said over his shoulder.

The door closed and Henry got up. "I must be going. Can I call on thee sometime soon?"

Susan smiled coquettishly. "Fifteen miles is a long way."

" 'Twouldn't seem far if I was coming to see thee."

"Do you say pretty things like that to all the girls?"

"Just to the specially nice ones. How about next Seventh Day?"

"Seventh Day?"

Henry laughed. "You call it Saturday. Can I come over next Saturday evening?"

"I'll expect you. Come for supper and I'll bake you a pie."

"I'll be here." He put on his flat black hat with the wide brim. "It's been nice meeting thee, Susan." He took her hand. "Good night, I'll see thee Saturday."

In spite of his narrow escape from the law, Henry was in high spirits as he drove home through the mist and rain.

4 ——————————— *1815*

LUCRETIA SILENTLY SET BOILED potatoes, dandelion greens and fried salt pork on the table. Henry noticed his mother's missing front teeth and gray-streaked hair. His father, too, was aging. They were satisfied with their monotonous slow-paced life, but he wanted more than this. He wanted adventure, success and money to buy expensive things. And he wanted to share his life with Susan.

After the usual moment of meditation which preceded Quaker meals, Ed said, "Thee are very quiet, Henry. What is on thy mind?"

"Thee will not be surprised that Susan and I will marry." He piled his plate with the plain food.

For several moments no one spoke. Then Lucretia said hesitantly, "Are thee sure thee wants to marry?"

" 'Tis a big step," Ed commented.

"Thee would like me to marry a Quaker girl, I know. But from the first time I saw her I wanted Susan for my wife. Thee don't want me to marry a Methodist. Is that it?"

"They are different from us. 'Tis not good to have two religions in the home," Lucretia said.

"Quakers and Methodists pray to the same God," Henry

remarked. A long silence followed.

Finally Lucretia asked, "Has thee told Susan about thyself?"

"She knows I am an orphan."

"Thee hasn't told her about thy temper? She should know about thy—thy spells."

Henry shoved his chair away from the table. His face was contorted with anger. "Thee never lets me forget! Like everyone else thee thinks I'm a worthless orphan whose mother threw me away and left me to die in the cold! I'll show them all—thee and all the other sanctimonious Quakers! And I'll show my mother who—who threw me away! Someday I'll own more land and have more money than any of them!" He picked his chair up and slammed it down violently.

"Sit down, Son," Ed said. "I want to talk to thee—quietly." He waited until Henry finally returned to the table.

"Thy mother and I know it has been hard growing up where everyone knew about thee. We know children have teased thee, and we understand why there were so many arguments and fistfights. Thee came into this world screaming and thee has been screaming ever since. But screaming doesn't change anything. It only makes other people unhappy." He paused. Henry stared at his plate.

Lucretia continued. "We loved thee the moment we found thee. Thee has always been a greatly loved son, the only child we ever had. From what we've seen of her, we believe Susan is a fine Christian girl, though we do wish she was of the Quaker faith." She paused.

"But Son, thee should tell her about thy temper and that thee has never learned to control it. She has seen only the pleasant, polite Henry who knows how to make people like him. She hasn't seen the Henry who cannot stand the slightest criticism without flying into a rage and who says cruel things to those closest to him. Son, truly I fear for thy marriage to Susan unless—"

Henry jumped up. "That's right. Keep nagging. I'm a no good bastard! Thee feels like all the others! But I'll marry Susan and we'll get away from this damned Quaker settlement!" He went outside slamming the door so hard the cabin walls shook.

References

[1]Joseph Gaer, *How the Great Religions Began* (Dodd Mead and Co., 1956).

[2]*World Book Encyclopedia,* Q Book (*See* "Quakers").

Chapter Two
1816 — 1829

FAMILY RELATIONSHIPS

1816

1 ─────────────────────────────

Susan's father, the Rev. David Thompson, nervously ran his hand through his wavy white hair. John and Henry sat with him at the table in the parsonage while Susan rattled dishes in the kitchen. The young men studied the distraught older man.

"This has been a sorrowful week for our family," he said. Tears stood in his eyes. "Your mother's death, John—it's hard."

John nodded. "I'll take over as many of your ministerial duties as I can. You can advise me, and together we'll manage."

The older man's eyes fell on Henry. "You and Susan had planned to marry this fall before—before Josephine took sick."

Henry studied the cover of the Bible on the table. "I

understand that you need Susan here now."

Suddenly changing the subject the old man asked, "How is your family fixed for food this winter?"

"Like everyone else, they don't have much. The unbelievable summer of 1816 has passed, but its results will be felt for a year. There will be starvation this winter." He paused. " 'Tis hard to believe—frost every month all summer, snow until near the end of June, almost no sunshine—"[1]

John said, "They're calling 1816 'the year without a summer'—and they could add, 'the winter without food'."

Henry said, "My father will turn the livestock out to pick for themselves. He doesn't have much hay or grain. They'll come into the barn to get out of the cold, but there won't be food for them—or much for us. We'll manage by trapping muskrats to add to our meat supply, and we'll kill some of the animals when we're forced to. 'Twill be a long hard winter."

John said, "I read that there were frosts as far south as New Jersey. And what are people going to do for seed—corn, wheat, oats and barley—to grow their crops next summer? What do you suppose caused the cold dark summer?"

Rev. Thompson replied. "When I was in Watervliet a few days ago the town crier read an annoucement. He said that there was a terrific volcanic eruption on the island of Java earlier this year."

Henry asked, "Where's Java?"

"It's in the Indian Ocean off the southeast coast of Asia. This terrific volcanic eruption threw ashes and gases and dust into the air where they were carried by the wind until they blanketed the earth, shutting out the sunlight and causing a change in the weather."

"Hm-m-m," Henry mused. "Think that's possible?"

John yawned. "It's possible, I suppose."

Susan came in with cups and a pot of tea. She smiled at Henry when she caught his eye. "Like everyone else, we're rationing our food," she said. "There's not much flour and it's expensive, so we're not having our usual sweets with Sunday evening tea."

"My mother is rationing our food too."

Rev. Thompson sipped his tea thoughtfully. Finally he said, "I have a suggestion for you, Henry and Susan. Why don't you go ahead with your plans for marriage? Josephine would want it that way. Then you two could live here with John and me."

Henry's face brightened. "What do you think, Susan?"

She hesitated. "I couldn't have a big wedding so soon after Mama's death," she said slowly.

Rev. Thompson suggested, "It needn't be a big wedding. Just Henry's parents and a few of both of your friends. I'll tie the knot whenever you say."

Henry rubbed his chin. "Food is scarce this winter, and I'd be another mouth to feed."

"You'd earn your keep. Because of his mother's illness and death, John is studying at home most of the time. Next year he'll go back to finish his work at the university. Then he'll be an ordained Methodist minister.

"There'd be plenty for you to do, Henry—wood to cut, the cows to milk, snow to shovel—there's enough to keep you busy. And you could hunt and trap to add to our supply of meat."

Henry glanced at Susan questioningly. She smiled and nodded. "Let's do it. That way I can keep house for all three of my men."

The old minister got up slowly. "Good. It's been a long day," he said. "I'll leave you young people to make your plans." He went into the bedroom as they murmured goodnight.

John got up. "I have reading to do," he said. "I'm glad

you have decided to go ahead with your plans."

The fire snapped in the fireplace. It seemed loud in the quiet room. Henry went to sit by Susan. He took her hand as he said, "Perhaps people will gossip if we marry so soon after Mrs. Thompson's death."

"Father always says if a person's conscience is clear, that's what is important in making decisions. I'm sure Mother would have approved." After a moment she asked, "Why are you concerned about what people might say?"

After a long pause he said softly, "I've told thee about —about—that I'm not the Parkers' own son. I don't know my real name. All my life I've been pointed out and talked —speculated about. It's important to me what people think. I have to make a name for myself through hard work. I will show people that I'm as successful as those who are born into good families."

Susan squeezed his hand. "I'm sure you will."

He continued. "I've been thinking that if I could get work next summer on Governor Clinton's ditch, it would be better money than I'd make as a hired hand on a farm."

"But you'd be gone all the summer months. And I've read that it will be hot, muddy work. Is it worth it?"

"I'm not afraid of hard work. I'd make good money for twenty-eight days of work a month, plus my room and board. And it will be exciting to be doing important work. The Erie Canal is going to make big changes in our country."[2]

"It will be years before it is finished. Will you be gone every summer?"

"I don't know. Let's take it a year at a time until we get a nice little nest egg. Then, when we have enough ahead, we'll decide what to do." He was silent for a time before he said, "People are talking about taking up land in the Territory of Michigan."

"Henry, that wouldn't be a pleasant life. Michigan's

nothing but a wilderness filled with hostile Indians, wild animals and swamps."

He shrugged. " 'Tis only an idea. We can't do anything until we get some money ahead."

She got up abruptly and threw wood on the fire. "Let's sit here," she suggested, "and plan for our marriage day."

As they sat down he brushed her forehead with a light kiss. "I've always dreamed of having a home of my own. I knew that night when I first saw thee four years ago that I wanted thee for my wife. I've loved thee for four years."

"I didn't know right away," she said, "but you've been so sweet and pleasant that—"

He squeezed her hand. "I should tell thee that I have a hot temper. I'm not always a pleasant person to be around."

She laughed. "Your feelings about yourself are showing. I'll help you bring out your good traits. Now, let's decide on a date for our marriage. How about three weeks from yesterday? That would be a Saturday."

" 'Tis fine with me." He took her in his arms and held her close until the wood in the fireplace burned down and became a bed of glowing coals.

2 *1818*

In THE FIFTY YEARS FOLLOWING THE war of 1812, America went canal crazy. A network of many miles of artificial waterways was built in the eastern part of the country. These canals provided a safe cheap system of transportation while they gave employment to thousands of men. [3]

The Erie Canal which was referred to by the citizens of New York state as "Governor Clinton's Ditch" was started in July of 1817. Hundreds of farmers left their farms in the care of wives and sons as they worked on the canal which would connect Lake Erie at Buffalo with the Hudson River at Albany along the route followed by the old Genesee Road. When completed the project would join the entire Great Lakes system with the Atlantic Ocean.

The Erie Canal was to be 363 miles long. It crossed farms, swamps and miles of wooded area. There were no powerful machines to do the work. It would be man power, horse power and mule power which dug the canal. [4]

For two summers Henry had been a canal worker along with thousands of other men, among them, three thousand Irish immigrants known as bogtrotters. These newcomers to America were given the least desirable work on the project. As they felled trees on the sixty-foot-wide clearing necessary for the canal right-of-way, Henry meditated about the lot of the bogtrotters who toiled in waist-deep mud in the swamps west of Syracuse. Wearing only a shirt and slouch cap to shield them from the relentless sun, they toiled on day after day. Mercilessly driven by bosses hired by rich contractors who had brought them to the United States from Ireland, they arrived in the country as indentured men who were obligated to repay by their labor the money that had been advanced to them.

The bogtrotters were in only a slightly better condition than the slaves of the South. Their food was the cheapest and coarsest the contractors could provide. At night they slept on the floor in shacks with a dozen other men. But what could they do? They were in America to escape starvation caused by a potato famine in Ireland. As a bonus to these unfortunate men, a tot (shot) of whiskey was doled out to them every two hours. And for this they were paid eight dollars a month.

As he swung his axe day after day, seven days a week, Henry compared his lot with that of the bogtrotters. His life was not easy but he was progressing financially. In a few years if he continued summer work on the canal and clerked in Evans Department Store in Watervliet during the winter months when he was home, he and Susan would be able to buy a farm. Or perhaps his secret dream would be realized and they could purchase land in the Territory of Michigan.

His daydream was interrupted by the arrival of a stray mongrel dog which sought him out several times daily. He paused a few seconds to pat the animal's head. "No food for you this time, Pete," he said resuming the rhythmic swinging of the axe. The sounds of chopping axes and falling trees reverberated through the woods. The dog trotted on.

Only a few more months, Henry thought, and he'd be going home for the winter. Hard as it was being separated from Susan and little Fred, it was worth the sacrifice. The baby was already more than a year old. His child would never have to wonder who his parents were. He would always know they wanted him. They would train him carefully so that he could hold his head proudly in any company.

During the previous winter of 1817 Henry had first realized the joys of being a parent and of watching his son's mental and physical growth. He recalled the first time Fred held his arms out to be picked up, and the joy of cuddling the soft little body of his son.

There had been times, too, that Henry tried to put from his mind—the occasions when Fred cried incessantly and neither Susan or Henry could quiet him—the times when he had lost his temper with the baby and had shaken him so violently that Susan's eyes flashed blue sparks as she rescued the child. He recalled her words. "He never did this until you came home! I don't know you when you have these insane spells! You are two different people, Henry, and one of them I don't like!" Later that day he had asked

Susan's forgiveness. "I forgive you," she had replied, "but I'm not the one to ask. Fred is the one you've hurt."

That violent temper. In spite of resolutions to control it, at the least provocation it flared into a conflagration.

3   *1821*

L<small>UCRETIA</small> <small>STUDIED</small> <small>THE</small> <small>FACIAL</small> features of her tiny granddaughter. Though her sight was dim, in imagination she saw a beautiful baby girl.

"God has smiled on thee, Susan," she murmured. "Two children, and thee will have more." She placed the baby over her shoulder and patted her back gently until little Emily loudly expelled an air bubble along with a dribble of milk from her tiny mouth. She grimaced.

Lucretia smiled, her lined face and dim eyes glowing. "There, there, little one. Now thee will feel better."

"Mother Parker, I think I'll start a big kettle of stew for supper. Then there will be some left for dinner tomorrow."

Lucretia brushed back a lock of gray hair. "That would be nice. Freddy likes stew, doesn't thee, Freddy?"

The sturdy little four-year-old came to lean against his Grandmother's knee. "I yike hot chocolate better."

Lucretia chuckled. "Thy Uncle John spoils thee. Good stew will make you grow to be a big strong man like thy father."

Susan dropped a peeled potato into a kettle of water. "John does spoil Fred. I wish John would find a nice young woman and get married. But he says he's happy the way things are."

"He has so much to do," Lucretia sighed. "Full time

minister at thy father's old church, then driving fifteen miles to keep things going here on the farm—'tis too much for one man."

"It will be better when Henry is home," Susan replied.

"When's Pa coming?" Fred asked.

"Most any day now." She spoke to Lucretia. "He might be here for our fifth wedding anniversary."

"Five years," Lucretia replied. "So much has happened in those years. Thy parents, both gone, thee and Henry have two children—Ed is gone, and I'm an old woman."

"In some ways," Susan began, "It seems longer than five years. Fred and I haven't had Henry with us for more than half of the time. I've grown to really dislike the Erie Canal for it takes Henry away from us. I can't see the money he makes as being more important than his family. He missed so much in being away from Fred. I feel each time he comes home they are like strangers."

"I think he will not go back next spring," Lucretia said. When he finds his father left the farm to him, he'll stay with thee and the children."

"And you, Mother Parker."

Lucretia placed the sleeping baby in her cradle. "And me." She returned to her chair. "There are still good times for us though some of our loved ones are gone."

Fred played on the floor with his wooden blocks. "I'm making a house," he said. "A big house."

"Can you count the blocks in your house?" Susan asked.

Fred smiled. "One, two, free, four, five, six, seven, eight, nine, ten! There are ten blocks."

"You're right. Your father will be proud of you. You count very well."

"Emily can't count," the boy said, "and she can't sing."

"That's right. You're a big boy and you can do many things a baby can't do."

Fred laughed. "I don't mess my pants like she does."

"No. But you did when you were a baby. Babies can't help it. They don't know any better."

"Grandma, do you want to hear me sing 'Gentle Jesus'?"

Lucretia nodded. "I'd like that."

Fred stood straight and tall in the center of the floor. He took a deep breath, then he launched into the Charles Wesley hymn:

> *Gentle Jesus, meek and mild,*
> *Look upon a little child.*
> *Pity my simplicity*
> *Suffer me to come to Thee.*

"How's that, Grandma?"

"Thee has a nice voice, Freddy, and thee carries a tune very well. When thy father comes be sure to show him how well thee can sing."

Susan dropped vegetables into the kettle of simmering meat. "I'm going out to take the wash off the line," she said, throwing a shawl about her shoulders.

Suddenly old Yellow Boy, his tail waving, began high-pitched barking as he slowly limped toward the road. Susan shaded her eyes a moment, then she ran toward Henry who rushed into her outstretched arms. They met and embraced, a violent, hungry embrace. Finally he held her at arm's length as he studied her face.

"You're as pretty as I remembered. It's good to be home," Henry said as Yellow Boy yipped excitedly, begging for attention. He patted the old dog's head. "Good dog," he murmured.

Hand in hand they went inside. Fred shouted, "Pa!" Lucretia greeted her son warmly as the boy danced about waiting to be noticed. Everyone was talking at the same time.

"Pa! I can count!" Fred shouted. "One, two, free, four, five, six, seven, eight, nine, ten! Ain't that good?"

Henry picked up the child. "You have grown, Fred, and you count very well. But you must learn to talk plainly. Can you say 'three' instead of 'free'?"

"Free!"

"No, 'three.' Say it again. 'Three.' "

"Free."

"That's baby talk. Say 'th, th, three.' "

"Fr, fr, free!"

Susan interrupted. "Henry, come see Emily."

They went into the bedroom while Fred climbed on Lucretia's lap. "Grandma, I ain't a big boy. I talk like a baby." Tears filled his eyes.

The old woman held him close. "Thy Papa has never had a little boy before. Thee talks just fine." She hugged him.

A wail from the bedroom announced Emily's wakening. Henry came to stand before the fireplace holding his screaming daughter.

"Does she cry like this often?" he asked.

"Sometimes when she's wakened suddenly. I think it startled her when you picked her up," Susan said softly. "Let me take her."

In a moment the baby was quiet as she stared at her father. "It will take her a few days to get acquainted with you," Susan said.

Henry studied Emily's face. "She's a pretty little thing when she's not crying. She looks like you."

"That's what everyone says. And Fred looks like you."

The little boy still sat on his grandmother's lap. "Thy son looks just the way thee did when thee was four."

Henry smiled. "But I didn't talk baby talk." Fred covered his face with both hands. "Don't hide your face, Son. Don't you want to see what I brought you?" He opened his grip which he had dropped by the door. Searching through his clothing he pulled out a rattle. "For Emily," he said.

Fred's eyes were huge as he waited expectantly. Finally his father removed a book from the bottom of the grip. "This is a book of Bible stories."

"For me, Pa?"

"For you. You'll soon be learning to read. I read quite well when I was six, didn't I Mother?"

"Thee did. Thee was a smart child."

Fred carefully turned the pages of the new book. "I wish I could wead now," he said.

Henry glared disapprovingly at the boy. "You read, not *wead*. You *read*. Say 'read.' "

Fred closed the book and dropped it on the floor. He buried his face in Lucretia's bosom.

"Son, look at me."

With tear-filled eyes the child turned toward his father.

"Say read, read."

"Wead, wead." The tears spilled over and ran in streaks down Fred's face.

"Henry," Susan said softly, "let's drop it now."

"Drop it! The boy's going on five years old! If he doesn't learn to talk people will think he's half-witted! I'm surprised you've allowed this baby talk! He should have outgrown it by now!"

"Please, Henry," she whispered.

With flushed face the man glared threateningly at the child. "Pick your book up from the floor. That's a fine way to treat a new book. Pick it up!"

Yellow Boy barked furiously at the door. Fred slid from his grandmother's lap, grabbed the book, stamped to the door and with eyes flashing blue fire, he threw it outside. "I don't want the old book! I don't care if I never learn to wead! I don't yike you! I wish you hadn't come home!" He ran to the bedroom, climbed into his bed and covered his head.

The shouting had frightened Emily who was screaming her protest. Lucretia muttered, "Dear God, I'd hoped he'd changed." Red-faced with anger Henry charged into the bedroom where he repeatedly struck the crying boy.

Susan thrust the baby into Lucretia's arms and ran to the bedroom. "Henry!" she shouted. "Stop it!" She grabbed his arm. "Do you know what you're doing?"

Suddenly he calmed and walked from the room to stare outside into the afternoon sunshine. The Bible story book lay in the yard, the pages flipping in the wind. Without a word he went outside and walked rapidly toward the barn.

An hour later Henry returned to the house. Smiling, he went to his mother. "The barn doesn't seem right without Father out there. He was a good man. We'll all miss him."

Susan continued silently placing dishes on the table. He went to her and tipped her face up to his. "And you're a good woman, Susan. I'm sorry I lost my temper with the boy. Forgive me and help me to control myself."

"I forgive you," she said quietly.

Henry walked briskly into the bedroom, a smile on his handsome bearded face. Fred did not look up. "Freddy, I'm sorry I lost my temper with you. You're my only son and I love you. Will you forgive me?"

The boy did not answer. He stared fiercely into his father's eyes.

"Let's make a new start. We'll try another time to help you talk right. Forgive me?"

Fred silently turned his face to the wall.

4 ———————————————————— *1825*

Sᴜꜱᴀɴ, ʜᴇʀ ꜰᴀᴄᴇ ᴘᴀʟᴇ ᴀɴᴅ ᴅʀᴀᴡɴ, came from the bedroom. Lucretia hung her cane on a chair within easy reach while she washed and rinsed the dishes. She turned toward Susan.

"How is she?" There was a quiver in the old voice.

"No change." Susan dropped soiled sheets on a pile of dirty clothes on the kitchen floor. "I have to get at the washing, Mother. I'll call Fred to sit with Emily. The baby will sleep for a while, I hope." She bent over the cradle to chase a fly from the sleeping baby's face. She sighed. "Henry is no help when there's sickness. He says he can't stand to see anyone suffer."

Lucretia limped to the cupboard and felt to find the pile of plates. "I'm not much help to thee. 'Tis hard to be blind." She paused. "I remember when Henry was a child. He cried for days when his first calf died. He has always been unable to stand to see suffering. He goes to the barn or fields to get away from it. And thee knows how he grieved when old Yellow Boy died."

A weak wailing voice from the bedroom called, "Mama, Mama."

"Yes, Emily. I'm coming." Susan stroked the burning forehead of her four-year-old daughter who wheezed noisily as she panted for breath. Reaching under the child's shoulders she placed a second pillow beneath Emily's head. A violent coughing spell resulted in the expulsion of a large quantity of phlegm.

"There, there," Susan said. "Now you'll breathe easier." She straightened the covers. "Maybe you can sleep now." The child sighed and closed her eyes.

Fred, a sturdy eight-year-old, stood inside the kitchen door holding a yellow kitten in his arms. "Is—is—is—sh-sh-she better?" he stammered.

Susan tossed white clothes into a tub of hot water on the bench. "About the same, Freddy. Would you sit with her while I work out here?"

"Y-y-yes, Mama. Maybe she'd l-l-l-like to s-s-see the kitten."

"When she wakes up. You sit by her and let me know if you need me. Better close the door so we don't wake her."

Lucretia emptied the dishwater into a large pail in the corner, unaware that she had spilled part of it on the floor.

Susan scrubbed a stubborn stain on a pillow case. "The herbs I've been using on Emily leave stains," she commented. "Sometimes I wonder how much good they do, but we don't know—she might be worse without them."

"Mustard plasters are good to cure lung fever," Lucretia said.

"I've stopped using them. Her chest is blistered."

"Poor child," Lucretia sighed.

"I'm going to keep on with the cowslip flower and dried elderberry teas. It seems to me she's raising more phlegm today, and it seems looser. She's sweating, too, and that's good." Susan wrung the water from a sheet and tossed it into the rinse tub. "If we can clear her lungs, the fever'll go down."

"I've been praying for her," Lucretia said.

Susan brushed back a lock of blonde hair with her wet hands. "I think God works through us to bring about healing. He directs our thoughts to remedies that may help."

The bedroom door opened. "M-M-Mama," Fred called. "Emily n-n-n-needs you."

Drying her hands on her apron, Susan went to her daughter. "What is it?" she asked.

The little girl's flushed face and glassy eyes were evidence of a high fever. As she pulled the quilt about Emily's neck the child whined, "I'm so hot, but Freddy says I have to stay under the quilt."

"He's right, dear. You're wringing wet with sweat, but that's good. It's a sign the fever's breaking. Keep covered so you don't take cold."

"Do I have to take more elderberry tea?"

Susan took the cup from the bureau. "Just a few sips."

As Emily drank, Fred held up the kitten. "L-l-look, Emily. Since you've b-b-b-been sick, S-S-Sally's had kittens."

Susan smiled. "Want to hold the kitten?"

Emily held her hands out for the tiny animal. "He's getting his eyes open. He's so pretty. I like yellow cats. Can he be my kitty?"

"Ask Freddy. The mother cat belongs to him."

"He's y-y-yours. S-S-Sally has f-four others." The boy grimaced as he struggled with his speech. "Ar-r-r-e you feeling b-better?"

"Uh-huh. I'm so tired." She drifted off to sleep.

5　　　　　　　　　*1828*

Rᴇᴠ. Jᴏʜɴ Tʜᴏᴍᴘꜱᴏɴ ᴛɪᴇᴅ ʜɪꜱ bay horse at the hitching post in the Parker yard.

"Uncle John!" Seven-year-old Emily and three-year-old Josephine shouted as they ran to welcome him.

The young minister put an arm about Emily's shoulders. "You're getting so big I hardly know you," he commented. He swung Josephine to his shoulder. "And Josie, you look more like your Grandmother Thompson every time I see you."

Josephine stuck out her lips. "I don't want to look like

somebody else! I want to look like me!"

John laughed. "You're a spunky little rascal." He patted Emily's shoulder. "And you—I remember when your mother looked just like you do now."

"Uh-huh. I like to look like Mama. When I'm big I want to be just like her."

"Where's Fred?"

Emily replied, "He's picking up stones for Pa. And Mama's baking bread. Just wait until you see Jimmy. He's three months old already."

Josie squirmed to get down. She said, "I'm three years old! I'll always be older than Jimmy, won't I?"

John laughed. "That's right."

Susan opened the door. "John," she said as they embraced, "Henry said only yesterday that we haven't seen you for some time. Not since you preached Mother Parker's funeral sermon. We miss her. But we should all be so fortunate as to die quietly in our sleep."

"She was a good Quaker woman."

Emily exclaimed, "Come see Jimmy!"

The baby beat a tattoo on the foot of his cradle as he kicked violently with his right leg. His large blue eyes stared at the faces hovering above him. A sudden smile slid across his face.

John chuckled. "You have nice children, Susan." He picked the baby up and held him over his shoulder. "I wonder what he'll do when he grows up? I expect he'll have Henry's winning ways, judging by that smile."

For a moment Susan didn't answer. Then she said, "He is a good-natured baby. He hardly ever cries and that pleases Henry. He's always been annoyed when our babies cried, especially at night. Of course Jimmy gets so much attention—all of us spoil him. And Emily is like a little mother. She helps me with the dishes and she takes care of Jimmy and watches Josephine."

Josephine pouted. "I don't need watching! I'm three years old! This many." She held up three fingers.

John put the baby in the cradle where he again began the rhythmic kicking. He smiled as Emily gently rocked the crib.

"I'm going out to see Henry and Fred. Where are they?"

"In the cornfield behind the barn. You can stay for dinner, can't you?"

"I'd planned to have some of your good cooking. That's one reason I came." He laughed.

Henry welcomed his brother-in-law. "Let's sit here under the oak tree. This October sun feels like August."

"Pretty hot work cutting corn?"

"You bet. Someday they'll invent something so we don't have to cut one stalk at a time with a sickle."

"Yeah. But you like farming. And you're going to have two boys to help you. Fred out there is working hard picking up stones." John hesitated. "I thought he'd be over to see me right away."

Henry cleared his throat. "He doesn't like to meet people—his speech, you know. He's a funny boy. He's eleven years old and still can't talk without stammering. I've tried and tried to help him, but he resents it. He doesn't talk to me much."

"That's too bad."

"But little Jimmy—I'm pinning all my hopes on him."

From across the field Fred waved to his uncle, then returned to picking up stones.

Henry said quietly, "Have you had any more slave contacts?"

John shook his head. "It's been quiet. I think the Quakers in Pennsylvania are getting them through to Canada."

"Yeah. There aren't many Quakers in this part of New York anymore."

John mused, "I'm just as well satisfied that we are

pretty much out of it. Of course, I'd transport them if they called on me, but it's dangerous business. Your family and mine were nearly caught a couple times."

"I'm glad we helped a few escape. Sooner or later, slavery in the United States will have to go." Henry chewed on a piece of timothy, the seeds falling into his beard. "There aren't many of the old Quakers here now. They've died, like my folks, and the next generation has drifted away."

"Do you still consider yourself a Quaker? I've noticed you'd dropped the 'thee' and 'thy' when you came home from working on the Erie Canal."

Henry nodded. "Quakers are good people but I married a Methodist. I could be one as easy as the other." He hesitated. "But speaking of the Erie Canal, it's changed our country since it was finished in 1825. Know what I'd like to do? I'd like to sell this farm and buy land in the Michigan Territory."

John exclaimed, "Sell the farm your folks left you?"

"I've never really liked this place. As a child I was teased about my parents not wanting me—my natural parents, that is. Things that happen to you in childhood leave a mark." He watched Fred, speculating. "Michigan might be good for him. New people—a fresh start." He continued, "I couldn't make a move while Mother was living, but now I could sell the farm, pack up my family and go to a new land."

"Hm-m-m-m. It sounds interesting."

"Why don't you go with me? We'd go by way of the Erie Canal and Lake Erie next spring to look things over. If I liked it, I'd buy land at the land office in Detroit. Then we'd come home and I'd sell everything and take my family to Michigan in 1830."

"Hm-m-m-m." John said again, "I'd have to find someone to substitute for me as a minister. I have a friend who will be ordained next spring—he might take the parish for me." His eyes sparkled. "I've never mentioned it, but I've always had a hankering to be a circuit rider, or perhaps a missionary to the Indians."

"Michigan would be a perfect place for you. There are few churches in the center of the territory and there are Indians galore."

"Well—I'll have to think about it. What does Susan think of the idea?"

"She might consent if you were going. I have only hinted that I'd like to try it. She wasn't enthusiastic about leaving here. I'll break it to her a little at a time."

References

[1]Stan Perkins, *Lore of Wolverine Country* (Broadblade Press, 1984), p. 199.

[2, 4]*World Book Encyclopedia,* E Book *(See* "Erie Canal.")

[3]Harry Sinclair, *Canal Days in America* (Drago Bramhall House).

Chapter Three
1830

WESTWARD BOUND

1830

1

Susan wakened with a start. For a moment she couldn't remember where she was. Then the events of the previous day flooded her mind. They were on an Erie Canal packet boat headed for Michigan Territory where Henry had bought land in July.

In the dim pre-dawn light of a September morning, she raised her head. Emily and Josephine slept soundly on her right and little Jimmy snuggled close on her left. She hugged her youngest child, the two-year-old whom the family adored because of his amusing ways and sweet disposition.

The cabin of the canalboat was quiet except for the relaxed breathing of other sleeping women and children. In the dim light Susan could see the tables and chairs which were pushed aside each night to provide sleeping space for women, girls and infants. Soon the place would come to life as people wakened, folded their bedding and prepared for breakfast. [1]

The past night was the family's first on the canalboat. Susan wondered how Henry, Fred, and her brother John were resting in the men's room at the rear. She sighed. Though she dreaded living in the Michigan wilderness, this life had been a dream of Henry's for many years. And Fred —poor Fred. She hoped he would like life in Michigan. If only Henry wasn't so hard on the boy; after all, he was only thirteen.

A shout of "Whoa!" from the young hoggee who guided the four tandem-hitched horses that pulled the canalboat, *Lion of the West,* brought Susan's thoughts back to the present. [2]

Four-year-old Josephine sat up. "What are they doing?" she asked sleepily.

"Sh-h-h-h," her mother whispered. "They're changing horses. Lie down and rest."

"I don't want to. I want to see what they're doing."

Susan patted Josephine's arm as she whispered. "We mustn't wake the others." The little girl settled down next to her sleeping sister.

Two hours later when bedding was folded and put away and tables and chairs were in place, families gathered for breakfast. The women brought out food which had been prepared and packed for the three-day canal trip to Buffalo. Bread, cold ham and boiled eggs with cookies for dessert were served three times a day.

The Parker family bowed their heads as John said grace. "Father, we thank thee for watching over us during the night. Guide us today, and bless this food to our use. Amen."

The packet boat slid through the water at four miles an hour pulled by the straining horses on the towpath. Henry took a huge bite of bread and ham. "This is the way to travel," he said. "Those poor fellows that go the whole way to Michigan by wagon through mud, sand and swamps, are to be pitied."

John nodded. "It takes determination and courage to make the trip by ox team and wagon. We are fortunate to be able to go by water. It costs five dollars per person by steamer from Buffalo to Detroit, plus the expense of the canal trip across New York state—many people can't afford that kind of money."

"I'm hungry!" Jimmy announced.

Henry glanced at Fred who was wolfing down his breakfast. "Hey, Stupid!" he shouted. "Your job is to look after your little brother! Give him some bread and cut up his meat!"

Fred's face flushed. "Y-y-yes, Pa," he stammered as he hurried to obey.

People at tables near the Parkers were watching. Susan caught Henry's eye and shook her head. John stared silently at his plate as Emily patted Fred's arm.

Josephine's blue eyes flashed. "Freddy is hungry too, Papa!"

Henry brushed bread crumbs from his beard. He smiled, well aware of the attention directed his way. "I'm sorry, Son," he said so all could hear. "I didn't sleep much last night."

Between meals many of the passengers sat in chairs on the flat roof of the canalboat as boats moved endlessly back and forth from Albany to Buffalo. Straining, sweating horses and mules, followed by drivers with whip in hand, had worn a deep groove in the towpath along the side of the Erie Canal.

There were freight boats with wagons, animals and supplies like the one which followed the *Lion of the West* and which carried the Parker family's possessions; there were packet boats crowded with tired passengers; all came westward in a never ending line on the narrow blue ribbon of the Erie Canal.

From the flat roof of the boat the passengers watched as they passed the little cabins of the lock keepers.

A middle aged woman sitting beside Susan remarked, "We've already gone through several locks. I wonder how many there are between Albany and Buffalo?"

Susan brushed back a stray lock of blonde hair. "My husband worked on the canal for several summers. I remember he said there were twenty-seven locks between Albany and Schnectady. I believe he said there are seventy-two in all."

The woman remarked, "Must have cost a pretty penny to build the canal."

Susan nodded. "It took eight years to build and my husband said it cost eight million dollars—a million a year."

"Hm-m-m-m," the woman mused. " 'Twill raise the price of wheat and other crops the farmers sell, I expect." In a moment she continued. "Where are you going to settle?"

"Michigan Territory."

"That's still wilderness. Think you'll like it?"

Susan shrugged. "I'll try."

"We've bought land in northern Ohio near my brother's family. It's settled there, and it's been a state since 1803."

Emily stood behind her mother's chair. "Mama, will there be Indians near our place?"

"I expect there are Indians in most of southern Michigan."

The older woman smiled. "There are Indians, bears, wolves, and all kinds of wild animals in Michigan, and there's that ague sickness most everybody gets. 'Twill be a hard life for a woman."

Susan put her arm about Emily's shoulders. "We will manage," she said confidently.

Jimmy ran to his mother and climbed on her lap. He

smiled at the woman, a smile remarkably like the winning smile of his father.

"You're a nice boy," she said. "What's your name?"

"Jim-mee."

"He's learning to talk," Susan said, "and he makes friends easily."

" 'Tis his smile," the woman said.

Suddenly the captain bellowed, "Low bridge! Everybody down!" The people who were standing stooped as the boat passed beneath the bridge.

Josephine sat on the floor beside her mother. "Why are there so many bridges?" she asked.

Susan explained, "The canal cut through farms so farmers couldn't get their animals from one side to the other. When that happened, these low bridges were built. There must be hundreds of them."

A canal boat coming east from Buffalo passed the *Lion of the West* on the forty-foot-wide waterway. These eastward-bound boats carried goods from the West. Some were filled with wheat and corn; others carried barrels of cider, salt pork and bags of corn meal or flour that had been ground in small gristmills on rivers to the west. The boats also carried crates of eggs, hams and bacon from the smokehouses, along with live, squealing, grunting hogs and bawling cattle. Other boats were loaded with lumber. All were going to eastern markets along the Erie Canal.

"There's no end to them," Susan said softly. "All day and night the canal boats move along."

Emily said, "I feel sorry for the horses and mules on the towpath. The drivers hit them with whips. Look how they're sweating."

Susan nodded. "They change teams often; then they can rest." She brushed a fly from sleeping Jimmy's face.

Josephine stood at her mother's elbow. She studied the faces of passengers. Some were dressed in odd-looking clothes and they conversed in languages which she could not understand. They appeared uncomfortable. Others, like her family, were laughing and chatting.

"Mama," Josephine whispered, "who are those people? I can't understand what they're saying, and their clothes look funny."

"They came from far away, over across the Atlantic Ocean in Europe. Some are from Germany, and some from Norway and Sweden. It's far, far away."

"Why are they here?"

"I expect they're going to buy land for farms just like Papa did."

Emily whispered, "Some of those people are old. See that lady with the black scarf over her head? She hasn't any teeth and she can hardly walk. Why would she leave her old home?"

" 'Tis likely some of her children are going to settle in America and they didn't want to leave her alone in the old country." Susan glanced to the left. "Papa and Fred are coming," she said.

"Are our animals all right?" Emily asked.

Henry smiled. "Everything is fine. They're a little crowded on the barge, but they have hay and water. Isn't this great?" he asked enthusiastically. "I can hardly wait to get to Buffalo so we can get things loaded on the steamship and be on our way to Detroit."

"Where's Uncle John?" Josephine asked.

"He's found a man who knows about Indian tribes in lower Michigan. Uncle John thinks he might do missionary work among the Indians while he's riding his circuit as a minister."

"When will we get to Buffalo?" Susan asked.

"Sometime tomorrow afternoon."

Fred glaced behind him. "L-l-look!" he pointed excitedly, just as the captain shouted, "Everybody down!"

Henry and Fred stooped as did all people who were standing. The passengers resumed their conversation when the boat had passed under the bridge. Most of the men were farmers who viewed with satisfaction the well-kept buildings and fields of northern New York.

2 ——————————— *1830*

JUST AFTER BREAKFAST THE *Lion of the West* with the barge close behind docked at Buffalo amid shouts and confusion. Mothers called their children to help gather possessions in preparation for landing; men talked loudly in anticipation of transferring their personal possessions and livestock to the *Commodore Perry* which was docked nearby. The captain shouted directions to passengers through his funnel-shaped trumpet and from the barge came sounds of horses neighing, cattle bawling, dogs barking and chickens cackling. The noise and confusion created a scene of utter pandemonium.

Susan gathered her children about her. "Freddy!" she shouted. "Take Jimmy's and Josephine's hands and keep them with you so they don't get lost. Stay here until I come for you." Fred nodded.

"Emily, you come with me to be sure we have our things together, then we'll all wait for Papa and Uncle John."

"Where are they?" Josephine asked.

Susan bent to the children's level and shouted, "They're putting our animals, wagons and barrels on the steamship." She straightened. "Freddy, hold tight to their hands." Again the boy nodded.

Most of the passengers from the canalboat were trans-

ferring to the *Commodore Perry*. There were farmers and
their families from the eatern states, single men, young
couples, middle-aged men and their wives and elderly ladies
and men who could not be left behind. The strangely
dressed, foreign-speaking immigrants milled about in confusion.

On the shore the children could see people carrying
boxes and baskets aboard the *Commodore Perry* where they
were stacked on deck. "L-l-look, Josie! In-Indians!" Fred
shouted.

Silently they stared at two Indian men whose bodies
were draped in red woolen blankets which covered them
from head to knees and which they held closely around
themselves. They wore trousers reaching the middle of
their thighs. On their feet were deerskin moccasins. From
their ears hung glittering silk bands. Their faces were a
sooty brown and black eyes stared out from beneath deep
brows.

"Will they hurt us?" Josie shouted as Jimmy squealed,
pointed at the Indians and tried to break away from
Freddy, but the boy maintained his grasp.

"I d-d-don't know. They're g-going on the st-steamer!"

Susan and Emily returned. "Mama! We saw Indians!"
Josephine exclaimed. "Will they scalp us?"

Emily stood close to her mother as though for protection. Susan smiled. "They won't harm us. Won't it be interesting to have them on the ship with us?"

Soon Susan said, "They're taking teams and wagons up
the gangplank onto the steamer. And there is someone's
cow."

"There's Papa and Uncle John in line!" Emily said. She
laughed. "Brindle and Blacky don't like being tied behind
the wagon. They're trying to get away."

Jimmy squealed and pulled on Fred's hand. Susan
reached for the little boy. "I'll watch him now, Fred."

Henry, with his black team pulling the covered wagon went first. The horses hesitated and praced nervously as Henry urged them forward. A Negro member of the ship's crew came down the ten-foot-wide gangplank to grasp each horse's bridle as he led them onto the deck of the *Commodore Perry*. He directed Henry to the proper spot on the deck.

John walked beside his pair of oxen, urging them on. They hesitated until a crew member escorted John, the oxen, wagon and the nervous cattle aboard. On top of barrels and boxes in the wagon were three wooden crates containing a grunting red hog, a barking dog, a glaring cat and a crate of cackling chickens.

Fred pointed. "P-P-Pa's taking the wh-wheels off!"

"Why's he doing that?" Josephine asked.

Susan shifted her other hand to Jimmy's wrist. "Sometimes there are storms on Lake Erie. The men take the wheels off the wagons and tie them to the boat so the wagons won't roll around and cause damage if we should run into a storm. The wagon boxes will set on their axles on deck and we'll live in them on the way to Detroit."

"Where will the animals be put?" Emily asked.

"Below deck in the hold."

At last when the wagons were loaded, the waiting families streamed aboard carrying luggage and boxes. Henry and John waited beside the wagons, their eyes shining with excitement. Henry seized Jimmy and tossed him into the air as the child squealed and grabbed his father's beard.

"Fun, Pa! More!" the little boy shrieked.

Henry, laughing, again tossed the child into the air. "Pa likes to hear you talk," he said. "You speak so well."

Fred turned his back to hide his hurt expression. His attention was drawn to a man who was off-loading cords of wood which were transferred by crew members to a pile close to the boiler room of the *Commodore Perry*. Two passengers also watched.

"It takes a heap o' wood to keep the boilers hot," one man remarked. "When I bought my land in Michigan last summer I went by steamer. Wherever the ship stops along the northern shore of Ohio, wood is thrown aboard to keep the boilers humming."

"Who furnishes the wood?" another man asked.

"Farmers that have settled in the region haul it to the docks. They get cash for it so they can buy sugar, flour, salt, gunpowder and guns, axes and other supplies."

"Once in a while the steam pressure gets too high for the boiler and it blows up," the first man said.

"I remember reading that one blew up last year killing some passengers," the second man added. "Hope the fireman knows his business on this ship," he grinned.

Finally with a hoarse toot of the whistle the *Commodore Perry* pulled away from the dock and pushed westward across Lake Erie. The turning paddle wheels left a foaming trail behind in the blue water. Sparks flew upward from the smokestack and hot ashes drifted down onto the passengers and deck.

The Parker family watched from their seats in and about their wagons. John carried on a conversation with two brothers, Joe and Tom Arnold. Dressed in deerskin jackets, they carried guns and hunting sacks and had knives in their belts. They were fur hunters and trappers who were on their way north to the Michigan rivers and forests.

"We're going to our land in southern Michigan," John explained. "It's a few days southwest of Detroit. Can you tell me anything about the Indians in the area?"

Joe Arnold fingered the handle of the knife at his belt. "There are three main tribes," he began. "Ottawas, Chippewas and the Potawatomi. What did you want to know about them?"

"I'm a Protestant minister. Have the Indians had any

contact with Christianity in the area where we're going?"

"Some. The tribes move about from north to south with the seasons. Some of them know a little French and English through contact with Jesuit missionaries and fur traders in the northern part of the Territory of Michigan, and they profess to be Christians."

Tom Arnold commented. "There's a chief named Black Hawk that I often hear mentioned. His tribe's summer home is near the northwestern tip of the Michigan peninsula. They move south in winter. I've never met Black Hawk but I've been told he's a strong, reasonable leader for his people."

John stood up. "I hope to do missionary work with the Indians. I'm looking forward to it as a part of my work as a Methodist circuit rider."

Jimmy stirred and opened his eyes. He lay on a pile of quilts beside his mother at the front of the covered wagon. He yawned and sat up. "You had a long rest," Susan said, her eyes following Jimmy's gaze at the two blanketed Indians who sat by the rail. All afternoon they sat immobile, staring moodily before them, each holding his blanket tightly around his body. Perhaps this was their only possession for they had no baggage.

No one spoke to the brown-skinned men, and they seldom spoke to one another, but when they did speak they used a series of short grunts.

Susan thought these Indians could not be wild for they were allowed to travel among white people. But they sat apart, ignored by the other passengers who walked past them in silence. Really, there was something dark, threatening, almost cruel in their looks, something that caused her to feel fear.

"Man!" Jimmy exclaimed pointing at the Indians.

Their dark eyes bored into hers. Susan looked away. John came from behind the wagon. "I'll take Jimmy," he offered as he took the child. "We'll go for a walk around the boat."

Susan rummaged through her basket of food. "While you're gone I'll put out something for our supper. We'll eat only a little tonight. I've heard people talking. They think there's a storm brewing, and too much food might make us seasick."

John shaded his eyes against the sun. "Thunderheads are piling up there in the southwest." He swung Jimmy to his shoulder. "Want to go with us, Fred?"

"Y-y-yes."

"We'll be ready to eat in a few minutes," Susan called.

The steamer had a large crew. They seemed to be everywhere—bosuns, engineers, stokers and deckhands. Negroes were serving in many capacities. For those who wished it, they served food; they loaded and cleaned the ship and busied themselves everywhere. From conversation with them John learned the black crewmen were free.

John, Fred and Jimmy went below to explore the steerage area. Most of these passengers were immigrants who were sorely in need of scrubbing with boiled-lye soap. Children appeared never to have touched water. Washing buckets set about but the water looked as though it never was changed. People dipped their hands and rinsed their faces in the buckets of black, thick water. The same towel passed from one hand to another—there was only one for all the steerage passengers.

There were no spittoons in the hold and the deck was awash from the tobacco-chewing menfolk's spittle. Small children were crawling and creeping on their hands and knees on the filthy floor.

Jimmy squirmed on John's shoulders. "Down," he said, "Down."

"No. You ride on my shoulders," John said as they passed two Negro slaves shackled in foot chains. He recalled having heard a man on the upper deck say he owned two slaves in steerage who must be chained because they had wild tempers.

Fred pulled on his uncle's sleeve. "L-l-let's get out of here!" he said softly. When they were back on the upper deck he asked, "Why were the N-N-Negroes chained?"

"They're slaves. Their master has caught them and he's likely going to get off at some Ohio port and take them back south."

"Wi-l-l he b-b-beat them?"

"I hope not."

They made their way back toward the family's wagon. Many people stood or sat near their wagons eating a cold supper. The stoic Indian men stared past them as they approached.

"Man!" Jimmy cried from John's shoulders.

John smiled at the deadpan, expressionless faces. "The boy wants to say, 'Hello.' He's learning to talk."

The set facial expressions relaxed slightly as they nodded.

While the Parker family ate, they discussed the steerage conditions. Josephine whispered, "The Indians aren't eating. Could we take them something?"

John said, "I think they understand some English. I'll take them bread and ham and a couple apples." He boosted Jimmy to his shoulders and as the others watched, he approached the Indians. "Jimmy brought you something to eat," he said motioning to the child who was reaching for one of the glittering silk bands that hung from the men's ears.

As they silently took the food, their eyes met John's. They nodded and the younger brave, in his mid-forties, removed the bright red band from one ear and gave it to Jimmy. The boy grasped the gewgaw and smiled happily.

"Tell him 'thank you'," John prompted.

"Thank you, Man," he said without looking away from the colorful band.

Back at the wagon Susan said softly, "They seem friendly now, but this afternoon they stared at Jimmy and me until I was frightened."

" 'Tis their way," Henry remarked. He shaded his eyes against the setting sun. "Wouldn't be surprised if we had a thunderstorm before long. He pointed. "See that curdly sky?"

Emily added, "A curdly sky never lets the world go dry."

"That's right," her father replied. "And over there to the southwest the clouds are looking more like a storm every minute."

"We won't get wet inside the covered wagon," Josephine said as she wiped her sweaty face on her sleeve. "It's awful hot."

Susan and Emily packed the food away. "Those clouds are rolling in fast," Susan remarked. "A shower would cool things off. There's not a breath of air stirring."

The Captain's voice broke in loud and forceful. "A storm is coming. We are battening down the hatches to the lower decks. People should remain inside their wagons. If the wind is strong, do not go out on deck. It may get rough, but remain inside your covered wagons."

Emily took her mother's hand. "I'm scared," she whispered.

Henry placed Jimmy inside the wagon. " 'Tis moving in fast! Everyone grab something and get it in the wagon. Then get inside and stay there!"

There was confusion as passengers hurried to get under cover. The noise of shouting men and screaming children rose above the sudden blast of wind which struck the little steamer.

The Parkers were inside when John shouted, "The Indi-

ans! I'm going to ask them in with us!" He dashed across the
windy deck just as the skies opened and rain swept down in
torrents.

The Indians stood stoically holding the red blankets
over their heads. "Come!" John shouted, grasping each one
by the shoulder. They ran and quickly climbed into the
wagon when John motioned to them. The nine people were
crowded and wedged into every available space near the
top of the heavily loaded canvas-covered wagon.

"Whew!" Susan gasped. "It's stifling! There's no air!" She
shifted Jimmy to Henry's lap. The ship lurched sending her
into one of the bow-shaped ribs which supported the canvas
above them.

Henry quickly handed Jimmy to the Indian beside him.
The younger Indian cradled the child in his arms as Henry
reached to help Susan.

"I'm all right," she said. "It's just a little bump on the
head."

Henry shouted above the roar of the storm and the
creaking of the tossing ship. "Find something to hold onto
—the side of the wagon or a bow!"

Through the tiny slit in the canvass opening at the
front of the wagon they viewed the deserted rain-swept
deck. Jimmy squealed with glee each time the ship lurched.

In a short time the sound of retching came from the
back of the wagon. "Might know. 'Tis Fred." Henry's voice
revealed his disgust.

Emily wailed, "I'm sick too, Mama."

Her mother rummaged about in a box below. At last
she brought out a tin wash basin. "Use this," she said.
"Freddy!" she shouted. "Hold your head outside if you must
vomit."

The wind tore at the canvas-covered wagon which
rocked violently with each new blast. "Hope the canvas
holds," John murmured to himself. Time after time the ship

pitched and rolled. The minister shouted, "Join me in prayer!"

Emily and Fred continued retching as John prayed: "Father, we come to Thee and ask that if it be Thy will Thou will protect this ship and bring us safely through the storm. Be with all the passengers. Be with the poor souls in steerage. We pray no lives will be lost. Protect us, we pray. We ask it in Thy name. Amen."

Like a powerful broom wave after wave swept over the deck taking anything into the lake that was not fastened down.

Susan whispered to Henry. "Might the ship go down?"

"Some have," he replied.

Josephine called, "I'm sick. I need the basin."

Five minutes later all of the group except the Indians were retching violently. Jimmy hung to the neck of the younger Indian at the front of the wagon as the man emptied the basin onto the rain-swept deck. The older man had worked his way to the back where he emptied the utensil when it was passed to him. In the close quarters of the wagon the stench of regurgitated food was nauseating.

After an hour the rain stopped and the wind lessened in intensity. " 'Tis passing over," Henry said as he opened the front of the canvas top. Fresh, clean air rushed in to flush out the repulsive odor of vomit. Still the sickness continued as they retched and strained to quiet already empty stomachs.

Suddenly an ear-splitting shriek cut through the air. Heads popped out of wagon openings on every side. A woman, perhaps thirty-five years old, leaned against the side of a wagon as she held her head and rocked her body back and forth uttering shriek after ear-splitting shriek.

John climbed out as the younger Indian man put Jimmy in Henry's arms. Their eyes met briefly as Henry murmured, "Thanks for looking after him." The man almost smiled as he and the older Indian left the wagon.

John approached the screaming woman. "Can I help?" he inquired. In the fading evening light he saw a dark-haired woman, her face lined and tortured.

"My father and my son! They've drowned!" she screamed. "My father was sick. He went to stand by the rail to throw up. When he didn't come back, my son—thirteen years old—went to find him. The storm—the awful storm —the wind and waves—they must have been swept away!"

John said quietly, "Perhaps they're somewhere on board."

"No! They're gone! My husband still is searching, but they're gone! Why did we ever leave home? This awful lake has killed them!"

"Are you alone?"

"My husband will be back." She wiped her eyes.

"Maybe he'll have good news."

She shook her head. "They're gone. My father and my only child—drowned." Her shoulders shook as she sobbed.

People ignored their queasy stomachs and streamed from the wagons offering help, but little could be done. Lake Erie had claimed two more lives.

Though the wind and rain had stopped, the waves still tossed the *Commodore Perry*. Night had come but most passengers were unable to sleep. Many still were nauseated while others were unable to put the events of the past hours from their minds.

The next morning the sun was shining and waves on Lake Erie had subsided. The ship docked at a village on Ohio's north shore to take on a supply of wood. Most of the passengers were Northerners who watched with disapproval as the slave owner and his overseer escorted the two chained Negroes from the ship.

"I don't suppose there'll be much we can do about the slavery problem in Michigan," John said. "I'm glad we helped a few Negroes escape back in York State."

"We were lucky we were not caught," Susan commented, "but I'd do it again if I had a chance."

"When I'm big I'm going to do something to help the Negroes," Josephine stated firmly. The adults smiled at the child's determination.

All day the *Commodore Perry* steamed toward the northwest. "When will we be in Detroit, Papa?" Emily asked.

"Tomorrow afternoon," Henry answered. "I'll be glad to get our animals on solid land again. They must have been as scared as we were during the storm. Brindle isn't giving much milk, and the rest of the animals look rough and bedraggled."

The next afternoon as the ship left the broad waters of Lake Erie and steamed up the wide mouth of the Detroit River past Fort Malden on the Canadian side and Grosse Ile on the American, the passengers on their third day out of Buffalo looked with approval at the autumn forested shores on either side. To the beauty of the forest was added the strangeness of Indian villages on the western shore.

Henry and John stood by the rail viewing again scenes they had observed when they had been in Michigan a few months earlier.

"M-m-maybe the t-t-two Indians l-live there," Fred said as he pointed to a small village.

"Maybe," Susan replied. "They were nice to Jimmy, but—" She didn't finish.

"Didn't you like them, Mama?" Emily asked.

Susan frowned. "They were strange."

Emily pointed. "Why are all those little white cabins back from the river?"

"Your father told me French people live in them. Their narrow farms go from their buildings to the river."

Fred stammered, "See their f-f-funny w-windmills."

"Uh-huh. I expect they have windmills with wide wings like that in France."

Women and children lined the rails of the steamer as the ship docked while the men hurried to assemble their wagons.

Henry gave orders to his family. "Fred, you keep the children together for your mother. Hold Jimmy's hand so he doesn't get lost. Emily, you stay with Mama and help whenever you can. John and I will get the animals and we'll meet you to the left of the gangplank. Watch for us to come off."

Already wagons were rolling ashore. People, boxes and bundles spilled from the hold, along with babies, older children, axes, shovels and pieces of cherished furniture and cooking utensils. Susan and Emily carried luggage followed by Fred with Jimmy and Josephine in tow.

Susan selected a spot near the end of the gangplank. "Let's wait here," she said as she paused beside a wooden barrel. "Jimmy can stand on the barrel so he can see." Fred lifted him up. "Now," Susan continued, "everyone stay here until the men come."

Such pandemonium they had never seen or heard. Added to the noise of settlers getting their families and teams and wagons ashore were the criers who called out the names of one of the local hotels or inns for which they were drumming up business. Cries of "Mansion House," "Eagle Hotel," "American" and "Steamboat Hotel" were heard above the confusion as the drummers tried to entice settlers to their frontier inns.

One after another wagons pulled by horses or oxen came down the gangplank. Suddenly Emily shouted, "A cow is loose!"

A red and white cow with a strap dangling from her neck ran along beside a loaded wagon. Shouting men rushed at her from in front and behind. Confused, the animal tried to turn back. She skidded and fell into the water beside the pier. Only her head and back could be seen above the water. A curious crowd gathered to see the rescue. The cow struggled like a sea monster, snorting and bawling as water squirted from her nostrils. Finally the men succeeded in getting a rope around her horns and pulling her on shore.

"She's safe now," Susan said turning to look at her children. Her heart jumped. "Jimmy!" she cried. "Jimmy's gone!" The color left her face and for a moment she thought she would faint.

"I-I-I'll find him!" Fred yelled, dashing into the crowd.

Emily and Josephine clung to their mother's skirts and sobbed. "Stop it!" she ordered. "Help me look! He must be near here!"

Ten minutes later Fred returned. He sobbed, "I couldn't f-f-find him!"

References ———————————————

[1]Ferris E. Lewis, *Michigan Yesterday and Today*. (Hillsdale Educational Publishers, 1956, pp. 179-181).

[2]Harry Sinclair, *Canal Days in America* (Drago Bramhall House).

Chapter Four
1830

THE SEARCH

1 ——————————————————————

J IMMY COULDN'T BE GONE! HE WAS here just minutes ago. Susan's thoughts were confused. Where were Henry and John? Why didn't they come? She must do something. She couldn't just stand here worrying.

"Stay with the girls and watch for Papa!" she shouted to Fred. "I'll search."

She approached a crier who called out the name of the Eagle Hotel. "Have you seen a little two-year-old boy wandering around alone?" she asked the neatly dressed man.

He lowered his voice. "In this crowd I wouldn't notice. He's around somewhere." He turned back to the people leaving the ship. "Stay tonight at the Eagle Hotel! Rooms to sleep six, only one dollar!"

Susan picked up her skirts and circled the end of the gangplank where women and children waited for their men. A woman with five small children caught her eye.

"Have you seen a little two-year-old boy by himself?" she shouted above the uproar. The woman shook her head and mumbled words Susan couldn't understand. Immigrants.

She went on to another hotel crier who was calling, "Stay at the Steamboat Hotel! Put up your family at our hotel and your animals in our barn!"

"Sir!" she shouted. "Have you seen a little two-year-old boy wandering around by himself?"

"Lost your little fellow, lady?"

"Yes. Where can I find a policeman?"

The crier scanned the crowd. He pointed. "The man in the blue suit with red whiskers. Hope he can help you."

Frantically Susan dashed around people and boxes to reach the policeman. "Please sir," she panted. "I've lost my little boy—he's two years old. Will you help me find him?"

The man smiled condescendingly. "Happens all the time, lady. Most every ship that docks, some youngster's lost. He'll turn up."

"You'll watch for him? He's just starting to talk. He says his name is 'Jim-mee.' His name is Jimmy Parker. He has blue eyes, brown hair and a beautiful smile. I'm so worried." She turned. "My husband's wagon is coming from the ship!" She ran up the gangplank to meet Henry and John.

"Henry!" she shouted over the clatter of wagon wheels on the gangplank. "Jimmy's lost!"

"I can't hear you! Meet me after I get the team off the gangplank!" He motioned.

Picking up her skirts Susan ran back to the spot where Fred, Emily and Josephine waited. All three children were crying. "I couldn't find him," she said. Tears stood in her eyes.

Henry, followed by John's ox-drawn wagon, pulled his team clear of the gangplank. He jumped from the wagon. "What's wrong?" he shouted.

"Jimmy's gone!" Susan, Emily and Josephine screamed

in unison.

For a moment Henry was speechless as he glared at Fred. Suddenly his voice exploded. "I told you to watch him! My God, can't you do *anything* right?"

Susan rushed to Fred's defense. "It wasn't his fault any more than mine. We stood him on a barrel and he—he disappeared!"

"We'll settle this later. Now we have to find Jimmy." He scanned the crowd.

The crier from the Steamboat Hotel stood nearby. "Find your little fellow?" he asked.

Susan shook her head.

"Both of these wagons belong to your family?"

Henry nodded silently as he studied the crowd. John stood by the ox team.

The crier continued. "The Steamboat Hotel is close. Take a room and stable privileges for your animals and you'll have more time to search."

"We'll take them," John said. "I'll drive the ox team and the girls can go with me. Fred can follow with the horses. We'll wait for you at the Steamboat Hotel."

Susan nodded silently. Henry's accusing eyes were fastened on Fred. "He'll likely lose the team and wagon," he muttered.

"Henry," Susan sobbed, "what are we going to do? I've searched and talked to a policeman and other people. I went through the crowd. He's—just—gone."

"Could—could he have fallen in the river?"

"We were right with him. He was standing on this barrel watching everything."

"Did Fred or you have hold of his hand?"

"No."

"I told Fred to hold onto him. And you should have known how he slips away."

"I know." She wiped her eyes.

"The Steamboat Hotel's there." Henry pointed. "We'll separate and search in opposite directions. He can't be far away, unless—" He looked toward the river. Finally he turned. "We'll meet at the hotel." He stalked away.

2   *1830*

At eight o'clock that night Susan stumbled into the hotel. The owner's wife, Mrs. Woodworth, met her. "You didn't find him?" she asked.

Susan shook her head. "Has my husband come back?"

"No. Your brother and children told us what had happened. The little fellow must be near here. Perhaps he is with another family and they haven't reported it. Yes, that must be what happened. I'm sure you'll hear something soon."

Susan rubbed her forehead. "I hope so, but I can't imagine anyone not reporting that they'd found a two-year-old boy." She hesitated. "Unless—unless they were immigrants and can't speak our language."

Mrs. Woodworth smoothed the apron over her broad hips. "That could be. Children often become separated from their families at the pier, but usually they're found in a few minutes. I'm sure he'll turn up soon—they always have."

Susan didn't reply. In a moment the woman continued. "You need food. I'll have something for you in a minute. Sit there at the table." She pointed to a long vacant table in the hotel dining room.

"Thanks. I'm not hungry." Susan rubbed her forehead.

"You need food and a cup of tea to cure that headache." Mrs. Woodworth disappeared into the kitchen.

Too weary to argue Susan dropped into a chair at the

table. Her temples throbbed. Almost immediately Mrs. Woodworth was back with a steaming mug of tea, a plate of bread and a dish of applesauce. She chatted as Susan sipped tea and picked at her food.

"My husband will spread the news about your little boy. The more people that know about his being gone, the better the chance of finding him soon. Your brother told us how he was dressed and that he's a friendly little fellow."

Susan slowly sipped her tea. "You're very kind. Thanks." She got up. "Where is our room?"

"Five doors to the right." She pointed to a long hall. "Room 10. Your brother and the children are there. When your husband comes in, I'll fix him something to eat."

"Thanks." Wearily she made her way down the hall to their room. She had never known such physical exhaustion. All afternoon she had prayed silently that Jimmy would be found. She pushed open the rough board door of Room 10. The children rushed to her, their eyes wide and frightened.

"Did you find him?" the girls asked.

Susan dropped on the bed. "No."

John put on his black hat and stood up. "Now that you're here with the children, I'll search."

"Please. I pray you'll find him." He patted her arm and closed the door behind him.

The girls sobbed. Fred, his eyes red, stared silently at the floor. Finally he blurted, "It's m-m-my f-f-fault. P-P-P-Pa's right. I'm n-no good. I n-n-n-never do anything r-r-right!"

Susan put her arms around the unhappy boy. "No one is to blame, certainly not you any more than I. Papa didn't mean what he said. You know how he is when he's angry. He's probably already sorry he said those things to you. But I can't understand how Jimmy climbed off that barrel without one of us seeing him."

Emily wiped her eyes. "We were all watching the cow

that fell in the water, remember?"

Susan said softly, "Did you see anyone talking to Jimmy?"

The children shook their heads. Emily said, "We only saw the Indians and other people that were on the boat and they didn't talk to us."

"Where—where could he be?" Susan whispered. "I searched and asked up and down the river, and Papa must have too."

"Maybe Papa will have him when he comes," Josephine said.

But it was not to be.

3
_____ *1830*

E~ARLY RISERS AT THE S~TEAMBOAT Hotel gathered at the table for breakfast. Most, like Henry and John, had cared for their animals at the barn, and many would be leaving that day for the last leg of their journey, the trip to their land in the wilderness.

The rough bearded men ate quantities of salt pork, biscuits, fried potatoes and coffee served to them by Mrs. Woodworth. The conversation was loud and boisterous as they discussed plans for the future.

"I'm settlin' my family out near Marshall," one man said. "The land's good an' there's oak clearings so maybe I can plant a little wheat this fall."

"They ain't no oak clearings on my land near Livingston Center," another settler replied. "I can't plant wheat 'til I get land cleared. 'Twill be slim pickings for a year or two." He paused. "My wife ain't happy 'bout comin' to Michigan. She's scared of the Indians, bears and wolves—an' she says we'll starve to death."

"Yeah," another man agreed. "Wimmin folk don't gen'rally like comin' to Michigan. But in a few years there'll be churches an' schools an' they'll have neighbors. They'll like it then."

Mrs. Woodworth passed the biscuits to Henry. "My husband says you should talk to Tom Mason about your little boy," she said softly. "He would spread the word."

A huge man asked, "You the feller that lost his little boy?"

The table erupted with questions and exclamations. Briefly Henry explained. After giving a description of Jimmy, he added, "We'd appreciate it if you'd watch for him." They murmured their sympathy and promises.

"Where could we find Tom Mason?" John asked.

Mrs. Woodworth answered, "He's at the Territorial Capitol. He's acting Territorial Secretary when his father is gone. Though he's only eighteen years old, he gets things done." [1]

"How do we get to the Capitol?" Henry asked.

Mrs. Woodworth passed a platter of salt pork. "You take Randolph to Jefferson, turn left one block to Woodward, then right to Michigan Avenue and left to Griswold. Look to the right and you'll see the Capitol. It's a white two-story building. Mason will be there early." She paused. "How's your wife?"

"She's holding up. She's still hopeful. She'll be down soon for breakfast with the children."

Outside the late September sun was shining. Henry and John hurried along wooden sidewalks to muddy Jefferson and on to Woodward. Near the corner French farmers were setting out their fruits and vegetables at the market. Children played about their fathers' crates of produce. As they walked John and Henry watched closely for Jimmy. They followed Woodward and crossed foul-smelling Savoyard

Creek.

Soon they arrived at the Capitol, a white, two-story frame building with a high square tower topped by a cupola. Six columns graced the south front entrance. It was an elegant appearing building uncommon in the little city of twenty-five hundred people.

Hurrying through the front entrance they entered the ninety by sixty foot building. The hall was dark, the only light coming from windows at either end, and from a few open doors. A meeting room bore the sign TERRITORIAL COUNCIL. A table surrounded by thirteen chairs was centered in the room. A tall young man came toward the door.

"I'm Tom Mason," he smiled. "We're glad to have you visit the Capitol. I'm alone here now—the others come in at eight—but I'll show you around."

"Thanks," Henry said, "but we're here because we have lost our two-year-old boy." He motioned toward John. "This is my brother-in-law, John Thompson, and I'm Henry Parker. Mrs. Woodworth at the hotel said you might help us find Jimmy."

Sympathy and concern were evident on young Tom Mason's face. He asked questions and listened attentively as Henry told of Jimmy's disappearance.

"Hm-m-m. It's strange. You say the boy is just learning to talk?"

"That's right. We hope he is with a family who doesn't know how to find us. There were many families of immigrants on the ship."

Mason nodded. "I'll make up signs and we'll post them all over town. Before night everyone in Detroit will know of your missing boy. Perhaps he will turn up before we have the signs done. You'll be at the Steamboat Hotel?"

"That's right." Henry held out his hand. "Thank you for helping us, Governor. That little boy is pretty special to us." Tears stood in his eyes.

"We're glad to help. Let me know when you find him."

Henry and John returned to the muddy street and turned left on Gratiot. "There's a crowd of people across Woodward," John said. "We may as well look there."

"Must be some kind of celebration," Henry said, "but it's early for that many people to gather."

"They have boards set up for seats and people are eating. What's going on?" John's eyes fell on the word at the front of the building. " 'Tis the penitentiary—the jail," he murmured.

A drunken fight erupted between two rough-appearing men near the street as several people scrambled to take the seats vacated by the men.

"My God," Henry gasped. "There's a gallows on that platform in front of the jail. This crowd is here for a hanging!"

A band at the right of the platform struck up loud music. Several boys laughed loudly as they stuffed themselves with peanuts. People applauded and stamped their feet and children yelled as the crowd anticipated the thrilling climax of the event—a hanging.

John spoke to a silent man beside him dressed in the garb of a priest. "Is there going to be a hanging?"

The elderly priest sighed. "Tom Mason and a few of us have tried to stop it but the people are wild for revenge."

"What's it all about?" John asked while Henry's eyes searched for his little son.

The priest shouted to be heard above the band music. "The prisoner, Jess Simmons, was convicted of killing his wife in a drunken rage. She was a well-liked lady and the public is furious. Simmons was sentenced to death by the territorial court. When the sheriff refused to act as hangman, Ben Woodworth, owner of the Steamboat Hotel, volunteered to take his place. There was nothing we could do to stop it. The people want revenge—an eye for an eye." [2]

John stared at the gallows. The rope with the noose at the end swung gently in the breeze. "We should talk to them," he paused. "Maybe together we could stop the hanging. I'm John Thompson, a Methodist minister," he explained.

The priest nodded. "I'm Father Gabriel Richard. I'm an old man, and I've tried many times to prevent public hangings. This morning I tried once more. It was a vain attempt. They must have their revenge." He hesitated. "It will soon be over. Woodworth is coming out with the prisoner."[3]

The band struck up another spirited tune. As one enormous voice the crowd cheered when, led by Woodworth, his head lowered and with a guard on either side, the prisoner came out of the jail. With his hands tied, the man raised his head and looked out over the spectators. The sentence of the court was read to him but because of the commotion Henry, John and the priest were unable to hear the words.

A blindfold was tied over Simmons' eyes and the noose was slipped over his head. Suddenly his lips began to move and in a quivering voice he sang. The crowd quieted as they listened to the words of the hymn, "My Faith Looks Up To Thee."

> *My faith looks up to Thee,*
> *Thou Lamb of Calvary*
> *Savior divine!*
> *Now hear me while I pray;*
> *Take all my guilt away;*
> *O let me from this day*
> *Be wholly thine.*

Woodworth waited until the last note of the hymn died away. Then the trap was sprung. The crowd's cheer was deafening.

Henry cleared his throat. "Let's get out of here." People were beginning to leave. They had had their vengeance.

John bade the priest farewell and followed Henry down the board walk across muddy Monroe and Michigan Avenue and past beautiful St. Anne's Catholic Church.

"That priest was Father Gabriel Richard," he explained. "If Jimmy isn't at the hotel, I'll find Father Richard. He might have suggestions."

Henry plodded through the mud. "Must have had heavy rains," he commented absently. After a time he said, "I am sick at heart. Jimmy—gone. I can't believe it. And I'm angry—angry at Fred and Susan that they didn't watch him. How could they be so careless?" He wiped a tear away. "I had placed all my hopes on that little boy. He was the child I would have liked to have been. Happy, smiling, even-tempered—the opposite of me, only he looked like me. I had great plans for the two of us."

John remonstrated, "But you have Fred, and we'll likely find Jimmy."

"Fred! I'm disappointed in the boy. And he despises me! I have a feeling Jimmy is dead—drowned in that damned river." He motioned toward the docks at the end of Randolph Street.

"We can't give up hope." John pointed. "There's the Methodist Church. Let's stop there to pray."

Inside they knelt in the cool semi-darkness of the church. John prayed aloud for Jimmy's safe return as Henry, his head in his hands, made silent supplication to the Almighty, though he felt in his heart the prayers would be unanswered.

4

Two days later there still had
been no word of the missing child. Tom Mason had had
posters put up at all the main intersections in downtown
Detroit, but no one came forward to say they had seen a
lost child.

"He's gone," Henry agonized sadly, "gone because of
carelessness." He glanced at Fred and Susan. The boy
walked to the window and stared silently into Randolph
Street. Supply-filled canvas-covered wagons rolled through
the muddy streets. Entire families bundled up against the
raw wet wind huddled inside. The wide-rimmed wheels cut
deep tracks so that teams of horses and oxen strained to
keep the wagons moving, ever fearful of a cut from the
driver's whip.

"Where's Uncle John?" Josephine asked.

"He's gone to talk to Father Gabriel Richard," Henry
said. "Father Richard said if Jimmy turns up they will keep
him at the orphanage until some of us are in Detroit." His
tortured eyes were tear-filled. "But he won't turn up. He's
dead and we may as well leave this damned place. I wish I'd
never heard of Michigan."

Susan said quietly, "You want to go back to York
State?"

"Hell, no! There's nothing there for us. The farm's sold
and most of the money is spent for land and supplies. We
will leave tomorrow. The animals are eating a dollar's
worth of hay a day, our room's costing a dollar every night,
and eating here at the hotel is expensive. There's no use
staying any longer."

"Henry," Susan hesitated. "The children and I have
been praying and we have an answer to our prayers."

"Yeah?"

"God has told me Jimmy is alive."

Henry snorted. "Did He tell you where he is?"

"No. But he is alive. I believe he has been kidnapped."

Fred turned to watch his father as Emily and Josephine nodded their agreement.

"Humph! We'll never see the boy again! And why would anyone kidnap him?"

Susan continued. "Because he's a sweet, friendly child and someone, probably a woman who has no children, just— just took him. And anyone who wanted a child enough to kidnap him surely will be good to him."

All eyes were on Henry. He stared at each of the children and then at Susan. "You believe what your mother says?"

"Yes, Papa," the girls murmured. Fred nodded.

"Humph! I guess that crazy idea makes you feel better."

Emily remonstrated, "But God told Mama Jimmy is safe."

"Well, He hasn't told Uncle John and he's one of His ministers." No one spoke for a time.

Henry suddenly got up, his eyes blazing with anger. "Everything happens to me! All my life it has been this way! Bad luck, bad luck! Nothing goes right for me! Life isn't worth living! You all hate me, I see it in your eyes. Jimmy was the only one that cared about me and you've taken him away from me! I'm getting out of here!" He crammed his hat on his head and slammed the door.

Emily worried, "Where will he go?"

Susan sighed. "You know how Papa is. He'll calm down and be sorry in a little while. He'll probably go somewhere and buy a few tools to take with us. We'll leave tomorrow for the new land."

"M-M-Mama," Fred said. "Are you s-s-sure Jimmy's alive?"

"I truly feel he is. We must all try to help Papa. Promise?"

"We promise," the girls said. Fred was silent.

References

[1, 2, 3]Harlan L. Hagman, *Bright Michigan Morning* (Green Oak Press, 1981), pp. 28, 39.

Chapter Five
1830

PIONEER TRAVEL

1830

1 ————————————————————

HENRY, JOHN AND FRED WORKED silently as they loaded the wagons and prepared for the journey to the Parkers' new land. Brindle and Blacky, the heifer, were tied behind Henry's wagon. The sow in her box beside Rusty, the dog, and Cat in her crate all peered out at the activity near the stable of the Steamboat Hotel. A crate of cackling chickens topped the load. Fog horns bellowed mournfully on the Detroit River which was invisible through the fog, though it was less than a block away.

"Uncle J-J-John," Fred began. "Where c-c-can I t-t-tie Roamer?"

"How would you like to ride him?"

"Your n-n-new horse? C-c-could I?"

"It would be good for him. He may as well get used to the wilderness. That's about all he'll see from now on. Did you hear the man I bought him from say he came from northern Ohio?" Fred nodded.

"You can break him in and get him used to Michigan trails. Maybe he'll see a wolf or a bear. He might be skittish at first, but just hold the reins tight."

"I-I-I can do it!" Fred exclaimed with a smile, the first time he had smiled in several days.

"May as well get started," Henry stated shortly. "Fred, get your mother and the girls."

Fifteen minutes later the solemn group began the trek to the new land. As they neared the market at the intersection of Woodward and Jefferson, Susan said, "We should lay in a supply of vegetables."

Henry changed the reins to his left hand and brushed tears from his eyes. "Yeah. I almost forgot." He pulled the team to the edge of the street beside the market of the French farmers and signaled to John and Fred. The little procession stopped.

A dark-haired, dark-skinned man approached the wagon. Behind him were other men and numerous crates of potatoes, carrots, turnips, onions, cabbages and apples.

"You want zee potatoes?" the ragged farmer asked.

Henry nodded silently as he spoke to Susan. "Tell him what you want and remember there won't be any more until we grow it next summer."

Quietly she ordered various kinds of vegetables which the farmer carried to the wagon. "Mama," Josephine called. "Could we have some apples?"

Susan nodded. "And we'd like five bushel of—better give us greenings. They keep better."

As Henry and John distributed the purchases between the two wagons the farmer asked, "Where eez your land?"

Henry pointed to the southwest. "Out toward Adrian."

"Take tree, four days—when eet eez dry. Now, much mud, and more rain comin'."

Henry paid the farmer before he asked, "You seen a little two-year-old lost boy around here?"

The French farmer's dark eyes showed his interest. "You are zee family what lost zee little boy? Zat is ver-r-ry bad." He shook his head. "I not see heem."

"If you or your friends see him, would you tell Father Richard? He will take care of him."

The Frenchman nodded. "We will watch good. Zanks for zee business." He turned to wait on another customer.

Silently the two wagons, followed by Fred riding John's horse, made their way through the busy streets. Dozens of people hurried along the wooden sidewalks between muddy intersections. Bearded men, some dressed in deerskin clothes, a few women carrying parcels or baskets of vegetables from the market, society ladies with exquisite hats and outer wraps, children following their mothers or holding to their skirts, businessmen and government officials in dark suits with white shirts and wide-brimmed black hats, all hurried about their business. Numerous Indians and French people mingled with the frontier men who dressed in the accepted shirt and knicker-type pantaloons above knee-high knitted socks and heavy shoes. Though each was different in some way, they all had one trait in common—their shoes were caked with mud.

There were many carts and wagons in the streets. Susan wondered if these people also were going to the Michigan wilderness to make their home. Silently she studied a stylishly dressed couple whose horse splashed through the mud pulling the now-familiar wide-rimmed two-wheeled cart commonly used in the muddy streets. The cart had an open box with benches set lengthwise, and a tailgate which could be opened. Some of the vehicles carried people while others transported goods. Matrons bowed to friends and acquaintances on the sidewalk. Many conducted business with the French market owners from the carts.

Silently they passed the Episcopal and Presbyterian churches on the right side of Woodward. As they neared

Michigan Avenue at the Campus Martius Square, Josephine called, "What are all those people doing?"

"They're standing in a circle watching something," Emily murmured.

" 'Tis a whipping post," Henry explained, "and a man is tied to it."

"Why's he got his shirt off?" Josephine asked. "What are they going to do to him?"

"Let's go on," Susan urged. "I don't want the children to see this."

Henry replied, "We can't get through. We'll have to wait."

The hands of the young man were tied to the post above his head. People from the circle about him jeered. "Serves ya right, ya thievin' bugger," a man yelled. Another shouted, "If I catch you in my chicken coop you won't live to get to the whippin' post!"

A large man holding a blacksnake whip with a long, tapering rawhide thong stood ready to administer the punishment. The crowd continued shouting and murmuring.

"What did he do?" Emily asked.

"Likely stole chickens from somebody's chicken coop," Henry answered. "Listen. He's talking."

The young man looked over his shoulder. His frightened blue eyes went from person to person as though he was searching for someone. Finally his glance stopped. "Eric," he began, "I'm sorry I stole your hen, but little Sally was sick and she begged for chicken soup. I didn't have the money to buy a chicken."

A rough-appearing farmer answered. "If you'd asked for a chicken, I'd have given you one. Thieves have to be punished." He spoke to the man with the whip. "Let's get on with it."

"Twenty lashes!" the bailiff shouted as he lifted the whip and brought the snapping thong down on the young man's bare back.

"One!" the crowd shouted as the victim flinched and a red welt appeared on his back. "Two! Three! Four! Five! Six! Seven! Eight! Nine! Ten!"

Blood was flowing from the torn back of the thief who twisted and turned with the force of each lash.

"Mama, I'm sick," Emily gasped.

"Turn your head. Don't watch."

"Eleven! Twelve! Thirteen! Fourteen! Fifteen!" A piercing scream came from the tortured man's lips. "Sixteen! Seventeen! Eighteen! Nineteen! Twenty!" He slumped against the post. The bailiff released the victim's hands and he struggled to his feet and staggered away with blood dripping onto the soiled shirt which hung from his waist.

"He got what was comin' to him," someone said as the crowd melted away.

Henry clucked to the horses and motioned to John with the ox team and Fred on horseback. They pulled left onto Michigan Avenue which became the Chicago Road outside of Detroit.

"That was awful," Emily gasped.

"He was a thief but he stole to feed his sick child," Susan murmured.

Henry said, "I remember something the Quakers used to say about punishment. I think it's from the Bible. 'A whip for the horse, a bridle for the ass, and a rod for the fool's back.' "

Suddenly Josephine said, "Papa, is that the way they whip the slaves?"

"I expect it is—only worse."

"Someday when I'm big I'm going to help them."

Susan smiled at the child. "I believe you will."

They were silent for a long time as the wagon bumped along on the rut-filled trail outside Detroit. The miles passed slowly on the narrow Indian trail which was bor-

dered by water filled ditches. When two wagons met, one
would pull to the side and stop until the other passed. As
soon as they were outside Detroit the Michigan wilderness
closed in, the leafless trees arching over the narrow trail.

At noon they stopped beside a creek for a lunch packed
that morning by Mrs. Woodworth. Gathered about Henry's
wagon they ate bread and cold ham and drank water
dipped from the creek. Susan filled a quart dipper with
milk. Everyone drank from the container and passed it on.

"Brindle's milk tastes good," Emily said. "I wish Jimmy
was here to have some."

No one spoke. Finally Henry blurted, "We may as well
get used to it. Jimmy's gone—for good."

Fred turned away to wipe his eyes. John took a big bite
of bread before he said, "We have to accept whatever is
God's will."

" 'Tis a strange God that would end a little boy's life,"
Henry replied bitterly.

Susan turned. "All of you listen to me! Jimmy is alive!
Don't ever let me hear any of you speak as though he is
dead!"

Henry got up. "You're living in a dream world. Get
used to it, Susan. He's not coming back to us. Now we have
to get going. 'Tis a long way to our land."

Susan stood before Henry and stared into his eyes. "I
know he is alive. I feel it in my heart. We will see him
again, Henry."

As Fred walked past Rusty's crate the dog barked impatiently. "I-I'm going to l-l-let you out. You n-n-need to
r-r-run."

The dog raced about jumping and barking at the horses
and oxen, then spinning in a circle he chased his tail. Fred
gave the dog a friendly pat. *You're thanking me for letting
you out,* he thought.

The silent, somber group slowly made their way westward, each one deep in thought. As the wagon jolted along Susan pulled her shawl about her shoulders for protection against the misty cold air. She pondered the future with concern. They had left the security of their York State home and neighborhood to face the dangers of the Michigan wilderness. They had lost Jimmy. They would be facing uncivilized Indians and dangerous wild animals. She sighed. They had made their choice. She would do her best to hold the family together. She hoped Henry would try to control his impatience with them and that he would not expect perfection from Fred.

Henry coughed and slapped the reins against Major's shiny black rump. "Gee!" he shouted. Why had he ever decided to come to Michigan? He'd had everything a man could want in York State. A good farm left to him by his parents, a fair house, a fine wife and children—all but Fred, that is. He didn't expect much from Fred. But Jimmy —poor little Jimmy. He must not think of him. They had burned their bridges behind them. There was no returning. He would have to make his way in Michigan. Work and a farm that produced good yields of grain—that was all he had to look forward to. He was thankful he still had money left from the sale of the farm.

Emily cradled her rag doll. Everyone seemed so sad. They all missed Jimmy. She would believe like Mama that he was alive. Some day they would see him. And she would help Mama all she could when they got to their land. The scene at the whipping post returned to plague her. Her stomach twisted.

Josephine perched on a barrel of corn meal. She watched the woods hoping to see an Indian or a bear. She liked the excitement of the trip. First the canal boat, then the steamship and the storm, the Indian men and—and then Jimmy was lost. That was the bad part. She missed her little brother's smile and baby chatter. She thought of the poor man who had been whipped. His bleeding back had been a horrible sight.

John, walking beside the pair of oxen, guided them with commands of "Gee" and "Haw" together with a light touch of the whip he carried. He was glad he was in Michigan, but perhaps it was a mistake for Henry to have brought his family to this wilderness. Susan was strong, but could she bear up indefinitely to the hardships of a frontier woman's life? And little Jimmy—though John believed the child was dead, it was easier for his sister to pretend he was alive. He'd do what he could to help Henry build a cabin and barn and he'd remain with them during the winter, but next spring he would begin his work as a circuit rider and Christian missionary to the Indians. He glanced back at Fred. The boy's head was down. He seemed deep in though as Roamer followed close to the covered wagon.

Fred thought, *Pa will never forgive me for losing Jimmy. He loved Jimmy better than me. He has never liked me. I remember the day he came home from working on the canal. I was four years old. He said I was a baby because I couldn't talk plain. He always says I'm stupid. I know I'm not stupid but I don't talk right. But I can read and write real good. I don't talk much because it's too hard and people laugh or they look away so they don't see the way I twist my face when I can't say words. But Pa is the worst. He thinks I stammer to bother him. I wish I could talk right; then he would like me better.*

Brindle bawled as Rusty ran barking beside her. With each jolt of the wagon on the rut-filled trail, loose items inside the wagon jingled and pails and tubs tied on the outside rattled. Susan and the girls swayed with the jouncing wagon. When they dropped into an unusually deep hole in the road, the chickens cackled and the sow grunted as they voiced their complaints.

Silently Henry drove the team past an abandoned wagon. John called to Fred, "Someone broke a wheel on that hole and they left their wagon."

Fred nodded. John continued. "Must have happened to-day or else the good wheels would be gone."

"Why?"

"Many wheels are broken on these rough trails. People take what they need from abandoned wagons."

"That's s-s-stealing!"

"You're right. These people were only half a day out of Detroit. They must have piled everything on another wagon because this one is empty."

Roamer pricked up his ears and shied at a buzzing sound beside the trail. Fred tightened the reins. "R-R-Roamer's s-s-scared. 'Tis a rattler!" he shouted.

"Horses are afraid of rattlesnakes. There's lots of them in southern Michigan. This one didn't harm us. We'll let him live." In a moment John asked, "How do you like Roamer?"

"I-I-I like him."

"He and I will be good friends," John said. "When I ride the trails he will be my only companion."

"I-I-I'd like a horse of m-m-my own."

"You'll have one someday."

"Where will we s-s-stay tonight?"

"Your father said Ten Eyacks, if we get that far. It's on the Rouge River."

The afternoon passed slowly for Susan and the girls. The constant jolting and swaying of the wagon was tiring. Henry was moody and silent except when he spoke to the horses. Finally Susan said, "I hope we reach Ten Eyack's Inn soon."

Henry replied shortly, "I'm going as fast as I can. You want me to drive pell-mell and break a wheel like that wagon back there?" Susan didn't reply.

The misty afternoon sky suddenly became dark as a heavy cloud hung over them. Soon a few drops of cold rain changed to a heavy downpour. No one spoke as the wagon jolted on. Emily hugged her doll and Josephine peered soberly into the dripping forest. Cat mewed as rain splashed into her cage. The chickens stood with their tails low so the rain would more easily run off their backs.

John, Fred and Henry had pulled on their oiled jackets. John splashed along beside the oxen in the slippery mud. In a short time the wet clay of the trail oozed up beside the turning wheels making deep tracks. It seeped up through the cloven hooves of the oxen and cows and was sucked downward with a sticky sound as John and the animals raised their feet from the slippery paste. It stuck to the slowly turning wheels and gradually filled the spaces between the spokes until the wheels looked solid.

They had not met a wagon since before the noon lunch. It was as though they were the only people in the area. The downpour continued. Huge puddles rapidly collected on ground already saturated with fall rains.

Early darkness was descending on the little group when John called jovially, "A light ahead! Must be Ten Eyacks!"

Five minutes later they pulled up in front of the little inn. Henry went inside. In a moment he returned. "They have room for us," he announced. "Susan, take the girls and go inside while we stable the animals."

A welcome fire crackled in the large fireplace. Several kettles hung suspended from cranes over the fires. Appetizing odors drifted into the twenty- by thirty-foot room.

"I'm hungry," Josephine said.

A buxom woman came to greet them. "We have plenty of food. Would you like to go to your room before you have supper?"

Susan removed her shawl. "Yes, please. We'll wait to eat with the men." Several frontier men lounged about the room smoking corncob pipes and drinking beer.

"Your room is the third door on the left. You'll find water in the pitcher."

"Thank you." Susan and the girls walked down a narrow rough board floor to their room. She pushed the door open to pitch darkness. "Hold the door open, Emily. Yes. Here's a table with a candle." A moment later the dim light gave them a view of the room. Two beds, a small table with a pitcher of water and a rough towel, a slop bucket, a straight chair and a four drawer chest. Susan sighed. "It's good to be out of the wagon and inside where it's dry," she said as she hung her shawl over the chair. "Girls, wash your hands and face so you'll be ready for supper." The rain beat a tattoo on the west window.

Half an hour later they sat down to a supper of boiled potatoes and cabbage, salt pork, bread, applesauce and milk. Shortly after they began eating, two men came from the hall to join them at the table.

John said, "Susan, these fellows are Sam and Joe Gross. We met them at the stable. They have a nice horse they'd like to sell."

"How do you do?" Susan motioned. "The girls are our daughters." The children looked up from their plates and smiled.

"Nice family, you have, Parker," one of the men said. Henry nodded as he kept his eyes on his plate. Finally he asked, "You fellows come from the west?"

"Yeah," Sam Gross replied. "Trail's bad. Mud holes, deep ones. It's bad going for loaded wagons."

"Why you selling that horse?"

"Joe and me are riding horseback to Detroit. We been here all summer. Built a cabin and barn and got some wheat out. We're going back to York State for the winter, then next spring we'll bring our families to stay. We had two teams. They worked good. We sold one horse to a fellow near Tecumseh and we want to sell the second one, too. In Detroit we'll get rid of the two we're riding and buy new ones next spring. You fellows interested?"

"I might be," Henry replied. "I've got oak clearings on my land. The sod's mighty tough. Plowing would be easier with a three-horse team." He hesitated. "Let me think about it until morning."

All night the rain pounded on the tavern roof. Susan and the girls slept restlessly in one bed while Henry, John and Fred slept in the other. They were up before daylight. It still was raining. Fred and the men went to the barn to feed and care for the livestock. The Gross brothers were there ahead of them.

"Still interested in the mare? I'll make you a good price," Sam Gross said as he threw the saddle on his horse.

Fred walked over to the ginger-colored mare the men were discussing. He rubbed her velvety nose and she whinnied softly and nuzzled his face. He could love this horse. He patted her neck.

"Like her, Son?"

Fred started. His father never called him "Son." That was the name he called Jimmy. Fred smiled. "Y-yes sir. She's nice."

"I've bought her for you. She's yours, only I'd like to use her sometimes with my two."

Tears filled Fred's eyes. "Thank you, Pa. Thank you."

"Her name's Ginger. Want to ride her today? Uncle John says you can use his saddle and we'll lead Roamer behind my wagon."

Fred wiped his eyes on the back of his hand. "Th-thank you, Pa," he said again.

"I'm sorry, Son. I've not been nice to you. Let's start over." Henry put his arm about Fred's shoulder.

"Y-yes Pa. I'll be good." He hesitated. "Who's that man w-w-watching us?"

"I don't know. He came in just as I was paying Sam for Ginger. Maybe he thinks he's seen me somewhere. Let's feed the animals and milk Brindle. Then we'll go to breakfast and tell Mama and the girls about your horse."

John smiled approvingly as he curried Roamer. He hoped the reconciliation between Henry and his son would be lasting.

Chapter Six
1830

TROUBLE ON THE TRAIL

1830

1 _____

As THEY FOLLOWED THE OLD CHI-
cago Road Trail westward toward Ypsilanti, the Parkers
occasionally passed clearings in the forest where families
had built tiny log cabins. Smoke wafted upward in the
damp air and drifted off among the forest treetops. Around
the cabins amid girdled trees were patches of winter wheat
and corn shocks. Bright orange pumpkins lay on the ground
waiting to be gathered.

Usually a settler's dog barked furiously and ran to chal-
lenge Rusty who capably defended himself while the settler
waved at the travelers. Slowly they made their way over
the muddy, bumpy trail through a wilderness of hardwood
trees: elm, maple, oak, hickory, ash and beech.

As they passed a small farm with numerous girdled
trees, Josephine asked, "Why has someone cut bark off
some of the trees?"

" 'Tis the quickest way to kill a tree," Henry replied. "If you cut off a ring of bark with an axe, the tree will die. See where the man had corn growing between the dead trees?"

"Why doesn't he cut them down?"

"He will when he has time."

Emily asked, "Will you cut rings around the trees on our land?"

"Our land has a few oak openings—places where there aren't any trees. We'll plant crops there next year. Later we'll clear more land so we can have big fields of wheat."

As they paused for the noon lunch, an ox-drawn wagon came from the west. The man, dressed in deerskin clothing, paused to talk. "Jest want to tell you folks there's a bad place in the road a few miles west. Turrible mud, jest turrible. My oxen could hardly get the empty wagon through. The north side of the trail might be harder than the middle."

"Thanks," Henry called. "Are there other bad places 'tween here and Ypsilanti?"

"Some. But the first one is the worst. Good luck!" He waved and touched his oxen lightly with the whip.

While they stood about eating the lunch, prepared by the cook at Ten Eyack's Inn, Henry said to Fred, "How'd you like riding your new horse?"

The boy smiled. "Sh-she's great!"

Rusty barked and ran into the forest. "A deer!" Emily shouted. "He's chasing a deer!"

John smiled. "I wonder what he'll do when he meets a bear? He'll likely run in the other direction."

Henry put his arm about Susan's shoulders. "You're mighty quiet today," he said.

"I've been thinking how pleasant everyone has been this morning. It's nice when we're like this."

He kissed her lightly on the cheek. "Young 'uns, we're lucky to have your mother. She's special." The children nodded.

An hour later the procession halted at Henry's signal. A marshy swamp lay ahead. "This must be the place that's bad," John said as the men went to investigate. Fred rode Ginger behind them.

Henry spoke to Fred, "Ride back and get the axe from inside the back of my wagon. We'll cut a stick to see how deep the mud is." the boy turned the horse and rode the short distance to the wagons.

Henry paced impatiently. "This looks bad. Hope we're not held up too long."

"We may have to cut logs to throw into the mud," John said.

"That would hold us up." He turned. "Where is that boy?"

Two or three minutes later Fred trotted up on his horse carrying the axe. "It took you long enough," Henry growled as he took the axe and cut a sapling with one chop. Quickly he removed the small branches and began testing the depth of the mud.

"Doesn't look good," John commented. "Mud's more than a foot deep."

Henry tried the north edge of the trail. " 'Tis no better here. We may as well start cutting trees to throw across the mud." His voice showed anger. "I don't know why things can't go right," he grumbled. "Fred, get the other axe out of Uncle John's wagon. And hurry!"

The men chopped numerous trees about three inches in diameter which were thrown across the mud hole at six-inch intervals. while they cut down the trees, Fred and Emily dragged the poles to the mudhole.

Susan and Josephine climbed from the wagon and wandered about. "It feels good to get out and walk," Josephine sighed. In a moment she asked, "What are those orange berries on the vine?"

"Bittersweet."

"They're pretty. Are they good to eat?"

"No. They're poison. But a little of the juice from the vine will stop pain. That, and tea made from willow twigs are about all we have for pain."

Susan walked on. "This bush is sassafras. When people have inflammation of the lungs or when children don't break out as they should with measles, sassafras tea will make them sweat. That's good. It helps them to get better."

"How do you know these things, Mama?"

"My mother, your Grandma Thompson, told me just as I'm telling you."

"It would be nice to be a nurse and to help sick people get well."

Henry's impatient voice came to them through the trees. "Gol darn it, boy! You're slower than molasses in January! Get a move on, and you, too, Emily! Seems like you could place these poles as fast as John and I cut them!"

From a distance Rusty barked. A few seconds later two does raced across the trail, their white tails held high as the dog yipped at their heels. The commotion set the chickens to cackling and the sow to squealing.

" 'Spoze there are Indians out there?" Josephine asked as she gazed into the forest.

Susan brushed an insect from her hair. "There might be."

"Are you scared?"

"I guess not. Those Indian men on the ship seemed friendly."

"They liked Jimmy."

Susan sighed. "Everyone loves Jimmy. I hope he's with some nice family." She wiped her eyes. "I miss him so."

Josephine turned. "I'll go help Fred and Emily. Papa's yelling at them again."

Susan rubbed her forehead as she returned to the

wagon. Her head ached as it often did when Henry was in a bad mood. She recalled what his mother once had said. "Henry's like two people. One sweet and loving, the other angry and abusive. And he can change from one to the other as fast as a flash of lightning. He'll not be easy for thee to live with, Susan."

Two hours later after much shouting, Henry declared they were ready to cross the mudhole. "I'll drive the horses," he said, "and everyone else get behind and push."

John removed the cattle from the back of the wagon and tied them to the wheel of the ox drawn vehicle.

"When the team starts, push for all you're worth!" Henry shouted. He clucked to the horses. "Get up!" His voice was forceful. The wagon began to move. "Push!" he shouted as he struck both animals with the end of the reins. They lunged forward, up and over the first log. Straining, they heaved the heavy load over the second pole as pots and pans rattled and chickens cackled. Banging and clanging over the corduroy-like roadway the horses snaked the heavy load forward with the help of the family pushing at the back. At last they were again on solid ground.

"One more to go!" Henry shouted triumphantly as he jumped from the wagon and led the others back to the second vehicle. Half an hour later both wagons and the animals were across the mudhole.

"If we don't have more trouble we might still reach Ypsilanti before dark," John said.

"I hope we can. I'd like to sleep in a bed rather than under the wagon," Susan replied.

Josephine grinned. " 'Twould be fun to sleep under the wagon and to cook over a campfire."

Henry cuffed her good-naturedly. "You'll get enough of that kind of life after we reach our land. It'll take several days to get a little cabin built." He patted his hip pocket. "We're more lucky than some settlers. We have money to stay at inns along the way."

They reached Ypsilanti before dark and found food and lodging for the family and animals at Arnold's Inn.

The next morning at breakfast John nudged Henry. "The man just coming in—isn't he the one we saw at Ten Eyack's stable where you bought Fred's horse?"

Henry nodded. The man seated himself across from them. "You must be going west, too," Henry commented.

The man glanced up but his eyes failed to meet Henry's. Gruffly he growled, "I'm on my way to Detroit."

"Didn't we see you at Ten Eyack's?"

"Nope. I'll be there tonight."

John said, "You must have a double—a brother, maybe?"

"Nope."

The conversation turned to other topics of interest as the fifteen guests consumed the bounteous breakfast. John and Henry were silent, each one wondering why the rough-appearing man denied being at Ten Eyack's.

Eager to return to the trail the Parker family left shortly after daylight. "We have a long day ahead of us if we are to reach Oak Plains tonight," Henry remarked. "The men in the saloon at Ypsilanti said there are no bad mud-holes between here and Oak Plains."

"When will we see Indians?" Josephine asked.

Henry smiled. "They're likely out there in the woods watching us most of the time."

Emily moved close to her mother as Josephine scanned the forest. "There's none out there," she declared.

"Papa's joking," Susan said. " 'Twill be a nice day. The sun's coming up."

"There are no good days for me since Jimmy's gone," Henry said, his mood suddenly swinging from a jocular to a morose one. No one replied.

Fred rode Ginger beside John. "I-I wish I could dr-drive

the oxen so you c-c-could ride." His face twisted with the effort required for speaking.

"I don't mind. You enjoy your horse while you can. Your father, you and I have many hard days ahead of us before we get our shelter built on the new farm."

"L-l-log b-buildings?"

"The cabin will be logs. Perhaps we'll build a pole barn for the animals. It's easier." He flicked one of the oxen with his stick and thong whip. "Gee, Red," he called.

"Wh-what will we d-d-do all winter?"

"We'll hunt deer and fish through the ice and maybe we can get acquainted with the Indians. There's a tribe that winters on the Raisin River near our place."

Fred's eyes sparkled. "I-I-I'd like that."

"And there's reading to do on bad days. I'll be teacher. We can't have the Parker young ones growing up ignorant," he laughed.

"W-w-we don't have many b-b-books."

"I packed some and so did your mother. We'll have enough." He hesitated. "Fred."

"Y-y-yes."

"I know your stuttering bothers you. I have some ideas that may help you to break the habit. If you like, we'll work on it together."

Fred's eyes filled. He turned his head to brush away the tears. "I-I-I'd like that. I w-w-wish Pa was l-l-like you."

"We're all different. God made us so that no two are alike. This winter we'll see what we can do about the stuttering." John glanced behind them. "There's someone coming on horseback," he said. A few minutes later he muttered, "It's the man we saw at Ten Eyack's stable and again this morning at the Ypsilanti Inn."

"He—he said he was going to Deee-troit," Fred stammered.

"Yeah. He's carrying a rifle."

As the man approached them John called, "You're headed the wrong way."

"Nope. I'm headed right where I want to go. Right here." He dismounted holding the rifle. "I want to talk to the other feller. We have business to take care of." Striding ahead to Henry's wagon he spit tobacco juice on a flaming sumac shrub and wiped his beard on his hand. When he was abreast of the covered wagon he shouted, "Thought I'd catch you 'fore this!"

"I'm surprised to see you," Henry said. "Thought you'd be on the way east by now. What's wrong, did we leave something at Ypsilanti?"

The man's eyes were piercing. "Nope. But you will leave something here."

Susan, Emily and Josephine peered from inside the wagon at the uncouth character who repeatedly spit and wiped his mouth on his hand or sleeve. Fred rode Ginger behind the man and John stood beside Henry's team.

The man patted his rifle. "Old Betsy here says you'd better give me the purse you're carrying in your hip pocket."

For a moment there was dead silence as the family stared in disbelief at the robber. Suddenly Fred sprang from his horse and jumped astride the man's back knocking the rifle from his hands. John seized the gun and tossed it aside. Henry hit the ground and landed a forceful punch on the man's jaw. Fred hung on the robber's back, his arms locked in a vise-like grip about the thief's neck while Henry continued slugging him. Finally his knees buckled. Rusty barked furiously.

"Get a rope!" Henry shouted as he stood over the struggling man.

Shortly the robber was helpless, his hands tied behind his back. "What you gonna do?" he pleaded between swollen cut lips.

"We ought to let Old Betsy take care of you," Henry said picking up the rifle. "But we're not murderers. We'll take you to the next inn and they can send you back to the sheriff at Ypsilanti. We don't need your kind on the trails." He turned to Fred. "Thanks, Son. You saved our money." Fred smiled and nodded.

Henry pushed the man behind his wagon. "We'll tie you between Brindle and Blacky. You can walk."

"Can't I ride my horse?" the robber whined.

"You'll walk between the beasts. That's where you belong," Henry replied as he tied a rope around the man's neck and fastened it to the wagon box. "Tie his horse beside Roamer at the back of your wagon, John. And Fred, you ride behind and keep an eye on this fellow."

"Y-y-yes sir."

The procession soon was on its way. With pans rattling, animals complaining, chickens cackling and Rusty barking, there wasn't a quiet moment.

Inside the wagon Henry said, "We are in luck. If that fellow had stolen our money we wouldn't have had a cent left. We can thank Fred for quick thinking."

"He's a good boy," Susan said. "But he's sensitive and his feelings are easily hurt."

Josephine remarked, "I'd have liked to punch that man like Papa did!"

"Little girls don't punch people," Susan said. "Ladies don't fight."

"Then I wish I was a boy."

The remark was ignored. Riding silently through the wilderness each one was deep in thought. Josephine imagined she was a boy starting on a journey to an unknown area. She would be strong, brave and she'd do exciting things. She would live with Indians and ride her pony like the wind.

Emily planned how she would help her mother. She'd

learn to cook, bake and sew. And she would be a good housekeeper.

Susan said a silent prayer of thanksgiving that no one had been hurt in the scuffle with the robber. She would be glad when they turned him over to the people at the next inn. Her mind wandered to what the future held for them. It did not look pleasant. Nothing but hard work in a floorless rough log cabin. And though she didn't voice her feelings, she feared Indians. They had scalped many people years before in New York. And bears and wolves—she feared for her children and their animals.

Henry silently reminisced about Jimmy. He was bitter that God had taken his favorite son. Of course Fred had moments when he showed promise; jumping on that robber's back had taken courage and it saved the family's money. He would try to be more patient with the boy—if only he could control his unreasonable temper. But Fred's stuttering annoyed him. Why couldn't the child talk correctly? Was he stuttering to annoy as a way of getting even for past happenings?

John plodded along beside the oxen. "Haw, Brindle!" he shouted. His mind wandered. That fellow that tried to rob them—what had his life been like? Was he desperate for money to support a family, or was he lazy and of the belief that the world owed him a living? John hoped he'd have a chance to talk with the fellow before they reached the next inn.

Fred patted Ginger's neck. The horse whinnied softly. He kept his eyes on the man tied between the two cattle. It must be hard walking over the rough trail with your hands tied behind your back. Well, he deserved whatever sentence he received. Fred remembered his father's words of praise and he felt proud to have helped the family. He wished his father liked him. Maybe if Uncle John could help him to stop stuttering, his father would like him more.

The day passed slowly. At noon they ate a lunch of milk, johnny cake and hard boiled eggs which had been prepared for them by the cook at the Ypsilanti inn. Silently the robber stumbled along, his eyes on the ground. No one spoke to him. It was as though he wasn't there.

In mid-afternoon a shout from Henry alerted the family. "A man on horseback!" As he came nearer Henry murmured, "I'll be jiggered. I think 'tis the sheriff."

The traveler stopped his horse. "Afternoon, folks," he called. The sun glared on the silver star pinned to his jacket. "Where ya headed?"

Rusty yipped and barked before the man's white horse. "Down below Adrian," Henry replied. "We own land there. We're glad to see you, Sheriff. We have a prisoner for you. Want to get rid of him soon's we can."

The sheriff glanced into the wagon, then back at John and Fred. "One of these fellows?"

Henry laughed. "Hardly. They're part of my family. The prisoner's tied at the back of the wagon 'tween our cows. He tried to rob us." Henry reached behind him. "Here's the rifle he used. My son back there outsmarted him."

"Oh?" The sheriff went behind the wagon followed by Henry. The robber refused to look up. "What's your name?"

"Zeke Farmer," the man mumbled.

"You try to rob these people?" There was no answer. The sheriff untied the rope from the wagon and pulled the man to face him. "Answer me! Did you try to rob these people?" He waited, then gave the rope a yank. The robber's head snapped forward, then back. "Did you try to rob these people?" the sheriff demanded loudly. Rusty barked furiously.

"Yeah," the thief said softly. "But I didn't hurt them."

"Lucky for you. You're going with me to the jail." He turned to Henry. "Are one of the horses Farmer's?"

"Yeah. The one on the left. And here is his rifle. We are the Parkers. I'm Henry."

The sheriff grinned. "I most forgot to find out who this fellow tried to rob." He unfastened the rope from Farmer's neck. "Bet you're the feller that's been robbing folks along the Chicago Trail for the past few weeks. We'll put a stop to that kind of business. Get on your horse. You'll have to ride with your hands tied behind you."

"Thank you, Sheriff, for taking this fellow off our hands," Henry said as the little procession started toward the southwest.

"How far to the next inn?" John asked.

"I figger about ten miles but the trail's good. You should be there by dark."

They settled down for the last part of the day's journey. The horses tossed their heads, impatient with the slow pace of the oxen. Now and then they would turn their sensitive ears toward the underbrush where wild creatures were hidden. John and Fred told jokes to pass away the time.

Fred said, "A f-father said to his b-b-boy, 'You're a p-p-pig. Do you know what a p-p-pig is?'

"The boy said, 'Y-y-yes. A p-p-pig is a hog's little boy.' "

John laughed. "Here's one about a little girl. Her mother said, 'Milly, you're pretty dirty.' The little girl said, 'I know. I'm even prettier clean.' "

Fred chuckled. "That could be about J-J-Josephine. She gets pretty d-d-dirty."

John continued, "Hank said to Pete, 'Did you hear about the fish that had the measles?'

"Pete said, 'No. How's he getting along?'

"Hank answered, 'Pretty well. He just had them on a small scale.' "

Fred roared. "I-I-I like your jokes. Tell another one."

John scratched his head. Finally he said, "Three men were in a boat halfway across a lake. The first man said,

'Shucks! I forgot my lunch,' so he got out of the boat and walked to shore on top of the water.

"Later the second man said, 'Shucks! I forgot my fishing pole,' and he also walked across the water to shore.

"By this time the third man thought, 'They're not going to outsmart me.' He said, 'I forgot my bait can,' and he started across the water, but he sank.

"The first man turned to the second man and asked, 'Do you think we should have told him where the rocks are?' "

Again Fred laughed heartily. Then he said, "Did you hear about the m-m-man that said, 'I was sh-sh-shot through the l-l-leg'?

"His friend asked, 'Have a scar?'

"The first man said, 'N-no thanks. I d-d-don't smoke.' "

Susan smiled at the sounds of laughter coming from behind their wagon. "It's nice to hear Fred laugh. John is good for him."

"I wish we knew what they're laughing at," Josephine said. "I'd like to laugh too. I'm tired of riding in this bumpy wagon."

"When we get to the inn we'll have a good supper," Susan said. She glanced at the sky. "It looks like rain again."

When they reached the inn they found the place had only two buildings, an unfinished log cabin of a settler who was willing to feed and lodge them, and a pole barn.

"Next year we'll finish our cabin and build a real inn for travelers," Alpheus Kies, a whiskered pioneer, explained.

Mrs. Kies, a tall washed-out appearing blonde woman with straggly hair greeted them. "Come in. Our place ain't fancy, but we can feed you and put you up for the night. How many of you are there?"

"Six," Susan answered as she noticed the primitive unfinished cabin. A blanket served for the door, only half of the roof was on and there was no floor.

"Sit there on the trunk, Mrs.—"

"Parker," Susan replied. "And my daughters are Emily and Josephine."

"You have any boys?"

"Two. Fred and Jimmy." She hesitated. "Jimmy isn't with us."

"We don't have no young ones," Mrs. Kies said as she threw wood on the coals in the fireplace. "We just got here this summer and we've had guests many nights." She glanced up at the unfinished roof. "Al's got to get the roof done. Rains in like blazes sometimes."

An hour later they sat down at a rough-hewn table for a supper of boiled potatoes, salt pork, johnny cake and milk. Henry and Al drank whiskey with the meal.

Susan studied the crude cabin with its hard-packed dirt floor. She scarcely heard the conversation around the table. Mrs. Kies' dress was dirty. Susan's stomach lurched as Al frequently spit into the fire, barely missing the half-filled kettle of boiled potatoes on the hearth.

Suddenly rain spattered through the unfinished roof and onto the hard clay floor which soon turned to slippery mud.

Al and his wife laughed. Al wiped his mouth on his hand. "Take your plates, folks, and stand in front of the fireplace. Glad we got half of the cabin roofed."

Wind blowing through the open roof caused candles to flicker and go out. They finished eating by the light from the fireplace.

One corner in the roofed part of the cabin contained a bed which was partitioned off by hanging quilts. As Mrs. Kies collected the plates from her guests she said, "Mrs. Parker, you and your girls can sleep in the bed. Al and the men will sleep in the barn."

"Where will you sleep?" Josephine asked.

"On the floor under the bed." She carried the dirty

dishes to a pail of water on the hearth where she hastily rinsed them. The rain continued to drip through the open roof.

The men made light of the situation. "Guess we'll soon have a cozy little home like this, Susan," Henry laughed. Susan didn't answer.

After the men had gone to the barn and the cabin was quiet, Susan pulled the quilt high above the girls' necks. "The damp night air isn't good for you," she whispered.

A weird howl came from the nearby woods causing goose pimples to pop up on Susan's arms. Almost immediately other wolf voices answered. Rusty's barks joined the chorus until the woods echoes with the sounds.

"I'm scared," Emily whispered.

Mrs. Kies spoke from beneath the bed, "Wolves won't hurt us here. Course they might try to get your chickens or pig."

"Go to sleep," Susan whispered. "We're safe here."

At times the wolf pack and Rusty were silent. At other times a weird medley of whines, whimpers, howls and snarls reached the ears of the restless family. Finally a chorus of howls, yelps and barks together with shouts from the men, nearly deafened the women. Cattle bawled, the sow squealed and added to the pandemonium. Rifle shots rang out followed by sudden silence.

"Hope they got the varmints," Mrs. Kies muttered beneath the bed. "They was after your chickens." In a moment she continued, "You go to sleep now."

The rain dripped monotonously on the rough table. Henry shouted, "Think they'll be back?"

"Naw!" Al Kies called. "We hit two of 'em. That'll scare 'em off." Next morning two dead wolves lay a few feet from the wagons.

Emily wakened with a sore throat. Susan said, " 'Twas the damp night air. 'Tis not good for us."

A few minutes later Mrs. Kies mixed a weak salt solution in a tin cup which Emily carried outside in the rain where she hurried to gargle. Running inside, her teeth chattering, she murmured, "I'm so cold, Mama."

"Climb back in bed with Josephine. 'Tis warm there." Checking the child's temperature by laying her hand on her daughter's forehead, Susan said softly, "You have a fever. Cover up and keep warm."

The rain rattled against the half of the cabin that was roofed with split basswood logs. Mrs. Kies added wood to the fire and hung a kettle of water from the crane. "We'll have hot cornmeal mush and milk for breakfast. 'Twill stick to your ribs on a cold day." She worked by the flickering light from the fireplace.

An hour later as they ate standing before the fire in the dry half of the sixteen by twenty foot cabin, the conversation was of the wolf attack of the previous night.

"You'd think the varmints would learn," Al remarked. "About every week I shoot one or two of 'em."

"D-d-d-o they ever hurt people?" Fred asked.

"Naw. Course I wouldn't trust a pack if they was hungry and I didn't have my rifle."

Susan carried a bowl of hot mush to Emily. "Sit up, dear, and eat. 'Twill make you feel better."

"I can't Mama. I'm sick to my stomach." She threw the covers aside and rushed outside. The sound of retching drifted through the quilt which served as a door.

John finished his breakfast and set the bowl on the hearth. "I'll fix a place in the wagon so she can lie down." He went outside where he could be heard sympathizing with Emily.

No one spoke for several seconds. Finally Henry said, "Just our luck for someone to get sick. Everything seems to be against us."

"I wish I had some raspberry leaves to make tea," Susan

mused. "It quiets a sick stomach."

"Al," Mrs. Kies said, "Go see if there are a few leaves left on the raspberry bushes behind the barn."

The raspberry tea temporarily relieved Emily's nausea. John made a bed on top of the boxes and barrels in the wagon where the child lay covered over her head.

"I'm so cold," she whispered.

Susan comforted her. "You'll soon be warm in your little nest."

The rain rattled against the canvas top of the wagon. Josephine rode in John's ox-drawn vehicle. "I wanted to ride with you, Uncle John," she said. "I heard you and Fred laughing and telling jokes yesterday, and today Papa's cross, Emily's sick and Mama's worried." The wagon wheels hit an exposed root which threw Josephine against a side bow. "Ou-ouch! My head!" she complained.

"You'll l-l-live," Fred grinned.

The hours passed slowly. Cold and wet, the little group moved on. Emily vomited frequently and complained of her sore throat, muscle pains and headache.

"She has the grippe," Susan said softly to Henry. "This cold damp air is not good for her. When will we get to our land?"

"If we don't have trouble, I figger sometime tomorrow. Tecumseh is only a few miles ahead. We'll get something to eat at the inn."

"Is Tecumseh the Quaker settlement?" Susan asked.

"Both Tecumseh and Adrian." He paused. "Though I don't think of myself as being a Quaker, I feel comfortable with them. I understand their ways."

"They're nice people. I'm glad they'll be near us."

"Mama, I feel awful!" Emily wailed.

Susan rubbed the child's forehead. "I know," she soothed.

About one o'clock the wet, cold group entered the settlement of Tecumseh. "It's grown since I was here last year," Henry remarked. "Then there was only a sawmill and a tannery, besides the inn. Now they have a gristmill and several new cabins." They pulled up at the inn where a hearty meal was served. [1]

Susan carried a cup of warm milk and some bread to Emily who remained in the wagon.

"I'm not hungry," the ill child complained as she swallowed a few sips of milk and ate a couple bites of bread and butter. "I'm so hot."

"You have a fever. Keep your arms covered."

Back on the trail Emily fell into a restless sleep. Henry and Susan talked in low tones. "Most of the people in Tecumseh were dressed like Quakers," Susan said. "Their clothes are very plain."

"Yeah. I didn't tell them I was brought up a Quaker. Last year they told me Tecumseh was started by men named Wing, Evans and Brown. The next settlement, Adrian, was started by a Quaker named Comstock. I hope we can get there by night." [2]

"We should get Emily inside as soon as we can. This damp weather is bad for her."

"Yeah. Well, we'll stop at a settler's home, if we find one, and ask if they will put us up for the night."

Emily slept on though she had developed a hoarse cough since the midday stop. Finally they sighted a cabin, a barn and a small cleared field.

Henry stopped and called to John. "I'm going to stop and see if they'll put us up. Emily's pretty sick."

A young dark-haired woman came to the door. She looked at them questioningly. A small boy clung to her skirts.

Henry tipped his hat and smiled. "Ma'am, could you give us supper and breakfast and sleep us tonight? We'll pay you."

She responded to the question with a dazzling smile which revealed even, white teeth. "I wish I could, but we are low on food. I have barely enough for my son and myself. My husband will be back any time with supplies."

"Hm-m-m." After a moment Henry said, "We have cornmeal and ham and potatoes. Would you cook us a meal?"

The young woman again flashed the dazzling smile. "I'd be happy to, and also for you to stay overnight. It's lonely here with just Teddy for company. I had expected Zeke to be back before this. Bring your family inside and you can put your animals in the barn."

Henry tipped his cap. "Thank you, ma'am."

The young woman threw a shawl over her head. "I'll be right back," she said to the little boy who stared wide-eyed at Henry. Running towards the wagons she called to Susan, "Come in!"

Half an hour later when Emily was in bed, the animals were in the barn and the group was soaking up the heat from the fireplace, Henry said, "I'll get some of our supplies so you can fix supper, Mrs.—"

"Farmer, and your name is?"

Everyone stared at Mrs. Farmer. The silence grew uncomfortable. Finally Henry said softly, "Mrs. Zeke Farmer?"

"That's my name. Nancy Farmer. Did you meet Zeke somewhere?"

"Er—I think so. Between Kies Inn and Ypsilanti."

"That would be Zeke. We are so low on supplies, and winter's coming, so Zeke has been going over on the Chicago Trail to work for the innkeepers. When he gets a little money ahead he buys supplies and brings them home to us."

John asked, "Didn't you grow anything for food this year?"

"Just potatoes and a few vegetables. Zeke hunts when he's here so we have meat, but he's gone so much." She paused. "What did you say your name is?"

"I'm John Thompson and my sister's family are the Parkers."

"I'm glad you stopped." Her son clung to her skirts. Emily's raspy cough alerted Nancy Farmer. "Your little girl been sick long?"

"Since yesterday," Susan answered. "Henry, get Mrs. Farmer a pan of cornmeal and some salt pork from the wagon. A hot meal will make us all feel better. I wish the rain would stop."

When he returned Henry remarked, "I noticed deer tracks in the mud near the barn. Maybe we could get one for you so you'd have meat."

Nancy's dark eyes filled with tears. "You're so kind. Zeke took his rifle or I'd have tried to get a deer or some rabbits."

John and Henry, carrying their rifles, went into the woods behind the barn. Half an hour later they returned with a fat buck suspended from a pole between their shoulders. By the time it was dressed and packed in a wooden chest in a lean-to at the back of the cabin, Nancy called them to supper.

Fred came from the barn. "The wolves are t-t-tuning up," he remarked.

"They smell the venison," Nancy said. "Are your animals in the barn?"

"They're safe," Henry replied.

As the others sat at the rough table Susan mashed a hot boiled potato and poured half a cup of warm milk over it. She stirred in a bit of butter as she called to Emily, "Come have some potato soup!"

The little girl silently came to the table and sat beside her mother. The conversation was of wolves, the rainy weather and of the amount of work facing the Parker family when they reached their land.

Emily ate only a few spoonfuls of her soup before she began coughing violently. "Sounds like a croupy cough," Nancy said. "Teddy and I both have bad coughs and we take some syrup I made from honey mixed with coltsfoot. Sometimes it helps." She left the table to rummage in a box in the corner until she found a large bottle. "Take a big spoonful, Emily." Silently the child obeyed and the cough stopped temporarily.

Josephine asked, "Feel better?"

Emily shook her head. "I'm hot and my throat's awful sore and my legs and back hurt."

"Crawl back in bed," Susan suggested. "You'll feel better tomorrow."

The night seemed long. Susan, Josephine and Emily slept in one bed, Nancy and Teddy occupied a smaller bed while the men lay on the floor before the fireplace. There were numerous sounds to interrupt their sleep; Rusty barked constantly as sniffing sounds came from outside the door, while Emily alternately talked in her sleep or coughed.

Josephine whispered, "Mama, are those wolves sniffing at the door?"

"I think so. They can't get inside. Go to sleep."

Finally the rain stopped and morning came. After breakfast Nancy packed venison and cornbread for their lunch while the men repacked the wagons and prepared to continue their journey.

Susan thanked Nancy for her kindness and wished her well as she hurried Emily to her bed in the wagon. She was concerned that the child still was running a high fever. The fear of lung fever weighed on her mind.

Henry generously left a pan of cornmeal with Nancy as he handed her two dollars. "Will you be all right?" he asked softly.

She brushed away a tear. "Thanks to you, we will be fine. Zeke likely will be home today."

Henry patted her shoulder. "I wish we were going to be closer so we could help you."

"Thanks. We'll be fine when Zeke's home."

He patted Teddy's head and walked briskly to the wagon. When they were under way, Henry said, "What's going to happen to her?"

"Do you think we should have told her that Zeke's in jail?"

"I don't know. I didn't have the heart to tell her Zeke is a robber. She's a nice little woman." He hesitated. "Maybe the punishment will be a flogging at the whipping post. It would be over fast and he could get home."

"Would he be whipped like the man we saw in Detroit?" Josephine asked. "That was awful. His back was bleeding."

"Don't think about it," Susan said.

Henry continued. "Robbery is a serious crime. I doubt if he'll get off with a flogging. According to the sheriff, he's likely been working the trail for several weeks. He'll probably spend a long time in jail." He paused. "I don't know what will happen to Nancy and Teddy if he's gone all winter. Teddy's about the age Jimmy was."

"Uh-huh."

They passed through the settlement of Adrian which was situated at the confluence of two branches of the River Raisin. Henry was silent. He carefully guided the horses around mud holes but he appeared lost in thought for the remainder of the forenoon. Even when Emily cried out it seemed he didn't hear her.

Susan broke into his reverie. "Henry, I'm really worried about Emily. She's not talking right. It must be the fever. She's very sick and I don't know what to do for her."

"Huh? Oh—Emily. She's just got a bad cold."

"But she's burning up with fever! We should have stopped in Adrian to see if there's a doctor there."

"Damn it, Susan! Now I'm to blame 'cause Emily's sick! I should have done this, I should have done that! Everything that does wrong is my fault! According to you, I never to anything right!"

Susan ignored the outburst and crawled back to hold Emily's head in her lap. The child rolled restlessly from side to side. "Make them go 'way. They'll get me. They're sniffing at the door. They're coming in!" she screamed.

Susan stroked the child's forehead. "We're here with you. Everything is all right." Gradually Emily relaxed and closed her eyes.

Susan peered at the little girl's neck, then gently she pulled aside her clothing and briefly inspected the inflamed, mottled chest. "Scarlet fever," she whispered.

Reference

[1,2] Clara Waldron, *One Hundred Years a Country Town* (Thomas A. Riordan, 1966).

Chapter Seven
1830

AN ILL WIND

1830

1

Henry's voice was jubilant. "Another two, three hours and we'll be home!" The horses plodded on. Susan didn't answer. Perhaps she didn't hear as she carefully tucked blankets about Emily's neck.

Henry leaned from the wagon to shout to John and Fred. "Two, three hours and we'll be home!" he yelled.

"We're ready," John replied, "but the trail is full of holes."

"We've seen worse! I can't wait to get there. Let's speed up a little! Get up!" He shouted slapping the reins against the horses' sides. The team broke into a trot causing the wagon to rock dangerously. Suddenly the front wheel dropped into a hole. A cracking, splintering sound came from beneath the wagon.

"Damn!" Henry yelled. He yanked on the reins. "Whoa! Whoa!" The horses tossed their heads nervously as he sprang to the ground to inspect the damage. Rusty yipped at the side of the wagon.

Fred rode up on Ginger. "Wh-a-a-at happened?" he stammered.

"Damn wheel broke!" Henry scratched his head as John came to look at the damage. "Wish we had an extra wheel. This one's done for."

Susan worried, "We have to get Emily somewhere so she can rest. She has scarlet fever, Henry."

"Scarlet fever! My God, what else can happen? Nothing —nothing goes right for me!" He tramped back and forth as he raged.

Susan remonstrated calmly, "This trip was your idea."

"Yeah! Yeah! I'm to blame. If something happens, it's always my fault!"

"You ran the horses."

"I didn't lose Jimmy! That's once you can't blame me for what happened!"

"Are you forgetting we have a very sick child and no place to put her so she can rest?"

John suggested, "We could load her in my wagon and go on to the land and put up a little make-shift shelter. Then tomorrow we'll come back with a wheel from my wagon."

Henry grumbled. "Guess that's all we can do."

While Susan and John got Emily situated in the ox-drawn wagon, Henry and Fred transferred blankets and a small amount of food. After some delay, the odd procession started.

John's wagon contained Susan, Emily and Josephine and was followed by Henry who walked behind his team of horses as he led the two cows while Fred came last leading John's horse, Roamer.

Emily, in delirium, frequently cried out as the wagon jolted over exposed roots and holes in the trail. "The wolves! They'll get me!" she cried.

Susan stroked the child's feverish head. "You're safe. Just a little longer and we'll stop."

Josephine asked, "Have I had scarlet fever?"

"No. Fred had it when he was a baby."

"Will I get it?"

"We hope not."

The oxen plodded slowly along the wilderness trail. They had not passed a cabin since leaving Adrian. Susan wondered why Henry hadn't purchased land where there were neighbors. He had said a tribe of Indians had a camp near them on the River Raisin, but they were not like a friendly settler's family. She was fearful of the future. She said a silent prayer for the family, and especially for Emily. She tried to put from her mind the memory of friends in New York who had lost three young children to scarlet fever.

"There's the river!" Henry called. "We're almost there!"

Ten minutes later the procession pulled into an oak clearing near the trail. "This is it," John said quietly.

"Everybody out! There's work to do!" Henry shouted as he tied his team to a colorful maple. "Tie the cattle and Ginger and Roamer. Don't want them wandering off. Fred, gather some wood for a fire so your mother can cook supper. I'm starved!"

John spoke to Susan. "You may as well stay with Emily until Fred has a fire going. We'll start making a little shelter next to the wagon."

After the animals were cared for, Henry cut four slender elm trees to a length of about ten feet and leaned them against the covered wagon. The bottom of each pole was braced against a stick driven into the ground. By the time quilts and blankets were fastened to cover the lean-to, Fred had a fire started and Susan climbed from the wagon.

"Josie," she said quietly. "You sit with Emily while I fix

supper." Taking potatoes in a pail she went to the river. It was a larger stream than she had expected. At least they would have plenty of water.

She stooped to wash the potatoes, keeping a wary eye on the dark forest on the opposite shore. She thought something moved, then it was gone. Hurrying she took the pail of potatoes and hung it over the fire to boil. Tomorrow she'd make johnny cake. Tonight they'd have to do with ham, potatoes, fresh milk and apples.

Rusty hastily explored the area, barking with excitement when he reached the river. "Probably sees a deer," John said setting a pail of milk near the shelter.

Henry carried Emily inside the lean-to and covered her. "Wolves," she complained. "I hear wolves."

"That's Rusty barking. We're at our new home, Emily. When you're well, you'll like it here." He patted her hand.

Some time later the family sat inside the blanket-covered shelter as they ate a leisurely supper. Susan fed Emily a few spoonfuls of potato soup before she fell into a deep sleep. Night was descending and the fire cast flickering shadows on the inside of the lean-to.

"Tomorrow we'll get the other wagon," Henry planned. "Then we'll have to work like blazes to get a cabin and barn up before cold weather."

"Listen," Susan said softly. "Something's walking out there."

"Likely deer," Henry said.

"C-c-could be a b-bear," Fred said, "or w-o-olves."

John glanced at his sister. "I doubt it."

Fred and Josephine helped their mother clean up after the meal. The woods were dark. Susan kept an eye on the nearby forest.

Suddenly from the distance a lonesome howl drifted through the trees. At the same moment Rusty barked wildly. Susan silently went inside to sit with Emily.

"Will they come here?" Josephine asked.

"They won't come near the fire," her father answered. But almost at once howls came from the opposite direction. Gradually the weird howls came closer.

Henry said, "Maybe we'd better fetch the crate of chickens and put it near the lean-to."

John led the cattle and horses and tied them between the campfire and wagon. "Don't think they'd bother the larger animals, but they might's well be here where we can watch them."

Fred threw more wood on the fire. The animals were uneasy, peering into the darkness, shaking their heads, stamping the ground and pulling on their tethers. "We'd b-b-better get the sow up here."

Josephine pointed. "Look! There's eyes out there!"

Susan crawled to the opening. "My goodness. They're just beyond the fire." Her heart pounded in her throat as the wolves yipped and whined beyond the circle of firelight. Rusty crawled under the wagon, his tail between his legs.

"Pull the chicken crate under the middle of the wagon," Henry said. Fred nodded.

John tossed wood on the fire. "We'll keep the fire burning all night. They won't hurt us. They're after the chickens." Susan silently stared into the darkness.

From the distance the call of a lone wolf drifted through the air. The whispering of owls' wings in the treetops overhead had an eerie sound.

"Michigan's a wild place. I feel as though we're the only humans on earth," Susan commented.

"I'm not scared," Josephine boasted.

Fred chuckled. "G-g-good for you, J-J-Josie."

Henry tossed more wood on the fire. "All of you might's well go to bed. When I get sleepy Fred or John can spell me."

Susan stared at the eyes beyond the fire. "I'm glad Emily's drifted off to sleep. Those wolves would scare her to death."

"All of you go to bed," Henry ordered. "It's no use to sit here and stew."

During the night John and Fred alternated with Henry in taking turns at two hour watches. At times the wolf pack was silent. At other times a weird medley of whines, whimpers, howls and snarls reached the ears of the restless family. On several occasions a chorus of barks and yelps nearly deafened them, each time causing panic in the domestic animals who pulled and jerked on the leather straps which rocked the wagon and caused the lean-to to sway.

As they changed shifts John spoke quietly to Henry. "I had a mind to shoot into the pack, but the cattle and horses are so uneasy, I was afraid they'd break loose."

Henry nodded. "There's a bunch of the critters out there. They're ornery beasts. I don't think they'd bother anything but the chickens, but 'tis best to be safe. They'll be gone when it's daylight." Gradually the howling lessened and the weary family arose.

Emily had slept soundly all night beside Josephine. She opened her eyes and stared into the top of the lean-to. "Where are we?" she asked. "And where is Mama?"

Josephine said, "We're at our new land in a lean-to. Mama's cooking breakfast."

"I don't remember getting here."

"You have scarlet fever. Mama says you must keep warm. You were real sick for two days." Josephine swallowed with difficulty. "I've got a sore throat and my head hurts."

Wrapped in blankets the sisters ate a few spoonfuls of cornmeal mush before again burrowing beneath layers of quilts. Susan tucked them in. "We're glad you're better, Emily, but you must keep warm so that cough doesn't settle in your lungs. And Josie, I hope you only have a cold. Stay covered."

She went outside. "Both girls are sick and the shelter is cold and damp. I don't have a thing for medicine. All my herbs are in the other wagon." She sighed.

Fred stared at his mother. There were lines in her forehead and about her mouth that had not been there when they left New York. She was thirty years old, but she appeared older. His glance traveled to his father. Damn him! Damn him for bringing them to the Michigan wilderness which had brought nothing but disaster to the family. Jimmy gone, likely dead; the girls sick with no warm dry place to recover. Children sometimes died with scarlet fever. And his mother, she already was exhausted, and they'd only arrived. He turned rebellious eyes on his father.

Henry bellowed orders. "Fred, tie the cattle so they can pasture and let the sow and chickens out to pick for themselves. You and I will go back to get the other wagon. Tomorrow we've got to start on the cabin. Come on, boy! Get a move on!"

The sound of John's axe echoed through the forest. Soon he dragged a strong ten-foot pole to the camp and returned to the edge of the clearing for a large block of wood. Using the pole as a lever, John and Henry raised the wagon while Fred slid the block under the axle so the wheel could be removed.

Shouting directions to the boy as he finally forced the block in place, Henry grumbled, "He's so gol-darned slow!"

Susan remonstrated. "Fred's going as fast as he can." In a moment she went on, "I'll do what I can to fix some food, but most of our supplies are on the other wagon."

John wiped his brow. "I'll start cutting logs today and tomorrow the three of us will make the chips fly." He squinted into the early morning sun. "It's good the rain has stopped." Going to the wagon he returned with a small

Bible. "We should take a few minutes for morning devotions."

Ignoring Henry's impatient gesture John flipped the pages of the Bible "I'll read the third verse of the Thirty-Seventh Psalm. Listen: 'Trust in the Lord and do good; so shall thou dwell in the land, and verily thou shall be fed.' There's a message in those few words for us. We have God's promise that if we live according to his word he will care for us." He looked at Henry. "We should be kind, we should have patience with one another. Harsh words sometimes cut like a knife. Let us pray."

The family knelt on the damp ground as John prayed. "Our Father, we come to Thee asking for Thy guidance in this new land. Be with Emily and Josephine and bring them through this sickness. Comfort us in the loss of little Jimmy. Give us strength and courage to meet the hardships of wilderness life. We ask it in Thy name. Amen."

Fifteen minutes later Henry and Fred walked behind the team of horses on the long trek back to the broken-down wagon. They talked little, each one busy with his own thoughts. The wagon wheel bumped along the ground behind the horses.

The October morning air was crisp. Angry squalls of a pair of blue jays and a shrill *Caw! Caw!* of a crow wakened a pair of fox squirrels who chattered from a branch overhead. These watchdogs of the forest warned the wildlife of approaching danger. A mist still hung above the tops of the trees which the sun barely penetrated. A doe and a buck cleared the trail in one leap, then disappeared into the heavy underbrush.

Numerous kinds of trees made up the forest. Maple, beech, oak, poplar, elm, shagbark hickory, black walnut and butternut were common. In swampy places willow branches, their leaves yellow, drooped gracefully over cat-tails gone to seed, the silky down-like fluff sailing away on the slightest breeze. Bright orange bittersweet berries hung from vines on trees along the trail.

A fat woodchuck sat on his haunches watching the intruders. Suddenly Fred stammered, "I saw a b-b-bear!"

"Where?"

He pointed. "Up-up-up ahead! He crossed the tr-trail!"

"I expect they are all around here. Hope they don't bother our animals. We'll have an exciting life here, Freddy."

Finally Henry announced, "There it is—wagon's just ahead." A minute or two later he exploded, "It's wrecked! The canvas is in shreds!" He clucked to the horses and they broke into a fast trot with harnesses jingling and the wagon wheel bumping along behind. Fred and Henry stretched their legs to keep up with the team.

"Wh-what did it?"

Henry stared in disbelief at the wagon. For a moment he was speechless. He scratched his head as he studied the ruined canvas top.

Fred peered inside. "Gosh! Everything's sp-sp-spilled!"

Henry swore, a string of oaths poured from his lips as he investigated the damage to his possessions and the family's store of food. The barrels of cornmeal and flour lay on their sides, the contents mixed on the floor among smashed apples and winter vegetables, bedding, clothing, dishes and odds and ends. Finally he dropped on the wagon seat, his head in his hands.

"This about finishes us—our food for the winter—gone."

"Who d-d-did it?"

"Bear. There's claw marks on the wagon where she crawled in. Maybe a she bear and cubs."

Fred continued poking about in the hodge-podge mess while his father brooded. Finally Henry exploded. "Why can't anything ever go right for me? A hundred other settlers could come down that trail and nothing would happen 'til I came!"

"They p-p-probably didn't leave their wagon."

Henry jumped to the ground. "You're just like your mother! You're blaming me because the wheel broke!"

Fred didn't answer. He righted the flour and cornmeal barrels. They still were about half full. He sorted the whole apples and vegetables and returned them to the overturned crates. The damaged ones, the smashed squash, potatoes and apples, he placed in separate crates. Perhaps his mother could salvage some of them.

Henry returned with a pole and a block of wood. "Get out of there and help me raise the wagon!" he ordered.

"C-c-can we do it?"

"We have to. Shove the block under the axle when I raise it. Get it in place fast for I can't hold it long."

Though he strained and pushed with all his might, the wagon barely moved. Finally he grumbled, "We'll have to unload the damn thing." An hour later the boxes, barrels, crates and trunks were at the side of the trail. Soon the wagon, with the new wheel, was in a level position.

A gentle breeze blew the tattered canvas. Blue jays and crows perched overhead as they scolded the intruders.

Henry viewed the untidy wagon box with distaste. "Half of our winter's bread and johnny cake is there on the floor," he grumbled. "Open the trunk and get two of your mother's sheets. We'll put them in the barrels over the good flour and cornmeal and clean up this mixture in the wagon box and put it on top. 'Tisn't too clean, but maybe 'twill keep us from starving."

"C-c-can't we b-buy food in Adrian?"

"I don't know. Everyone brings in their own supplies." He picked up a crate. "Let's get loaded and on our way."

Silently they drove back through the colorful autumn forest.

Chapter Eight
1830

INDIAN NEIGHBORS

1830

1 ——————————————————————

T HE SOUND OF JOHN'S AXE RANG through the forest. Susan hovered over her sick children.

"Do I have scarlet fever?" Josephine asked. "My throat's awful sore."

"I know. I wish I had my herbs. They're in the other wagon, but Papa will be here by night. I think both of you have scarlet fever." She pulled the covers high about the children's necks as she laid a hand on each child's forehead.

"I feel a little better," Emily said. Talking started another coughing spell.

"Josie has a fever too," Susan mused. She stepped outside the lean-to and looked toward the river. "I saw willow trees down there last night. I'll make some willow tea for you. It will make you more comfortable. I'll be back soon."

Picking her way through the underbrush, Susan peered ahead. The willow trees were to the right, their late fall leaves still clinging to the graceful branches.

She gathered an armful of the boughs and stood for a few minutes watching the river. The current was swift, the result of the heavy fall rains. Fred would enjoy fishing here. Down the river a short distance a muskrat ran along the water's edge. Trapping would be good, too. The willows would be beautiful in summer, their slender branches hanging gracefully over the river.

The wind stirred the slender boughs. Susan sighed. *They're at the mercy of the wind*, she thought. *We're like that —like willows in the wind.*

Her daydream was shattered by the girls' piercing screams and Rusty's savage barks. Still holding the willow branches she picked up her skirts and ran toward camp arriving just as John, with axe in hand, dashed up from the opposite direction.

They ran into the lean-to where an Indian man and child stood peering down at the screaming children. "Mama!" Emily wailed. "They'll scalp us!"

Both the boy and his father were dressed in identical deerskin clothing and moccasins. The boy, his dark eyes puzzled, stared at the girls. "*Au-to-go!*" he exclaimed.

The tall Indian man stepped outside followed by John and Susan. He carried a large piece of fresh meat which was wrapped in corn husks. "Stay here?" he inquired.

John smiled. "Yes. We will build a house."

The man extended his hand toward John. "For you. Deer."

"Thank you. This will be good for the girls. They're sick."

"Sick?"

"John!" Susan exclaimed. "We must get the boy out of there! He'll get scarlet fever! You tell him." She rushed inside to lead the Indian child to the open air.

"*Au-to-go. Au-to-go,*" he repeated.

"We don't want your boy to get sick like the girls." There was a long silence. Finally John said, "You live near here?"

The man pointed to the east. John nodded. "Thank you for the meat." He went to the wagon and returned with half a dozen apples. "For you and your boy."

Silently the Indian accepted the apples, then he and the child walked away toward the east. Emily still sobbed quietly inside the shelter. Josephine's raspy voice declared, "They are gone now. I won't be afraid the next time they come."

Emily said softly, "I will. They scalp people."

Susan called, "The Indian brought venison. I'll make broth and soup for you. 'Twill make your throat better, Josie."

"I'm awful hot," Josephine complained, "and my head hurts and my legs and back ache."

"I know. I'll fix willow tea for both of you. It's good to stop pain. Try to rest." She broke the willow twigs into a kettle of water and hung it over the fire to steep.

"The man speaks some English," Susan said to John. "I'm surprised."

"They must have had contact with other settlers. I want to go to their camp when I can get away." John piled wood under the kettle of twigs. "Maybe this is their winter camp. I understand some tribes come to southern Michigan in winter and travel north in summer, especially those along the shore of Lake Michigan."

"Why do they do that?"

"They're wanderers. In early spring they tap maples and make maple sugar here, and in summer camp they grow corn, squash and other vegetables. They pick berries and other wild fruit and nuts. And they hunt deer and turkeys for food. But some of them live here all year."

"Sounds like a good life." John returned to his work and

Susan prepared johnny cake and venison for the family.

Nearby the chickens picked at the soil searching for late fall insects. The cattle and Roamer and Ginger browsed on tender shoots of shrubs. The sow rooted in the earth for grubs. Cat mewed softly to draw Susan's attention to the limp mouse she held in her mouth. She petted the cat. "You're a good hunter."

"Mama!" Josephine called. "I feel awful! Now I'm cold!"

Susan dipped two half-cups of willow tea from the steaming kettle and stooped as she entered the shelter. "Sip this. It will help you sleep." She handed each child a tin cup and felt their foreheads. "Your fever is down, Emily."

"But I still feel awful. Has Josie really got scarlet fever?"

"I think so. I hope that little Indian boy doesn't get it."

"My ears ache," Josephine complained as she swallowed the willow tea.

"Scarlet fever sometimes causes all the aches and pains you're having."

"Do people die from it?" Emily asked.

"Perhaps sometimes. Uncle John prayed for you this morning. I think you'll both feel better in a few days."

Emily sighed. "If Jimmy was here, he'd get it too."

Susan turned. "I have to put wood on the fire."

Several hours later Henry and Fred returned with the tattered covered wagon and damaged food. After complaining bitterly about his hard luck Henry shouted orders to the family.

"Susan, sort through the apples and vegetables and save what you can. That damn bear! Fred, store the corn meal and flour under the wagon. We have to keep it dry. Looks like a hard winter ahead. I've got to help John cut logs for the cabin. Fred, unharness the team."

2

A WEEK LATER A ROUGH CABIN stood in the middle of the oak clearing. While John and Henry placed thirty-inch-long shakes on the roof and held them in place with hickory and beech withes, Fred filled the chinks between the logs with clay and moss.

A low fire burned in the fireplace. The chimney was made from sticks and mud. Susan hung a kettle of venison from the crane above the fire. She turned, attempting to visualize the crude home as it would look when completed. For the present, they would have a dirt floor. Henry's and her bedroom with the rough homemade bed was built into a corner. Someday she likely would give birth in this bed.

Their home was crude, but she and Henry would be together with the children—all but Jimmy. Henry was a good man and she loved him in spite of his violent temper. Away from home with friends and acquaintances he always was courteous and helpful. During their marriage she had observed many times how women reacted to his charm and to the friendly little pats on hand or shoulder. She didn't mind. She knew Henry craved approval and could not tolerate criticism. She understood him. His confusing personality was the result of his unfortunate birth. Because his natural mother had discarded him he felt that he was unworthy of affection. Though Susan tried to give him love and approval, somehow it was never enough. But they loved one another. They both had faults. She would try harder to keep things on an even keel.

She turned to observe the main room of the cabin. They had no furniture but blocks of wood would serve as chairs and the men would fashion a table by driving posts into the ground to serve as legs which would be topped with small split basswood logs with the flat side up.

A window at the right of the fireplace let in so little light that even when the sun was shining, the cabin was dark. Susan glanced at the ladder on the left of the fireplace which led to the loft where John and the children would sleep. She sighed. A wave of homesickness washed over her as she compared the rough cabin with the comfortable Parker home she had known in New York.

As Susan returned to the shelter, Emily called, "Mama! I want to get up. I feel good today, only my skin is peeling off."

"Scarlet fever does that. Stay up a while, then go back to bed. You've been very sick."

Josephine's voice was listless. "I don't want to get up."

Susan placed her hand on Josephine's head. "The fever is about gone. You'll soon be better if we can stop that cough."

Suddenly Rusty tore down the trail barking furiously. " 'Tis the Indian," John said from his vantage point on the roof. The man's spotted pony tossed his head nervously as Rusty jumped at his nose.

Henry whistled. "Rusty! Rusty! Come here!" he shouted. The dog returned to the clearing followed by the Indian on his pony.

"Hello!" John called as he and Henry came down from the roof.

The Indian grunted, his eyes sweeping the scene before him. "Good horses," he muttered as he sized up the four horses pasturing nearby.

John nodded. "Where is your boy?"

The Indian stared past the family toward the river. "Boy sick. Boy sick. Maybe he die."

"Scarlet fever," John said softly. "He caught it from the girls."

"You make him better?"

"I'm not a doctor, but I'll go with you and try to help." John hurried to saddle Roamer.

The Indian grunted. Susan reached into the wagon, then carrying half a pail of milk she went toward the Indian. "Milk," she said. " 'Tis good for sick boy."

Silently he accepted the pail. There was a pause. Finally Henry said, "I'm Henry Parker."

The Indian grunted. "Whiskey?"

Henry shook his head. "No whiskey."

John rode up beside the Indian. "I'll be back as soon as I can," he called. The family watched, their faces reflecting feelings of doubt and bewilderment as the two men silently rode into the wilderness.

After a few minutes John said, "I am John Thompson, a minister. I do what I can to help people and to tell them about God. What is your name?"

"Me Joseph Black Bear."

"How many children do you have?"

The Indian held up one finger. "Little Beaver, Jake, he sick. Maybe he die. You help?"

"I'll try."

They rode in silence for several minutes. Joseph led the way to the banks of the river. Through the trees John could see a dozen dome-shaped wigwams which were used by the Potawatomi tribe in the area. Indian ponies grazed nearby. Several mangy dogs ran barking to meet them.

Three squaws were cooking over open fires. Children played before the wigwams.

John dismounted and tied Roamer to a small tree. Joseph jumped from his horse's back and slapped the animal's rump. The pony trotted away. Carefully carrying the pail of milk the Indian said gruffly, "Little Beaver here." He led the way into a wigwam.

It took a few moments for John's eyes to adjust to the

dusky light inside the thatched bark home. He saw a young
squaw crouched beside the blanket-wrapped body of the
boy. He laid his hand on the child's forehead. It was burning hot.

Joseph said, "He no move."

"How long has he been sick?"

"Three suns."

"Does he eat?"

Joseph shook his head and grasped his throat. "Hurt
here. Why he not move?"

"It's the fever. He's sleeping to get better. When he
wakes up we'll give him milk. It's good for sick children."

"You make him better? You medicine man?"

John shook his head. "But I will ask God, the Great
Spirit, to make Little Beaver better. I hope the Great Spirit
will tell me what to do. I will pray for your boy."

"Pray?"

"Ask God, your Great Spirit, to help him." John closed
his eyes and knelt beside the sleeping boy. He laid his hands
on the boy's burning forehead. "Dear God," he began, "we
come to Thee asking that You touch Little Beaver. Guide
us to know how to help him so that he will return to good
health. Protect the other children in this camp and help us
to show these people the power of prayer. We ask it in Thy
name. Amen."

Joseph asked, "He get better now?"

John got up. "We hope so. What do you do for him?"

"Squaw put water on face. Too hot. Give bee honey
when he cough."

"Good. Does squaw sit with him for long time?"

"Three suns."

"Tell her to rest. I will sit with Little Beaver."

Joseph Black Bear spoke rapidly in the gutteral Indian
tongue. His wife nodded and stiffly got to her feet and
went outside. Joseph followed her.

Alone in the dome-shaped wigwam John studied the interior of the bark-covered shelter. Deerskin clothing hung from the pole framework together with a few cotton garments for which Joseph likely had bartered in Tecumseh or Adrian.

Little Beaver was wrapped in a bright woolen blanket. The boy stirred and moaned softly but did not open his eyes. His face and neck were covered with the fire-red rash of scarlet fever. John gently stroked his forehead as he continued observing the interior of the wigwam.

Several bows and quivers of arrows and a rifle hung near the door. Furniture consisted of a rough bench and a rickety table covered with half a dozen wooden bowls and a smoke-blackened kettle. A pile of animal skins and blankets at one side apparently served as the bed. A stone-encircled fire ring in the center of the wigwam was directly below the smoke hole above. Since the squaws were cooking outside, John thought the fire ring likely was used only in disagreeable weather.

Through the open door John saw Joseph and several other Indian men in earnest conversation. Children frequently peeped inside to stare at him before they ran away.

Little Beaver opened his eyes. He silently stared at the strange white man. "I'm John." He continued stroking the boy's forehead.

The dark eyes showed fright but he did not cry out as a white child might have. Softly he murmured, "*Au-to-go. Au-to-go,*" before he was seized by a severe coughing spell. The boy's mother hurried inside, took a roughly carved wooden spoon from the table and dipped it into a bowl of honey. John moved away as she spooned the honey into the little mouth.

Joseph's voice came from the doorway. "Little Beaver better. He move."

"*Au-to-go,*" the child gasped between rasping coughs.

Joseph bent over his son and spoke briefly. The boy relaxed.

"What does he say?" John asked. "What does '*Au-to-go*' mean?"

"He not know you. He 'fraid. '*Au-to-go*' mean he is 'fraid. I tell him you talk to Great Spirit and he get better."

John remained with the family for several hours during which time Little Beaver drank a few spoonfuls of milk and a little venison broth. He left in mid-afternoon promising to return the following day.

3 ────────────────── *1830*

For two weeks John spent part of each day at the Indian camp. Five children were ill with scarlet fever. With the squaws' help and the dosing with Indian remedies, the children gradually improved.

Every time he went to the camp John prayed at the side of each ill child. The adults watched silently. They were deeply impressed.

At the cabin, Susan was concerned. "If it hadn't been for Little Beaver coming here, those children would not have been sick. I feel responsible," she said repeatedly. She sent milk, apples and bread to tempt delicate appetites.

For three weeks in October, Michigan enjoyed beautiful Indian summer weather. Though many deciduous trees had shed their colorful leaves, the oaks in their scarlet and rust apparel and the willows along the river garbed in faded yellow plainly told of the approaching end of autumn weather.

Henry, resentful of the amount of time John spent at the Indian camp, drove his family relentlessly. Emily and

Josephine, as soon as they were able, were sent to gather and shuck hickory and walnuts from the trees which grew near the edge of the oak opening. Fred and Henry worked from daylight to dark completing the cabin and building a pole barn for the animals. They boxed in a spring close to the shore of the river which formed an ever-fresh tank of water for the family.

Susan made the rustic cabin as homelike as possible. She and the girls also chinked spots between the logs where daylight could be seen.

John, Henry and Fred cut and piled a large supply of wood. Wild turkeys and deer were plentiful. Susan and the girls picked quarts of cranberries. Everyone was busy. By mid-November they were prepared for winter. Daytime temperatures hovered around the freezing point and occasional snow showers left a dusting of white on roofs.

Evenings after the children were in bed in the loft, the adults planned for winter. " 'Twill be slim pickin' for the animals this winter," Henry worried. "I don't have any hay or grain for them. They'll have to survive on tall hay."

"What's that?" Susan asked.

"Tender shoots from brush and the low branches of trees. 'Tain't much, but it's all we have."

"They'll starve."

"I'm more worried about the wolves. A pack could pull down the sow or a lone cow."

John said, "Perhaps it will be an open winter so the wolves can find rabbits and mice."

A sudden howl nearby alerted Susan. "They're out there again. Every night they're out there." She shivered. "I'm afraid of them. If we had a little one they could carry off a small child—like—like Jimmy."

Henry silently took his rifle from the corner and yanked the door open. He aimed at one of several fleeing shadows and fired. A sharp yip told him he'd made a hit.

"You'd think the darn critters would learn," he muttered. "That makes five I've killed since we've been here."

John said, "When you go to Adrian or Tecumseh you might inquire if there is a wolf bounty here. I've read that it is five dollars a scalp in some places. I've saved the scalps."

"Yeah." In a moment Henry asked, "Will you be spending much time at the Indian camp now?"

"The children have recovered. I'm thankful. I won't be there much for a time. Why?"

"I've been thinking of Nancy Farmer and Teddy. I expect they're low on meat by now."

"I hope the little boy didn't get scarlet fever," Susan said. "Maybe Nancy's husband is out of jail by now so he can look after them."

Henry snorted. "How? By robbing people? I feel sorry for that little woman. If you're going to be here for a couple days, John, I might ride over to see how she's getting along."

"I'll be here. Fred and I will build the shed at the end of the cabin that we talked about. A lean-to would be a good place to store venison and hams."

Susan said, "I'd like that. Our meat would be safer there than hanging from a tree branch. Besides it calls the wolves and I noticed birds picking at it today." She hesitated. "When will you go to Farmers, Henry?"

"Tomorrow morning. I feel we owe something to Nancy. After all, we are responsible for Zeke's being in jail. I'll not be gone long."

Chapter Nine
1830

A TANGLED WEB

1830

1

T HE FAMILY STOOD BEFORE THE cabin in the bright November sunshine to bid Henry goodbye. He hugged the girls as he kissed each one. He shook Fred's hand. "Help Uncle John and your mother." Fred nodded.

Holding Susan tightly he kissed her on the lips. "I'm going to miss you," he whispered. He swung into the saddle. She waved as he called, "Take care of my family, John!"

John shouted, "They'll be fine!"

Ginger trotted into the wilderness as the little group waved furiously. "Hurry back!" Susan called.

A flock of wild turkeys crossed the trail. Henry aimed his rifle and pulled the trigger. Amid beating wings and frightened squawks a hen lay flopping on the ground. Henry wrung her neck and placed her in the saddle bag. " 'Twill be a change from venison for Nancy and Teddy," he said aloud.

Arriving at the village of Adrian, he stopped at the French Hotel. Isaac French, the owner, introduced him to Addison Comstock. "He's Adrian's mill owner, postmaster, and one of our first settlers," French explained. [1, 2]

"Glad to meet thee, Parker," the man said.

"When did you settle here?" Henry asked.

"In 1826. There were eighteen people in our party. Thee knows we are Quakers." He smiled. "My wife, Sarah, named the town 'Adrian.' She'd read about a Roman emperor called 'Hadrian.' He was a political leader in his time and she admired the efforts he made to set up a lasting government."

"So she dropped the 'h' from 'Hadrian'?"

Comstock nodded. "Has thee a family?"

"Two girls and a boy. We lost our two-year-old son in Detroit." Henry paused. "Are most of Adrian's settlers of the Quaker faith?"

"Many are. We don't have a meeting house as they do in Tecumseh, but sometimes we attend Methodist Episcopal services. Jacob Hill, a circuit rider from Monroe, preaches here. He has five members, but anyone is welcome."

Henry hesitated, then said, "I was brought up in the Quaker faith."

"Thee was? Thee don't speak as a Friend."

Henry laughed. "I married a Methodist preacher's daughter and her brother also is a Methodist minister. I grew away from the faith when I worked on the Erie Canal for five summers."

Addison Comstock nodded. "I, too, worked on the Erie Canal. Thee and I seem to have much in common."

French explained, "Addison and his father-in-law built a mill north of Adrian on the Raisin River. Everyone calls it 'The Old Red Mill.' There's a mill at Tecumseh, too."

Henry smiled. "That will be handy after I grow some

grain."

French continued. "The land's good here and the Indians usually are friendly—that is, if they don't get to drinking. Tecumseh had a mill before Adrian. It broke down one winter and settlers had to make the trip to Monroe to get flour made. The Cadmus family lived east of Tecumseh. They ran out of food in the dead of winter. The situation became serious so the father started out for Monroe with a bag of grain on his back. He got caught in a blizzard. His frozen body was found not far from his home in the spring."

"What happened to the family?"

"The Browns, Joseph and Cornelia, in Tecumseh, took them to their place." In a minute he went on, "There was another family, the Brainards, who ran out of food while the mill was down. He also ran into a bad storm and below-zero weather. After two weeks his family had given him up for dead, but he finally returned with the flour."

"Where had he been?"

"He'd been very sick with lung fever, but he'd wandered into an Indian village and they took care of him until he was able to travel. When he came back with the flour his family had eaten every scrap of food. They even had cooked some of the precious seed beans for the next year's planting."[3]

Addison Comstock stroked his beard. "Life is not easy in the Michigan wilderness. Thee said thee lost a child in Detroit. Sarah and I had a little son, Leander, but he only lived two months. Measles and lung fever. That was in 1827. Now Adrian has two doctors. E. Conant Winter and Dr. Ormsby. Winter came here last year."

"We're lucky to have him," French said. "He's built a store that's the headquarters for all the Indian tribes near here. They come to the store for supplies. Dr. Winter speaks the Indian language." He laughed. "They call him

'McIntosh.' He spends more time trading with the Indians than doctoring."

"Why do they call him 'McIntosh'?"

"I don't know, but they like him. There's always Indians hanging around his store."

Henry said, "There's an Indian camp near our land. Joseph Black Bear has been to our place. He speaks some English. My brother-in-law, John Thompson, the Methodist minister, has spent a lot of time with the Indians since we've been here. They seem friendly. Joseph did ask for whiskey, but I didn't give him any."

Comstock replied, "Joseph's a good Indian, but even the good ones get mean when they get hold of 'firewater' as they call it. The Spafford family live near Tecumseh. Mrs. Spafford and her daughters were alone while the men were in town. An Indian chief and several braves from the vicinity walked into the cabin. 'Me want whiskey,' the chief said. Mrs. Spafford replied, 'Me no whiskey.' She was nearly frightened to death but she stood her ground. He walked up to her, put his hands on her shoulders and said, 'Me no hurt Chimoka Man's squaw!' "[4]

"That would scare a woman," Henry said.

French nodded. "Ira Goodrich told me something that happened. He had gone into town and his wife and children were alone. There's a small Indian camp near Goodrich's place between here and Tecumseh, and they must have seen him leave because soon several drunken Indians demanded to be admitted to the cabin. Mrs. Goodrich and the children barricaded the door. One Indian began to use an axe to break it down. Mrs. Goodrich and the children fled to the loft, drawing up the ladder after them. Mrs. Goodrich stood by the opening with a club and she threatened to 'brain' the first man who tried to climb up. They left, but they broke the two windows in the cabin before they went."[5]

"There must be many Indian camps near here."

Comstock nodded. "There's a large one at Devil's Lake northwest of here. They live on the banks of the lake in summer but they move into the deep wilderness in winter."

He continued, "Another tribe lives on Round Lake which is close to Devil's Lake. 'Tis about twenty miles as the crow flies. Chief Metau heads the Round Lake group. They say he was a brave under Chief Tecumseh. Sometimes a young man, Baw-Beese, is with old Meteau when they come to trade. They seem like gentlemen."[6]

"They're of the Potawatomi tribe?" Henry asked.

Comstock nodded. "We're lucky because the Potawatomis are the least aggressive of Michigan's Indians, though the Chippewas and Ottawas are more friendly than they once were."

French said thoughtfully, "They've been pretty well beaten down by the white man."

Henry shook his head. "Man's inhumanity to man. I guess it will always be that way."

Addison Comstock shoved his black hat back on his head. "Both France and Great Britain wanted North America and both countries tried to win help from the Indians by bribing them with liquor and guns."

"People in this part of the Michigan Territory haven't forgotten the past. Even though the Indians seem friendly, the settlers remember things, and so would thee and me if we'd been here then."

"Has something happened recently?"

"Last year the Blissfield colony had a tragic thing happen," French said.

"Blissfield is between Adrian and Monroe?" Henry asked.

French nodded. "The Tubbs family had a small son kidnapped by the Indians."

"Are they sure he was kidnapped? Couldn't something else have happened?"

Comstock shook his head. "The parents are fairly sure. The little fellow had taken a liking to the people at the camp. I think he was about three years old. He played with the Indian children and spoke their language. One day he didn't come home. When the boy's father went to look for him he found the camp deserted. Not one of the tribe has ever been seen since." [7]

Comstock went on. "Another thing happened back in 1813 that people around here haven't forgotten. That was seventeen years ago, but they still remember. At that time the British held Detroit. The Americans planned how to recapture it. A force of seven hundred Americans led by Colonel Lewis crossed frozen Lake Erie from Toledo to Monroe because the people of that settlement had sent an urgent appeal for protection against the Indians who had threatened their lives and property."

Comstock paused. "But a force of British and Indians already were in Monroe. The Americans drove them out and forced them back to Fort Malden."

Henry said, "Is that fort on the east bank of the Detroit River?"

"About twenty miles north of Monroe." Comstock went on. "The Americans waited for reinforcements. As they relaxed, they were surprised by an early morning attack of Britishers and Indians."

Henry scratched his head. "I remember reading about that battle."

Comstock nodded. "The British were driven back but their general threatened the American general that unless he surrendered, the Indians could not be stopped from murdering the American prisoners they had taken. So, the American general agreed to surrender if the prisoners would be protected from the fury of the Indians.

"The British returned to Fort Malden taking prisoners who could walk but leaving behind the wounded Americans. Early the next morning two hundred drunken Indians roared into town. They murdered and scalped wounded prisoners and burned houses."

No one spoke for a time. Finally Henry said, "And people still remember."

French cleared his throat. "The battle of the River Raisin was the bloodiest battle ever fought on Michigan soil. Only sixty survivors were left of the force of around a thousand. Even today, old timers in Monroe are wary of becoming too friendly with the Indians. They haven't forgotten the old battle cry, "Remember the River Raisin!" [8]

Henry said, "I recall several battles on Lake Erie between Lieutenant Oliver Hazard Perry and the British fleet. The victories won by Perry opened the road to the capture of Detroit." After a moment he said, "Perhaps I'll make myself unpopular by the statement I'm about to make, but I feel we have wronged the Indians. They were here first, happy in living their life. Then the white man came in, and the goverment bought their lands. They didn't understand for they believed no one owned the land, that people only used it, and that they were just giving the white man the right to use it."

Both French and Comstock nodded. "They aren't stupid. They see what is coming. But they're so beaten down by all that has happened that there's no fight left in them unless they have firewater. Then the old rage comes out," Comstock said.

Henry mused, "The Indians and the Negroes—we have done them wrong. In the past—back in New York—I helped a few Negroes escape to Canada. I don't suppose we get any through here."

Comstock's and French's eyes met. Silently they shook their heads. Henry got up. "It's been nice talking with you. Can I buy a few supplies at the Winter store? I'll need flour and cornmeal mostly."

"Thee are out of supplies so soon?"

"I'm not in real good shape. A darn bear got into one of my wagons and ruined part of our supplies. But I'm getting a few pounds of cornmeal and flour to take to a friend between Adrian and Tecumseh."

"Anyone we might know?" Comstock asked.

"The Farmers."

"Glad thee mentioned the name. There's a letter for a Mrs. Zeke Farmer at my place. 'Tis been there for two or three weeks. I'll go get it and thee can take it to her. 'Course thee will have to pay the twenty-five cent postage."

"I'll be glad to. People don't get many letters here, do they?"

Comstock laughed. "I don't work too hard at being post master, but the mill keeps me busy. Come, I'll get the letter."

2 _____ *1830*

DEEP IN THOUGHT OF HIS CONVER-sation with Comstock and French, Henry was unaware of the darkening sky. He was glad Susan and Emily hadn't heard the stories about settlers' experiences with Indians.

Nancy Farmer. He hoped she hadn't been threatened by Indians as other women had been. If Zeke was still in jail she likely was short of food.

A sudden blast of wind caused Henry to turn up his coat collar. The sky to the northwest was dark. "Looks like bad weather," he said aloud.

He clucked to Ginger. An hour later he tied his horse to the bell post in Farmers' yard. Smoke came from the chimney. He knocked on the rough board door. "Hello!" he shouted. "Anybody home?"

The door opened. "Henry Parker!" Nancy gasped. "I'm so glad you came." Tears stood in her eyes and spilled down her cheeks.

He stepped inside. Teddy, thin and wan, stared up at him as he clung to Nancy's skirt. Henry patted her shoulder. "What has happened?"

Touched by his concern, Nancy sobbed softly. "I'm desperate. Teddy's been so sick—scarlet fever, I think. He's better now, but he can't hear." She broke into a flood of tears.

Henry gave her his handkerchief. "His hearing may come back." He patted her shoulder. "I'll do what I can to help you. Has your husband returned?"

Nancy shook her head. "Something has happened to him. I've worried until I'm about crazy."

Henry reached into his pocket for the letter. "The postmaster in Adrian said this came for you several weeks ago."

"Zeke's handwriting!" she exclaimed as she frantically tore open the envelope and scanned the page. She looked up, her dark eyes huge and frightened. "He's in jail," she said almost inaudibly. "He's been sentenced to six months in the Ypsilanti jail for attempted robbery. He says he's innocent, but they didn't believe him."

"I'm sorry." He smiled at Teddy. "What's your name, young fellow?"

The child stared blankly and clung to his mother. She wiped her eyes. "He can't hear you, Henry. He was just learning to talk and now—" her voice caught, "he'll grow up deaf and dumb."

"Maybe not. His hearing may come back."

They were silent for a few moments, then Henry said, "Will you be able to stay here until your husband returns? 'Twill be a long winter for you."

She spoke softly. Her voice had a desperate tone. "We don't have food. I'm nearly out of wood. Teddy has been so sick I couldn't leave him long enough to cut wood and with his ears so bad, I don't want to take him out in the cold."

"Do you have relatives? Where was your home?"

"Vermont. I have a sister there. My parents are dead." She blew her nose. "I don't have any money to go back and my sister and her husband have a large family. They couldn't pay my fare."

Henry glanced outside. "It's starting to snow. I'll see if I can get a deer for you before the weather worsens." He opened the door. "I shot a turkey on the way over and bought you a few supplies in Adrian. You can make a good dinner while I'm hunting."

"Thank you. Thank you for helping us. I haven't seen another soul, except Teddy, since your family left two months ago."

He shook his head sympathetically. "No Indians?"

"They ride by on the trail but they don't stop. I'm afraid of them. I'd die of fright if they came in."

"No settlers traveling between Tecumseh and Adrian?"

"A few. But I can't beg from strangers. Most of them don't have anything to spare. I don't know what to do."

He shook his head. "It's tough." He strode to his horse and returned with the turkey and supplies. "I'll tie Ginger in your barn."

Snow was falling rapidly. "Not a good day to hunt," he remarked. "Deer likely are deep in the swamps when it snows this hard, but I'll try. Maybe I'll get something— another turkey or a rabbit or two."

Several hours later with snow swirling about him in an oak opening, Henry decided to return to the cabin with two rabbits, the results of an afternoon of hunting. He followed his tracks in the snow for a distance but soon the footprints were no longer visible. Though it was not yet four o'clock, darkness was approaching in the dense forest. He brushed the snow from his eyelashes and strode on. Half an hour later he quickened his pace. It couldn't be far to the cabin. The snow-filled air darkened the forest.

Just my luck, Henry thought. Mid-November was too early for a blizzard. Now snow mixed with rain sailed through the bare trees driven by a brisk northwest wind. The cold penetrated his clothing and cut his face like a knife-edge. The wind increased in velocity. In the air high above the trees a heavy roar could be heard. The trees swayed and the snow-laden tops of the pines bent under the weight. Soon even large tree trunks were swaying. Snow-hail whipped his face. Occasionally masses of snow struck with mighty force. Everything was enveloped with snow— hurling, whipping, smarting snow.

"Damn," he murmured as he shielded his face from the stinging sleet. "I've got to get back to the cabin." But a doubt was gnawing at his mind. Where was the cabin? He plodded on.

A wolf howled nearby. Henry shivered. He was lost in the wilderness in a raging blizzard. He must find shelter. But where? He leaned against a swaying tree trunk. A pine branch, heavy with snow and ice, slapped him in the face. Working his way to the trunk of the tree he climbed among the lower branches where there was some protection from the weather. The wolf howled again.

Suddenly a heavy crashing sound cut through the roar of the blizzard. Brushing the snow from his eyes he could make out the outline of a giant tree that had fallen where he stood minutes before.

He could go no further. He'd rest for a time. Again the cry of the wolf followed by the hair-raising snarl of a wild-cat came from somewhere nearby. In the distance a bell was ringing. Strange. You'd expect the wild animals to be in protected places in such weather as this.

Time passed. Henry fought to stay awake. If he slept he'd freeze to death. He beat his numb hands together to restore circulation. Again and again the wind carried the sound of a ringing bell. He wondered if he could be hallucinating.

His heart lurched. Nancy! Nancy had a dinner bell in her yard! She was trying to guide him back to the cabin!

Stiffly he climbed from the pine. He listened. The sound of the bell seemed to be to the left. He stumbled in that direction. The bell stopped ringing. He walked on, stepped in a hole and fell flat. Swearing softly he got to his feet and blundered on.

The bloodcurdling howl of the wolf seemed only a few feet behind him. He turned and fired his rifle in the direction of the howl. A moment of silence, then there came the snarling cry of the wildcat. Again Henry wondered if he could be hallucinating. Wolves and wildcats wouldn't travel together. He struggled on. It seemed a long time since he'd heard the bell. Maybe Nancy had given up—or maybe he had imagined he heard a bell. He waited—there it was again! Bearing a bit more to the left he stumbled on. Beating his numb hands together and stamping hard with each step to restore circulation, he struggled toward the sound of the bell. He must have been wandering in a circle for he'd have sworn Nancy's cabin was to his right. The ringing stopped.

Again he waited—and waited—and waited. The bell did not ring again. With his back to the storm he leaned against a swaying tree trunk to rest. There was no use to keep walking. Without the sound of the bell to guide him he was completely disoriented. He slid to the ground and leaned his head against the tree. He wondered how long it was until morning.

Damn, he was stupid! Going into the forest on a stormy day with no matches! Susan didn't approve of men smoking, and since it hadn't mattered to him, he'd humored her. The decision likely would cost him his life. No matches. He sighed. It didn't matter. Things were running true to form. From the moment his mother had abandoned him shortly after his birth until now, he'd never been happy. He tried hard to make people like him but deep down he knew what he'd been doing. He was buying affection and approval. Susan knew, and the children, and John. And his parents had known. If he didn't make it through the night, John would care for his family. Little Jimmy. He'd loved that boy. Maybe it was better for Jimmy that he had died young; he wouldn't have to face the trials of life. He was at rest.

Henry shivered. His wet clothing was becoming stiff. He laid the rifle across his knees and warmed his hands in his armpits. The wolf howled. If he fell asleep the animal would attack. Shaking his head to rouse himself, Henry got to his feet. He was so tired. He leaned his head against a tree and slid to the ground, breathing deeply.

The vicious snarl of the wildcat came from only a few feet away, but Henry slept on. A shadowy figure appeared to bend over the man.

"Get up!" a raspy voice commanded. Henry did not stir. The figure seized his shoulders and shook him violently. "Wake up!" the voice ordered.

Slowly he raised his head. He must be dreaming. "Who are you?"

"Sal. Crazy Sal," the strange voice croaked. "Get up. I'll take you to my shanty."

Silently he stumbled to his feet and followed the shadowy figure. Her long coat dragged in the snow. Was this a weird dream? Was he freezing to death and this was a last hallucination of his befuddled mind?

"Move along," the voice directed. A moment later the lonely wolf cry followed by the wildcat snarl came from directly in front of him. It wasn't animals howling—it was that old crone!

Now he knew he was hallucinating. No old woman would be out on a night like this. Silently he followed the bedraggled, howling, snarling figure before him. At last she stopped.

"Where are we?"

"Where you think we are? My shanty! Get inside!" She pushed him roughly through the door.

A few coals glowed in the fireplace. The woman threw dry wood on the coals and it caught quickly. In the light from the blazing wood Henry stared at the bedraggled woman. Straggly gray hair hung to her shoulders from beneath a ragged black bonnet. Her wrinkled face was dead white against the dusty black coat and bonnet. Her feet were covered by heavy men's boots.

"Quit starin'! How you 'spect a crazy woman to look? Get that wet coat off!" Meekly he obeyed. "Set there by the fire and thaw out! Ya can do that, can't you?"

"Yes, mam."

The old woman cackled a raucous laugh. "Men! Ya all think ya are so almighty smart but ya don't know nothin'! Ya would 'ave froze to death out there. I don't know why I bother with any of your kind. The world would be better if all men was dead."

Henry stared silently at the fire trying to ignore the pain in his chilled hands and feet. Crazy—the old crone was crazy as a loon.

She took off her bonnet and coat and brushed the ratty gray hair from her face. Opening the door, she howled a long quivering wolf cry. In a moment there came an answering howl. "My friends," she explained. "They don't think I'm crazy."

Sal rattled around among her pots and pans. "Spoze ya are hungry. Men's always hungry. They're too lazy to cook anything themselves but they ain't too lazy to eat what women cook."

Henry didn't answer. He didn't know what to say to this strange woman.

"Hey! Can't ya talk? Be ya hungry?"

"Yes, Mam."

The old crone cackled, "Yes, Mam! He! He! He! Ain't nobody said 'yes Mam' to me in a coon's age. Ya want some potato, carrot and onion soup?"

"Please. That would be good."

She puttered about before the fire as the soup heated. Finally Henry asked, "You know where the Farmers live?"

"Don't ya?"

"I was trying to find the cabin."

"He! He! He! Not very smart are ya?"

"I was lost."

Again Sal cackled. "Ya was walkin' in a circle for four hours. Ya call that smart? And all the time ya wasn't never a mile from the cabin."

"After I eat will you guide me there?"

Sal shrieked with laughter. "Lord! Lord! This big, brave, smart man's askin' Crazy Sal a favor! Lord! Lord!"

"Miss Sal, I do thank you for saving my life. I'll admit I was not very bright."

She gave Henry a bowl of soup, a spoon and two huge slices of bread. "That'll warm yer insides. Then I'll take ya back to the Farmers. What ya doin' there? Ya ain't the woman's husband."

"No. He's away. I'm tryin' to help her out."

Again Sal cackled. "I'll bet ya are. I'll take ya back. Wouldn't want ya stayin' here with me all night. Folks might talk. He! He! He!"

Henry looked at his pocket watch. Half past eight. He set the soup bowl on the table. "Can we go now?"

"Hold yer horses. There ain't no rush." Sal threw another log on the fire and put on her bonnet and coat.

As they stepped outside an icy blast hit them full in the face. Henry turned up his damp coat collar and shouldered his rifle as he followed Sal's shadowy figure. Now and then she would howl her wolf cry and snarl the wildcat call. Fifteen minutes later they came out behind the Farmer barn.

"Thank you, Miss Sal. You saved my life tonight," Henry said earnestly. "Would you keep watch of Mrs. Farmer? She'd be glad for company."

"Won't say I won't and won't say I will." The old woman turned back toward the forest.

The cabin was dark. Henry pounded on the door. "I'm back!" he shouted as he entered.

Through the darkness Nancy ran to him, sobbing. "Thank God, thank God. I thought you were lost in the storm."

A log shifted in the fireplace and in the resulting flames Henry saw Nancy, her hands over her face, as she wept. He went to her. "Don't cry. I can't stand to see women cry. I'm all right." He threw off his damp coat.

"I rang the bell. When—when you didn't come I was sure you were lost and it was my fault."

He put his arms around her to comfort her. "It's all right. Poor girl, you've had too many things to worry you. There. There." He stroked her hair.

She snuggled close to him as she sobbed softly, "You make me feel safe. I haven't felt safe in so long. I'd like to stay like this forever."

He kissed her forehead. "I'll hold you for a while, until you feel better." She sighed. He thought of Susan, but Nancy's attraction was strong. He kissed her full on the lips. They needed one another.

Outside the storm raged in all its fury as they took their pleasure throughout the long night.

3 —————————————————————— *1830*

J OHN AND FRED STAMPED THE SNOW from their feet. Inside the cabin they hung their heavy woolen coats on wooden pegs to the left of the door before they washed in the tin basin on the low bench.

"Breakfast's ready," Susan said as she dished up steaming bowls of cornmeal mush.

After John said grace, Emily asked, "Will Papa be home today?"

Susan looked at John. "What do you think?"

"Even though the snow has stopped the wind still is piling up huge drifts. He might stay at Farmers until the weather moderates."

Josephine complained, "He's been there two days."

Susan stared into the fire. "He knows we are all right. With Uncle John and Fred to take care of us he won't worry."

"Mrs. Farmer is a pretty lady," Emily said. "She has beautiful brown eyes."

Fred watched his mother. A frightened expression flashed across her face to be replaced by a frozen smile. "She is pretty, and young," Susan murmured.

After morning devotions during which John read scripture and he and Susan prayed for guidance, they arose from their knees.

"Today we start school," John announced. "Can't have you pioneer young ones growing up ignorant."

"Goody!" Josephine shouted. "Our books are in the loft."

Later as Susan helped the girls with reading, John and Fred tackled the stuttering problem.

"I have some ideas about stuttering," John said. "We'll

make this our winter project. It's not easy to break the habit. Are you willing to put great effort into it?"

"Y-y-yes. T-t-t-tell me what to do-do."

"I'm no expert, Fred, but when I was in school I had a friend who stuttered. He tried many things, but one of them helped him so that today he doesn't stutter at all."

Fred's eyes sparkled. "T-t-tell me 'b-b-bout it!"

"Let's take a simple word like 'on.' We will stretch every syllable to about two seconds, like this: the word 'on' becomes 'o-o-o-o-o-o-n-n-n-n-n.' Try it. Two long smooth sounds."

Fred grimaced and blinked his eyes. "O-o-o-o-o-o-n-n-n-n-n-n."

"Good. Keep saying it. You see, you're not stuttering. You're stretching out the sounds."

After several minutes, John said, "Let's try another word. You pick one."

"C-c-cabin."

"Stretch out the two syllables."

"Ca-a-a-a-a-bin-n-n-n-n." Grimacing, Fred repeated the exercise many times, alternating with "on."

After twenty minutes of intense work, John said, "Try to say 'on the cabin' by stretching out the words."

"O-o-o-o-o-o-n-n-n-n-n-n th-e-e-e-e-e-e ca-a-a-a-a-a-bin-n-n-n-n." Fred smiled.

"You can practice by yourself," John suggested. "When you're doing chores or working outside, practice new words. Practice, practice, practice. I believe you're going to talk without stuttering. This is only the first time you've tried. It will get easier."

"Wi-i-i-i-l-l-l-l-l I-I-I-I-I al-l-l-l-l-ways-s-s-s t-t-t-t-alk sl-l-l-o-o-o-o-ow?"

"For a time you may talk more slowly, but you will go faster when you're more confident. Just remember to make your stretched out syllables *smooth*. Don't allow the stutter to come out. Now let's work arithmetic."

The forenoon passed quickly for the children. After the mid-day meal John and Fred opened the barn so the animals could drink at the river. Afterward they browsed from tender shoots on shrubs and low-hanging branches.

"This winter," John said, "they'll exist on tall hay."

They spent several hours splitting and piling wood near the cabin. Late in the afternoon John straightened up. "This work is hard on the back," he muttered.

Fred laughed. His expression changed as a call came from the drifted trail and he saw his father riding Ginger as she floundered through the snow.

"Hello!" Henry shouted jubilantly. "Glad to see you fellows are hard at work. After I put Ginger in the barn, I'll be in!"

"Pretty hard getting through?" John asked.

"Tough. Ginger waded drifts the whole way. Wish I had grain for her. She deserves it." He rode on toward the barn.

Five minutes later Henry and Susan embraced. "How are you?" she whispered.

He nuzzled her neck. "Better now that I'm with you. I missed you."

After Henry greeted the girls Susan asked, "How was Mrs. Farmer?" She watched Henry's face.

"She's having a rough time. Zeke's still in jail—I took her a letter from him from the Adrian post office, and Teddy has had scarlet fever. I'm afraid he's deaf."

"He caught it from us!" Emily exclaimed. "We're to blame if he is deaf!"

"I'm so sorry," Susan murmured. "What will she do?"

"She was about out of food. I finally got a deer for her this morning and I got up enough wood to last for a while. She hadn't seen anyone since we were there."

Henry hesitated. "It's a long way in winter, but I feel I should look after her. We're to blame for her troubles. We turned Zeke in to the sheriff and we gave Teddy scarlet fever. I feel it's my responsibility to help her."

John sat at the table turning the pages of a school book. "Between us, Henry, we'll keep her supplied with meat and wood."

Henry stared at the floor. "It's my responsibility."

Susan turned suddenly and poked the fire until flames raced up the chimney. Intuition told her to beware.

References ——————————

[1]*Early Adrian* (American Association of University Women).

[2, 6, 7]Richard Illenden Bonner, *Memories of Lenawee County* (Western History Association, 1909).

[3, 4, 5]Clara Waldron, *One Hundred Years a Country Town* (Thomas A. Riordan, 1968).

[8]Willis F. Dunbar, *Michigan* (William Eerdmans Publishing Co., 1965), p. 213.

Chapter Ten
1831

TO PAY THE PIPER

1831

1

THE MARCH SUNSHINE GAVE SIGNS of approaching spring. Snow banks melted, crows cawed and squirrels chattered. A fox pounced on an adventurous mouse. The earth was wakening after a hard winter.

Henry's spirits were high. Soon he would dispose of a nagging problem that had tormented him for weeks. He clucked to Ginger.

Nancy Farmer, pregnant with his child—just his luck. He had spent two days each month since November at Nancy's place. He had hunted and cut wood for her and he'd bought supplies so she and Teddy could exist. And old Crazy Sal—she had looked in on Nancy now and then.

Now he had hit on the right solution for all of them. He would be rid of Nancy, and Susan and his family and friends in Adrian need never know of his tempestuous hours with Nancy. He wasn't sorry—just sorry she was in the family way. She was a beautiful woman, and therefore to be won. A quote flashed through his mind—he couldn't remember who said it but it fit his temperament. "Blessed is the wooing that is not long a-doing."

Nancy was beautiful, vivacious and spirited, but morally she couldn't hold a candle to Susan. She was perfect for a tempestuous romance, but a faithful wife she wasn't. Well—they'd had their fling and now it was time to pay the piper.

Henry tied his horse to the bell post and hurried to the cabin. They should get started soon. He opened the door. "Hello!" he shouted boisterously.

Nancy turned, her thickened figure showing her pregnancy. "We'll be ready in a minute, Henry." She slid Teddy's arms into his coat.

"He! He! He! He!" A cackle came from a shadowy corner.

"Miss—Miss Sal! I didn't expect to see you."

"He! He! He! I'll bet you didn't." Her voice became strident. "Men! I shoulda let you die in that storm! All of you got only one thing in mind! If I'd let you die out there this girl wouldn't have to pay for what you did. But now the ox is in the ditch! Men are animals—no, that's an insult to the animals!"

Henry stammered, "We—we have a solution."

"He! He! And what of your nice little wife?"

"What do you know about my wife?"

"He! He! He! Crazy Sal knows you got a wife and three young 'uns and a preacher brother-in-law. Know how I know? 'Cause I got a shanty on the River Raisin near the Injun camp. I got two shanties. I know 'bout people 'round Adrian and Tecumseh."

Nancy continued dressing Teddy as Henry stared in shocked silence at Crazy Sal. The old woman, her gray hair straggling over her face, continued, "Watch your step,

Henry Parker. Your wife and family and your high-falutin' Adrian Quaker Friends might like to know what kind of a hypocrite you are. And I just might tell 'em! He! He! He! He! Makes you squirm, don't it? He! He! He!"

Henry turned abruptly. "Let's go, Nancy." He picked up her grip. She draped a shawl over her head and took Teddy's hand. Turning to take a last look at the cabin, she went to Sal.

"You have been good to us. Thank you. Use the cabin if you'd like. Zeke won't be back." She kissed the old woman's wrinkled cheek. "Goodbye," she whispered.

Henry helped Nancy into the saddle, then lifted Teddy up before her. "Comfortable?" he asked.

"We're fine. I wish you didn't have to walk."

He unsnapped one side of Ginger's rein. "I don't mind. I'll lead the horse. We won't go fast."

When they were a quarter mile down the trail the mournful cry of a wolf drifted through the air followed by the angry snarl of the wildcat. "Sal's howling again," Henry remarked. "She's crazy as a bedbug."

Nancy didn't reply. Teddy looked about at birds and squirrels. He pointed excitedly as a doe bounded across the trail. Finally Nancy said, "He's never going to hear."

Henry didn't reply. After a time he asked, "You don't think Zeke will come back?"

She shook her head. "The letter you brought last month said he was going West when he was out of jail. He's deserted us." She coughed, a long racking cough. "I hope my cold gets better when warm weather comes."

"Yeah. You've coughed all winter."

"Henry, I can never repay you for giving us the fare to Vermont. After the baby comes I'll try to find day work among my sister's friends. If I can get the money together, I'll repay you."

"Don't, Nancy. I owe you that much."

About two in the afternoon they arrived at Al Kies' place on the Chicago Road. Henry laughed. "Al has the roof on. When we were here last fall we had to stand in front of the fireplace to keep dry." He lifted Teddy down and helped Nancy to dismount. Reaching into his pocket, he gave her an envelope. "There's enough in here to get you home, and maybe a little extra. The stage for Detroit will be here tomorrow forenoon."

"Thanks, Henry." She kissed him lightly.

He patted Teddy's head, " 'Bye, young fellow." Puzzled, the child stared about him.

The door of the inn opened. "Henry Parker!" The innkeeper called. "Come in!"

Henry shook his head. "I've brought a friend and her boy. They will take the stage to Detroit tomorrow. You'll put them up tonight?"

"Sure. Nice to see you."

Henry swung into the saddle. Nancy called, "Remember to take our cow when you go home!"

"I will!" He waved and headed Ginger south on the trail. He felt as though a great weight had been lifted from his shoulders. He had paid his debt, and no one would ever know—if that damn old crone kept her mouth shut.

1831

2

THE SOUND OF HENRY'S AXE echoed through the forest. During the cold damp spring he and Fred had worked at the tiresome task of clearing their land. Great piles of logs waited to be burned. On dry days a thick haze of blue smoke hung over the forest from smoldering logs and brush.

This first summer Henry planned to plant as much corn and oats as possible on the cleared land. They would work the soil around the stumps which would be removed the following fall and spring to be used for fences. There would be no wheat crop in 1831 which would make it necessary to buy grain in Adrian to be made into flour. But in the fall of the year they would plant the oak openings to winter wheat. In the summer of 1832 they should have a good crop. He hoped their money would hold out until then. The amount he spent for Nancy's and Teddy's fare to Vermont had cut into their reserves.

He set his axe beside a stump to watch Fred, who was piling brush. They talked very little. Henry felt his son's dislike. He also saw it in Fred's eyes and in the way he avoided being with him. He had picked on the boy because of his stuttering, but he'd tried to make it up to him by doing things he'd like.

Fred loved Ginger and when the two of them rode into Adrian together no one would have guessed there was a great gulf between father and son. If Jimmy had lived—no use to think about that.

Josephine and Jake the Indian boy came whooping out of the forest. Fred grinned. "Are you go-o-ing to sc-scalp us?"

The children brandished sticks as they advanced. "We scalp you!" Josie shrieked. Her playmate imitated her. "We scalp you!" he echoed.

Henry chuckled. "Your Ma wishes you'd play ladylike games. She doesn't like this rough stuff."

Rusty flushed a covey of quails from a brush pile. Yipping wildly he ran after the birds as they lifted into the air.

Josephine stamped her foot. "I don't like dolls and sewing! I like climbing trees and yelling and—and— scalping people! Don't we Jake?" The little deerskin-clad boy nodded silently.

Her father grinned. "What would you do if you met a big bear?"

Josephine slammed her stick on the ground. "I'd hit him —and then I'd scalp him!"

Henry laughed. "I'll bet you'd try." He picked up the axe and returned to work.

"Papa, can I go to the Indian camp with Jake?"

"You play here at our place."

"But I know the way."

"It's too far. You can't go."

Fred dragged a branch to the brush pile. "A bear m-m-might get you."

"Sometime I'm going to Jake's camp. He wants me to, don't you?" Solemnly the boy nodded.

"Run along now," Henry said.

Whooping and yelling the children raced through the woods.

"Josie should have been a boy," Henry said.

Fred didn't answer. They worked silently for the remainder of the afternoon. On the way back to the cabin, with Rusty's help, they rounded up the cattle and drove them to the barn. Henry brought the horses in and tied them after which he and Fred milked the cows. Returning to the cabin in the early twilight, Susan met them at the door.

"Is Josephine with you?"

Henry's face reflected concern. "She and Jake were playing—must have been about the middle of the afternoon. Didn't they come to the house?"

Emily stood behind her mother, her eyes huge with fright. "She said they were going out where you were working." In the dim light Susan's face seemed pale.

Henry took his rifle from the corner. "Fred, saddle the horses. We have to find her before dark." Fred ran toward the barn.

Susan wrung her hands. "Where can she be?"

Angrily Henry replied, "The Indian camp! She asked to go with Jake, but I told her 'No.' "

"I wish John was here," Susan said. "He knows how to talk to the Indians."

Henry stormed, "She has to learn to mind. That girl is stubborn and she lacks self control! You've spoiled her by allowing her to have her own way! We'll go get her, but when she's home, I'll handle the punishment!"

Susan turned away. "Please, Henry, just go find her. It's almost dark." She shivered as a wolf howled in the distance.

Fifteen minutes later Fred and his father rode into the Indian camp. They were met by several mangy barking dogs. Women were cooking over bonfires while the braves lounged about waiting for their food. Joseph Black Bear strode forward.

"My girl," Henry began. "My girl Josephine. Is she here?"

"Not here."

Henry sucked in his breath. "Jake. Is Jake here?"

"Jake here." The boy came from one of the dome-shaped wigwams.

Henry bent low over his horses neck until he was on a level with Jake's face. "Where is Josephine?" he demanded.

"Not here," the boy said.

"Did she come here with you?"

"No come."

The entire camp had gathered in a circle about Henry and Fred. On the outside of the group the women hovered.

Henry spoke to Joseph. "She was with Jake. Ask him where she went."

Joseph talked in a low gutteral tone to the boy who responded briefly. "He say she come with him. She go back."

"My God, she's lost!" Henry gasped.

"We help," Joseph said briefly. Already several braves

were jumping astride their ponies that had been tethered at the edge of the camp. Some went to the right on the trail, while others turned left.

Henry and Fred rode slowly, calling as they went. "Josephine! Josephine!" Henry's voice boomed and echoed through the woods.

Now and then Fred shouted, "Jo-o-si-i-e-e!"

Henry was plagued by the memory of the Tubbs child at Blissfield that Addison Comstock had told of who was kidnapped by the Indians. Joseph Black Bear's group seemed friendly, they were helping in the search, but—had some of them already carried little Josephine off? He put the frightening thought from his mind. They would find her. It couldn't happen that two of his children would disappear.

The gutteral voices of the braves seemed to come from all directions. "Josephine! Josephine!" they shouted, but no childish voice replied.

The weird howl of a lone wolf sent shivers up the backs of Henry and Fred. What chance would a small child have against a pack of vicious wolves?

The moon shone brightly in the crisp, spring air, and still the unsuccessful search continued. Finally Henry said abruptly, "We may as well go home. She's gone—gone just like Jimmy."

"No!" Fred shouted. "We-e-e-'ll find her!"

"I don't know where else to look. If she's anywhere near the Indian camp she would have heard some of us calling." He turned his horse around on the trail. They met Joseph.

"No find Josephine?" he asked.

"No. We're going back to the cabin." Almost in a whisper he said, "Maybe she's home now."

"We look more," Joseph said.

"Thanks. Thank everyone for helping." They rode down the trail toward home.

1831

3

Josie and the Indian boy made their way slowly along the narrow trail. Woods creatures were enjoying the warm April sunshine. Squirrels chattered, cardinals whistled and woodpeckers drummed on dead trees searching for insects. A hawk silhouetted against the blue sky shrieked, "Fierce, fierce, fierce."

Jake ran to push on a dead oak sapling. He rocked it back and forth. Josie joined in the play. They laughed as the dead roots of the small tree released their hold in the loose soil and the sapling crashed to the ground.

"We're strong!" Josephine laughed. "We pushed a tree over!"

Jake jumped to grasp the branch of a maple. He pulled himself up and straddled the branch. "Come!" he shouted.

Not to be outdone by an Indian boy, Josie selected a limb on the opposite side of the tree and with skirts flying, she struggled until she managed to get a leg over the branch. Perching proudly oppposite her friend, she said, "Let's climb."

Up they went a limb at a time until they were standing on branches twenty feet from the ground.

"I'm a crow!" Josie shouted. "Caw! Caw! Caw!"

Jake joined in the call and they giggled when a crow answered them. Soon two of the noisy black birds came to investigate, scolding angrily as they flapped away.

Time passed rapidly. Josie finally said, "I have to go. Come to my house again, Jake." She turned and he started toward the camp.

A chipmunk crossed the trail, his tail flicking as he made his way to a stump where he perched to munch on a store of beechnuts. He nibbled rapidly, his bright eyes watching Josie. Slowly she moved toward him until she was within six feet of the stump. Standing quietly she studied the sleek little animal. The light colored stripes on his face, back and sides were bordered with black, the rest of his back, legs and tail were reddish-brown while his chest and stomach were a grayish-white.

"You're pretty," she said softly. "I'd like to have you for my pet."

Suddenly the little animal streaked across the dry leaves where he disappeared. Josie followed. There he was at the foot of a giant oak. Slowly she advanced, but again he zigzagged away from her. Finally she gave up. "You're too scary. I don't think you'd make a good pet."

She looked around. Which way was the trail? Walking aimlessly, she searched. She stopped to listen for the ringing sound of Henry's axe. She heard nothing but the whisper of the wind ruffling dry leaves. She wished Rusty was with her. He'd know the way home. She plodded on. Surely she'd soon come to the trail.

There was a building ahead, a little shanty. Maybe someone lived there. She knocked on the door and called, "Can I come in?"

A scraping sound as though someone was moving something came from inside. The door opened. Josie stepped back in surprise at the outline of the strange hunched old woman before her. She looked like the picture of a witch in one of Josie's books.

"He! He! He! Come in, Josephine Parker," the woman cackled.

"You know my name?"

"Crazy Sal knows everything 'bout everybody 'round here. He! He! He!" Josephine hesitated outside the door. "Come in. Don't be scared. Sal won't hurt you."

Reluctantly Josie went into the dark little shack lighted

only by a low fire in the fireplace.

"I seen you today with the Injun boy. You like him?"

"Yes, Mam."

"He! He! He! Girls and women's all alike."

"Yes, Mam."

"Don't you want to know why?"

"Yes, Mam." Josephine was in awe of this strange woman.

"Ya know any other words than 'yes, Mam'?"

"Yes, Mam. Why are girls and women all alike?"

"He! He! He! I'll tell ya why. They all likes men and boys too much. I hate the critters."

"Why?"

"Never mind why." The old woman stepped over a block of wood and went to the cluttered little table. "Hungry?"

"Yes, Mam."

"Here's some dried apples." Josie held her hands out. "Now why do ya like the Injun boy?"

Josie munched a slice of the tough dry fruit. " 'Cause he climbs trees and—and—I like to do boys' things. My sister, Emily, sews and does ladylike things. I wish I was a boy."

"Be glad ya are a girl. Little boys grow up to be men. I hate men!"

Josephine silently studied the fire. After a few moments she said, "My father's a man."

"He! He! He! I know 'bout your father. He's just like all the others."

"How do you know him?"

"He! He! He! I know him. Ask him if I don't."

"Mam. What is your name?"

"Everybody calls me Crazy Sal." In a minute she asked, "You're lost, ain't you?"

"It got dark and I couldn't find the trail."

"I'll take ya home. Your ma must be worried. I don't

care how worried your pa is. Serves him right."

The old woman put on her black bonnet and the long black coat. "Come, we'll go."

Outside it was pitch dark. Crazy Sal took Josephine's hand. " 'Tis quite a spell to your place."

The child jumped as a wolf howled nearby followed by the snarl of a wildcat. She clung tightly to Crazy Sal's hand. After listening intently to several of the animal-like cries, Josie asked, "Mam, are you making those noises?"

"He! He! He! I can sound like any animal or bird 'round here. They're my friends. Soon they'll answer me. Who—who—whooo!"

An owl directly overhead answered. "See?" Crazy Sal cackled. "In a minute you'll hear the wolves and wildcats." Again she howled and snarled.

Suddenly the wilderness rang with the howls of the wolf pack and the snarls of a wildcat.

Josephine stumbled. "Won't they hurt us?"

"I told ya. They're my friends. They talk to me."

Silently Josie plodded on clinging to the old woman's hand. Periodically Crazy Sal howled, snarled and hooted like an owl, and invariably she was answered by the wild creatures.

"Miss Crazy Sal, you're very smart to know how to talk to the animals."

The old woman cackled. "He! He! He! Nobody's thought I was smart for many a moon. He! He! He! For a time she was silent, then she asked, "Would you like to talk to the animals?"

"Oh, yes!"

"Come to my place this summer and I'll show you."

"I couldn't find your place."

"I'll be round about. Sometime I'll stop at your cabin. I sell berries to people. Maybe your ma'll want some. And some day I'll show you the way to my shanty."

"Miss Crazy Sal—I like you."

The old woman squeezed Josephine's hand. "We're almost to your cabin. I won't come in tonight, but I won't forget. I can learn you many things, little Josie."

The dim light from the candle showed through the window of the Parker cabin. " 'Bye," Josephine said. "Thank you for bringing me home." She hesitated. "Papa is going to be mad 'cause I got lost."

"You tell him Crazy Sal said he'd better hold his tongue and that if he whips you, Crazy Sal will cook his goose. He! He!"

"What do you mean?"

"Never mind. Just tell him. He'll know what I mean."

The old woman turned back into the wilderness and Josie reluctantly shoved the cabin door open.

Chapter Eleven
1832

THE BLACK HAWK WAR

1832

1

F<small>RED AND HIS SISTERS SAT ON THE</small> wash bench outside the cabin in the fading May sunlight. Josephine wiggled impatiently. "Why are you always whittling, Fred?"

He hesitated a moment before he spoke slowly. "I like to whittle." Shavings fell from his pocket knife as he shaped a small block of wood into a rough figure of a bird.

"But you whittled all last winter, and you're always cutting yourself. I can't see why you like it. There are scars all over your hands."

"Yeah."

Emily slapped a mosquito. "You make nice things, Freddy. Mama likes the bird you made for her."

Josephine jumped up. "Papa thinks it's stupid to spend so much time whittling."

Fred didn't answer. Silently, almost with pleasure, he

observed the deep cut in his thumb from which blood dripped to the ground.

"There! You've done it again!" Josephine shouted as Emily hurried inside to get a damp cloth to wrap around the thumb.

"Does it hurt?" Josephine asked.

"Nope." He observed the wound. A smile played about his mouth. "I'm—I'm tough."

"I think you're half-baked to keep doing something when you hurt yourself!"

Emily silently tightened the damp handkerchief about the bleeding thumb. "Don't pay no heed to what she says," she whispered.

Josephine exclaimed, "Drat those mosquitoes! I'll itch so I can't sleep tonight. I'm going to make a smudge pot." Quickly gathering Fred's wood shavings, she threw them into a rusty pan and covered the shavings with pieces of damp grass. After carrying the pan inside for smoldering coals, she returned with a smoking smudge pot which repelled annoying mosquitoes for yards around.

The children continued their conversation about the pros and cons of Fred's passion for whittling while the drone of the adults voices could be heard inside the cabin.

Susan said softly, "I don't understand why Fred cuts himself all the time. He needs a sharp knife to shape the things he makes, but his hands and arms are always covered with gashes and scabs."

Henry grumbled, "He's too stupid to know enough to stop whittling. 'Tis a waste of time."

"Fred is a bright boy, Henry," John protested. "He's worked hard all winter to break the stuttering habit. He's done well, though occasionally he still falls back into the old way of speaking." When Henry didn't reply, John continued in a low voice. "I think he has a poor opinion of himself. He wants to please you but he feels you don't approve of him. I wonder if he is cutting himself as punishment for being a disappointment to you."

"Humph."

Susan gasped. "You think that's possible?"

The children came inside which put an end to the discussion. When they were in bed in the loft, John said, "I wonder what will come of this Black Hawk scare. I was in Tecumseh and Adrian today and rumors are flying. Joseph Brown was advised by the Indian agent at Chicago that the Sauk and Fox tribes west of Lake Michigan are on the warpath and that they may advance into southern Michigan."

Henry laughed. "Rumors—just rumors. The Indians here are friendly. I hope something doesn't happen to get them stirred up. Is this Joseph Brown at Tecumseh the Quaker?"

"Yes. And he says the people in Lenawee County haven't forgotten the Raisin River Massacre at Monroe. They're nervous."

"Who is this Black Hawk?" Susan asked.

John stroked his beard thoughtfully. "He is a chief of the Sauk tribe. Though the Sauk and Fox tribes agreed in 1804 to give the United States their land east of the Mississippi, Black Hawk refused to accept the contract. He insisted, and he probably was right, that the chiefs had been given firewater before they signed the documents."

"Hm-m-m. That's interesting," Susan mused.

John continued. "Black Hawk and five hundred of his braves fought with the British in the War of 1812. Between 1804, when the contract to give up their land was signed, and 1830, most of the Sauk and Fox Indians had moved to a reservation west of the Mississippi. But Black Hawk's tribe refused to move. They still are fighting the whites for their land." [1]

Henry slapped a mosquito on his hand. "We're lucky

the Potawatomi Indians around here are friendly. Joseph Black Bear and his people are good neighbors."

Susan nodded. "Josephine is very fond of little Jake. She likes climbing trees with him."

Henry said, "John, you've spent many days with the Potawatomi at Devil's Lake, Blissfield and Tecumseh. Have you seen any signs of trouble with them?"

John shook his head. "They've been receptive to the gospel. To them, God is their Great Spirit. They have moral commandments somewhat like our Ten Commandments. One of them is that they shall fear the Great Creator who is ruler of all things. Another is that they shall not commit any crime because the Great Spirit is always watching."

"They don't sound like savages," Henry said. "Do they have other commandments like ours?"

"They have twenty-one to our ten; among them they are told to honor their father and mother, to be truthful, not to cheat or steal, and to feed the hungry. There are many more, and all are appropriate commandments for humans in dealing with one another." [2]

Susan said, "It sounds to me as though they are reasonable people."

"Yeah," Henry added, "but remember Black Hawk, and perhaps all of them, feel that the whites are taking their land away from them."

John explained, "Indians believe land cannot belong to one person. The Great Spirit gave them the land to use to support the life of the tribe. They resent the white man's belief that he can own a piece of land. People in Tecumseh and Adrian are worried. The men are talking of joining to go west to meet Black Hawk if his warriors enter Michigan. There is fighting now between his group and the whites in Indiana and Illinois."

Henry went to the water pail in the corner where he drank from a long-handled dipper. Wiping his mouth, he said, "Rumors. I think we're borrowing trouble. Probably 'tis only a small disagreement between neighbors and 'twill all blow over."

John shook his head. "I hope so."

For a time no one spoke. Each one was occupied with his own thoughts and doubts about the possibility of trouble with the Indians. Finally John said, "I'm starting Detroit way tomorrow."

"Oh?" Susan's voice revealed her surprise. In a moment she asked, "You'll see Father Gabriel Richard to learn if he's heard anything of Jimmy?"

"Yes, Sis. But it's been eighteen months since Jimmy disappeared. Father Richard knows where we are. He would have written if there was news."

"I suppose so. But someday we'll see Jimmy again."

"You'll hold services along the way?" Henry asked.

John nodded. "Tecumseh and Adrian have their circuit riders and the Quakers are holding regular services in Adrian at Addison Comstock's home, so I'll stop in areas where there are no circuit riders. Some of the settlers are sorely in need of a minister for weddings and baptisms. Most funerals and burials are conducted by the family with the help of neighbors if there are any."

"How many people do you figger on before you have a service?" Henry asked.

John laughed. "No set number. Sometimes one or two families, and more if the word gets around."

"Will you work at Indian camps on the way to Detroit?" Susan asked.

"Anywhere I'm needed and welcomed. I'll do what I can."

"You don't make much money doing your work," Henry said.

"That's true. Settlers feed me, give me shelter and when they have it, they give me a few coins. The Indians have no money but I've learned to like Indian food—and they allow me to sleep in a wigwam. I don't need much money—and I still have most of the money from the settlement of our parents' estate. Susan and I shared alike."

Henry got up. "Susan still has most of hers, too. She hoards it. Mine is going fast. We spent quite a bit last winter for cornmeal and flour because that damn bear ruined half of our supply." He hesitated. "And it took a good bit to send Nancy and her boy to Vermont."

Susan nodded. "I'm glad you're kind-hearted," she said softly.

1832

2

HENRY PARKER, ADDISON COMstock, Charles Haviland and Sylvanus Westgate were gathered at Comstock's Red Mill in Adrian. Their faces were somber as they listened intently while Joseph Brown from Tecumseh spoke.

"Friends," he began, "we have a serious threat facing us. The Sauk and Fox tribes near Chicago are on the warpath against white settlers. Black Hawk has refused to give up his village on the Mississippi River in western Illinois as the Indians agreed to do by contract with the United States Government in 1804.

"As you know, I am a former military man. I have been made Brigadier General of the 3rd Brigade under Acting Governor Mason, and as such I'm the highest ranking officer in the Michigan Territorial Militia. I've been put in command of all operations."

"What operations?" Henry asked.

"Because Black Hawk warriors are moving rapidly we

believe they may sweep into southern Michigan after they
conquer northern Illinois and Indiana. To prevent loss of
our land and homes, Governor Mason received an urgent
call from the governor of Illinois for help. He has ordered
us to volunteer for service to prevent the ravage of southern Michigan. We believe the enemy will make a desperate
attempt to reach Fort Malden on the east shore of the Detroit River, and this likely would mean Detroit would be
captured." Brigadier General Brown paused to solemnly
study the faces of the men around him.

He continued, "We, the volunteers from Adrian,
Tecumseh and Clinton, which was formerly called Oak
Plains, will be the 8th Regiment led by Colonel William
McNair of Tecumseh. Our regimental surgeon is Dr. M. A.
Patterson of Tecumseh. Also joining us will be volunteers
from other areas, for Acting Governor Mason has called
for a total of three hundred men. Two groups have re-
sponded from Detroit, the Detroit City Guards and the
Light Dragoons. They're already on the Chicago Road,
headed west.

"I will go ahead to complete preparations for the arrival of the troops at Niles. From there we all will proceed
to Chicago." He paused.

"I'm asking for volunteers. Any questions?"

Henry cleared his throat. "Won't this action destroy our
friendship with the Potawatomi?"

Brigadier General Brown stared into the forest beyond
the River Raisin. "I fear it already is destroyed. Not an Indian is to be found anywhere in this region. I believe they
have gone to join Black Hawk to help him drive us from
our land."

There was dead silence. After a time the man continued. "I will leave for Niles tomorrow. Any of you who
wish to volunteer should meet Colonel McNair at Clinton
two days from now. Bring only your rifle or flintlock mus-

ket and a change of clothing.

"Spread the word. We need all the volunteers we can get. We hope you'll not be gone long for most of us have spring farm work waiting. If you are convinced your patriotic duty to your country is greater than your desire to remain at home, then join the troops at Clinton in two days." He turned to put on his flat black Quaker hat. "I'm sure I'll see most of you at Niles." He strode to his horse and galloped toward Tecumseh. [3, 4, 5]

3 — 1832

Henry, deep in thought, allowed Ginger to choose her pace on the trail toward home. His mind was in a state of confusion. He supposed his duty was to join the volunteers, but this meant no spring planting. He also had a duty to Susan and the children. With John gone for several months, he disliked leaving them alone. Susan and Emily were terrified of bears and wolves. The oats were planted but there would be no corn this fall unless it was in the ground very soon. They likely would have a fair crop of wheat, but it should be harvested in August and he might not be home by then—if he came home at all. Drat his luck!

And the Indians—were they really gone? As he neared the cabin, Rusty ran barking to meet him, closely followed by Josephine. He greeted her, calling as he rode on, "Tell your mother I'm going to the Indian camp."

"Can I go, Pa?" Josie begged.

"No. I'll be back soon."

As he urged Ginger into a gallop he knew that if the Indians were gone, the situation was serious. Joseph Brown said the Potawatomi from the Tecumseh, Adrian, Blissfield and Devil's Lake areas all had mysteriously disappeared. There could be only one reason—to help Black Hawk drive the whites from the land. But they had appeared friendly. John had told of experiences with Chief Meteau at Round Lake. He seemed to be a reasonable and a moral man. John had talked with a neighbor of Meteau's tribe who told of an experience with the old chief who, though intoxicated, came to the settler's home to demand whiskey. When his white friends refused him, Meteau tried to help himself. The chief was roughly thrown from the cabin. He whooped his loudest Indian call and ran away.

A few days later Meteau returned, sober and begging for peace and friendship, saying, "I boss Injun, you boss *che-mo-ka-man*"—white man.

John also told of Chief Baw-Beese from the Devil's Lake, Round Lake area who often called on settlers asking for meals but wanting to pay "two shilling like white man."

And Joseph Black Bear and his braves had been good neighbors. During the past winter they brought meat, wild honey and fish for which the Parker family had traded salt, apples and hand-knitted sweaters. Then, recently the braves had turned out to search for Josephine. They had searched as earnestly as though one of their children was lost.

As he neared the Indian camp Henry half-expected a group of barking dogs to meet him. Instead there was the silence of the wilderness broken only by the raucous call of a crow. The camp was empty of any sign of human life. Only the deserted wigwams and fire rings with dead ashes remained. Reluctantly he rode back to the cabin to inform his family that he would soon be leaving to fight Black Hawk's warriors.

Susan and Fred received the news of Henry's decision to volunteer with solemn silence. Emily burst into tears. Josephine alone was elated at the news. "I wish I was a man so I could go!" she exclaimed.

Ignoring her statement, Henry said, "We must plan. I'll leave day after tomorrow for Clinton. Fred, you ride Ginger and I'll take Major, and you'll bring both horses home. Think you can manage?"

"I-I can do it. I'll take care of the animals and—and I'll plow and plant corn."

" 'Tis a big job, and hard work. Damn, I wish John was here."

"I can do—do it. I'm fourteen."

Josephine asked, "If you send Major home with Fred, how will you get to Niles?"

"We'll walk." He grinned. "We're foot soldiers." In a moment he continued, "I'll leave the rifle for you, Fred. I'll take the old musket." He glanced at Susan. "You haven't said a word." He put his arm about her shoulders. "I'll miss you. I love my family. You're all very dear to me."

Fred stared silently into the dying coals in the fireplace. Henry wondered what he was thinking. Did the boy secretly hope he wouldn't return? Swallowing, he choked back tears as he remembered little Jimmy.

Two days later Henry told his family goodbye in an affectionate farewell. Susan and Emily kissed him repeatedly, but Josie, after a quick peck at his lips said, "Pa, remember everything so you can tell me. I wish I was a man going to war. Don't you wish you were going, Fred?"

"Nope." His eyes met Henry's. "Some—somebody has to take care of Mama and you girls."

After another round of kisses and hugs, Henry said, "Come, Fred. Time to start." They swung into their saddles, waving as the wilderness closed behind them.

Late that afternoon Fred returned leading Major. After turning the horses loose he and Rusty rounded up the cows for milking. Finally, when the chores were done, he went inside for supper.

Susan and the girls were filled with questions. Were there many volunteers? How were the men dressed? Did they seem to dread going? When would the march to Niles begin?

Fred answered in as few words as possible. There were about seventy-five men when he left. They seemed jovial. Dressed in their everyday work clothes and carrying firearms, they likely would leave the following day.

The boy ate slowly without raising his eyes from his plate. Susan sensed his concern. Watching him closely she asked, "Did you and your father have angry words?"

"No, Mama."

After several more minutes of silence, Susan said, "Something is worrying you. Is it all the work you have to do?"

"No, Mama."

"Fred, tell me. We have to work things out together. What is wrong?"

Silently he drew a letter from his pocket and passed it to his mother. "On the way home I-I stopped at the post office. Mrs. Comstock gave me this letter for Pa. I paid the twenty-five cent postage from the money you gave me." He stared at the floor a moment before he glanced at his mother. Her face was pale. Quietly she opened the letter. " 'Tis from Nancy Farmer," she whispered.

"What does she say? What does she say?" Josie demanded.

Susan's eyes skimmed the lines as the children watched. Emily broke the silence. "How is Teddy? Can he hear now?"

Susan read on, oblivious to the children's questions. Finally she dropped the letter in her lap. There was a note of quiet resignation in her voice when she spoke. "Teddy died of lung fever a few days after Nancy and he arrived in Vermont."

"Poor Teddy," Emily said. "I gave him scarlet fever. It was my fault he was deaf."

Susan patted the child's shoulder. " 'Twas one of those things that happen. When we stopped at the Farmers we thought you had a cold. 'Twas not your fault." In a moment she continued. "Nancy is not well. She has consumption."

"You—you don't get o-v-ver consumption," Fred stammered.

"No. She thinks she may have only a few months to live."

"That's awful!" Emily gasped.

Susan rubbed her head. "There's more. She has a baby boy that will be a year old in August. She named him for your father—because Henry was so good to her, she said." Susan glanced at Fred, wondering if he had the same disturbing thoughts she was experiencing. The boy's flushed angry face assured her of his suspicions.

Josephine asked, "If Nancy dies, what will happen to the baby?"

"She wants us to take him."

Fred jumped up, his tin cup spilling milk over the floor. "What? I-I-I don't believe it! That—that woman! Mama, you can't take that—that child!"

Susan sighed. "I don't have much choice. He's already on his way to Adrian with a family named Martin. They'll be here in July."

Emily smiled. "It will be nice to have a baby. Did Mr. Farmer come back to live with them?"

"No. She doesn't know where he is. Nancy says if she didn't send the baby to us he would have to go to an orphanage because her sister has a large family and she's sick too."

Fred stamped back and forth from the door to the table. "So we're elected to bring up her—her—b-b—"

Susan raised her hand. "Don't say it!"

"Don't say what, Mama?" Josie asked.

"Nothing, dear. You and Emily will help me. He'll be like a little—little brother."

Fred snorted. "S-s-some br-br-brother!" He stamped outside without another word.

4 ───────────────────────── *1832*

Brigadier General Joseph Brown urged his horse along the trail. Plans were racing through his mind as he contemplated his responsibility for carrying out orders given him by acting Governor Mason. Arrangements must be made for three hundred volunteers who would arrive in Niles about May 30th. From the rumors, he expected a hard battle with Black Hawk's braves before victory was won. Tales had reached him of the shocking murder of settlers, men, women and children in the Fox River country where Black Hawk's tribe refused to give up their land.

As a Quaker, Joseph Brown disliked war, but when ownership of American land purchased from the government was threatened, he was willing to fight Black Hawk until he was defeated.

But a surprise awaited Joseph Brown in Niles. He learned that the regular army in the west had already met Black Hawk and that reports of future danger were greatly exaggerated. Under attack from the Illinois militia and some Federal troops, Black Hawk withdrew. He then began moving his people toward the Mississippi River.

Frustrated and uncertain as to how to proceed, the Brigadier General sent an order by messenger to Colonel McNair, who Brown thought was at Jonesville with the marching volunteers, to return his men to Tecumseh. But somehow the message was not delivered. In his report to Governor Mason at the capitol in Detroit, General Brown said, "I hope you will do all in your power to silence the alarm, for with the arms you sent me I feel sure the people here can protect themselves."

While the volunteers continued the march to Niles, Brigadier General Brown and a mounted scouting party pressed on to Black Hawk country west of Chicago. There they found first hand evidence of the murder of fifteen settlers by the Indians, before the massacre had been stopped by the regular army.

Hurrying back to the Carey Mission in Niles, Brown found an Indian Council in progress. All of the Potawatomi from southern Michigan were camped in the nearby wilderness. Chiefs Meteau, Baw-Beese, Joseph Black Bear and several others had brought their tribes to the council.

Joseph Brown spoke with Chief Meteau, the senior chief. "Why did you come here? No one is left in your camps."

Old Meteau pulled his blanket about his frail shoulders as though for protection from some danger. "Black Hawk," the old man said.

"Do you take your squaws and children into battle?"

"No battle. Meteau no fight."

"But your young men. Did they come to help Black Hawk drive the whites out of Michigan Territory?"

"We no help Black Hawk. No like Black Hawk. No want to fight *che-mo-ka-man*. Meteau *che-mo-ka-man*'s friend."

Joseph Brown wiped the perspiration from his forehead. "The other chiefs—they don't like Black Hawk?"

"Potawatomi friendly Injuns. Potawatomi not bad Injuns like Sauk and Fox. We want fight no more with white man." The chief's sharp old eyes met Brown's. "If Black

Hawk come here, Potawatomi young men help you drive him away. We no like Sauk and Fox Injuns."

"Thank you, Chief Meteau. Your people are good neighbors." A half-smile flickered across the wrinkled old face as he turned, ending the conversation.

The Brigadier General met with Colonel McNair and Regimental surgeon Dr. M. A. Patterson. A decision must be made. Since the volunteers had arrived, should they be sent home or should they remain at Niles until Black Hawk was forced to surrender by the general United States Army? It would be several days before orders arrived from Detroit. It was decided the men would remain as back-up troops in the event they were needed.

Colonel McNair scratched his head. "The men are going to be sore. We march them miles across the Territory, they'll wait around here doing nothing, while at home their spring planting goes undone. Then, we'll march them home. 'Tis a wild goose chase."

Dr. Patterson smiled. "I agree. They've already been here several days, and they're the laughing stock of the young Indian men."

"They are? Why?" Joseph Brown asked.

McNair smiled as Dr. Patterson continued. "When they have target practice they can't hit the broad side of a barn with their old flintlock muskets. 'Tis laughable, but 'twouldn't be if they were in a serious battle."

McNair went on. "Last night a sentry fired a shot and killed one of Sylvanus Blackman's hogs that had crossed the line without giving the countersign." He chuckled at the recollection.

Patterson asked, "How long should we hold the men here?"

"The Brigadier General replied, "Let's take it a week at a time. I figger 'tis about over for Black Hawk. Surely in a month or six weeks he will have surrendered."

References

[1]Harlan L. Hagman, *Bright Michigan Morning* (Green Oak Press, 1981), pp. 34-37.

[2]Andrew J. Blackbird, *History of the Ottawa and Chippewa Indians in Michigan* (Ypsilanti: Job Printing House, 1887).

[3]Clara Waldron, *One Hundred Years a Country Town* (Thomas A. Riordan, 1968).

[4]*Early Adrian* (American Association of University Women).

[5]Willis T. Dunbar, *Michigan* (William B. Eerdmans, 1965).

Chapter Twelve
1832

CHOLERA

1832

1

J OHN LEFT ADRIAN IN MID-MAY. The following six weeks were spent visiting remote families where he held services, performed the rites of marriage and baptism, and on two occasions, he conducted funeral services. In addition he visited Indian camps where he received friendly welcomes. He had no schedule but followed suggestions made by families he visited about areas where there was a need for the services of a minister. Generally, he traveled in a northeasterly direction.

As they neared Detroit the circuit rider leaned forward in the saddle to affectionately slap Roamer's neck. "Old Boy, we're going to the city. You'll have it easy with nothing do do but eat and sleep in the stable at the Steamboat Hotel." Roamer nickered.

There were changes in the city since he had arrived with the Parkers nearly two years earlier. The formerly muddy intersection of Woodward and Jefferson now was paved with cobblestones. A large dry goods store, Disbrow's, stood at the northeast corner, and King's clothing store was at the southeast. Across from them on the northwest corner was the new Thomas Cook Drug Store. South on Woodward was the long, low-roofed shed of market stalls. On either side of the market were stores, warehouses, saloons and small cottages.

John glimpsed the Detroit River and the dock from which Jimmy had disappeared. Small ferries, one steam-powered, crossed the river to Richmond, as Windsor was known until 1836.

To the north Woodward sloped down toward the wooden bridge over Savoyard Creek, a smelly, slow-moving stream only inches deep in the heat of summer. Refuse and garbage littered the little creek and clouds of mosquitoes hovered near the muddy water.

On the east side of Woodward were three churches in a row, the Presbyterian at the northeast corner of Larned, the Episcopal St. Paul's Church in the middle of the block and the Methodist on Gratiot just off Woodward. Ste. Anne's Catholic Church stood at Larned and Bates. [1]

John rode slowly as he observed the busy streets. Two-wheeled carts pulled by a single horse or pony carried well-dressed women in voluminous gowns, their children by their sides. With parasols over their heads, they bowed to acquaintances on the wooden sidewalks, attempting as much dignity as possible while riding in their rumbling, jolting carts. An occasional family carriage pulled by a sleek team passed through the dusty streets.

On the wooden sidewalks John viewed a cross section of Detroit's population. Indian men with colorful blankets about their shoulders, bedraggled women whose numerous offspring trailed behind, businessmen in suits and tall black hats, French farmers shouting their bargains in produce from the market stalls, and settlers, newcomers and those who had come to the city for supplies, all served to produce a kaleidoscope of the people of the Michigan Territory.

After Roamer was stabled at the Steamboat Hotel barn, John walked the short distance to Ste. Anne's Church where he hoped to find Father Gabriel Richard. His first duty was to inquire about Jimmy, and then to post a letter to Susan.

He found Father Richard in the rose garden behind the church. The white-haired old man appeared taller and thinner than he remembered. He greeted John warmly.

"Rev. John Parker!" he exclaimed, extending his hand. " 'Tis good to see a fellow servant of God. Come into the parsonage." He motioned toward a nearby cottage. He explained as he led the way to the back door, "Mary, my Indian housekeeper, will fix us a cool drink."

When they were seated at the dining room table John hastened to ask, "Have you had any news of little Jimmy?"

The lines in the old priest's face deepened as he fingered his tumbler. "I have heard nothing of the boy."

John sighed. "My sister insists God told her Jimmy is alive. She believes he was kidnapped and that some day he will find his family."

"Only God knows. Perhaps it is well she has this hope to cling to. It makes the uncertainty easier."

The men conversed as Mary silently glided about in deerskin moccasins refilling tumblers and attending to household duties.

"When did you come to Michigan Territory?" John asked.

Before he answered the old man produced a snuffbox from within his robe and slowly took a pinch of snuff, placed it on the back of his hand and sniffed vigorously. "Like some?" he asked.

"No thanks."

"Well, I came to Michigan Territory in 1798 as a missionary to the Indians. I was thirty-one years old and full of Christian zeal. That was thirty-four years ago. I have guided some of them to a Christian life, but I've failed many times—too many." He pondered silently and finally continued, "I'm a priest at Ste. Anne's, as you know. Most of the French settlers are of the Catholic faith."

"You've done much good," John said softly. "Have you been at Detroit for thirty-four years?"

"This is my home, but my charge takes in the Michigan peninsulas and the land west of Lake Michigan. In fact, my charge is the entire Michigan Territory. In 1822 my parish included nine hundred twenty six families, mostly French-Canadians in six Catholic churches in the Territory. Now we have many more churches."

John said, "I work with the Indians as much as with the settlers. I've heard you spend time visiting northern Indian settlements. I'd like to do that."

The old priest smiled. "I was first sent on a missionary tour to the northern lake region in 1799. Though the thirteen hundred Indians of L'Arbre Croche had had no resident priest for many years, they had not abandoned the Christian faith. Efforts are now made to provide them with a priest from time to time. Their Chief Blackbird, though uneducated, is a fine leader. He encourages the Ottawas and Chippewas of L'Arbre Croche to accept Christianity. Several times in his younger days he led warriors on the warpath against the white man, and he was known for his daring. But for many years now, he has been a peaceful man who counsels his people to live a moral life."

John asked. "Where is L'Arbre Croche?"

"It is built along the Lake Michigan shore of Michigan's northwestern lower peninsula. It stretches along the lake shore for many miles." [2]

John brushed a fly from his face. "Tell me about some

of your early experiences."

The priest walked to the window. His long black robe caused him to appear unusually tall and thin. As he looked toward the Detroit River he seemed to be thinking aloud as he said, "Hm-m-m—1799. That was the year I went to Mackinac Island. Fur trading dominated the way of life there. Though Americans took part in the trade, the business management was almost entirely in the hands of the Britishers. The only symbol of United States authority over the region was the fort with its small garrison flying the American flag."

"Was there a Catholic church there?"

The old priest returned to his chair. Thoughtfully rubbing his forehead he replied. "A church was there but they had no resident priest. Conditions were bad for the Indians. Liquor was prevalent and generally was used in trading with them. The street was filled with drunken Indians. They were not like the Ottawas and Chippewas of L'Arbre Croche for they were uninterested in religion. They had no strong chief such as Chief Blackbird of L'Arbre Croche. Former converts had even forgotten the sign of the cross."

John smiled. "We Methodists would say they were backsliders."

Father Richard nodded. "I did what I could but it wasn't enough. They needed a resident priest. A few baptisms and masses weren't a drop in the bucket to meet the need."

"I've heard many of the Frenchmen have taken Indian wives. Is this a common practice?"

"Very common. Usually 'tis a matter of convenience. The man profits from the arrangements but the Indian woman often is left with fatherless children when the fur trapper moves on where he likely will take another Indian woman into his wigwam."

"What can we do to be of the most help to the Indians?

That is in addition to telling them of the benefits of Christianity?"

"Education." The old man shook his head. " 'Tis an immense problem, and progress is slow. In 1808 I started a plan here for the education of Indian children. It included crafts as well as common school education. The government in Washington finally gave us a small subsidy for the school. We had a printing press and we produced a child's spelling book. We had enthusiastic plans in those days. We were going to save souls and educate people. But even now, years later, white children must pay 'rate bills' to attend school. Most of the French and many Americans who live here do not have money to pay for their children's education. I've always been a firm believer in the need for education, but though I've pushed and prodded from the local level to the Congress in Washington, I feel I've failed."

"You were a representative from Michigan Territory to Congress?"

"Yes. A poor one, I fear. I was first elected in 1823. I've dabbled in many areas. Perhaps I would have accomplished more if I'd concentrated on one. A man of God shouldn't dabble in politics. In 1825 and 1827 I had some influence in getting Congress to provide money for extending the Sauk Trail to the Indiana line. Congress liked the name Chicago Military Road. The road is having a positive effect on settlement in southern Michigan."

"Father Richard, you've had great influence upon the people of Michigan."

The old man smiled a tired smile. "Perhaps, some. But nothing is completed. Souls brought to God, education of our children, better roads—I'm impatient for I see the end of my life approaching. John, you and other young men must carry on." He got up abruptly. "You will have supper with me?"

"Thanks. I'd like to."

The old man called, "Mary!" The Indian woman instantly appeared. As the priest and Mary discussed the evening menu, John studied his appearance, thinking that the priest must have been quite a curiosity in the national capitol. In spite of his education and correct use of the English language, he spoke with a French accent. He wore knee breeches, silk stockings and a long black coat with a voluminous collar over a huge skirt extending almost to his ankles.

Concluding the conversation with Mary, Father Richard returned to his chair. Again he indulged himself in a pinch of snuff. "I'm enjoying our conversation," he said genially.

"I've looked forward to talking with you since we were here in 1830. There are many things I'd like to ask you. You have an orphanage here, I remember."

"It's still operating. Those children may not have parents but the Church is raising and educating them. Since 1817 Rev. John Monteith and I have tried to get a university started here in Detroit. We have been unsuccessful thus far, but some day we'll succeed. We refer to it as the "First College of Michigania." [*] We have been able to start schools for the Indians at Monroe and Mackinac Island, but there truly is little interest by parents or children." He was silent for a moment. Then he asked, "When did the Methodist circuit riders first come to Michigan?"

"In 1810. The first Methodist society in Michigan was formed by people living along the River Rouge. At first services were held in homes, much as we do today in the wilderness. Now we have several circuit riders and a few resident pastors.

---

[*] In 1817 the University of Michigan opened at Ann Arbor. This was the college Father Richard had hoped would be located in Detroit.

"At Adrian and Tecumseh several Quaker families have settled. They are strongly opposed to Negro slavery, as are most Michigan people. However they discuss the problem freely in their monthly meetings, I'm told by my brother-in-law Henry Parker, who was brought up as a Quaker. Two Quaker women, Margaret Chandler and Laura Smith Haviland are noted leaders among Adrian's Quaker Society."[3]

Father Richard got up. "While Mary's cooking supper, let's stroll down to the docks."

The priest greeted people warmly and John sensed the respect and affection with which he was regarded. Suddenly the old man chuckled. "We've been very serious in our conversation. I just remembered an unusual incident which happened shortly after I arrived in Detroit. About the year 1800 a small pipe organ was installed in Ste. Anne's. The Indians were so fascinated and amazed by the instrument that they stole the pipes."

John laughed. "They must have been disappointed that the single pipes couldn't produce music."

"They were like children. It gave me a chance to teach a lesson in honesty, but we never did get the pipes back. However, we did secure another small organ for the church."

"I don't suppose there are many musicians here."

"That's right. But the few we have are appreciated. Many years ago the first piano arrived. Prior to that there were two harpsichords. The first piano was carried from Marietta, Ohio, on horseback. Another piano was brought to Ann Arbor from Detroit by ox team. The driver was somewhat frightened of the box in which it was packed because he said 'it thundered so.' That was the first piano taken west of Detroit—about 1827, I think."

"Were the Indians impressed by piano music?"

"The chief is said to have offered half a dozen ponies

for the instrument and the young lady who played it." He chuckled.

"Your life has been a busy one. You are priest, missionary, reformer, educator, politician and a friend of humanity," John remarked. "Is there any ambition you haven't achieved?"

Father Richard sighed. "There is one, but I will never realize it." He hesitated. "I may as well tell you." He paused to indulge in a pinch of snuff. Somewhat reluctantly he continued. "Remember I said priests shouldn't dabble in politics?"

"Yes."

"I learned that fact too late. In the election for delegate to Congress in 1823 I won largely because of the support of the French people. Colonel Biddle also was a candidate—he was clerk of the Detroit land office—and he attempted to contest the election on the grounds that I was not a citizen, but a congressional committee decided in my favor. When I returned to Detroit in the spring of 1824 after Congress had adjourned, I was put in jail."

"What?"

"My opponent had been at work while I was gone. Some months before the election, from the pulpit, I had condemned an adulterer and had excommunicated a man named Labadie who had divorced one wife and married another. Labadie brought suit for damages against me and the court awarded the man a judgment of $1,116. I refused to pay because it seemed to me the civil authorities should have no power over purely ecclesiastical concerns. So—I was jailed for three weeks but was released when my friends gave bond that insured I would remain in Wayne County." [4]

"Then you couldn't return to Congress in the fall?"

"Henry Clay was Speaker of the House. He informed me that as a member of Congress I could claim immunity from arrest, so I returned to Washington. But, John, this thing still plagues me. It is the greatest disappointment of my life that I was never consecrated as a bishop."

"You think the Labadie case was responsible?"

"That, together with my involvement in a number of controversial affairs."

They walked on until they approached the dock where Jimmy had disappeared. A steamer was unloading and families were milling about among their possessions piled beside the dock.

In the middle of the river the steamship *Henry Clay* and three other transports waited to approach the dock. The priest explained, "They're carrying Federal troops who are going 'round to Chicago. They're being sent to defeat Black Hawk."

"I heard a rumor at Ypsilanti that the Black Hawk situation is not serious and that Governor Tom Mason acted hastily in calling up volunteers," John remarked.

The old priest's eyes followed the movement on the dock. "I suspect the rumor is correct. The *Courier* carried a report that none of the Indian tribes had joined Black Hawk's cause. The Illinois militia and some Federal troops attacked and Black Hawk withdrew up the Rock River where he was defeated."

"Then why is the goverment sending more troops to Fort Dearborn at Chicago?"

Father Richard shook his head. "I suppose their orders still are in effect. The *Courier* also carried a report that Black Hawk tried to put his tribe's women and children in boats to carry them across the Mississippi. But a Federal gunboat fired into the huddled Indians while the troops on land joined in killing most of the Indians on the spot. Black Hawk is defeated, though he hasn't surrendered." [5]

John shook his head. "It was cruel, useless slaughter. The whole situation seems as futile as the slavery problem.

The Indians and the Negroes—where will it end? My brother-in-law says when he was a child the Quakers said, "If we sow the wind we will reap the whirlwind." They were referring to the slavery problem. Perhaps it also refers to the Indian difficulty."

Conversation stopped as the steamer moved away to make room for the *Henry Clay*. Soon young uniformed troops were pouring ashore. They appeared serious and in a hurry to leave the ship. Bits of conversation were picked up by John and the priest. "The sickness—filthy ship—poor food—doctor can't help—Tom and Sam died—cholera."

"Cholera!" John exclaimed.

"Perhaps they're wrong," Father Richard replied, but even as he spoke the bodies of several dead were brought ashore to lie near the dock awaiting burial.

A few days later on a hot, steamy July 6, two cases of cholera were found among Detroit citizens. Rumors were rampant which soon proved to be true. The medical officer of the *Henry Clay* abandoned ship leaving the care of the sick on board to local doctors who had not yet realized the extent of the danger.

Governor Mason, Father Richard and other leading citizens were concerned. They had read that the disease first appeared in Russia in 1831 and was brought to America by an immigrant ship and that soon many cholera deaths were reported on the eastern seaboard. [6]

In Detroit the disease spread rapidly. The four troop carrying ships still were docked in the Detroit River. More soldiers became ill. Bodies of the dead men were carried ashore to lie near the dock until burial arrangements were made. A warehouse became a temporary hospital. [7]

Tom Mason conferred with the few medical people. The ships were ordered to move away from the city and to continue up the river and through the lakes. One transport docked beside Hog Island (now Belle Isle) while attempts were made to care for the dead and dying.

Father Richard and John Thompson were tireless in their efforts to aid the unfortunate victims before the *Henry Clay* steamed northward where it docked at Fort Gratiot north of Port Huron. There, putting ashore for wood to stoke the boiler, many of the frantic troops who were either ill or were fearful of becoming ill with cholera, fled the ship. Many died in the fields and woods, but others made it back to Detroit carrying with them the dread disease.

By the second week in July there were twenty-eight cases of cholera. Almost nothing was known about what could be done to prevent the spread of the disease or what treatment might be helpful. The second floor of the capitol was hurriedly made into a hospital. People on the street wore masks over their noses and mouths and carried torches of burning pitch in the belief that breathing the smoky fumes would prevent contagion.

Clergymen and medical people worked tirelessly, but still the epidemic raged. Church bells tolled endlessly as the custom of tolling for another death was followed.

Father Richard welcomed John's help in ministering to the sick and dying. The disease struck its victims suddenly. Persons in excellent health suddenly were stricken with a feeling of uneasiness to be followed with a consuming fever and a craving for cold drinks, followed by vomiting, intestinal cramps, weakness and death. Some became seriously ill but recovered. For those who survived, the disease ran its course in three to five days.

On his visits to the ill on the capitol's second floor, John often spoke with the concerned young governor. Twenty-year-old Tom Mason had aged. His face was haggard as he spoke with quiet desperation. "John, I don't know what to do. We don't know how this sickness spreads. We've passed ordinances requiring streets and Savoyard Creek to be kept free of refuse and garbage, but the people are too ill or too concerned with sick and dying relatives to comply. I believe carelessness with rotting garbage and the hundreds of rats that are everywhere have something to do with spreading the sickness because it seems to strike hardest in the poor neighborhoods of our French people."

John nodded. "Those are the people who live in overcrowded homes and who do not have proper food. It spreads through a family like wildfire. The old and weak are the first to go."

Tom Mason stared toward the Detroit River. "Granny Peg, our old colored cook, died yesterday. She has been with our family since before I was born. She was like one of the family." He wiped away a tear. "She died in my sister's arms."

"I'm sorry." The church bells tolled mournfully.

Tom Mason shook his head. "We've got to stop tolling those bells for every death! 'Tis bad enough without having the bells everlastingly reminding us of this tragedy. Come into my office, John. I need to talk to someone."

They removed their masks and sat quietly for a time. Finally the governor said, "I feel so utterly helpless. Nothing we do seems to stop the thing. People are trying to run away from the city. But that would only spread it outstate. I've ordered barricades at the border of villages and towns to keep the cholera confined to this area. But people are determined to escape. At Ypsilanti armed guards were forced to shoot one of the horses on the stage because the driver refused to stop."

"They're desperate," John agreed.

Mason continued. "This thing spreads in spite of anything we do. Out at Marshall more than one-fourth of their people have it. We have learned to accept the ague which we don't know how to prevent, but few die from ague. We've learned to live with it."

Through the open windows the sound of horses' hooves clopping on the street and the clatter of a wagon was followed by a call, "Bring out your dead! Bring out your dead!"

Neither man spoke. At last John said, "How many so far?"

"In the nineties. 'Twill soon reach a hundred. We no longer can keep up with digging the graves. They're burying about thirty in a common grave this morning." He paused, then continued as he brushed a fly from his face. "I appreciate what you and Father Richard have done in working day and night to give aid to the dying and in consoling grieving families."

John gestured impatiently. "As servants of God we wish we could do more. We've prayed with the sick and dying and have tried to give comfort where we could. But it's so little." He hesitated a moment. "Father Richard is not a young man. I think he's not well."

The governor sat bolt upright. "Not cholera?"

"I don't think so. 'Tis more like he's worn out— exhausted. For the first time since the cholera started he didn't leave the house this morning. He's been with the sick and dying every day and night for almost two months."

"And so have you."

"But I'm a young man. Father Richard is sixty-five."

"I'll stop to see him later today. He is a great force for good in our city. Perhaps with a few days' rest, he'll be better."

But it was not to be. In September after the epidemic ended, Father Gabriel Richard died, not of cholera but probably from exhaustion. His body lay in state while Detroit's citizens filed past the bier of the old priest in a final tearful farewell. His body was placed in a crypt under Ste. Anne's church at Bates and Larned where it remained until it was moved to the new Ste. Anne's church on Howard Street.

With the coming of cool autumn weather, the terrible cholera epidemic passed.

References

[1, 7, 8]Harlan L. Hagman, *Bright Michigan Morning* (Green Oak Press, 1981), pp. 24-25 [1]; pp. 37-41 [7]; pp. 39, 145 [8].

[2, 4, 5, 6]Willis F. Dunbar, *Michigan* (William B. Eerdmans, 1965), p. 185 [2]; pp. 277-278 [4]; pp. 265-266 [5]; pp. 266-267 [6].

[3]*Early Adrian* (American Association of University Women).

Chapter Thirteen
1832

FATHER AND SONS

1832

1

HENRY, HIS OLD MUSKET AND A bundle of clothes over his shoulder, took giant strides along the wilderness trail. He was going home. The Black Hawk War had been an exercise in futility, and though the Michigan volunteers had wasted the summer waiting in Niles for a call that never came, they would be home in time for the wheat harvest. He quickened his pace. 'Twould be good to be home. He'd missed Susan and the girls—and Fred, too. The boy must have had a heavy load if he had done the summer work alone. Henry vowed he would be more lenient with his son.

"Hm-m-m," he said aloud. "New neighbors." A rough cabin, only partially completed, set to the right of the trail. No one was in sight. Though he was curious, Henry hurried on. There would be plenty of time to meet the new neighbors.

A few minutes later he walked in the door of the cabin. "Hello!" he bellowed. "I'm home!"

For a moment there was wild confusion as the family jumped up from the noonday meal. The girls rushed to him with welcoming cries. He bent to embrace them. Straightening, he saw Fred still at the table intent upon the food on his plate. Susan started toward him, but she stopped short at his shout.

"Jimmy! My God, Jimmy's back!" Henry stood as though frozen to the spot.

A small child stared up at him from his place at the table. Suddenly the blue eyes filled with tears, the little chin quivered and the boy shrieked at the top of his voice.

Fred jumped up knocking over the block of wood he used for a chair. Red-faced and angry, he stamped outside.

"Papa!" Josie said. "That's not Jimmy. That's Henry!"

Susan, her face drained of color, gripped the edge of the table. Emily carried little Henry to the bedroom where she comforted him.

"Who—who is that baby?" Henry gasped.

Susan bit her lip until teeth marks remained. "He does resemble Jimmy, doesn't he? They look enough alike to be—brothers."

"Who is he?" Henry demanded, "and what is he doing here?"

"He lives here," Josie answered.

Susan suddenly rushed outside. A moment later sounds of retching came from behind the cabin.

"What's going on?" Henry roared. "This is a fine welcome I get after being gone all summer!" He rushed out to find Susan. Josie followed.

Susan, her face colorless, straightened to wipe her mouth on her apron. She leaned against an oak and drew a quivering breath.

"Where did that baby come from?" Henry shouted.

"Josie," Susan said, "Please feed Rusty and clear the table." She turned to Henry.

"He's the baby of your friend Nancy Farmer."

Henry's face flushed blood-red. For a moment he was speechless. Then he exploded in a noisy tirade of accusations. "Damn it! You're accusing me! I wasn't the only man Nancy Farmer knew! I did my damndest to help the woman and what do I get from my wife? Accusations! You're just like everyone else. You think I'm no good! People always think the worst of me. And Fred—now he'll hate me more than ever."

"The boy's not blind, Henry."

"You've turned him against me! You two have plotted behind my back!"

Susan sighed. "Don't you wonder how the baby got here?"

"I suppose his mother brought him. She took advantage of my kindness and dumped the boy on us. He likely belongs to Farmer."

Susan shook her head. "His birthday is August 15. Nine months after you started 'helping' her. Nancy Farmer died of consumption in early June. She named the boy for you and sent him here with the Martin family who settled up the trail a few weeks ago. Her other boy, Teddy, died of lung fever."

"Humph! Well—I suppose we can put the baby in an orphanage at Ypsilanti."

Susan said glumly, "After all these years I'm beginning to see the kind of man you are. You'd put your own son in an orphanage to protect your good name. You would try to cover shame with shame."

"There's no use talking to you! You're convinced I'm his father! Think the worst of me if it makes you feel better! You may see the day when you'll regret your accusations!" He stormed off toward the river where he wandered aimlessly, his mind in turmoil. He would never be able to convince Susan that he was not that child's father. He cringed; she thought less of him now. He couldn't tolerate disapproval. And Fred—

Sweating profusely Henry made his way through the wilderness to the Martin homestead. He had to find out how much they knew about the child and what Nancy had told them.

Amos Martin and his young son were coming from the cabin as Henry emerged from the forest. He threw up his hand in greeting. He called, " 'Afternoon, neighbor! I'm Henry Parker!"

A smiling young woman appeared in the doorway. Amos shouted, "Glad you're home from the war!"

"Yeah. 'Twas a wild goose chase."

Amos introduced his wife, Beth, and son, Charley. "We've all been looking forward to your coming home. That boy of yours is a worker. The way he took over—well, you don't see anything like that once in a blue moon."

Beth nodded. "He's a good example for Charley. You must be proud of him."

Henry smiled. "He's made of good stuff."

Amos continued. "I've been to your place a few times. Fred is always working. The corn he put in looks good. He keeps the weeds out slick as a whistle. It's good you're home in time for the wheat harvest. Both the wheat and oats are turning color."

"Yeah." Henry hesitated before he inquired cautiously, "How was the trip from Vermont?"

"Tiring," Beth answered. "It was very hard for little Henry. We knew it would be, but we had promised Nancy we would take him to your family."

"My wife said Nancy and Teddy both were dead."

Beth nodded. " 'Tis sad. Nancy didn't have an easy life with Zeke. He never was worth a hill of beans. Can you imagine? He left her, she was in the family way—and he just didn't come back. Left her with deaf little Teddy, almost no food, and in the family way. He was worthless."

Henry shifted his weight from one foot to the other. "Yeah, I guess so."

"She'd have starved if it hadn't been for you," Amos commented. "Nancy told us you kept her in wood and food through the winter, and that you gave her money to go back to Vermont."

"I felt sorry for the poor woman. I did what I could. 'Twas only my Christian duty." Henry hesitated. "I wonder why she decided to send the baby to us?"

Beth explained. "Her sister has three small children and she's not well. I think she may have consumption, too. Anyway, she has an awful cough. There are no other relatives. Nancy couldn't stand the idea of putting little Henry in an orphanage. He's a sweet baby. And you know what happens to orphanage boys when they reach the age of ten or eleven."

"Yeah."

"What happens to them?" Charley asked.

"They're bound out," Amos said.

"What's that?"

"They're given to a family where they are forced to work early and late in good weather or bad."

"Can't they go to school?"

"No. They're lucky if they're able to write their name. They're bound out until they're twenty-one. They are treated about like slaves." [1]

Beth went on. "Nancy said she disliked imposing on you and your wife, but because yours is a Christian home and you are a generous, kind-hearted man, she believed you would raise Henry." She smiled. "You'll get your reward in heaven."

Henry flushed. "I'll do the best I can for the little fellow." As he turned to go he said, "I'm glad we have neighbors now. It will be good for Susan to have a woman friend."

Beth smiled. " 'Tis nice for me, too."

Back at the Parker cabin Henry was jovial. "I met the Martins. They're fine people." Susan was entering the cabin with a pail of water. "Here, let me do that." He took the pail from her hand. "You shouldn't be carrying heavy things when you have a man in the house." He placed the pail on the kitchen table. "It's good to be home." He put his hand on her shoulders and looked into her eyes. "I'm sorry I lost my temper. Help me to do better, will you?"

"You'll have to help yourself, Henry. 'Tis your problem, not mine."

"You say things that upset me."

"I told you the truth."

"It's the way you said it. You always expect the worst of me. You accused me of being the baby's father."

She turned away. "You know how I feel. I'll not mention it again."

"Where are the girls—and the baby?"

"In the cornfield with Fred. He's hoeing corn. He's worked from daylight to dark most every day since you've been gone. He's held things together."

"Yeah. He wasn't glad to see me. He didn't even speak."

"He's growing up. He'll soon be fifteen. He's forming opinions for himself."

For a time it was silent in the cabin. The sound of Susan's paring knife scraping new potatoes seemed loud. Finally he said, "You have any problems with wolves and bears this summer?"

"The wolves howl most every night. Sometimes they sniff at the door. Rusty goes wild when they come near the cabin. They've got most of our chickens, and foxes are bothersome, too. Fred has shot several wolves. He takes the scalps to Tecumseh and collects the five-dollar bounty."

"Five dollars, huh? Bears get any of our animals?"

"Two of the young pigs. Josephine saw a bear carry off one of them. The pigs got through the pole fence and a bear charged out of the woods, snatched him up and walking on his hind legs just carried him away. The squealing was awful. Emily is afraid to go outside the cabin after dark—and I'm as frightened as she is." Susan hung a kettle of potatoes over the fire.

Henry walked to the door. "I'm sorry we came to Michigan. There's been nothing but trouble for us."

Susan carried the dishes to the table. " 'Tis no use to cry over spilled milk," she commented. "And now you'll have little Henry to take Jimmy's place."

"No one can take Jimmy's place."

"The Indians are back. Little Jake often comes to play with Josie. They fish in the river and play in the woods. I wish she wasn't such a tomboy."

"Does she still see Crazy Sal?"

"They're great friends. Sal brings wild strawberries and dandelion greens to us. I pay her, of course. I'm afraid for the girls to go by themselves in the woods, so I'm glad she comes. She says she knows you—then she laughs that—that crazy laugh."

"Yeah, I've met her."

"Where?"

"Well—she has a shack near the Farmer place."

Susan was silent. At last she said softly, "I see."

Henry got up abruptly. "I'd better go have a look at things. Fred might need some advice." Susan didn't reply.

Walking slowly Henry went to the barn, then to the oak clearing where Fred was hoeing. The girls, giggling, sat beneath a maple tree where they braided strands of grass into long ropes. The baby crept nearby, busily occupied by pulling leaves from a small maple branch.

"Papa!" the girls shouted. Fred, his back turned, did not look up. The baby stared wide-eyed at Henry.

He stooped to tickle the child's chin. "Hello, Hank."

Josie said critically, "His name's Henry, Papa."

"I'll call him Hank. Two Henry's are too many. I'm glad you're taking care of him. You girls are a big help to your mother."

Emily smiled. "Do all little babies look alike?"

Henry shook his head. "Of course not. Why do you ask?"

"Josie and I remember when Jimmy was a year old. He looked just like little Henry does now."

Henry coughed. "Their hair and eyes are the same color—but it's been so long, you've forgotten." He stalked down a corn row toward Fred.

"Corn looks good!" he called.

"Yeah."

" 'Course the rows are crooked."

"Yeah." Fred viciously attacked a purslane plant without glancing up.

"Your mother says you've worked hard all summer."

"Yeah."

"Made much money from the wolf bounty?"

"Some."

Henry glanced to the left where the amber wheat gently rippled in the sunlight. "Wheat looks good. Have to get it cradled soon." Fred, his back to his father, moved on silently.

"Get any land cleared this summer?"

"No."

"We've got to keep working at it. If we're to make money farming, we have to plant more wheat. There's lots of work here. Your mother said two pigs got through the barnyard fence and a bear got them. You should have cut more poles and made the fence tight. We can't afford to lose pigs."

Fred turned to face his father. "Not when we have another mouth to feed—and—and—you never can tell when some—somebody will drop off another baby that—that looks like you."

Henry sprang over two rows of corn to land a blow squarely on Fred's nose. The boy staggered and fell. With blood streaming from his nostrils, he jumped up, fists flailing.

The girls screamed, "Stop it! Stop it!" The baby shrieked.

"Go call Mama!" Josie yelled to Emily while she ran toward the angry pair. She grasped Fred by the collar as he again struggled to his feet. "Stop it!" she shouted.

Fred flung her away as though she was a rag doll. With blood dripping from his chin he threw a punch with all his weight behind it, striking Henry on the side of the head. He went down, his legs twitching.

"You've killed him! You've killed Papa!" Josie screamed. "Mama! Hurry! Hurry!"

Susan, holding her skirts high, dashed down the corn rows to where Fred stood over his motionless father. Henry opened his eyes to see his family standing above him. A few feet away little Henry crept toward them screaming.

"You two!" Susan exclaimed, her voice revealing disgust. "Are you all right Henry?"

He wobbled to his feet, fists held high. "I'm well enough to lick that young whippersnapper!"

Fred wiped his nose on his sleeve as he squared off. "Prove it!"

Susan stepped between them. "There will be no more fighting. I'm ashamed of both of you! Go to the cabin and clean up. We have some talking to do when you cool off."

Fred muttered to his father, "I've wanted to deck you since I was four years old. Now I know I can."

That evening after the girls and little Henry were asleep Susan prepared a smudge pot which she placed near the cabin door. When the air was free of annoying mosquitoes, Fred and his parents went outside where they sat on the wash bench.

Susan began. "I'm warning both of you—keep your voices down. The girls don't need to know about our—problem. Let's talk about it."

Crickets chirped. A barn owl hooted eerily. In the distance wolves tuned up for an evening symphony. Rusty barked. Neither Henry nor Fred spoke.

Finally Susan said, "You start, Henry. Why were you fighting?"

"He insulted me—accused me of things. He's always hated me."

"What do you have to say, Fred?"

"He's a—a—hyp—hypocrite! He pretends to be a Christian. When he's with other people he's friendly and helpful. I've watched him. I know him like a book. He can't do enough for people when he's buying their good opinion. And especially the way he acts with women—a friendly pat on the arm, a smile, a long look into their eyes. They—they like it and tell their friends what a good man he is. But at home, he's mean—disagreeable—disgusting! Mama, I don't know how you can stay with him when you have put up with so much—and now little Henry!"

Henry jumped to his feet. "Get out of my house!" he roared. "I never want to lay eyes on you again!"

Fred remained seated. He spoke calmly. "I plan to leave. I can't live here and watch you abuse Mama any longer. With you gone we've had a good summer. But I want to tell you something—you caused my stuttering when I was little. I was never able to do anything to please you. I thought there was something wrong with me that you didn't like me. But Uncle John helped me stop stuttering. And he said I was cutting myself when I whittled as a punishment for not being the son you wanted. And he said I had a good mind.

"I've done a lot of thinking this summer and I'd decided I'd leave when you came home. One more thing—I'm glad I knocked you down!"

Henry picked up the smudge pot and slammed it against a tree before he stalked toward the barn.

2   *1832*

T HE OCTOBER MOON CAST A YEL-low gleam through the trees of the Lenawee County wilderness. Henry clucked to the horses. The wagon jolted over the rough trail.

"I'm glad we're going to the meeting," Josie said.

"Me, too," Emily added.

"You'll hear unpleasant things there," Susan warned, "but you may as well know about slavery."

A wolf howl came from nearby. Josie answered, following the wolf call by that of a snarling wildcat.

"Stop that!" Henry ordered. "You sound like that old hag, Crazy Sal!"

"We talk to the animals," Josie giggled.

Susan shifted little Henry's weight to her other arm. "I hope he sleeps through the meeting," she commented.

The Quaker meeting house in the Raisin River Valley was dimly lighted by flickering candles. Several people already were seated. Addison Comstock was speaking.

"Most of you know I was raised as an orthodox Quaker and that my father was a Quaker preacher. Like some others, I have dropped the Quaker way of speaking, the 'thees' and 'thous.'

"But I haven't dropped our convictions about slavery. In fact, I feel more opposed to this blight on our country with each passing year. I know from talking with many of you that your sympathy lies with the southern slaves.

"Five years ago in 1827 our territorial legislature passed a law entitled 'An Act to Regulate Blacks and Mulattoes.' According to this act, Negroes living in Michigan are neither citizens nor persons with civil rights. Any Negroes coming to Michigan are to have in their possession a legal document stating they are free born persons and they must register with the county clerk and post a five hundred dollar bond for good behavior. [2]

"You know as well as I do that such an act is unenforceable. Very few of us, and no Negroes, have five hundred dollars in ready cash, and Negroes' legal certificates are easily destroyed or lost even if one had been given when they were freed. The census in 1830 listed 139 free Negro males and 102 free females in Michigan. We know there are more than that in the Territory who are not free. Some of us feel we have a responsibility to these unfortunate people—even though it means we are not within the law in helping them.

"For some of you this is the first meeting of the Friends you've attended. We began meeting a year ago. Tonight a talented Quakeress and poetess, Miss Elizabeth Margaret Chandler, will speak to us. She has been influential in opposing slavery in the preparative meetings of Friends at Farmington in Oakland County and in Palmyra in our own county. Her poems and articles are published in Boston in the *Liberator* which is William Lloyd Garrison's newspaper, and also in a paper called the *Genius of Universal Emancipation*. Both are anti-slavery papers. [3, 4]

"Friends, Miss Elizabeth Margaret Chandler."

A tall, willowy woman dressed in black arose from the

women's side of the meeting house. Susan thought she appeared frail, but even in the dim light, she sensed the intensity and determination of the woman. Miss Chandler spoke with a clear, forceful voice:

"Friends, we have before us an enormous task if we are to have a beneficial effect on banishing the evils of slavery. It will be a long difficult fight which may take many years to complete. It will involve those of us who take part in the anti-slavery movement of being in danger of arrest for we will be lawbreakers when we aid Negroes to escape from their masters in the South. 'Twill not be easy, for we must be secretive, vigilant and unafraid. Some of us may face jail sentences for the crime of helping unfortunate people.

"But we will not be alone. All over the North the anti-slavery movement is growing, and especially in Quaker communities the Lord is laying on the people the burden of the Negroes' suffering.

"Now the question is, what can we do to influence the loosening of the chains of slavery? How can we people from the North have any effect upon southern plantation slave owners? I say we can hit them where it hurts—in the pocketbook! Yes, it can be done."

Miss Chandler brushed back a lock of hair and adjusted her black bonnet. She continued, her voice rising. "We can boycott any product produced by slave labor! Can you imagine the effect upon the South if northern people refused to buy cotton goods?"

The small audience stirred—a whispered murmur here and there until a low hum swept over the meeting house.

Miss Chandler waited for silence. "I realize this may be a new idea. I'm sure some of you wish to speak. Thank you for listening." She returned to her seat.

A young woman passed her baby to an elder daughter. She stood facing the group. "I'm Laura Haviland," she smiled. "We're glad to see the newcomers at this meeting.

All are welcome whether or not they are of the Quaker faith. My husband, Charles, and I came here from New York in 1829 with the early settlers. We have long been interested in the anti-slavery movement. I like the idea of the cotton boycott suggested by Miss Chandler. We need to make a statement that will get the attention of slave owners." She sat down after which she was seized with a violent spell of coughing.

One after another men and women rose to testify their support of anti-slavery actions. Often there was a period of silent meditation between speakers. If anyone present was opposed, they did not voice an opinion.

Addison Comstock stood. "We have had a profitable discussion this evening. Miss Chandler has given us food for thought. Our next meeting will be four weeks from tonight. Come prepared to offer suggestions which we Raisin Valley members can act upon."

The meeting closed with a short prayer by Mrs. Haviland. For a few minutes the men gathered to visit while the women dressed sleepy children in outdoor clothing. Susan spoke to several of the women who invited her to return. She explained she was in agreement with their views on slavery and that she was of the Methodist faith, though her husband was raised a Quaker.

Little Henry whined. "We must go," she said as she followed Emily and Josie outside. The moon shone brightly. At the foot of the steps to the meeting house a sound caught their attention. "P-s-s-s-s-s-t!"

Turning, they walked a few feet to the dark side of the building. "Mama! 'Tis Fred," he whispered.

Susan thrust the baby into Emily's arms. "Freddy!" she cried. "I didn't know where you went. Are you all right?"

"We miss you," Josie whispered.

"Tell me—quick. Where are you staying?" Susan asked.

"I'm living in Tecumseh with Serrill LeBaron and his

wife. He has started an academical school. It's an advanced course of study, but—Mama—I can do the work!"

"Of course you can. Do you have money?"

"It costs five dollars per quarter. I'm using my wolf bounty money."

Susan whispered, "Good. Stay there and get your education. If you need money, I have some."

"I work around Mr. LeBaron's place for my meals and lodging. I—I—I'm doing fine."

"How did you get here?" Josie whispered.

"I still have Ginger. I heard Miss Chandler was speaking and I thought you might come."

"Were you inside?"

"Yeah. Back in a dark corner where Pa couldn't see me." He put his hand on his mother's arm. "Are you all right?"

"I'm fine, Freddy. We have to go now. I'm so glad you came tonight." She kissed him. " 'Bye, Son. I'm proud of you."

" 'Bye Freddy," the girls said. They turned and trudged toward Henry's wagon.

References

[1]Richard I. Bonner, *Memories of Lenawee County* (Western History Association, 1909).

[2,3]Ferris E. Lewis, *Michigan Yesterday and Today* (Hillsdale Educational Publishers, 1956), p. 234.

[4]Willis F. Dunbar, *Michigan* (William B. Eerdmans Publishing Co., 1965), p. 290.

Chapter Fourteen
1833

DARKENING CLOUDS

1 ———————————————————————

A REGULAR THUD, THUD, ECHOED through the forest. Guided by the sound Josephine skipped through the woods until she saw her father swinging the axe as it bit through the rough outer bark of the tree and then with each stroke sank deeper into the clean sappy wood beneath. Damp white chips snapped out with each swing of the axe and fell among dry leaves and twigs at the foot of the trees.

Josephine called, "I'm going to help you, Papa!"

Henry leaned the axe against the tree. "Going to drag brush to the brush pile?"

"Yeah. I wish I could swing an axe like you do."

" 'Tis hard work, Josie. 'Tis no work for a girl."

"I can do anything a boy can!"

Henry laughed. "Think you'd like to chop down trees for a whole year to clear five acres? That's how long it has taken me and I still have to burn brush and logs."

"Amos Martin will help—and so will I."

Henry picked up the axe. "Amos is a good neighbor, and there are more settlers moving in every month. Next year your mother thinks we should build a little school. Guess she's tired of being your teacher." He resumed chopping. Soon the trunk swayed slightly.

"Run 'way back!" Henry warned. "Tree's going to fall soon." A moment later it crashed to the ground with a ripping, thundering sound. As he trimmed branches from the huge oak trunk, they talked.

"Mama's lying down. I don't think she feels good," Josephine commented as she dragged a branch toward the brush pile.

Henry rubbed his forehead. "She should see a doctor. She's looking tired and wore out."

"She works hard. 'Course, Emily helps her and she looks after Hank most of the time."

"We have two nice girls in our family—and Hank, of course."

"If Jimmy and Fred was here, we'd have two more boys."

Henry didn't answer. After a time he said, "You going to help me make fences next year?"

"How?"

"We'll set the stumps up—after we get them out of the ground—and they'll make a fine fence."

"Yeah, I'll help. I'd rather work outside with you than in the house." She stared into the forest. "Something moved over there."

"Could be a deer, or one of the Indians. They move as quiet as a shadow. I see them watching me sometimes. I don't think they like us to cut down the trees."

"Why not? 'Tis our land and trees."

"But it was their hunting ground. Since so many settlers

are moving in, there's not as much game."

"Jake said sometimes they were hungry last winter," Josie said softly. " 'Twould be nice to be an Indian. They go on long trips to get berries and last year they all went to Niles for a meeting. I don't ever go anywhere only to the Indian camp and Crazy Sal's and Martin's."

"Better stay away from Crazy Sal."

"I like her." Josie giggled. "She smokes a pipe."

"Humph."

"She says lots of settlers' wives smoke pipes but Mama or Beth Martin don't. I might try it sometime."

"You'd better not let your mother hear you say that."

Rusty's sharp barks echoed through the forest. Josephine shaded her eyes and stared across the clearing toward the cabin. " 'Tis Uncle John!" she exclaimed. "He's tying Roamer! I'm going, Papa!"

Racing toward the cabin, her sunbonnet and pigtails streaming behind her, the little girl puffed up to her uncle as he removed the saddle bags from his horse. "Uncle John!" she shouted.

He swung her into the air. "You're getting 'most too big for this!" he laughed as he put her down.

Josie pulled his hand. "Come see Mama."

Rusty's barks of welcome brought Emily to the door. "Sh-h-h," she cautioned. "Mama and Hank are sleeping." She took John's hand. "Come in."

"You look more like your mother every time I come home," John said approvingly. "I remember when she looked just as you do now. You're about twelve, aren't you?"

"Uh-huh. I'm glad I look like Mama. I want to be like her too."

A wail from the bedroom announced that Hank was awake. Rubbing his eyes the two-year-old boy staggered through the door. Emily rushed to him. "Hank, Uncle John is here." The howling continued.

John said, "He doesn't remember me."

Emily sat down and pulled the child to her lap. He quieted immediately. Susan called, "I'll be right out." A moment later she appeared to greet her brother. After they embraced he held her at arm's length and studied her face.

"What's wrong? Have you been sick?"

She dropped onto a block of wood beside the table. "I'll be all right. I'm just tired all the time."

"Have you seen a doctor?" She shook her head.

"You're going tomorrow. Why hasn't Henry taken you?"

"He's busy. There's so much to do."

"How long have you been like this?"

"A few months. Emily's such a help. She can get a meal on and she cares for Hank."

Josie bristled. "I wipe dishes, Mama."

"Of course you do. And you help Papa outside."

John studied the little boy. "Hank's growing. Does he talk yet?"

Emily smiled. "He says 'Em-e-e-e' and 'Mama' and 'Papa.' Don't you think he looks like Jimmy did the last time we saw him?"

John glanced at Susan. "A little, but I expect all two-year-old boys look a little alike if their coloring is the same." He paused, then added, "How is Fred getting along at the Academical School?"

"Very well. I'm proud of him. He's sixteen now. He lives with the teacher's family and works for his food and lodging. This is his second year there and he's taking the regular courses—arithmetic, geography and grammar. Mr. LeBaron, the teacher, encouraged him to take a composition course. Fred likes writing. He showed me a paper he had done about our trip on the Erie Canal. He got a grade of ninety-seven."

"Does Henry pay his tuition?"

"No. It's five dollars a quarter and I'm taking care of it.
I'm glad I haven't spent the money from our parents' estate.
Last year Fred used his wolf bounty money and paid his
own way."

"Does he come home?"

Susan shook her head. "Henry told him to never darken
our door again. I think he's sorry now but he won't apolo-
gize. We've been attending the monthly meetings of the
Raisin Valley Friends. Fred sometimes comes and the girls
and I get to talk with him a few minutes. Henry goes out to
the shed where the horses are tied and waits for us."

Changing the subject, Susan inquired, "Where have you
been in the past few months?"

"North of here seventy or eighty miles. There are several Indian tribes there that I've worked with near Knaggs'
Place on the Shiawassee River. 'Tis the first settlement in
Shiawassee County and a popular meeting place for the Indians, settlers, traders and travelers. The Williams Brothers
have bought land at a spot called Big Rapids. They have
two hundred acres about ten miles northwest of Knaggs'
Place on the Shiawassee River."[1]

"Are you going back there soon?"

"As soon as we get you to the doctor and find out what
is wrong."

2 _____ *1833*

Susan PULLED THE SHAWL ABOUT
her shoulders against the chill October air. "I wish winter
wasn't coming. I'm always cold," she remarked.

John threw a blanket over her knees and tucked it

about her feet. The wagon jolted as the horses plodded along the wilderness trail. " 'Twill do you good to see something different," he said. "I hope Dr. Patterson can give you medicine to make you feel better."

" 'Tis so far to Tecumseh. Maybe we should have gone to Dr. Ormsby at Adrian."

"Distance isn't important. I've heard good reports of Dr. Patterson from Rev. John Baughman."

"He's the Methodist circuit rider at Tecumseh. We've not gone to hear him preach for we've been going to the Quaker meetings."

When they reached Tecumseh John helped Susan from the wagon before the doctor's office. "I'll take Henry's wheat and corn to the mill while you're here. When I'm finished I'll come back for you." She nodded and reluctantly entered the office. She seemed frail, almost too weak to walk, he thought.

A bell rang as she opened the door summoning Dr. Patterson from another room. He was a large, friendly-appearing man. "Can I help you?" he asked.

"I'm Susan Parker. I'm not feeling well."

"Come in here where you can sit. Are you tired?"

"Yes. We came from south of Adrian." She sat in a straight chair beside the desk.

"Tell me what your problem is."

"I'm tired all the time, and weak. I can hardly do my housework and I have bad pains low down across here." She motioned toward her lower abdomen.

"Are you having your periods?"

Her face flushed. "They're not regular and sometimes they last for three or four weeks."

"Is the bleeding heavy?"

"Yes. I think of it as being almost a hemorrhage. Is that what makes me tired and weak?"

"It could be. How many children do you have?"

"Er—four."

"What are their ages?"

"A boy sixteen, a girl twelve and another eight, and—and a boy two, though he's not mine, he lives with us." She gasped. For the first time she hadn't included Jimmy as one of her children.

"We'd better examine you."

"Oh," Susan said softly. "I have to undress?"

"Yes. You needn't be afraid. 'Tis the only way I can be sure what's wrong." He took a folded sheet from a drawer in his desk. "When you're undressed put the sheet around you and lie down on the table. I'll be back in a few minutes."

After he left Susan's body trembled. She felt as though she was going to participate in something indecent.

3 _____ *1833*

W HEN SUSAN LEFT THE DOCTOR'S office with John in mid-afternoon, she was quiet. Finally he asked, "What did the doctor say?"

"I don't want to talk about it."

" 'Twas bad news?"

"Yes."

"But you'll get better?"

She hesitated. "He gave me medicine. I don't want to talk about it. I need to think."

Silently they drove to the Academical School to see Fred. The teacher, Serrill LeBaron, was pleasant and generous with praise for Fred and his success in school. He noted Susan's tired wan expression.

"Mrs. Parker, my wife and I would be happy to have

you and your brother stay overnight at our home. We have room and you'd have the opportunity to visit with Fred."

Susan looked questioningly at John. "We'll accept the invitation," he answered. "My siser's not well. 'Tis a long trip and she's been at Dr. Patterson's since we got here."

Later in the afternoon at the LeBaron home they met Mrs. LeBaron who was a teacher that assisted her husband in teaching some of the classes at the Academical School. After supper, conversation turned to the recent "Negro Riot" in Detroit. Fred listened intently as John and the schoolmaster discussed the matter while Susan and Mrs. LeBaron chatted over the kitchen work. A cheerful fire crackled in the fireplace.

"This is only the beginning of our problem with the slavery issue," Serrill began. "In our little community of Tecumseh feelings generally are in sympathy with the Blackburns."

John noticed Fred's puzzled look. "The Blackburns were the Negroes who were involved in the Detroit riot," he explained. Fred nodded and John continued. "From what I've read in the papers Blackburn and his wife had several narrow escapes from the law on their way North. Slaveowners with dogs were on their trail and the authorities hounded them all the way, but through clever tricks they eventually arrived in Detroit. They were only a mile from freedom in Canada when they were arrested and jailed."

Serrill interjected, "Can you imagine the dejection they must have felt? They knew arrest meant they would be returned to the slaveowner and that punishment would be severe. 'Tis a crime that a white man can beat his slaves 'til they die from the beating. We Northerners are forced to take a stand."

"What caused the riot in Detroit?" Fred asked. [2]

John replied, "In some way Mrs. Blackburn escaped from the jail. The free Negroes in Detroit and many of the whites stormed the jail demanding that Blackburn be released. All business in Detroit stopped for a day or two. Feelings ran high among the crowd outside the jail.

"The sheriff and a few guards tried to take Mr. Blackburn to a steamer at the docks so he could be returned to the South, but the sheriff and his guards were attacked by enraged Negroes and whites with sticks and clubs. A shot was fired at the sheriff who was hit. Blackburn was rescued and he and his wife were hurried across the Detroit River to freedom in Canada."

"Good!" Fred exclaimed. "I hope I can do something to help end slavery, but it's such a huge problem. I think I'd like to write anti-slavery articles for newspapers."

John nodded. " 'Twill take years, I'm afraid, to put an end to slavery. By the way, Fred, I've brought you a dictionary that was prepared by Noah Webster in 1828. You can use it in your composition class. I'll get it from the wagon in the morning."

"Gee, thanks, Uncle John."

The circuit rider nodded. He continued. "Before your parents were married, the three of us and your Grandfather Parker helped a few slaves on their way to Canada."

"You did? When we lived in New York State? What year would that have been?"

John thought a moment. "About 1815, I think."

"Eighteen years ago," Fred murmured.

"The wheels of justice turn slowly," John replied.

1833

4 ————————————————————

THE FOLLOWING DAY SUSAN WAS welcomed home by the girls and Hank. The little boy climbed on her lap. "I'm glad you're home, Mama," he said.

Susan looked into the eyes that were so like Henry's. She smiled. "It's good to be here."

Emily hung her mother's shawl. "What did the doctor say?"

"He gave me some bad tasting medicine that's supposed to make me feel better."

Josephine said, "Crazy Sal says she will fix something for you that's made from herbs. She learned about it from the Indians."

After the family were in bed that evening Henry and Susan sat at the table.

"I'm going to buy you a rocking chair," Henry said. "They have them for sale in Adrian next to the mill."

"That would be nice. My back gets so tired."

There was a long silence. Finally Henry said, "I've been waiting for you to tell me what the doctor said. You'll soon be better, won't you?"

"I—I don't think so."

"What? What are you saying?"

"I don't like to think about it. He said—he said—I shouldn't have more children." She wiped her eyes. "I wanted another baby."

Henry patted her arm. "We have the girls and Hank. That's enough. Don't feel bad."

"Hank, yes. And Fred, and—and Jimmy." She hesitated. "But—but there's more. The doctor said I'd die if I had another baby. I can't ever get in the family way again if I want to live—and even that may not help."

Henry jumped up. "My God, what are you saying?"

"I'm saying I can't be a wife to you anymore."

"What? What does that old bastard know? He has no right to tell you that!" He paced back and forth pouring out his anger and heaping blame on Dr. Patterson. Meanwhile Susan sat calmly waiting for Henry's anger to wear itself out. At last he sat down.

"Tell me just what he said." Again his voice was soft and kind.

"He examined me carefully. I didn't like it. It hurt. He said my womb was all torn up from four births. The bleeding comes from open sores in the womb, but maybe they'll heal and the bleeding will stop." She paused. "But he warned me several times that another childbed means death."

The words were said and his ears heard them. "Another childbed means death." The full impact did not hit him. He was so shocked he could only close his eyes and feel dizzy.

At last Susan whispered, "I'm sorry. I've failed you as a wife."

Henry sat with bent head, his cheeks burned, his ears buzzed, there was a weight across his shoulders. He kept hearing the words, "Another childbed means death."

Susan went on. "Dr. Patterson said if I took the medicine, rested and ate good food, I might get well, but that you must never again make me pregnant." She rubbed her head. Her voice was weak. "I'm sorry." She put her hand on his arm.

Who was this doctor who dared to say he couldn't have his wife? What did he know? He tried to moisten his lips with his tongue, but his tongue was as dry as his lips. At last with great effort he managed to stammer a few words. "I'll—I'll sleep in the loft in Fred's bed. Hank—Hank can sleep with you."

Susan sighed. "I'm no good anymore. I'm a useless woman. You've no wife any longer." She was quiet a moment, then she continued. "I've thought a great deal about us. When we got here three years ago I was tired—the girls had been sick and life was hard with Jimmy gone. I wasn't a good wife to you, Henry. I know why you went to Nancy Farmer. I forgive you."

He put his arm about her and kissed her tenderly. "I'll manage. You have to get well for all of us."

References

[1]Adele Ball, *Early History of Owosso* (Michigan Historical Society, 1944).

[2]Ferris E. Lewis, *Michigan Yesterday and Today* (Hillsdale Educational Publishers, 1956).

Chapter Fifteen
1834

OWOSSO

1834

1

JOHN FOLLOWED INDIAN TRAILS
that led in a northerly direction through the wilderness.
His destination was the area around Knaggs Place on the
Shiawassee River. From a previous visit to Knaggs Trading
Post John believed he would have success there with con-
verting the Indians to Christianity. Several tribes lived in
the vicinity on three thousand acres of land reserved for
the Indians by the Saginaw Treaty of 1819. They named the
place *Ketch-a-wan-daug-o-ning*, but the white settlers called
it Knaggs Place. The trading post was a popular resort for
Indians, settlers, traders and travelers. General Cass and
other prominent men of the Michigan Territory came to
Knaggs Place.[1]

John had been told by trader Pierre Lefebvre and his
half-Indian wife, Marie, that the first white man who traveled the region was a French-Indian by the name of Henry

Bolieu. He was friendly with the Indians, and like them, he discovered the most convenient places to ford the streams. At these crossings he built himself rough log shanties, generally erected over a hole on the side of a hill and fashioned somewhat like a western dugout. At the spot later known as Knaggs Place he built a more typical log cabin. The Lefebvres had said that in 1820 Whitmore Knaggs, a French trader, built a second log house at the crossing. It was then that the spot became known to the Indians living in the valleys of the Shiawassee, Flint and Saginaw Rivers.

John looked forward with anticipation to again visiting the Lefebvres. Pierre, about sixty years of age, was an invalid who had been crippled by a stroke of apoplexy. Though his lower body was paralyzed, his mind was keen. He and Henry Bolieu once had been friends. Bolieu's half-Indian daughter, Angelique, had grown up with Marie Leval who later became Lefebvre's wife.

Since his last visit to Knaggs Place John had often thought of Marie. She had told him that when she was twelve, her father Jean Leval and Henry Bolieu had decided that their daughters should be sent to Detroit to receive their education. The half-Indian girls had absorbed the intellectual and social values of the female seminary in Detroit. Courses in sewing, literature, French and etiquette were offered in addition to mathematics, composition, history and geography. When they returned to Knaggs Place the two well-educated, vivacious young ladies of sixteen set about creating a social atmosphere in the little settlement. Marie and Angelique taught the young people to sing the songs of the day as well as the gay French songs. Knaggs Place became famous throughout the Michigan Territory for its gaiety.

Roamer suddenly pricked up his ears and shied. John patted the horse's neck. "What's wrong, Boy?" he asked as his eyes searched the forest. A brown bear lumbered into the middle of the trail and turned to stare at them before he disappeared into the forest. Crows protested loudly as John and his horse continued their journey in the bright October sunshine.

John's thoughts returned to Marie. He wondered why she had married Pierre, a man thirty years her senior. Now she was a young woman tied to a helpless invalid for the rest of his life. From what John had seen on his first visit to Knaggs Place there no longer was a lively social life. He recalled that Marie had said Angelique had gone to "The Flint" where she had married and now lived among her French and Indian girl cousins. He had thought he detected a note of envy in her voice as she told of Angelique's young French husband and babies.

There were occasional settlers' homes along the seventy-mile trail between Adrian and Knaggs Place. John stopped to spend the night with families along the way. When several families lived nearby he would remain a day or two to hold services. Marriages and baptisms were customary in addition to the regular two-hour sermon. Often people were converted and sometimes backsliders returned to the fold. Occasionally friendly Indians wandered in to join the group.

John always carried his Bible, his pitch pipe and the Methodist hymnal; these were his only clerical accoutrements. Singing was a popular part of every service. John would establish the pitch with his pitch pipe. Then the cabin walls would vibrate as the people shouted out the melodies and words of familiar old hymns. Favorites were: "Rock of Ages," "Just As I Am," "How Firm a Foundation," "Holy, Holy, Holy, Lord God Almighty," "Silent Night," "Joy To The World," "A Charge To Keep I Have," and many of the other old well-known hymns.

After the meeting people remained to socialize. The women brought food which was placed on the rough table where people served themselves before finding a spot to sit or stand while they ate.

Conversation invariably turned to the last disastrous cholera epidemic in Detroit. With the summer of 1834 came the second severe outbreak of the disease. Many people fled from the city. Ypsilanti and Ann Arbor were hit as hard as Detroit and offered no refuge. Many settlements barricaded themselves against Detroiters who attempted to escape the plague. Tom Mason's father returned to take his wife and three daughters to Virginia to remain until the terrible epidemic passed.

Between August 5 and September 1, three hundred nineteen people were buried in hastily dug graves. All persons on the street wore masks over their mouths and noses. There was much speculation about how the disease could be checked. People were advised to carry torches of burning pitch for it was believed that breathing the smoky fumes would keep the disease away.

Like Governor Tom Mason, some of the people thought the slow-moving polluted little stream of Savoyard Creek was a health hazard, but there was no basis for proof. As the city grew the little river had become an open sewer over-burdened with garbage and human excrement. Mosquitoes, rats and flies congregated about the filthy little stream.

Still the epidemic raged. Emergency hospitals were set up. Churches took in the ill and dying. As Father Gabriel Richard had done in 1832 prior to his death, Father Martin Kundig now became the hero of the community effort against the disease. He worked tirelessly to provide care for the ill and to help families left destitute by deaths of the fathers. He also helped doctors in attending ill patients. Many died, but many also recovered.

The epidemic passed in early September and the city once again resumed its normal life. [2]

As John came nearer to Knaggs Place he recalled that on his first visit he had met a few of the Indian braves at the trading post. He also had met the Willliams Brothers, Alfred and Benjamin O., who had purchased land on the Shiawassee River and had built a trading post a few miles from Knaggs Place which they called the "Shiawassee Exchange." It was an imposing structure with rooms lighted by large windows and was used as a trading post, storehouse, tavern and dwelling.

Because Chief Wasso and his braves spent many hours at the trading post of the Williams Brothers, the settlement about it gradually became known as "Wasso," but later it was changed to the present name of "Owosso." [3]

John tied Roamer before the Lefebvre cabin. A knock brought Marie to the door. Laughing, she welcomed the minister. Her dark eyes sparkled. "Come in! Come in! Pierre and I have been hoping you'd be back soon. Some of the people have been asking for you."

Pierre called from his chair. "Welcome, stranger!"

John shook hands with his friends, then he sat in a rocker near Pierre. "What's happened since I was here?" he asked.

Pierre stroked his gray beard. "Settlers are moving in. We have a dozen new families nearby. You'll find plenty to do both with the whites and Indians."

"Pierre and I think it would be nice if you stayed here while you're in the area. You're needed by our people."

John was aware of Marie's dark beauty. He wondered again about her life with Pierre. They seemed happy. It was none of his affair.

Pierre chuckled. "There are two or three nice unmarried girls among the settlers' daughters. You need a wife, John. And Marie has two half-Indian cousins that would make good wives. Every man needs a wife, and squaws try especially hard to please their man."

John shook his head, laughing. "I appreciate your concern, but marriage is not for me. The life I live, being gone for months at a time—it wouldn't be fair to a woman."

"A squaw would jump on her pony and go with you. She'd be a help in getting a tribe to accept you as a minister —and she can speak the language."

Marie got up quickly. "Stop pestering him, Pierre. He will know when he meets the right one." She threw wood on the smoldering fire. "I'm going to start supper. You'll stay with us while you're here?"

"Thanks for asking me. I'd like to. I'll try to earn my keep by cutting wood and hunting."

"It will be nice having you here. We get lonely, don't we Pierre?"

"You do. I'm contented sitting by the fire and talking with my friends."

John detected a note of criticism in Pierre's voice.

During this trip he planned to spend time in all of the nearby Indian camps. Chief Wasso's group knew him from an earlier visit. The next day as he crossed the river by canoe, dogs and children announced his arrival. The dome-shaped wigwams were ready for winter with extra layers of animal hides and tree bark.

Chief Wasso, tall and unsmiling, met the minister as he pulled his canoe up on the bank. "Good you come," he said. "You say more 'bout God?"

John's glance swept over the camp. Squaws continued pounding corn in a crude mortar fashioned from a hollowed-out tree stump. The pestle, a three-foot-long pole rounded on both ends and about three inches in diameter, was repeatedly banged with great force into the shelled corn in the hollow of the stump. [4]

John nodded. "I will tell you more about God."

Braves and children were gathering about to listen. The squaws continued cooking over open fires as the sounds of the *thump, thump, thump* of the pestle and the yipping of the dogs filled the air. "We will wait until the squaws can listen too."

Chief Wasso looked into John's eyes. "Squaws work. Cook. Sew. Squaws no have time."

The minister shook his head. "Squaws need to know about God, too. I'll wait. I have time."

"You stay? You eat with us? You sleep here?"

John smiled. "Yes."

"You hunt with Wasso?"

"I'd like to."

Chief Wasso motioned to a squaw who sat on the ground sewing a deerskin garment. "Get gun." He turned to John. "Gun for you. Bow for Wasso. We get deer."

John silently took the old musket, certain that he would have little success with the dilapidated gun. They entered the wilderness behind the camp. Looking back he saw the entire village staring in their direction.

Wasso and John did not speak. With moccasin-clad feet the Chief made no sound as he went through the waist-high maidenhair ferns and brush. Though John concentrated on placing his feet quietly, twigs snapped, alerting wild creatures of their approach. Wasso appeared to have a destination in mind and John followed. After an hour of tramping the Chief held up his hand. The forest was so silent John could hear Wasso breathing. He stared in the direction where the Indian was looking, his bow already fitted with an arrow. He decided Wasso was mistaken, for after several seconds nothing had appeared. The Chief sucked in his breath as a brown bear slowly walked into view and the silent arrow skimmed through the air. With a roar the bear lunged and with the arrow extending from his left shoulder, he came toward them shaking his head and roaring.

John fired. The recoil of the musket caused him to stagger backward, but in that split second he saw the bear fall. Silently they waited. At last Wasso said, "Come. He die now. You shoot good."

They cut a two-inch sapling and bound the animal's feet with vines before tying him to the pole which they carried over their shoulders. The trek to camp seemed long but at last they arrived with the bear hanging between them. Dogs and children ran to investigate.

Several squaws came from wigwams, their knives in hand. Silently they set about skinning and dressing the animal. For a few minutes the braves watched, talking among themselves. Wasso nodded toward the bear carcass. "Good meat," he said. "Two, three year old."

After a time the men drifted to the far end of the camp where they were making chert arrowheads. The chert first was soaked in water. Then they tapped the chert nodule sharply and chipped away unwanted material to form an arrowhead with a sharp cutting edge. [5]

A squaw, her black, greasy hair braided, bent over a fire stirring something in a smoke-blackened kettle. After a time she carried two hollowed-out wooden bowls of the mixture to Wasso and John. They squatted beside the Chief's wigwam to eat the food with crude wooden spoons.

John tasted the porridge-like mixture. "Corn?" he asked. Wasso nodded. John motioned toward the crude mortar. Again Wasso nodded. "Good," John said. " 'Tis sweet. Maple syrup?"

Wasso nodded and motioned toward the Indian woman who had prepared the porridge. "My squaw, she cook good. Good squaw."

John tried not to look at the dried food at the edge of his bowl and on the wooden spoon. He doubted they ever were washed. He wondered how many of the group had eaten from the unwashed bowl before him. He also was aware of the soiled clothing of the Indians. It was apparent that neither bodies, clothing or dishes were often washed.

There was much work to be done among these people both in religious and healthful living areas.

Several black-eyed somber papooses hung from tree branches near wigwams, their cradles swaying. Indian ponies grazed in the forest behind the camp. The women worked at cutting up the bear until the job was completed. Wasso distributed the meat so that each wigwam got a fair share based upon the size of the family.

After an outdoor evening meal of tough bear meat and beans, the squaws carried away the soiled wooden bowls and spoons which John now knew would reappear, still unwashed, for the next meal. It was no wonder disease spread like wildfire through an Indian camp.

The October evening air was chilly. Braves and children huddled about the campfire waiting for the squaws to nurse the papooses and to make them comfortable for the night. The unsmiling babies learned early in life to accept attention only when their silent mothers were ready to give it.

"Nice papooses," John commented.

"My boy." Wasso pointed to a papoose who still waited for his mother to take him down from the tree branch beside the wigwam. The Chief puffed on his stone pipe. After minutes of silence during which the Indian men smoked, Wasso announced, "Squaws come now. You talk 'bout God."

One by one the squaws and older children sat in an outer circle behind the men facing John. The fire blazed against the darkening sky.

"When I was here last spring," John began, "we talked about God who is much like your Great Spirit. God loves all men, women and chilren. He loves Indians and white people alike." A pony neighed.

Wasso grunted, "What is love?"

John thought a moment. "God likes all of us. Love is when you like someone very much. You love your children.

You love your squaws. God loves all people."

"Bad Injuns too?"

"He doesn't like the bad things people do, but He loves every person. If people are sorry for the bad things they do, and they say they won't do them again, He makes it all right. We say God forgives them. Do you understand?"

Several braves shook their heads. John explained. "You have a boy six years old. He wants to be big like you. He asks to hunt with your musket. You say, 'Use your bow and arrow.' He waits and when you are gone he takes your musket, gets in a canoe and paddles downstream. He sees a deer and shoots. The musket knocks him over, the canoe tips and your boy and your musket fall into the Shiawassee River." John paused.

The group was silent, waiting. He continued. "The boy gets to the shore but your musket is at the bottom of the river and the canoe has floated away. He knows he has done something bad. He knows you will be angry because he did what you said he should not. He comes to camp, dripping wet.

"You say, 'What did you do?' He tells you.

"You are angry. You say he did wrong. The boy is sorry. He says he will do what you say next time. You love him and you forgive him. That is the way it is with God. We are all God's children.

"God, too, has a son. His name is Jesus. Tomorrow I'll tell you more about God and Jesus. Now I'm going to pray —that means I'll talk to God."

A brave asked, "Can you see Him?"

"No, but I know He is everywhere—just like your Great Spirit is everywhere. I close my eyes so I can think better when I talk to God."

He kneeled and bowed his head. "Dear God, we come to you tonight asking that you help our Indian brothers and sisters to understand about your love for every person.

Help me to teach them so they will love You and serve You. We ask it in Your name. Amen."

The brief service ended with John singing the hymn, "Just As I Am."

That night he slept in the wigwam with Chief Wasso, his squaw and papoose. He suspected his blanket was less than clean. In the darkness he could not see the family, but their breathing was audible. Once the child whimpered but the sound stopped to be replaced by the sucking sounds of a nursing baby.

The only fresh air in the wigwam entered through the small smoke hole at the top. Though John was accustomed to roughing it in his travels, the odor of the three un-washed bodies near him was overwhelming. Finally he fell into a restless sleep.

When he wakened the wigwam was open. Bright sun-light streamed in to reveal the interior. At the back there were piles of pumpkins and squash topped by numerous heads of sunflowers. Cattail reed baskets contained beans and cranberries. From the framework of the wigwam hun-dreds of ears of corn were drying.

Wasso and the papoose still slept. Through the opening in the wigwam John could see the squaws at work. Several were cooking the morning meal; two were scraping the bearskin which later would be tanned, a long tiresome task performed by the squaws.

One woman could tan only a few deer skins a year. A skin was first carefully scraped to get off all the flesh and hair. Then it was treated with a tanning solution prepared from forest plants and buried in the ground for some time. Later the skins were dug up, treated, and then buried again. When the tanning was completed, doeskin and buckskin became a soft and pliable material which the squaws sewed into durable clothing. [6]

Breakfast consisted of a squash or pumpkin gruel

served in the unwashed wooden dishes. Though his stomach twisted, John forced himself to eat and to pretend enjoyment of the food by smacking his lips as the Indians did.

When the papooses had been fed and laced into their cradles, they were hung from the tree branches in the sunshine. Their solemn black eyes followed John's every movement. Wasso and his braves sat smoking while the squaws worked. Two women brought firewood from the forest. Two more were cutting bear meat into pieces about an inch square and stringing it on bark strings before it was hung above the fire to be dried and smoked. One woman carried water from the river in two reed pails made waterproof with resin from pine trees. Another sewed on a pair of deerskin moccasins.

Every woman was busy. John knew they did the gardening in addition to other chores. The work of the men was to provide food by hunting and fishing, but all else was done by the women.

Little boys raced about the camp with the dogs, while others climbed trees or went hunting with small bows and arrows. One came from the river carrying a few little fish.

After the noon meal John conducted a short service. He was uncomfortable for he felt Wasso and the braves resented his request that the squaws leave their work to join the circle. He was uncertain how much they understood as he told of the birth of the Christ Child, for the women did not go to the trading post where English was spoken as the braves did. Again the service was ended with prayer and singing. John suggested that they join in by humming "Just As I Am," and he was pleased that a few complied.

Promising to return, John paddled back to the Lefebvre home at Knaggs Place.

1834

2

JOHN TALKED WITH MARIE AND Pierre of his experiences at Chief Wasso's camp. "I felt I was not reaching the squaws," he complained. "They understand so little English."

Marie laughed. "You need an interpreter—or someone to teach you the Chippewa language." She hesitated. "I could teach you."

John caught the look of disapproval that flashed across Pierre's face. "Thanks. But would that help me when I work with the Potawatomi and the Ottawas?"

"The languages are much alike. I'll make a list of expressions used by all of them. They will be pleased if you know a few of their words."

"Do you plan to work here all winter?" Pierre asked.

"I'll stay as long as I feel we're making progress. Of course I'll hold services for the whites too, though I know many people are of the Roman Catholic faith."

"Chief Leopold Pokagon is a devout Catholic. His tribe spends most of their time southwest of here near Lake Michigan. They're of the Potawatomi tribe. Do you plan to work near there?" Marie asked. [7]

John shrugged. "The need is so great here and in the Saginaw area that I'd like to go there."

Pierre asked, "Have you met Chief Okemos?"

"No."

"He was born near here at a camp on the Shiawassee River. Sometimes he and his braves come to the trading post. He is peaceful now but he was a great warrior in the War of 1812. He was wounded and has a long deep scar over his right eye. They say the scar resulted from a terrible wound he received from a sabre cut in a fight with the American Cavalry near Sandusky." [8]

"Is his camp near here?"

Pierre shook his head. "His tribe of Chippewas live on the Red Cedar River, but Okemos is a friend of B. O. Williams."

Marie commented, "B. O. is a friend of all the Indians. He never cheats them and he respects them which is more than many of the whites do."

Pierre nodded. "B. O. has a basement with an outside entrance. The door is always unlocked and Indians who are here are welcome to sit or sleep there." He laughed. "Mrs. Williams says she has to step over sleeping Indians when she goes to her basement for vegetables." He paused a moment. "John, you could pick up a great deal of the Indian language if you'd spend time around the trading post. It might be more profitable than studying a list of expressions with Marie."

The young woman's face flushed. Her husband continued. "Have you heard of Chief Blackbird from Arbor Croche? That's where their summer camp is located." [9]

"No. Is that on Michigan's northwest side on Lake Michigan?"

"That's right. Chief Blackbird, like Pokagon, is a credit to his people. His tribe also are of the Roman Catholic faith. Their winter quarters are on the Muskegon River but sometimes he and some of his sons visit the trading post. They are—"

Pierre stopped speaking. A gurgling sound came from his throat. His eyes rolled back in their sockets and spittle drooled from his mouth.

"Pierre!" Marie shouted as she and John rushed to the unconscious man. "Help me get him to the bedroom. We can pull the chair with him in it."

Together they worked the chair across the rough board

floor to the bedroom. Pierre breathed irregularly. John seized his left wrist to search for the pulse. "His heart's beating too fast."

"Help me lift him into bed," Marie breathed. " 'Tis apoplexy."

Together they tugged and lifted Pierre's heavy body. He continued drooling from the left side of his mouth. At last he was lying flat in the bed.

"Pierre!" Marie called. "Can you hear me, Pierre?"

There was no response. She stroked his forehead. "Pierre, wake up," she said.

"He doesn't hear you," John said softly.

References

[1, 3, 8]Adele Ball, *Early History of Owosso* (Michigan Historical Society, 1944).

[2]Harlan L. Hagman, *Bright Michigan Morning* (Green Oak Press, 1981), pp. 46-47.

[4]Ethel Rowan Fasquelle, *When Michigan Was Young* (William B. Eerdmans Publishing Co., 1950).

[5, 6]Ferris E. Lewis, *Michigan Yesterday and Today* (Hillsdale Educational Publishers, 1956), pp. 55 and 55.

[7]Willis F. Dunbar, *Michigan* (William B. Eerdmans Publishing Co., 1956).

[9]Andrew J. Blackbird, *History of the Ottawa and Chippewa Indians of Michigan* (Ypsilanti: Job Printing House, 1887).

Chapter Sixteen
1840

THE EXODUS

1840

1 ——————————————————————————

Roamer FOLLOWED THE TRAIL from Saginaw to Owosso which ran parallel to the Shiawassee River. John enjoyed solitary trips through the wilderness for they gave him time for deep thought.

For ten years he had wandered the trails of Michigan. He had become fluent in speaking with the Potawatomi, Chippewa and Ottawa Indians. He visited, and sometimes lived for a time, in the camps of his Indian friends. Mentally he reviewed the past ten years. Joseph Black Bear near Adrian had been his first contact. John smiled to himself as he recalled that autumn day in 1830 when Joseph and his son Jake had walked into the Parker shelter frightening little Emily and Josephine who were ill with scarlet fever.

Old Chief Meteau and his tribe lived a few miles northwest of Adrian. He was a fine old man, though he was too fond of whiskey.

Chief Whimsey's people had a camp near Blissfield. Whimsey had a young nephew who doubless would be the tribe's next leader. He encouraged the members to barter with settlers. They traded venison or wild honey for salt, cornmeal, flour, tobacco and cows' milk. They were more prosperous than some tribes.

Chief Okemos, though civil to John when he visited the camp on the Red Cedar River in Ingham County, was somewhat of a beggar. He invariably needed "tobac, a shirt or whiskey," none of which John could supply.

Chief Wasso's group whose name was used when the Shiawassee River settlement near Knaggs Place chose the name Owosso, had progressed both in religious matters and in habits of healthful living. Though there still was room for improvement, they attended John's services and several had been converted. The squaws liked using the tin dishes the braves brought from the trading post and they washed them occasionally.

John had not met Chief Blackbird of Arbor Croche or Pokagon from the southwestern part of the Michigan peninsula. From Marie and from others in his travels John heard of these chiefs who seemed to be more educated than most Indians of the time. He understood that Chief Blackbird's son, Arthur J., and Pokagon's son, Simon, were very intelligent young Indians. Someday he would meet them.

Feeling hunger pangs, John glanced at the sun. "Time to eat, Boy," he said to Roamer. Dismounting, he took bread and a slice of ham from his saddle bag. Roamer grazed on the dry grass on the floor of the forest. A fox peered cautiously from behind a large rock on the shore of the river.

His thoughts returned to the Indian camps he had visited. Chief Ogemawkeketo from near Saginaw seemed less friendly than some of the other chiefs. The man, who ap-

peared to be in his mid-fifties, did not encourage John to
hold services at his camp, nor did he invite him to visit for
a period of time. A young Indian boy, the son of an older
brave, showed promise of someday being a leader of his
people. About twelve or thirteen years old, he was an expert marksman with the bow and arrow. He seemed to have
been selected by the teenage boys to act as their leader.
John suspected it was because of his intelligence. Though
his hair and skin were dark, his eyes were blue which gave
him an unusual appearance for an Indian. Perhaps an
English fur trader had passed this way and had fathered
the boy. Possibly this was the reason for Ogemawkeketo's
unfriendly attitude—he didn't trust English people.

The sun shone warmly through the partially leafless
trees. John leaned his head against a beech at his back.
Muckameet—Chief Muckameet was the head of another
Potawatomi tribe located near Owosso. Muckameet was a
strong-willed old chief who bragged to John that the government never would send him west of the Mississippi for
he would run away to Canada.

The missionary's heart ached for his Indian friends. The
white man had taken their land for a few dollars under the
guise of treaties. The Indians hadn't understood. Indians
never owned land, they only used it. In 1819 when Lewis
Cass was governor of Michigan Territory, white settlers
met with the tribes in Saginaw and persuaded them to give
some of their land to the government for one thousand
dollars in silver and the right to use the land until it was
settled. The Indians did not realize how much territory
they had given up.

The government set aside two reservations for the Shiawassee County Indians; one of ten thousand acres at Big
Rock (later Chesaning) and the other of three thousand
acres at Ketch-a-wan-daug-o-ning. (Knaggs Bridge). Before
long the settlers wanted the land in the reservations, and

the Treaty of 1837 forced the Indians to relinquish it. The people were deported to Kansas. However, due to an error, the reservation at Ketch-a-wan-daug-o-ning was omitted in the treaty, and another one was signed to take this land from them. It was not until 1840 that General Hugh Brady was under orders to capture Chief Muckameet and his two hundred Potawatomi men, women and children so that they might be deported west of the Mississippi. [1]

John stood up and stretched. He noticed Roamer, his ears erect, staring upstream on the Shiawassee River. Peering through the trees he saw a two-man canoe approaching. Brushing the leaves from his old greenish-black trousers, John walked to the river bank.

"Hello!" he shouted, waving.

The two Indian men paddled to the edge of the river. "Preacher Thompson," one of them said. "We are from Muckameet's tribe. Have you seen men on the trail?"

"No one since I left Saginaw. Why do you ask?"

"Army man named General Brady and three other white men, they look for Muckameet. They have soldiers in Owosso to catch Potawatomi, but Muckameet not there. Some more of us get away. We go to Canada."

"God speed!" John exclaimed. "God be with you!"

Silently they glided downstream. John wondered what their plans were. Evidently the Indians thought Muckameet was somewhere on the trail. John said a silent prayer for their safety.

Back in the saddle his thoughts turned to Marie. He had been gone from Owosso and Knaggs Place for several months and every day he had wondered how she was getting along. For five years she had cared for Pierre who was paralyzed and unable to speak. She had fed, bathed and diapered him like an infant. Her neighbor, a widow lady, helped with the care of Pierre and some of the housekeeping. Then suddenly, a year ago, Pierre had died in his sleep.

John's heart lurched as it always did at the thought that Marie now was free. Though he had never told her, John knew he had loved her since he first saw her ten years before. Now, a year after Pierre's death, he felt free to tell her of his love. Though nothing more than understanding glances had passed between them, John believed she, too, loved him.

The sound of voices roused him from his daydream. A quarter mile ahead several men on horseback shouted at one another. John clucked to Roamer who broke into a trot. Pulling up beside the group he recognized old Muckameet and three braves facing United States General Brady and two soldiers. John watched.

The general shouted, "Thought you'd get away, didn't you, Muckameet? You're slippery as an eel!"

Chief Muckameet, seeing that he was trapped, made an involuntary movement of defense, but in an instant he realized the hopelessness of resisting with bow and arrow while covered with the firearms of his opponents. [2]

The old Indian stared into General Brady's eyes. "Me not Muckameet." Cooly he demanded, "Why you stop me? I am Ogemawkeketo, the Saginaw Chief."

The white man sneered. "I have known Ogemawkeketo for many years. You are not he. You are Muckameet, the Potawatomi Chief, and you will go with us."

The old man saw there was no use to resist. Sadly, his eyes met John's. "Yes, it is true. I am the great Chief of the Potawatomi and it is well for you that you hid in the woods 'til we came along for otherwise Muckameet could not have been taken. I would fight you now, but it is too late! I will surrender! It is very hard, but I will go with you!"

The other Indians following the lead of their Chief, surrendered peaceably and were taken back to Owosso where they were held in a log cabin on the southeast corner of Main and Washington Streets. The building was a rendezvous for supporters of William Henry Harrison and John Tyler in the presidential campaign of 1840.

John, sad and depressed by the capture of the proud old chief, made his way to Marie's home. He greeted her solemnly. "You're looking well." Aware of her beauty and eligibility as a mate, together with the wealth she had inherited upon Pierre's death, he wondered how he dared hope she might marry him, a nearly penniless Indian missionary and Methodist circuit rider.

The joyous look of anticipation faded from her eyes. "Come in," she said softly. She noticed he still was wearing the same threadbare suit which had once been black.

"Thanks." He was at a loss for words. Finally he said, "General Brady captured Muckameet and three of his men. I rode in with them."

"I'm sorry!" Tears filled her eyes. "The others will give up and go into exile without Muckameet."

John nodded. "A few may run away. I met two who were going to Canada. I can't condone what our government is doing to the Indians."

They sat silently in rocking chairs before the fireplace. At last Marie said, "Chief Wasso and his tribe have disappeared."

"Where did they go?"

"No one knows. One day they were at the camp and the next day they were gone."

John said forcefully, "I hope they've gone to the northern wilderness. They might be safe there for a time. Muckameet should have done the same."

Marie changed the subject. "B. O. Williams has died. The Shiawassee Exchange Trading Post is not the same without him. His brother still is there but it was B. O. the Indians loved."

"He was an honest trader and he liked them. They've lost a good friend."

"Remember how they used to come to trade and if the weather was bad they'd sleep in B. O.'s cellar? Mrs. Williams said after B. O.'s death several of the braves came to the house and asked for B. O. She told them he was dead and they were so sad. They went back of the house on the high bank of the river, sat down in a circle with their arms folded and swaying back and forth, kept chanting his name, 'B. O., B. O.' over and over." [3]

"Hm-m-m," John mused. "That was their way of paying tribute to a dear friend."

Marie stared into the smoldering fire. "Soon they will all be gone. My relatives are near Saginaw, Wasso's people are gone, and soon they will be taking Muckameet and his tribe. Michigan is changing."

John said, "A large number of the Ottawas from Saginaw eluded government agents and went to Canada so they escaped the fate of the others. The Canadian government welcomes them and even provides them with annual presents. Perhaps your relatives are safe."

"I sometimes wonder why I was so fortunate as to have been born half-white. My father and Henry Bolieu and Pierre were friends. My father and Henry married Ottawa girls. My mother encouraged me to leave behind the customs of the tribe. She was glad I could go to school in Detroit. Though I'm half Indian, I feel that I'm white. When I see what is happening to the tribes, how they're being exiled to Kansas, I almost feel guilty that I'm safe." She hesitated. "My parents and Henry Bolieu and Pierre all are dead now." [4]

"Do—do you mind if I ask you a personal question?" John asked. "Don't answer unless you want to. Why—why did you marry Pierre?"

Marie sighed. "Pierre was a bachelor. He said he had waited for me to grow up. My parents were afraid I'd marry a brave and go back to the tribe. They encouraged me to marry Pierre so I'd always be taken care of." She shrugged. "He made much money as a trader. He was good to me. He left me well provided for."

"You repaid him by caring for him night and day for eight years."

"I don't regret it. 'Twas my duty."

"But—but now you are free." He reached across the arm of the chair to take her hand. "Marie, I've loved you for ten years. You're the only woman I've ever loved. I'm poor as a church mouse and I don't have much to offer you—only my love and devotion. The life of a Methodist circuit rider's wife is not easy. You'd be alone for weeks at a time, but you would know I'd always come back to you. Would you—would you marry me?"

Marie burst into tears. John dropped her hand. "I understand. 'Twouldn't be much of a life for you married to me."

She wiped her eyes and laughed through her tears. "No. No. I want to marry you. I thought you'd never ask me."

He pulled her to her feet and kissed her hungrily—her lips, her cheeks, her neck and her tear-stained eyes. She responded ardently.

Finally she pulled away, laughing. "I'm so happy. All of a sudden my whole life has changed." She blew her nose. "Indians aren't emotional—this must be my white blood showing."

He sat down and pulled her to his lap. "Whatever it is, I like it." She snuggled under his chin. He stroked her dark hair. "We'll have a good life," he said. "I'll have a reason now for hurrying home."

"Oh? I'm going with you."

John shook his head. " 'Tis no life for a woman. I'm out in all kinds of weather. There have been times when I was lost in a blizzard and in danger of freezing to death. You know what they say when the weather is very bad? They

say, 'Nobody's out but crows and Methodist circuit riders.' "
He chuckled. "But I'm glad you want to be with me." They
kissed.

Finally she stood. "I've something to say and I have to
tell you it's my final decision. I know about bad weather. I
can stand it. I won't complain. I can be of help to you in
your work. I'm as interested in helping my people as you
are. I know their ways and language. Together we can do a
lot of good. From now on, where you go, I go."

" 'Tis more than I'd hoped for. But let's think about it.
How soon can we be married?"

"Judge Elias Comstock would marry us." [5]

"I'd rather have a minister."

Marie laughed. "You're the only minister in Owosso.
Sometimes the Baptists have an itinerant preacher but he's
not here now. You know, beggars can't be choosers. Of
course we could wait until we can find one, or we could
ride one of the flat-bottomed boats of the Owosso and Saginaw Navigation Company to Saginaw. There are ministers
there."

"Yeah. Or we could ride the trail to Saginaw but—well,
I don't want to wait. Let's have Elias Comstock tie the
knot."

"Good." She rubbed her forehead. "There's so much to
do before we're ready."

"There is? I'm ready tomorrow."

"We'll want to invite everybody. Probably it should be
in the schoolhouse on Saturday if we can get ready. There
is food to prepare, and I should have a new dress made—
and—" She looked at John's threadbare faded suit.

"Yeah. My clothes are not very good." He grinned.
"Methodist circuit riders always look like paupers."

"Maybe we can borrow a suit for you. Or, let's see if
Ebenezer Gould might have one in his store that we could
buy. We'll ask him."

"Marie, I don't have the money to buy a suit."

"Don't worry. If Ebenezer has one that fits you, it will be my gift to you."

"I don't like having you pay for things. I should be the provider."

Playfully she shook her finger under his nose. "Now, see here, let's get this straight right now. What is mine is yours, and what is yours is mine—from now on."

"You're getting cheated. I don't have anything."

"If I have you, that's all I need," she said sincerely. "We should talk with the schoolmaster, Charles Parkhill, and Elias Comstock about our plans for Saturday."

John got up and put on his old black hat. "I'll do that."

"And after you see Charles Parkhill and Elias Comstock to set up the date, invite everybody to the wedding."

"Everybody?"

"If everyone comes there will only be about fifty or sixty. I want all my friends there."

"There's one thing we need to talk about," John said. "I don't want any liquor or dancing at our wedding."

"People will be disappointed."

"We'll spread the word before Saturday. They know Methodists don't drink or dance—and especially, Methodist preachers."

"All right. While you're gone I'll see what I can find to wear. It's fall, so a winter dress will do."

2 — *1840*

SATURDAY DAWNED, A CRISP, sunny October day. At eleven o'clock people dressed in their finest clothing entered the log schoolhouse on the corner of Washington and Williams Streets. The building served the community as a schoolhouse, church and court-room. The women carried baskets of food, for they had insisted Marie had enough to do without being concerned about feeding so many people.

Everyone was jubilant. Crops had been good in 1840 and settlers continued to come to the community. Improvements were being made. A new bridge had been built across the Shiawassee River at a cost of two hundred fifty dollars, which everyone appreciated for previously the river had to be forded. Owosso now had several business places including Sturtevant & Blood's Lumber Yard, a post office, a completed dam, a saw mill, a general store and the trading post. Though stumps still stood in some of the streets, and Main street west of the river was only a cart track across land owned by Elias Comstock, he was offering lots for sale at twenty-five dollars each. [6]

Elias Comstock, tall, dignified and stern-appearing in a black suit, white shirt and wide black cravat, talked with early wedding guests. Daniel Ball, the millright and his wife, the families of Rufus Collier, Simon Hall, John Griswold, William Hopkins, Harry Crooks, Daniel Fletcher and Henry Smith were among the first to arrive. Their wives chatted as they kept an eye on rambunctious children.

Daniel Gould, the surveyor and his merchant brother Ebenezer, talked with Anson B. Williams,, owner of the trading post, about business. Charles Parkhill, the schoolmaster, circulated through the crowd speaking with mothers about recent discipline problems with active boys. [7]

Mrs. Williams discussed her son, A. B. "Mr. Parkhill, I know A. B. can be a trial, but after being so sick with ague all summer, I'm almost glad to see him act up again. There were times when we wondered if he would pull through—it was one attack after another. Terrible chills and fever— why he'd be so cold his teeth chattered, and a while later he was sweating and burning up with fever. He got so weak he could hardly walk. He began to feel better when the weather got cooler."

Mr. Parkhill laughed. "He's full of life now. Did the rest of the family have ague?"

"Yes, but it seemed to hit A. B. the worst. We all dragged around with it until the hot weather was over. I wish we knew where it comes from. Some people say it comes from swamp gas and rotten leaves. I think night air is bad too. We kept our windows and doors shut, even when it was hot."

"Didn't quinine check it?"

"Some. But it doesn't cure the sickness. When it was gone we tried steeping tree bark and roots of wild plants, but that didn't help much."

Mr. Parkhill shook his head. "Last summer was a bad one for ague. At times it seemed like about every family had somebody down with it. I wonder if the rainy weather we had in June and July had something to do with it."

"It might be. But it seemed each time A. B. felt a little better he'd play in the swamp, and then he would have another attack."[8]

Mrs. Williams glanced at the front of the room. "Elias is speaking," she whispered.

"Friends," Judge Comstock began, "The wedding party is arriving. The ladies will sit on the benches and the gentlemen may stand at the back. Children should sit on the floor in front of the ladies. When the wedding party appears, we will sing the last stanza of Isaac Watt's and John Wesley's old hymn. You know it I believe. It begins, "Praise God From Whom All Blessings Flow." And sing in a joyful manner, please. Here they come."

Judge Comstock set the proper key on his tuning fork as the front and side doors opened together. Marie, on the arm of Pierre's brother, Jean Lefebvre, entered from the side while at the front door John, neatly attired in a new suit, stepped inside.

Judge Comstock gave the signal and the audience enthusiastically sang,

Praise God from Whom all blessings flow,
Praise Him all creatures here below,
Praise Him above ye heavenly host,
Praise Father, Son and Holy Ghost.

Marie, smiling and radiant in a rich maroon-colored, full-skirted dress made her way slowly to the altar as John, his serious blue eyes meeting hers, walked the few feet to her side. The music stopped and Jean Lefebvre sat beside his wife.

Judge Comstock spoke briefly of the sacredness of married life. The room was hushed as the bride and groom exchanged promises "to love, honor and cherish each other as long as they both shall live." Finally the Judge declared them husband and wife and concluded by saying, "Those whom God hath joined together, let not man put asunder." Softly he spoke to John, "You may kiss the bride."

Everyone smiled approvingly as John ardently kissed the blushing Marie. They turned to receive congratulations from friends and neighbors. The men joked as they stood in line to kiss the bride.

For a time it was bedlam as the building reverberated from the enthusiastic voices of the guests. Women set out the food they had brought on a makeshift table and passed out dishes and knives and forks to their families. Ladies who lived near the schoolhouse dashed home to return with huge pots of coffee. John and Marie, flushed and excited, circulated among the crowd. Finally Mrs. Williams insisted that they sit down and eat. When they had finished their

food the children went outside, almost immediately to return. "The Indians!" several shouted. "They've got the Indians!"

The guests poured outside to stare in disbelief. Old
Muckameet's tribe of nearly two hundred people were being herded down the street by General Brady and his
troops. Sad and dejected, the captives kept their eyes on the
ground. The braves no longer appeared physically strong
for their shoulders slumped. The squaws followed their
men, looking neither to right nor left. Only the children's
wide solemn eyes met the sympathetic glances of the wedding guests.

Marie sobbed, "John, can't you do something?"

Wearily he shook his head. "You can't fight Washington."

Several of the men suggested that they call on General
Brady the following day to make an appeal that Muckameet and his people be released, or perhaps that they be
sent to a Michigan reservation. John agreed to accompany
the group, but in his heart he knew it was useless.

Women among the wedding guests dabbed their eyes
with fancy handkerchiefs. "Why must the government do
this?" they asked one another. "How would we feel if
troops came and marched us away across the Mississippi?
It's not right. They're good neighbors."

The Indians were quartered in a wooden building
which had been erected for a hotel and a log cabin where
Muckameet was held prisoner. They would be held until
General Brady was sure Muckameet's entire tribe had been
captured.

The capture of the Indians cast a cloud over the hon-
eymoon days of Marie and John. They were granted per-
mission by General Brady to visit the Indians but no other
favors were given. John spent hours preaching, praying
with and counseling Muckameet and his men. Marie

worked with the women, speaking to them in their native tongue. Many of the group were converted to the Christian faith.

John and Marie attempted to prepare the Potawatomi for the difficult journey westward. They stressed the comfort the people would receive from prayer and placing trust in God.

The days passed as Brady's troops searched for additional members of the tribe. On the day of the capture, the large group, save for Muckameet and the two braves who already were held in the log cabin, were a few miles north gathering hickory and black walnuts along the Shiawassee River. They had no inkling of danger until the government troops appeared demanding their surrender.

As the days passed, only a few stragglers were brought into the prison quarters and placed under guard with their friends.

The Indians were kept in the crowded buildings for several weeks. When Brady was convinced there would be no more brought in, a number of four-horse wagons were loaded with older men, women, and children and their few utensils and other movable articles. Some of the men were allowed to ride their ponies, but most of the younger squaws and braves were forced to travel on foot.

The mournful Potawatomi caravan, closely guarded by mounted troops in front and rear, moved out on the road and sadly began their journey to the place of exile beyond the waters of the Mississippi.[9]

Their white friends stood sadly watching the exodus. Women and children, their eyes tear-filled, watched the departing tribes. Men stared at the ground, unable to witness the misery of the captives. A few people waved farewell but the Indians with lowered eyes and bowed heads did not respond. Old Muckameet had become a tired, withered old man, no longer the proud chief of the Potawatomi.

Marie clung to John's arm, her eyes brimming with unshed tears. "There, but for the grace of God, go I," she murmured.

John replied, "Blessed are they that mourn, for they shall be comforted."

References ————————————

1, 3, 5, 6, 7, 9Adele Ball, *Early History of Owosso* (Michigan Historical Society, 1944).

2*History of Shiawassee and Clinton Counties* (Philadelphia: D. W. Ensign and Co., 1880).

4R. F. Bauman, *Kansas, Canada or Starvation* (Michigan History, XXXVI, 1932).

8C. Cliver Bald, *Michigan in Four Centuries* (Harper & Bros., 1954), p. 160.

Chapter Seventeen
1841

TRAUMA

1841

1

F<small>RED ADJUSTED HIS GREEN EYE-</small>shade, pulled his shirt sleeves higher beneath the elastic sleeveholders and leaned back in his chair at the *Adrian Watchtower* newspaper office. He fingered a letter from his uncle, John Thompson, which was addressed to his parents. His mind was in turmoil. Should he take the letter to them? He hadn't seen his mother for several months but his intuitive feeling told him she wasn't well. Life had not been kind to her.

Fred glanced up as a gust of wind drove pellets of sleet against the window. "Miserable day," he muttered.

"You say something?" editor Tom Bowerman asked from his desk nearby.

"Just complaining about the weather. Winter is gloomy at best, but a sleet storm is the last straw."

"You're in a bad mood," Tom grinned.

"Yeah. I should take this letter to my parents. It came two days ago, but—you know how things are between my father and me." He hesitated. "I'd like to see my mother and sisters."

"This weather's not going to last. It's getting brighter already. Why don't you take the day off and ride out to your place with the letter? And your family would like to see the scrapbook you're keeping of your published articles. They'd be real proud."

"Not my father. He'll probably throw me out, but thanks, I will go."

That afternoon as he tied his horse he sized up the new Parker house. He was glad his mother had a nice clapboard home. She had lived in the old log cabin for more than ten years. He missed Rusty's bark. Perhaps he was in the barn.

Fred opened the door. "Hello! Anybody home?" he called.

Emily and Josie raced down the stairs as Susan clumsily made her way to the living room. "Freddy!" all three shouted.

He stared at his mother in disbelief. "Mama," he said softly. "I didn't know." He embraced her, reaching across her ponderous abdomen.

She smiled. "The child of my old age," she said softly.

Silently he turned to his sisters. Emily looked as he first remembered his mother, small, dainty and blonde. He kissed her. "It's good to see you. I'm glad you are with Mama," he whispered. She nodded.

"And Josie!" he exclaimed. "Let's see. You are sixteen now. Sweet sixteen," he laughed, "but I'll bet you've been kissed."

"Stop teasing, Freddy. There's no boys around here I'd let kiss me!"

"You'll change your mind." He turned to Susan. "Sit down, Mama. You look tired." She settled slowly into her rocker beside the round heating stove.

"I'm glad you have the new house and some decent furniture," he commented.

"We have a cast iron cooking range, too. I don't do much work anymore but 'tis nice for Emily."

"You're not well," he commented.

"I'll be better after the baby comes."

Fred bit his tongue to keep from speaking his opinion of his father. "Oh!" he exclaimed. "I brought you a letter from Uncle John and his new wife."

Susan quickly opened the envelope and skimmed the pages. Finally she laid it aside.

"What did he say?" Josie asked.

"They plan to spend the winter at Arbor Croche with the Indians who didn't go south. There's a young Indian man there named Andrew J. Blackbird that John likes very much."

"What does he say about his new wife?" Josie asked.

"She goes everywhere with him. He says Marie is a real helpmate. They'll come to see us this summer."

"When they come, tell them to stop in to see me at the newspaper office," Fred said. He unwrapped his scrapbook and passed it to his mother. "I thought you might like to see some of the things I've written."

Susan's eyes filled with tears as she skimmed the pages. "I had no idea you could write so well. This story about the first train and the one about the Toledo Boundary War—they're very well done."

"Thanks, Mama. I like to write."

Josie took the scrapbook from her mother. She skimmed a few paragraphs. "Damn! you *can* write!" she exclaimed.

"Josephine! Watch your language!" Susan commanded.

The girl grinned. "Yes, Mama. But listen to this. It's titled *The Boundary Question:* 'For months Michigan and

Ohio have bickered over the boundary between the two states. Ohio claimed most of the southern tier of Michigan counties. Governor Lucas of Ohio is ambitious for his state; young Tom Mason is equally ambitious for Michigan. Our Erie and Kalamazoo Railroad extends twelve miles into land unlawfully claimed by Ohio, according to Michigan authorities. Governor Lucas sent out surveyors and said Ohio would take possession of the land by force, if necessary.

" 'It was time for action. A posse of forty men was sent from Tecumseh under General Joseph Brown. They caught the surveying party and their military escort while they were drinking and relaxing in a house.

" 'What happened next was humorous. Colonel William McNair and Judge Stillman Blanchard from Tecumseh burst into the house demanding surrender. The half-drunk Ohio group became belligerent, shouting, "Shoot them! Shoot them!" Rifles were pointed at the men from Tecumseh.

" 'Meanwhile the posse outside shouted, shot into the air and stirred up so much confusion that the Ohio men could think of only one thing—escape. Falling over one another they dashed toward the door and ran pell-mell into the woods while General Brown and his men hurried them along by shooting over their heads.

" 'The result was that the Tecumseh group captured the surveyor and eight of the party, including three colonels who were taken to the county jail in Tecumseh. The rest of the surveying party was allowed to escape, the men being speeded along by the firing of guns over their heads. Back in Ohio rumors were circulated that depicted the Michigan men as bloodthirsty villians as brutal and vicious as the savage wolverine.

" 'The story of the Michigan-Ohio fracas during the next few weeks is filled with comic opera incidents. One event, which this reporter witnessed, was uproariously funny. Several judges were appointed by Governor Lucas to hold court in the disputed strip of land as a means of establishing Ohio's claim to jurisdiction. Though the judges were accompanied by armed guards, they were half scared out of their wits by fear of the Michigan militiamen. In the middle of the night they crept into a schoolhouse, covered the windows, lit a tallow candle, and went through the motions of holding court before they hurried to a nearby tavern to refresh their spirits.' "

Josie paused in her reading. "Isn't this interesting?"

"Go on. What happened next?" Emily asked. "You were there, Freddy?"

Fred chuckled. "I was at the tavern."

"Go on, Josephine," Emily begged.

She continued. " 'As they were about to have a second round of drinks, a local joker dashed in and shouted, "A company of Michigan militiamen are about to arrest you!" They dropped their tumblers, dashed to their horses and made off at top speed. But shortly the clerk of the court realized his tall stovepipe hat was missing, and inside it he had stowed the official records of the court session.

" 'The group was nervous about a clash with the bloodthirsty Michiganians but they retraced their route. The clerk's stovepipe hat was discovered under a tree where it had been knocked off by a low branch during the hasty retreat. They were so happy at finding the hat and records that two salutes were fired to celebrate their victory.' "

Susan asked, "Weren't they afraid the Michigan militiamen would hear them?"

Fred laughed. "The spot was near enough to the border so they could escape into Ohio if the shots were heard by the 'bloodthirsty wolverines.' "

Emily urged, "Josie, read what happened then."

"Freddy says, 'It is surprising that no one was killed in

the clashes between the two sides. There was only one casualty, which was not serious. One of our Michigan sheriffs was stabbed with a jackknife in a tavern scuffle by an Ohio man named Two Stickney. He is the son of B. F. Stickney who believes himself to be a military genius. B. F. has two sons named One and Two.' "

Josie giggled. "Are there Three and Four Stickneys too?"

"I don't know. But at last the dispute between Ohio and Michigan was settled. After many threats by both governors, the matter was referred to Congress and a compromise was reached. Michigan was to have the upper peninsula, which probably is worthless land. People in Michigan are disappointed for they feel Ohio got the best of the deal."

"Why?" Josie asked. "We got more land. They only have a little strip."

"We got more forests, which we don't need. They got acres of fertile soil. But as Uncle John says, "You can't fight Washington." The boundary trouble finally was settled and we then were admitted as a state on January 26, 1837." [1, 2]

Emily took Fred's scrapbook and leafed through it as Susan remarked, "We miss Joseph Black Bear and his tribe. They looked so forlorn when the government troops herded them down the trail like cattle."

Josie exclaimed, "They didn't get Jake! Crazy Sal and I hid him until the troops had gone."

"How did you do that?"

"I saw the troops coming down the trail. We expected them for they already had rounded up the Tecumseh and Devil's Lake Indians. I ran through the woods, cross lots, to the camp. It was bedlam. Joseph didn't know what to do. He said to Jake, 'You're young. You can get away. Go.'

"Jake and I ran to Crazy Sal's. He stayed there until it

was safe to leave—about two weeks."

Fred nodded. "You know where he went?"

Josie shook her head. "He said he was going north. I miss him. We understood each other." Wistfully she added, "We grew up together." For a moment she was silent, reminiscing. Then she said, "Emily, remember when we first came here and were sick with scarlet fever and Joseph and Jake walked into our shelter? We thought they were going to scalp us."

"I remember."

Susan remarked, "I feel sorry about what our government is doing to the Indians. And making them walk all the way to the Mississippi—Henry says half of them will die before they get there."

Josie exploded. "It's not right! And slavery's not right! If I get the chance I'll help slaves escape just like I helped Jake!"

Fred said quietly, " 'Tis against the law, Josie."

"I don't care! Buying and selling people should be against the law! Someday I'll do something about it!"

Susan glanced outside. "Hank should soon be coming home from school. He's a nice child, Freddy. I picture Jimmy as looking like him, only Jimmy is about three years older." She sighed. "Someday we'll find him."

Emily flipped the pages of Fred's scrapbook. "I like your story about the railroad. I didn't know the line from Toledo to Adrian was the first train west of Schenectady, New York." [3]

"That train in the fall of 1836 was a sight to behold."

"Did you see it the first time it came to Adrian?" Josie asked.

"Yeah. There was only one car of the Erie and Kalamazoo Railroad then and it was drawn by two horses that walked between the wooden rails. That was in November, 1836, and it not only was the first train in Michigan, but also the first train in the whole area that had once been the Northwest Territory."

Josie grinned. "We're famous for something. Go on, tell us more."

"The wooden rails had a grooved iron ribbon on top and farmers along the tracks could run their wagons on it. But by January of 1837 we had a steam locomotive named the *Adrian*. It had a high stack, a small boiler and one set of driving wheels. Wood for the firebox was carried on a flat car behind the engine."

"Could they carry enough wood for the whole trip?"

"No. There were piles a few miles apart beside the tracks. If they ran out of water for the steam engine, they'd dip it from the river or from ponds."

"How fast did it go?" Emily asked.

Fred smiled. "I remember one crew was scolded by the superintendent at Adrian because they had made the thirty-three mile run from Toledo in less than three hours. That was recklessly fast."

Susan said, "I've never seen the train. Tell us about the passenger car."

"The first one was top heavy because it had two levels. Men rode on benches on the lower level and women sat on sheepskin-padded seats on the upper. Now they also have a car that you enter by the side like a stagecoach. That can seat twenty-four passengers."

"Does it cost a lot to ride the train?" Josie asked.

"About twelve shillings from Toledo to Adrian with fifty pounds of baggage free. Freight is four shillings for one hundred pounds."[4]

Emily still held the scrapbook. "I notice you mention accidents in your article."

"The iron strips on top of the rails sometimes work loose. Then they fly up and derail the train."[5]

Susan watched Fred's expressive face. "I'm so proud of

you. You've made your own way since you were little more than a child. Now you have a good position, you're well educated, and you write beautifully."

"Thanks, Mama. You helped me by giving me your support. You encouraged me to go to the Academy at Tecumseh."

Josie broke in. "What happens to the passengers if the train has trouble in the wilderness?"

Fred laughed. "One time when I was on the train we ran out of wood. The passengers went into the forest to pick up sticks. Another time the coach was so heavily loaded that the men had to push to get it uphill."

"Jake used to talk about the train. He said he was going to ride it someday. His people called it the 'iron horse' or 'a hot water horse that spits hot water.' " Josie laughed.

The door opened suddenly. Henry, his hair and beard streaked with gray strode inside. He glanced at Fred. "Humph! It's you! See you got a new horse. Ginger wasn't good enough for you?"

"G-g-ginger br-o-o-ke her leg."

Susan grasped the arms of her rocker and pulled her heavy body to her feet. "Freddy's been showing us some of his work. It's things he has written for the *Adrian Watchtower*. You should read them."

Emily passed the book to her father. "Look, Papa," she begged.

Henry threw the scrapbook on the floor and glared at Fred. "Work? You call that work? You don't know what work is! You haven't done a day's work in nine years! Sitting behind a desk writing stories about what someone else has had the courage to do while you sit on your ass in an office, writing! You're a coward! I've seen some of your er—work in the *Adrian Watchtower*. I'm ashamed we bear the same name! I don't know why I had to lose a son like Jimmy and have one like you left! Just my usual luck!"

Fred's eyes flashed. "C-come outside! I have s-something to say before I l-l-leave!"

Susan dropped into her chair. "Please, please," she gasped. Emily stood, her hands over her face. As Henry turned to open the door Josie whispered, "Sock him!"

Fred went to his mother. " 'Bye, Mama," he said. "I'm sorry." He kissed her on the forehead. " 'Bye, girls." He followed Henry outside. His step was determined. As he closed the door he heard Susan praying, "Please, God. Don't let them fight."

Henry growled. "What you got to say that you couldn't say in there?"

Fred stood face to face with his father. His voice was low but vehement without a trace of the childhood stammering. "I should sock you, knock your brains out, but I have too much respect for Mama. You don't deserve her— you never have. How many women have you 'helped' like you helped Nancy Farmer? I know about you, the kind, generous Henry Parker. But the ladies don't know what you're like at home. And Mama—now you've made her pregnant. You knew the danger. Having this baby may kill her, and if it does it will be on your conscience. Maybe you'll have another son. I pray you don't. No boy should have a father like you. I even feel sorry for your little bastard, Hank." Fred jumped on his horse and galloped down the trail. Silently Henry watched him go.

2   *1841*

THE FEBRUARY WIND HOWLED down the chimney, a sad mournful sound. Emily shuddered. "I wish the wind would die down. It sounds so weird. It makes shivers run up and down my back."

Susan sat before the window sewing on a tiny white dress. "This baby will have more clothes than the rest of you had. I've done nothing but sew for months—just lie in bed or sew. Everything has been left for you girls to do."

"We don't mind," Emily said as she shoved a chunk of wood into the round heating stove.

The door burst open and nine-year-old Hank dashed in to the shouts of Susan and the girls. "Get out!" Josie yelled, holding her nose.

"Outside!" Emily commanded.

"Go to the barn at once!" Susan ordered.

"What's the matter?" the boy called.

"Get! Get out!" Josie screamed. "You stink to high heaven!"

"Don't you bring that awful skunk smell into the house!" Emily ordered.

"I don't smell anything. I got a nice skunk pelt."

"Outside! At once!" Susan said. "Go find your father. You'll have to change your clothes and take a bath in the barn."

"It's too cold out there!"

"Get out!" Josie screamed as she shoved him outside and slammed the door. His puppy stood nearby wagging his tail. Together they ran to the barn.

"Mix up a pail of vinegar and hot water, Emily," Susan said. "And Josie, get a set of clean clothes for Hank. Everything he has on will have to be buried to get rid of that smell—even his shoes."

"How long will it take to get the smell out?" Josie asked.

"Several days, and even then things will smell musty. That boy! Always trying to make money! I don't mind his trapping muskrats, but I draw the line at skunks."

Henry stamped snow from his feet on the wooden

porch and stuck his head inside. Laughing, he said, "I hear you kicked Hank out."

"You'd think he'd know better than to tangle with a skunk," Josie sputtered. She carried a pile of clean clothes to her father as Emily arrived with an unbleached towel and a pail of hot water and vinegar.

"How did it happen?" Susan asked.

Henry chuckled. "The puppy got the skunk trapped in a hole under an old stump and Hank pulled him out by the tail. He and the dog got the whole load in their faces. Hank said he rubbed snow in his eyes, but they still hurt. Ain't that boy something? Now he's what I call a real boy!"

"You help him clean up and then bury his clothes," Susan said. "He'll have to eat and sleep in the barn for a day or two. And when he's through with the vinegar water, scrub the dog, too."

" 'Tis winter. The dog will be wet and he'll take cold."

"Dry him with Hank's towel."

Still chuckling, Henry took the clothes and water and went toward the barn.

That night at supper Henry said, " 'Tis starting to rain. Hope we don't have an ice storm. The wind's shifting to the northwest."

"How's Hank getting along?"

Henry laughed. "He wolfed down the supper Emily put up for him."

Josie asked, "How does he smell?"

"Pretty musty. He'll have to stay there for two, three days. Brownie is curled up beside him in the haymow with horseblankets over both of them."

"I miss Rusty," Emily said. "He was our pet for so many years."

Urgent pounding at the door stopped conversation. Henry opened it. "Charles Haviland, come in," he said.

"Can you take four to the next station?" the man asked.

"They're with you?" Henry could see a team of horses and a wagon through the rain with figures huddled under blankets.

"They're hungry. Can you feed them and take them to Joseph's?"

"Sure. Bring them in." As he put on his heavy winter coat and boots, Henry talked to Emily and Josie. "Rustle up food for four. I want to leave as soon as I can."

Susan sighed. " 'Tis a terrible night. I wish you didn't have to go."

" 'Tis my duty. Charles has likely brought them from Blissfield." He opened the door to four wet bedraggled Negroes, two men and two women. "Come in, folks. We'll go soon." He closed the door behind him.

Susan lifted her heavy body to her feet. One of the women said, "Set down, Mrs."

"Stand by the fire and get warm." Susan dropped heavily into her chair. "Been on the road long?"

"Four days." A muscular young Negro added, "People is good to us."

"We pray you get to Canada," Susan said softly. "That is where you're going?"

"Yes, mam."

Josie commented, "The sheriff won't be out tonight —the weather's too bad. Here, sit down and eat."

The Negroes hungrily consumed ham, eggs, bread, applesauce and milk as Josie chatted.

"Did your owner whip you?"

"Yes, mam," the second man said. "He was goin' to sell us and keep our wives. He said me and Joe was strong young niggers and would bring him a good price."

The room became very quiet. Suddenly Henry burst inside. "Ready?" he asked.

The Negroes went toward the door. "Thank you," each one murmured.

"We'll pray for you," Susan promised.

Emily brought an armful of quilts. "They'll need these to keep warm," she said. Henry nodded.

He kissed Susan. "I'll be back as soon as I can."

They watched as the Negroes climbed into the wagon and wrapped themselves in the quilts. A cold damp wind blew fine mist from the northwest. Henry clucked to the horses and they moved onto the trail.

"They're already wet," Susan worried. "By the time they ride to Joseph Brown's at Tecumseh they'll be half-frozen. They're not used to Michigan winters."

Emily cleared the table. "Don't worry, Mama. We've done all we can."

Josie went to the door. "It's starting to snow." The cry of a lone wolf drifted through the air shortly to be joined by the harmonious voices of the pack. Josie answered, a long quivering howl.

"Josie, stop that," Susan scolded.

As she closed the door the girl said, "They're my friends —mine and Crazy Sal's."

Emily shuddered. "I wouldn't trust them, especially in the winter when they're hungry. You remember how they ate the sheep Papa left beside the barn."

"It was dead. They'll kill sheep and chickens and rabbits, but they won't bother people."

"I'm not so sure."

After Josie ran to the barn to check on Hank, the girls and their mother went to bed. An hour later Susan called. Her voice trembled as they came into the bedroom. "I—I think the baby's coming. The water has broken."

"Mama!" Emily's voice quavered. "We don't know what to do!"

Susan took charge. "Keep calm. It likely will be several hours, but the pains have started. Your father should be back in time."

"He won't know what to do," Josie said. "The horses are gone so I can't go to Adrian for Dr. Winter." She walked to the window. "What are we going to do? It's snowing hard. That will make Papa later."

Emily sighed. "I wish Martins hadn't gone back east. There aren't any neighbors near enough to help."

Susan bit her lip until the contraction passed. "We'll manage."

"Is the pain bad?" Josie asked.

"Not yet. I've had four babies. We'll get along."

As the night wore on the time between contractions shortened. Kettles of hot water steamed on the cookstove. A pile of baby clothes waited for the new arrival. Emily and Josie paced the floor from kitchen to bedroom to the outside door. Susan's moans frightened them for she usually bore discomfort silently.

By three o'clock, ten inches of snow lay on the ground and the west wind swirled it about the side of the house in deep drifts. Emily rubbed her head. "Papa can't come back with the wagon through these drifts. We're going to be alone with her when it happens."

"The pains are only five minutes apart now, and they last longer," Josie said.

Emily went to her mother. After the next contraction ended, Susan relaxed. "Get a sheet and I'll tell you how I want you to fix it. I need something to pull on when the pains come."

She directed Emily to twist and tie the sheet to the foot of the bed. When a contraction started she grasped the sheet and pulled as her abdominal muscles pushed down steadily until the exhausting contraction ended.

"How much longer will it be?" Josie asked.

Beads of perspiration stood on Susan's forehead. "I don't know," she panted. "It's taking longer this time."

Josie went outside the bedroom door and motioned to

Emily. They went into the kitchen. The wind howled down the chimney and snow slashed against the windows. "I'm going to get Crazy Sal," Josie whispered. "Maybe she'll know what to do."

"You'll get lost and freeze to death out there," Emily protested.

"I can't stand staying here and doing nothing. Mama's going to die if the baby doesn't come soon. She looks awful. The pain is killing her."

"Can you find the way in the storm?"

"I know every tree between here and Crazy Sal's."

Five minutes later Josie braved the storm and headed east through the wilderness. In places drifts were hip-high, then for a distance the wind had swept the ground bare. She plodded on. Suddenly there was a lull in the wind. Wolves howled nearby. She didn't have the breath or energy to answer them. She had covered half of the distance for there was the blackberry patch where she and Crazy Sal picked berries.

After wading through a deep drift, she paused to catch her breath. The wind had gone down and the moon was peeping from behind the clouds. Something caused her to look behind her. She gasped in surprise as she saw a pack of a dozen wolves standing a short distance behind. Throwing up her hand in a threatening gesture she shouted, "Get!" The gaunt animals snarled, but stood their ground.

Puzzled, Josie watched as the pack formed a semi-circle around her. Suddenly she realized they were cutting off her escape. Soon she would be surrounded. She grasped a stick and aimed at the closest one. "Scram!" she yelled. The animal snarled as he advanced a few steps. The circle began closing. In the moonlight she could see how gaunt and thin the wolves were. In a moment they would attack.

She backed against a tree with low hanging branches. Frantically Josie pulled herself up until she was six feet above the ground. Snapping and snarling, the hungry horde sprang toward her feet. She climbed higher and settled herself on a branch out of the wolves' reach. Staring down at the snarling animals she muttered, "Some friends you are."

Josie waited. The wolves continued the siege, alternating their tactics. One or two would howl as others snarled, circled the tree or sat expectantly glaring up at their prey.

"I can outwait you," Josie said aloud. But she wondered. Already she was cold, she had a cramp in one leg and again a fine rain was falling. A cloud passed over the moon. In the pitch darkness she clung to the branch and exercised her cramped leg.

Minutes stretched into hours. With numb mittened hands she clung to her precarious perch which she straddled, her feet dangling. Circulation was cut off and her feet prickled until numbness set in. Her wet clothing had frozen.

She had been captive so long. She was doubly concerned, not only by her own predicament but by what might be happening to her mother. In some way she must get to Crazy Sal's place. Emily was ignorant of what to do in childbirth and their father wouldn't be back. The drifts were too deep for a wagon. He should have taken the sleigh, but when he left, the rain had melted the small amount of snow on the trail.

Josie pulled a knee up and placed her foot on the branch. Holding on with one hand she massaged and pounded the foot and leg until they prickled. She tried to work on the other leg and nearly lost her balance. The wolves jumped against the tree trunk expecting she would fall among them.

"You bloodthirsty villains," she said. "I've always argued with Papa about wolf hunts. I've said you wouldn't attack people, that you only killed small animals. But if I fell out of this tree, you'd be on me in a second. Well, you're not going to get me. I know you well enough to know you'll leave when it's daylight."

She waited. The wolves waited. At last it began to grow light in the east. The rain had stopped. With full daylight, one at a time the wolves slunk off into the wilderness. Josie paused to be certain they didn't return.

Finally she stiffly climbed from the tree. For a time she was unable to step. After stamping her feet and beating her hands together for several minutes, she staggered in the direction of Crazy Sal's shack.

3   *1841*

Emily shoved folded sheets beneath her mother to protect the bed. She was frantic. Neither her father nor Josephine had returned and Susan was becoming weaker. The awful contractions now were less than a minute apart. Susan gasped in agony with each two minute contraction during which she moaned, bit her lip and pulled on the knotted sheet.

"Why doesn't that baby come?" she panted, too fatigued to speak clearly.

Emily wiped her mother's perspiring forehead. "Surely it will be here soon," she said softly.

Another contraction began, building in intensity until Susan screamed in agony and frustration. As the pain subsided, she said, "I can't push down anymore. I don't have the strength."

Someone stamped snow from their feet on the back porch. Emily rushed from the bedroom to face Hank. Her heart sank.

The boy grinned. "Can I come in? I don't think I stink

like skunk now."

"It's all right. Come in. Mama is awful sick. Don't go into the bedroom. Get yourself some bread and apple butter for breakfast. I can't leave Mama."

He threw his cap and coat in the corner. "Papa didn't come home?"

"Not yet."

"Where's Josie?"

"She went to get Crazy Sal. They haven't come yet."

"Want me to do the milking and barn chores?"

"That would be nice."

Susan screamed. A frightened look came over the boy's face. Emily explained. "She's having the baby. You eat and then go do the chores. Stay at the barn if you can't stand it here." She hurried to her mother.

The hours wore on as Susan's strength lessened. She now screamed weakly, but her moans tore at Emily's heart. "If the baby lives and I don't," Susan whispered, "Promise me you'll take care of it." She panted from exhaustion, dreading the next violent contraction.

"Yes, yes, Mama. But you can't leave us!"

A forceful contraction worked the cramping muscles of Susan's abdomen. She gasped. "I think it's coming." She pushed. "Look."

Emily pulled back the covers. "There's the feet!"

"No! It's wrong! The head should come first!"

Another powerful contraction racked Susan's body. "Pull on the feet. Pull hard," she ordered.

While her mother stuggled in intense labor, Emily grasped the baby's waxy feet and pulled vigorously. With each contraction the birth advanced slightly.

"We're getting somewhere now, Mama. It won't be long."

Susan sobbed. "But it's taking too long! The baby can't breathe!"

"Next time let's work together. You push hard and I'll pull."

Susan drew a deep breath. "Now," she said.

The labor seemed endless but at last it was over. Emily held the oily little body up for her mother to see. "A boy," she said.

Susan screamed, "He's not breathing! Slap his bottom! Hold him upside down! Make him cry!" She raised up on one elbow. "Hurry! Get him to breathe!"

Emily worked frantically. The baby's face was blue. Susan whispered a prayer as she watched. "Shake him! Slap him!" she repeated.

Finally after two or three minutes the baby drew a short breath and wailed weakly. Five minutes later he was breathing normally. Exhausted, Susan dropped back on the pillow. "You have to cut the cord." Briefly she described the procedure as the baby continued to cry.

Half an hour later, bathed and dressed in a tiny flannel nightgown and wrapped in a hand knitted blanket the baby was lying in his mother's arms.

Emily smiled. "We did it, Mama."

"Yes, we did it." Susan hesitated. "I've made a terrible mess of the bed. I wish Josie would come to help you. I'm worried something has happened to her. And your father, too. Why don't they come?"

At last Josie arrived with Crazy Sal. The old woman's long black coat dragged in the deep snow. Gray hair straggled over her wrinkled face.

"He! He! He!" she greeted Emily. "Josie thought I couldn't make it through the drifts, but Crazy Sal's a tough old hen. He! He! He!"

"How's Mama?" Josie asked.

"Sleeping, and the baby's beside her. A boy. What took you so long?"

"Sometime I'll tell you. The drifts are three feet deep in

places. Papa can't get home from Tecumseh."

Emily rubbed her head. "I hope he's all right."

The three of them peeped into the bedroom. The tooth-less old face and two fresh young ones, smiled.

1841

4

Emily silently wished Crazy Sal would go home for she distrusted the strange remedies the old woman suggested. They needed a doctor. Her mother was rapidly losing strength from excessive internal bleeding.

Josie came from the bedroom, her arms filled with blood-soaked bedding. "Look at this. She's no better. She can't have much blood left. What are we going to do?" She threw the sheets in a tub of water on the wash bench in the corner of the kitchen.

Emily shook her head. "I'm desperate. If only Papa would get home, he'd get the doctor. Two days now since he left—"

"Men," Crazy Sal hissed. "He's enjoying hisself in Tecumseh. He don't care 'bout nobody but hisself. They're all alike. They just use women, the worthless brutes!"

Josie said, "Maybe I could walk to Adrian to get the doctor."

"No! You'd never make it! Look at those drifts across the trail! We're not even sure Papa and the Negroes got to Joseph Brown's. If only we had a horse." Emily peeped into the bedroom. "She's sleeping, and the baby is too. Thank goodness he's all right."

Hank came in with a pail of milk. "Sh-h-h," Josie warned.

Crazy Sal, her hair hanging over her face, whispered to the boy. "Is there spiderwebs in the barn?"

He grinned. "Yeah. Want me to brush them down?"

The old woman picked up a cup from the table. "Git as many spiderwebs as you can. Try to git a cupful."

"What you going to do with 'em?"

The old eyes squinted into the snow laden forest. "Spiderwebs stops bleedin'. They'll help your mama."

"No!" Emily exclaimed. "That's crazy! Er—I mean, how can that help Mama?"

"He! He! He! Crazy Sal knows a few things. Spider webs makes the blood clot. That will stop the bleedin'." She shook a finger under Hank's nose. "Go! Go get the spiderwebs!"

Josie whispered, "Mama's skin is cold and clammy, and she's so white. I'm scared, Emily."

"He! He! He! Crazy Sal's spiderwebs will stop the bleedin'." The old woman wiped her soiled hands on her greasy dress.

The sisters ignored the remark. Emily said, "I can't understand why she sweats so much when her skin's cold."

A weary call came from the bedroom. "Emily—Josie."

"You slept," Emily said. "Feel better?"

"I don't hurt, but I'm so weak," she whispered feebly. "And I'm cold."

Josie placed another quilt over her mother. "The baby sleeps a lot," she said. "What are you going to name him?"

Susan sighed and closed her eyes. "David. I'm tired." She seemed asleep. The girls tiptoed out to the kitchen.

"You think she's sleeping?" Josie asked, "or is she unconscious?"

Emily sobbed. "I don't know. I'm—I'm afraid she's not going to get better. She made me promise I'd take care of David if she didn't—didn't get well."

Crazy Sal patted each girl on the shoulder. "Now, now.

Don't cross any bridges. When that slow-poke boy gets here, we'll stop the bleeding."

Emily wiped her eyes. "What do you do with the spiderwebs?"

Crazy Sal snorted. "He! He! He! What do you spoze? You put them on the place that's bleedin'."

"But it's inside her!"

"He! He! He! I'll push it up there."

The girls stared at Crazy Sal's scarred dirty hands. "No!" they both exclaimed.

"We won't let you!" Emily declared.

Crazy Sal dropped into the rocker. "Lan' sakes! I've never seen such ornery young ones. 'Tis up to you if you don't want to stop the bleedin'."

When Hank came with the cobwebs Josie quietly emptied them outside in the snow. Crazy Sal watched, a hurt expression in her eyes.

The hours passed and again it was night. The wind had stopped. "Surely Papa will be home tomorrow," Emily said.

"Hank, you and Crazy Sal might as well go to bed," Josie said. "We'll sit with Mama." She went into the bedroom and returned with Baby David. "He's a good little fellow. I thought babies cried a lot."

"I'll warm some cow's milk for him," Emily said. " 'Tis too bad Mama can't nurse him. He must be wet, Josie. Change his didy."

Finally the house was quiet. Only the sisters were awake. Emily said, "I don't believe she can last much longer."

They stood inside the bedroom door. Susan's breathing was shallow and weak and the sweat on her forehead was cold. Emily felt for her pulse. "Her heart—flutters," she said.

Susan opened her eyes. "My girls," she said softly. "Take care of little David," she panted, "and when you find

Jimmy, tell him his mother loved him. My last—last thoughts are of my children." She paused. "Freddy—all of you are good children." She rested a moment. "And your father. Tell him good-bye for me. I—I love all of you. I've prayed for you even though you thought I was sleeping. Soon—I'll—be—going."

With tears streaming down their faces the girls sobbed as each one kissed her mother. Susan smiled and closed her eyes. Her breathing ceased. Josie seized her wrist. The feeble heartbeat had stopped.

5 ———————————— *1841*

T HE PARKER PARENTAL BEDROOM door was closed. Emily, Josephine, Hank and Crazy Sal sat silently around the table.

"I'm not hungry," Hank said. He slid his chair away from the table and walked to an oak chest. The third drawer stood open and Baby David, his face red and wrinkled, slept in his makeshift crib.

Crazy Sal nibbled on a piece of bread. She glanced outside at the dazzling sunlight. "He! He! He!" she cackled. " 'Tis a pretty day. I'm going home." She got up from the table and slipped into her ragged black coat.

Josie roused herself. "Can you make it through the drifts?"

"He! He! He! 'Course I can. I'm a tough old bird." She pulled her dusty black hat over her straggly hair.

Josie and Emily went with her to the door. "Thanks for staying with us," Josie said.

"He! He! He! I wish you'd let me use the spiderwebs. It might have stopped the bleedin' you know." She opened the door, went outside and waded through the first huge drift.

Hank still stood staring down at the baby. He raised his head at Emily's voice. "Would you shovel a path to the barn? Papa will be home today, I'm sure."

The boy turned, his blue eyes brimming. He nodded. Emily, her eyes red from weeping, put her arms around the child. He sobbed. "She was the only mother I knew." Josie joined them and for a few minutes they mourned.

"We'll all miss her," Emily sobbed. "I'm afraid of what it will do to Papa."

Josie looked at the sleeping baby. She turned. "We have to make plans. Hank, were there some nice boards left when the house was built?"

The boy blew his nose. "Yeah."

"We have to make a coffin. You can help Papa when he gets here. Emily and I will line it with—with the lovely pink material Mama was saving for a Sunday summer dress."

Emily cleared the table. "Someone has to go to Adrian to tell Fred when Papa gets home with the horses—but they'll have to rest first."

Hank stood tall. "I'll go. I'm not very heavy."

The hours dragged. Hank did chores and shoveled paths. The girls washed the soiled laundry and threw it over a line in the yard to freeze dry. Several times they went to the bedroom to stand by Susan's body.

At mid-afternoon Henry arrived riding one horse as he led the other. The girls watched as he took the animals to the barn. "He had to leave the wagon at Tecumseh," Emily said dully.

A minute later Henry strode to the house followed by Hank who was weeping. The door burst open. "What's wrong?" Henry demanded. "This stupid boy won't tell me! Where's your mother?" Emily motioned toward the closed door.

"She's sleeping? In the daytime?" In three strides he was at the door, his hand on the doorknob.

"Wait Papa!" Josie ran to block the way. "Mama had the baby."

He pushed Josie aside and yanked the door open. "Susan!" he shouted. "Wake up! I'm home!" He jerked the sheet from over her face and laid his hand on her forehead. "My God!" he screamed. "She's dead!"

The girls and Hank rushed to comfort him but he flung them away and roared outside screaming incoherently and muttering oaths.

Shocked, the three clung together for comfort. Hank blew his nose. "Should I go find him?"

Emily shook her head. "He needs to be alone."

"He didn't ask about the baby," Josie said quietly.

Hank wiped his eyes. "David's like me. He don't have a mama."

A few hours later Henry returned. His face was drawn. Without a word he went to the bedroom to sit beside his dead wife. Silent and sullen, he refused to talk to anyone or to leave Susan's side. The girls quietly explained what had happened, but he seemed not to hear.

In a desperate attempt to rouse him, Emily carried little David to the bedroom. "See, Papa. See our brother David."

Henry refused to look. "Get him out of my sight!" he snarled. "I wish he'd die! He killed your mother!"

Shocked, they left him alone with his wife's body. Emily carried the sleeping baby to the kitchen where they spoke in whispers.

"We have to decide what to do," Josie said. "He's like a madman."

"Maybe he'll be more rational tomorrow," Emily whispered. "We have to get the coffin made and the grave dug. The ground is frozen."

Hank whispered, "I'll go get Fred tomorrow. He and I will make the coffin and dig Mama's grave. I hope Papa doesn't throw Fred out."

The baby stretched and whimpered faintly. Emily cuddled him. "Poor baby. It's not your fault." Again he dropped off to sleep. "I'm surprised he doesn't cry," she whispered. I thought all babies cried a lot. He has never cried really hard."

Josie remarked, "I guess we're lucky to have a good-natured baby." She tiptoed to the bedroom door. Her father, his head in his hands, sat before his wife's body.

References

[1, 3, 4]*Early Adrian* (American Association of University Women).

[2]Willis F. Dunbar, *Michigan* (William B. Eerdmans, 1965), pp. 309-312.

[5]Harlan L. Hagman, *Bright Michigan Morning* (Green Oaks Press, 1981), p. 95.

Chapter Eighteen
1841

THE INDIANS
OF ARBOR CROCHE

1841

1 ――――――――――――――――――――――

R<small>EV</small>. J<small>OHN</small> T<small>HOMPSON</small> <small>AND HIS</small>
wife, Marie, lived with the Ottawa and Chippewa Indians
of Arbor Croche in the spring of 1841. Chief Blackbird and
his son Arthur J. enjoyed John's and and Marie's company.
Many hours were spent talking of Michigan historical
events in which the Indians were involved.

The Blackbird family wigwam was clean. They were
Christians, having accepted the Roman Catholic religion
many years before.

Chief Blackbird's squaw, the mother of his ten children,
had died in 1828 at Little Traverse as the result of an accident. She had been making maple sugar in the woods and
was so badly burned that she lived only four days. At the
time of her death the youngest child, Arthur J., was eight
or nine years old. The older children consisting of five boys
and four girls scattered after the mother died. [1]

Chief Blackbird was uneducated but he told stories of the past in an impressive manner. As his son Arthur J. and the Thompsons sat around their rough table he recounted one of his earliest memories. He spoke of his father's first unfortunate experience with the white man.

The old man's expressive face revealed emotion as he spoke. "After Britain took Michigan from the French in 1763 my father, grandfather and great-grandfather wanted peace. Indians had taken Fort Michilimackinac (Mackinac) by a trick. Many British men killed.

"My father was a small boy then. My grandfather and some other Ottawas and Chippewas had not been a part of the group that killed the British soldiers at the Fort. They asked that they should not be blamed for the terrible killing and said the Indians that did the massacre were told to do it by Chief Bwondiac (Pontiac).

"The British government men made big promises to the Ottawas and thanked my grandfather and great-grandfather for coming to talk with them. They said the Ottawas would receive gifts—liquor, blankets, guns and ammunition."

The old chief hesitated, deep in thought. Finally he continued. "They asked them to go to Canada to get their gifts. They gave them liquor and blankets and guns and ammunition, and they gave them a box which must not be opened until they were home among the tribe.

"When they was home they opened the box. They found another—and another box inside. They went on until they came to a very small box about an inch long." Chief Blackbird paused.

"When they opened the little box they found moldy pieces—little pieces of something—in the box. The people looked at the stuff and handled it. Soon a terrible sickness started in the tribe. The medicine men were taken sick and died. Everyone that got sick with it died. Lodges were empty—nothing but dead people lying in the lodges. Many whole families died.

"Before the sickness there was one village fifteen or sixteen miles long from the Straits along the west shore of Michigan. Afterward not many Ottawas and Chippewas were left."

John asked, "The disease was smallpox?"

Old Chief Blackbird nodded. "The little box and the blankets spread the disease among us."

Marie exclaimed, "It was wholesale murder! Why did the British do it?"

"They wanted to kill us because we were friends of the French. They hated us and believed all Chippewas and Ottawas had agreed to the plan to massacre the British at Michilimackinac." The old man smoked his pipe. They waited for him to continue.

Finally Andrew J. said, "Father, tell John and Marie about Indian life when you were a child."

The wrinkled old face brightened. "When I was small we lived in Arbor Croche in summer. The squaws planted corn, potatoes, squash, beans and pumpkins. In summer it was nice here. We played a game called *'paw-kaw-do-way,'* we ran foot races, wrestled and tried to shoot more chipmunks and squirrels in a day with our bows and arrows than the other boys.

"There wasn't any bad language used. There were no swear words in our language, and hardly any Indians became drunk then—sometimes at a special time the old folks had a short spree, but in those days the young folks did not drink liquor—not like now."

"Was there much stealing?" John asked.

"We rested safely in our lodges with only a mat or blanket over the doorway. Our parents taught us what was right and wrong."

Arthur J. said, "My father has told me that their rules

for living a good life were almost the same as the Ten Commandments which God delivered to Moses on Mt. Sinai on the tablets of stone."

The old man puffed on his pipe. "Back then our people believed the eye of the Great Being or the Great Spirit sees everything. This kept us honest with one another. Our word was good."

"As good as a promissory note," Arthur J. said.

Chief Blackbird shook his head. "Now it's not the same. Some of our people rob and cheat and—and murder. We were better people before the white man came. Now our young men drink liquor. They do bad things."

Arthur J. changed the subject. "Father once was a great chief. He led his warriors several times on the warpath and my uncles said he was most daring in his younger days. Tell them about your brothers, Father."

The old man's pensive expression revealed his feelings. "My brother, Late Wing, fought with the Americans against Great Britain in the Revolutionary War. After that he was a great friend of Governor Lewis Cass of the Michigan Territory. He was pensioned for the rest of his life by the United States government for his help and bravery."

Arthur continued. "My mother's brother, Shaw-be-nee, served with the United States in the War of 1812. Now he travels free anywhere in the United States to repay him for his patriotism and bravery."

"Your family has been loyal to our government for many years," Marie remarked.

John said, "I'm wondering where you learned to speak English so well."

Chief Blackbird said, "You tell them, Arthur J."

The young Indian man began. "The Ottawas and Chippewas had bad things done to them by the white man. Our land was taken and treaties were not kept. Many Indian people were sent west of the Mississippi. Father was chosen to be head speaker for the Ottawas and Chippewas and he held this office for many years. He spoke easily and well and in dealing with the white man, he learned the English language."

Marie asked, "Wasn't it you, Chief Blackbird, who was friendly to education? Didn't you make an Indian alphabet so you could read and write in the Indian language?"

"Yes. I called it *'Paw-pa-pe-po.'* I taught grown persons. I had a wigwam sixty or seventy feet long where we lived in summer. It was like a big schoolhouse and I was the teacher. Many of our people came. We had good times."

Arthur J. continued. "One of my older brothers, Pe-taw-wannie-quot, called William when he was baptised into the Catholic religion, was quick to learn. When he was twelve or thirteen, my father sent him to the Protestant Mission School at Mackinac Island. In a year he was acting as an interpreter for the teacher. The mission closed and William came home for two years. Then Bishop Reese took him and my sister Margaret to Cincinnati where they were put in school. William graduated. Margaret stayed in school in Cincinnati, but Bishop Reese sent William to Rome to study for the priesthood."

John smiled. "I'm beginning to understand. Your family are educated people, Arthur J. Where is William now?"

"Dead. Since June 25, 1833. Almost eight years ago. He was assassinated."

"That's terrible!" Marie exclaimed. "Who would kill a priest?"

Chief Blackbird puffed on his pipe. His glance met Arthur J.'s questioning one. The old man nodded and the young man continued. "Like our father, William was a fine orator. The people in Rome considered him a promising man. While he was there the proposition came up in the United States government to buy out the Michigan Indians. William wrote to us here at Arbor Croche telling us not to sell or to make any contract with the United States government, but to wait for his return and he would help us in making out a contract or treaty.

"William was assassinated the very day he was to have been ordained a priest."

"Why? What was the reason?" John asked.

"We don't know. No motive was found. He had no known enemies, but we do know that several American students at Rome held a grudge and had a secret plot which originated in America to 'remove' William who had attained the highest marks in science and was their equal in other studies. It was said he was murdered because it was found out by the American government that he was advising us on the subject of our lands and treaties so that William's death would deprive us of a wise, educated counselor."

Marie was shocked. "You think our government approved of the secret plot?"

"We have no proof—only rumors."

John asked, "Where is your sister Margaret?"

"After William's death she taught at an orphan Catholic institution in Detroit until 1835 when she came to Little Traverse. She teaches at a Catholic mission there."

John asked, "Where were you educated?"

"The authorities at Rome asked that I take William's place, but Father said, 'No. They killed one of my sons after they educated him, and they will kill another.'

"So I started on my own when I was fourteen. I worked and attended school first in Detroit and later in Twinsburg, Ohio. I'm thankful for the education I have, but I still hope to improve it. I hope to someday counsel the Ottawas and Chippewas as my father did and as William would have, if he'd lived."

"Did you see many changes when you returned?"

"Yes. 'Tis not good. Too many of our people drink.

Many are lazy."

Marie said, "Though my mother was Indian, we always lived as the white man did. Tell us more about the way you used to live. You were at Arbor Croche in summer. Where did you go in winter?"

Chief Blackbird said, "As soon as our crops were stored we were ready to start south."

John was interested in details. "How did you store your crops?"

"The ears of corn were dried by the fire. Then they were beat with a flail to shell the kernels. The grain was put in sacks and placed in the ground inside a big roll of elm bark, and all of it was covered. It was safely stored for winter or summer use.

"After our grain was stored we started south. Some of our people went as far as Chicago to trap muskrats and beavers. Others went to the Grand River or Muskegon River to trap and hunt and to make maple sugar in the spring. Then we came back to Arbor Croche to spend the summer and raise crops."

"How did you travel?"

"We went in long bark canoes near the shore on Lake Michigan. The canoes were big enough to carry a family and enough supplies for the winter and were made of birch bark. They could stand a heavy sea. At night we landed and made wigwams with cedar poles that we carried in the canoes. We covered our wigwams with mats made of marsh reeds that were sewed together. Wigwams were good shelters from rain and wind. They were warm when there was a fire inside. We spread mats on the floor to sit and sleep on."

Marie said, "It sounds like a nice way to live. Were the mats like these on your floor?"

The old chief nodded. "The squaws cut green bullrushes, steamed them and laid them in the sun to bleach. Then they were colored and the squaws would weave them into mats four feet wide and six or eight feet long."

"They're pretty," Marie said. "Would the women show me how to do it?"

Chief Blackbird smiled. "They would be happy that you want to learn."

John asked, "Where did your family winter?"

"We liked a place on the Muskegon River above the Big Rapids."

"When you came back in the spring, did you bring furs and maple sugar?"

The old man stared into the distance, remembering. "Our bark canoes were loaded with sugar, furs, deer skins, prepared venison for summer use, bears' oil and bears' meat prepared in oil, deer tallow and honey."

He continued. "As soon as we were back in Arbor Croche, we hurried to look at our stores of corn and beans. Then we had good times. We had medicine dances, fire dances and feasting. Sometimes we danced around the fires in the wigwam which had places for two fires. 'Twas nice then—now 'tis not the same. We stay on the reservation. The white man has changed things for Indians since 1830. Then a mission was here and our children went to school. Life was good. Plenty of fish and all kinds of food."

Arthur J. took up the story of the tribe. "In March of 1836 a treaty was signed in Washington. The Indians did not like it but they were urged to sign. That year we were paid ten dollars cash per head besides some dry goods and provisions. There was a clause in the treaty that the Indians of Michigan were to be given one hundred fifty thousand dollars worth of dry goods until it all was paid. About ten thousand dollars was paid in 1836. There was waste in distributing the goods and much of it disappeared before it could be distributed. We asked the Indian agent, Honorable Henry Schoolcraft, for cash. He said he could not give us an answer then, but that he would make our wishes known to the Great Father in Washington, and he would inform us later. That was the last of it. At the time of the next payment there was neither goods nor money and no reply ever came."

John shook his head. "So you only got ten thousand dollars of the one hundred fifty thousand dollars promised?"

"That's right. If my brother William had lived, it might have been different."

They sat in silence for a time. Arthur J. said, "My father no longer trusts most white men. He has had too many bad things happen because of them."

Chief Blackbird nodded. He looked at John. "You are a man of God. I trust you as I trusted Father Gabriel Richard when he was here in 1800. But I told my children, 'Beware of the white man. They all are after the world's wealth, and to get it they will lie, steal, rob and murder. They talk with a smooth tongue while their heart is full of deceit. They do not intend us any good!' "

John shook his head. "I'm sorry. What you say is true. One of the reasons I work with the Indian people is that I want them to know they can trust in God and that He loves all people alike." He hesitated. "And our country is doing a terrible evil to the Negroes by allowing slavery—and again it is for money. The South says they cannot exist without slaves to produce cotton."

Arthur J. said softly, "Someday it will come to a head. Like a boil festering just below the surface, sooner or later it will erupt."

"My brother-in-law lives near Adrian," John said. "Many Quaker families there are violently opposed to slavery. I have a nephew who is not of the Quaker faith. He works for the *Adrian Watchtower* newspaper. He writes fiery articles about the slavery issue. Mrs. Laura Haviland is a powerful influence in southern Michigan. Laura's energy seems endless. Though she has a large family she is active in promoting education as well as the fight against slavery. In 1836 she started a school, the Raisin Institute, as a manual labor school for dependent children. A few years later the institute was raised to the preparatory level, open to boys and girls, colored and white." [2]

Marie murmured, "I'd like to know her."

Arthur J. asked, "Are there many Negroes living near Adrian?"

"There are a few 'free' Negroes who have their papers near Marshall, and an escaped family here and there in remote areas where they're protected by neighbors."

Marie enjoyed the spring of 1841 at Arbor Croche. She was well accepted by squaws and braves alike. She helped with tapping maple trees and the sugar making. She and John wandered along the Lake Michigan shore which is bordered and bottomed with glistening boulders, rocks and pebbles of many colors. The evergreens and white birches came down to the water. In places the shore consisted of yellow sand which the wind had blown into drifting dunes.

While John discussed religious matters with small groups Marie learned of the life her mother had lived before she married Jean Leval. The squaws taught her to work designs in beads or porcupine quills. Colors ran the gamut through yellow-greens of grasses to browns, soft reds and sooty blacks. These works of art were colored in soft tones of dyes made from roots, barks, fruit, fungi and lichens. The squaws said the colors would soften and mellow with age.

Marie was dismayed at the dirty and untidy conditions she found in some of the wigwams. In exchange for the squaws' knowledge in doing Indian crafts, she showed them new ways of cooking and stressed the health benefits of bathing, clean clothing and of washing dishes after each meal.

Marie wondered about Arthur J. Like herself, he was

'neither fish nor fowl,' for he too had adopted the life of the whites. He was a small man with hands and feet no larger than those of a woman; his body was straight and trim. His hair and eyes were coal black. His dress clothing consisted of a voluminous Prince Albert coat and a high stovepipe hat. On Sundays he wore shoes but on weekdays he preferred soft deerskin moccasins and traditional deerskin garments.[3]

Old Chief Blackbird no longer could cope with the younger generation. When Arthur returned from college in Ohio, he found his relatives and friends little better than beasts of the forest. He quickly took leadership among them and he was accepted as a wise counselor.

One evening while the old chief, Arthur J., Marie and John lingered over cups of *kinnikinnik*, Marie said, "I'd like to know how to make this tea."

Arthur laughed. "*Kinnikinnik* is good for many things—tea, smoking tobacco, or to cure bowel trouble. To make it you mix the bark of red osier (willow), leaves of sumac and bearberry and wintergreen. Dry, shred and mix these things and you have *kinnikinnik*. When our men have tobacco we mix it in and smoke it in our pipes. It makes a very blue smoke."[4]

"Hm-m-m," John mused. " 'Tis good for bowel trouble. We must remember that."

"We'll gather some tomorrow," Arthur J. promised. "We're going after passenger pigeons."

"Is it far?" Marie asked.

"We'll camp out for two or three days while the squaws smoke and salt the pigeons. Then they'll keep 'til next winter."

The next day the people of Arbor Croche packed for the pigeon hunting trek. They carried few supplies for they would build temporary wigwams and their chief food would be pigeons. A few blankets, cooking utensils and tin plates, salt for preserving the birds, cornmeal for cooking and a small amount of maple sugar would be sufficient. The hunters carried axes, poles, and bows and arrows. They were in high spirits for the monotonous diet of the winter soon would give way to delicious pigeon and squab preparations.

John and Marie were pleased to be included in the event. They were fully accepted by the tribe who did not often include whites in their festivals. Marie wore moccasins and a fringed deerskin dress on which she had worked Indian designs. Her dark hair in two braids was held back by a beaded headband. She laughed as John whispered, "You're my beautiful squaw."

The plan was to walk a few miles to the nesting area of the passenger pigeons where they would set up camp. The birds left during the day but returned to roost in the late afternoon when the hunt would begin.

Snowshoe hares, their color now a grayish-white, bounded away on long powerful legs while a slow-moving porcupine waddled away at his unhurried pace. An Indian boy threw a rock which made a direct hit. The animal instantly curled up in a ball. The dogs, wise in the way of porcupines, barked frantically but kept at a safe distance.

Chipmunks scolded the intruding party, *chuck-chuck-chuck,* before dashing into their underground burrows while gray squirrels scurried up and down trees, their bright eyes constantly watching.

Arthur J. walked with John and Marie. He was amused by Marie's interest in the ways of wild creatures. She inquired why Chief Blackbird did not accompany the group on the pigeon hunt.

"He is old and like some of the other old people, he stayed at the camp," Arthur J. answered. "This is the first year he hasn't gone with us."

"Pigeon hunting is a happy time for us. Winters at Arbor Croche are hard. Many times we are near starvation before spring. Then the passenger pigeons come by the millions. They are to us as manna was to the Israelites."

A scout who had gone ahead returned to say the roost was near and that they should make camp. Wigwams were quickly erected and covered with the reed mats. They lunched on dried venison. Then as the men smoked *kinnikinnik* the women hung kettles of beans over the campfires. Boys hunted squirrels with bows and arrows as the barking dogs raced through the woods.

"Won't all this commotion scare the pigeons away?" John asked.

Arthur J. replied, "They have nests of young squabs at the nesting place. They'll come back. Each day they leave but they return late in the afternoon. The squabs are better eating than the old birds, but all are good. You'll see."

Marie slapped a mosquito. As the sun began to go down, the annoying insects descended on the camp in hordes. Cans and jars of bear grease appeared which the Indians silently spread on skin not covered by clothing.

"Bear grease keeps mosquitoes from biting us," Arthur J. commented passing the jar to Marie. Though she was repulsed by the stickiness and odor of the grease, she found it was an effective preventive.

Clouds of mayflies hung over Lake Michigan. Swallows skimmed the air seeking their fill of the insects. Suddenly a shout went up as the braves jumped to their feet and pointed to the west.

A dark mass was rapidly moving toward the land. "Is it a huge swarm of bees?" John asked.

Everyone was standing and peering westward. "Passenger pigeons," Arthur J. said. "Hawks are chasing them. See how they swoop and drive the birds?"

A noise like the rumble of thunder came from the fluttering wings. The flock of pigeons divided into columns and descended in spirals like the coils of a long snake.

The men grabbed poles and axes and ran toward the point where the columns of birds were descending. Women and children followed as everyone ran the short distance to the pigeon roost. Noise was so great that human voices could not be heard though everyone was shouting. Cooing pigeons sounded like moans of pain to Marie and the whirring of wings reminded her of the coming of a storm. All of these noises were emphasized by the snapping and falling of limbs overweighed with birds.

The Indian hunters slashed down trees loaded with nests from which young ones were about to fly. As the squabs fluttered down women and children caught them and they were beheaded by a quick jerk and the quivering bodies were tossed into the family's heap. Nests on low branches were knocked down with poles.

Marie and John stared in horror at the slaughter. Below the pigeon roost, dung covered the ground looking like grayish snow. Broken tree branches were strewn about over bodies of pigeons killed by accident in the mad gathering of the enormous flock. Also mingled in the mass were many pure white eggs. The odor of dead birds, rotten eggs and dung made Marie feel as though she might suffocate.

At last darkness ended the killing. Men, women and children returned to camp loaded with adult pigeons and squabs.

"Tomorrow the squaws will clean and salt the birds," Arthur J. said. "They're good eating in winter when game is scarce." [5]

"Will you hunt more pigeons tomorrow?" John asked.

"We'll put out nets. We get hundreds that way."

That night, with John snoring beside her in their tiny wigwam, Marie listened to the night sounds. The eerie calls of the whippoorwill sounded like a spirit in the depth of the forest. *Whip-POOR-will, whip-POOR-will* was repeated

over and over. The wail of a screech owl, a plaintive
melancholy cry came from evergreens behind the camp, together with the *Who-who-who-who* of the barred owl. Finally she fell asleep to dream of the slaughter of the passenger pigeons.

Early next morning Marie wakened to the call of the
loon. Its halooing laugh had a human quality. A bittern
called from a nearby swamp, a heavy, regular, thumping
sound. She knew that to the Indians the bittern was the
spirit of the swamps, pools and bogs. Reluctantly Marie
faced another day of processing and hunting passenger pigeons. This was a part of Indian life with which she was
unfamiliar. She shuddered at the remembrance of squaws
and children beheading the young birds. In her mind's eye
she again saw the heaps of decapitated squabs, their bodies
jerking and quivering.

John stretched. "Something smells good. We'll have
roasted squab for breakfast."

Marie silently arose and slipped her feet into the deerskin moccasins. "I'm not sure I can eat any."

" 'Twas rather gruesome the way they killed the birds."

"John," she paused. "I'm more white than Indian. I
couldn't live as they do. But today I'll force myself to help
with cleaning the pigeons."

The squab were covered with scale-like feathers which
were easily removed by rubbing. Next the birds were
drawn, after which part of them were suspended above a
smudge to smoke, and the remainder were salted and
packed in receptacles to be taken back to camp.

John and the Indian men left to put out nets. They
chose low marshy spots from which all growth and leaves
were removed. Because pigeons like salt, the ground first
was saturated. On this tempting bit of ground, grain was
scattered. A stool pigeon, its eyes punched out, was tied to a
block with a cord arranged so that the fluttering bird could

be raised and lowered above the grain to attract pigeons high overhead. The net was eight feet wide and thirty feet long.

The trap was set by the adjustment of a rope and a spring pole at an edge of the net where a hunter hid forty feet away in a bough house. Toward evening he waited for the moment when the net was azure-blue with pigeons. Then the trap was sprung.

Except for the braves waiting to spring the traps, the entire village silently watched from the forest. Again the birds came in with a thunder of wings. Many were attracted by the fluttering stool pigeons and the grain. They swooped in to feast. When the net was covered with blue-feathered birds, the trap was sprung. Hundreds of glistening heads stretched up through the meshes of the nets as the frantic pigeons fluttered wildly to escape.

Several men ran to kill the birds. Standing in the mud and ooze of the pigeon trap they soon were plastered with mud, blood and feathers as, red-handed, they slaughtered their prey.

With thumb and fingers they gave the necks of the birds a remorseless twist. Blood burst from the eyes, the body quivered and the pigeon was dead.

Near one net Marie watched horrified as a brave would pick up a pigeon by the leg, flip it up so that its head went into his mouth where he crushed the head with his teeth. It was done so quickly that he threw as many azure-blue corpses in the pile as the other workers. His face was smeared from ear to ear and his nose and chin dripped gore and his clothes were covered with it.

Sick from watching the slaughter, Marie turned away. John stood nearby. "They must have caught several thousand," he remarked. "Arthur J. says twenty dozen per net is a good catch."

As dusk came on nighthawks zoomed about searching

the air for insects. The loud usual call of *Speek-speek* came again and again as they dove toward the earth with great speed, checking themselves just above the Indians' heads, then sweeping upward. As they checked their downward dive, they made a roaring sound similar to that produced by blowing hard in the mouth of a large bottle. Back at camp with the hundreds of pigeon carcasses, the Indians retired. Marie fell into the sleep of exhaustion. She was wakened by the rumble of thunder and flashes of lightning. A gentle rain pattered on the wigwam. Just as she was about to be lulled to sleep she heard a bloodcurdling scream like that of a human in distress. The unearthly sound was repeated several times until she sat bolt upright. John slept on.

She lay back down muttering softly. "I'm not much of an Indian to be scared of a wildcat."

References ————————————————

[1]Andrew J. Blackbird, *History of the Ottawa and Chippewa Indians of Michigan* (Ypsilanti: Job Printing House, 1887).

[2]*Early Adrian* (American Association of University Women).

[3, 4, 5]U. P. Hedrick, *The Land of the Crooked Tree* (Oxford University Press, 1948).

Chapter Nineteen
1842 — 1843

THE SOLUTION
TO A PUZZLE

1842

1

J OHN AND MARIE RODE SLOWLY through the Shiawassee County forest toward Indian Town (Chesaning). The summer of 1842 had plagued white and Indian farmers alike with late frosts and droughts, followed by heavy downpours of rain. Wherever they stopped they heard complaints about poor crops and fears that the harvest would be a failure.

Silently they followed the blazed-tree Indian path along the Shiawassee River. Finally John said, "I'd like to stop at the camp of Chief Ogemawkeketo."

"He's never very friendly. You think he'll talk to you?"

"I'll keep trying. I've not seen him since he moved what was left of his tribe from near Saginaw to Indian Town."

"Did many of his tribe escape the 1840 deportation?"

"I've heard there were only a few—perhaps a dozen."

Marie, eager to return to Owosso, argued, " 'Tis likely a

waste of time. He won't let you preach to his people."

John brushed away a fly that hung in the air before his face. "I feel I must stop and try again. I don't know what it is, but something tells me I'm needed there."

Barking dogs greeted the missionaries at the edge of camp. Four shacks, their doors ajar, were scattered beneath the trees. The old chief and a boy of perhaps sixteen years of age came from one of the shacks. Squaws stood outside, watching.

The old man came forward. "Preacher Thompson," he said. "Welcome. You will talk with my sister? She is sick. Maybe she die. You will talk to Great Spirit?"

"Yes, I'll pray with her, and my wife will too." They tied their horses and followed the old man toward a shack. John stared at the dark-haired, dark-skinned boy. He reminded him of someone. Who? This was the blue-eyed lad he had seen previously at Ogemawkeketo's camp near Saginaw. Marie, too, was studying the young Indian. Silently, in the way of Indians, he stared at the newcomers.

"He's likely a child of the wind," she whispered to John. "He may have one parent from the sky."

"Illegitimate? Is that what you mean?"

" 'Tis likely."

In the dusky interior of the shack they could make out a form lying on a mat. The chief spoke. "The preacher is here. He will pray to the Great Spirit."

The woman coughed, a tearing, racking cough. She raised her head to spit into a blood-spattered basin beside her.

Marie laid her hand on the woman's hot head. "We'll try to help you," she said softly. The boy stood inside the doorway watching. Another coughing spell followed.

Finally the squaw caught her breath. "My boy," she whispered to the young Indian. "Come." Silently the tall boy squatted beside the sick woman.

"Preacher man," again she coughed and gasped for air. Wiping her mouth on her hand she whispered, "I will die soon. I've been bad woman. Bad squaw."

The boy took her hands. "No. No. You are my mother. You are good squaw. My father say before he died, 'Your mother, she is good squaw.' "

"I must make peace with Great Spirit. I want preacher man to hear. He will talk to Great Spirit for me."

John kneeled beside the boy and his mother. "What is her name?" he whispered.

"Mary Fisher."

"Mary, tell me what is worrying you and we will pray about it."

She gasped for breath. "Once I was good squaw to my husband. I sew and cook. I want papoose. Two babies die. I feel bad. Other squaws have one, two papooses." She was interrupted by another violent fit of coughing. Marie stroked her forehead. Finally the woman continued.

"My husband feel sorry. He want papoose too. One time he go away. When he come back he bring me my papoose." She reached for the boy's hand.

"You have another papoose die?" the boy asked.

"No. No. You are the baby he bring me."

"Me? No! I am your son!"

"Yes, you are my son." The squaw spoke to the old chief. "You tell him."

The old man began. He looked at the boy. "Listen good. Your father go on long trip on steamship. When he come home, he bring you to Mary, his squaw."

"Where did you get me?"

"He steal you. He did it so Mary could have papoose."

"I—I don't understand. Where is my tribe?"

"You are white boy. He steal you from white family with name Parker. You are Jim Parker."

"My blue eyes—I've been teased about my blue eyes.

How will I find my family—the Parkers?"

John's heart pounded. Little Jimmy. Susan had been right—he was kidnapped. But she would never see him. He waited while the sick woman coughed and spit blood. Poor woman, she was dying of consumption.

"Jim," he said softly. "I know who you are. You're my sister's son. You were kidnapped in Detroit in October of 1830. I was with your parents. We searched for days but no one had seen you. My sister, your white mother, is dead, but your white father and brothers and sisters live near Adrian."

The boy clung to his mother's hand. "No," he said again. "You are my mother. I won't leave you."

"When I die you must find your family. Preacher Thompson is your uncle. You stay now, but after I die, go see them."

Talking irritated her damaged lungs. She closed her eyes to rest but they knew she listened.

Jim said softly, "My mother used walnut stain on my hands and face when I was small. She said I was too white."

John whispered, "We'll talk later, Jim." He turned to Mary. "Are there other things you want to say to Jim?"

"No. We did wrong to take him from his family. Will you talk to Great Spirit so I can die in peace?"

John motioned for the others to go outside. After a time he came out. "She is at peace. She feels she is forgiven. She wants you to sit with her, Jim."

That night with her son by her side, Mary Fisher died in her sleep. Marie and John remained to comfort Jim and to assist in the primitive Indian burial. Mary was laid to rest beside her husband, the man Jim had believed to be his father.

Chief Ogemawkeketo was appreciative of John's and Mary's help. While John preached to the men, Mary spoke with the women.

Jim wandered about in confusion. His feelings were ambivalent. Only a few months before his Indian father had died. Now his mother was gone. He felt as though he was Indian, but he was white. He thought like an Indian. Though he had envied the white boys he had seen in Saginaw and Owosso, he didn't understand their ways. Now the Chief, his Indian uncle, and Rev. Thompson, his white uncle, both said he should go to Adrian to meet his white family. Maybe they wouldn't like him. He knew how some white people felt about Indians. They called them savages. And white boys went to school. They could read and write. His white brothers and sisters would think he was an idiot. He was scared. An Indian should be brave—but he wasn't an Indian.

Once Jim had thought he sometime would be chief of his tribe, but two years ago the government had taken most of his tribe away—all but the old chief and three families who had escaped to Indian Town.

Then there was Owasco, his pretty Indian sweetheart. They had grown up together. Someday she would be his squaw—or would she? She might want a real Indian for her husband. Maybe she would be his friend Joe's squaw, after he went to Adrian. Confused and miserable Jim wandered for hours in the wilderness, his thoughts torturing him with the uncertainty of his future life.

2 ——————————————— *1842*

THE SEPTEMBER FOREST TOLD OF an end to summer. Here and there a few maple branches glowed red in the sunshine. Bluejays shrieked angrily as John, Marie and Jim rode toward the Parker home.

Jim, true to his Indian upbringing, was not given to idle chatter. He hid his emotions so well that John and Marie did not suspect the dread he felt at meeting his family. Though he had eaten very little, his stomach churned with nervousness.

Marie said, "Soon we'll be there. You look very handsome in your new suit." Jim did not answer but Marie suspected he preferred his Indian clothing. She had felt Jim would be better accepted by the family if he dressed as a white man. But the new outfit had caused friction between her and John for he resented the fact that her money had purchased it.

The solemn trio rode on. John glanced at Jim who stared into the forest. They needed something to make them laugh. After all, they were going to a family reunion, not a funeral. "I've just thought of a story," he began. "An old man was having trouble with the sight in his left eye, so he went to the doctor who examined his eyes. 'There's nothing wrong with your left eye. Your sight is dimming because of old age.' The old man said, 'Shucks. My right eye is the same age as the left and I see fine with it.' "

Marie laughed, but Jim gave no sign that he was amused, or that he had heard the joke. John continued. "You've seen a train, haven't you Jim?"

"Yes."

"One man said to another, 'A train passed not long ago.' The other man said, 'How do you know?' The first man said, 'I saw its tracks.' " A flicker of smile crossed the sober boy's face.

John peered through the trees. "See the house just ahead? That's your new home." Jim didn't answer.

Marie explained, "Your family don't know you're coming. They will be glad to see you, but when they saw you last, you were a baby. It will take time for you to get to know one another."

When they came to the door Emily rushed to embrace Marie and John. "It's so good to see you!" she exclaimed looking questioningly at Jim.

John said, "Emily, we have a happy surprise for the family. This is your little brother Jimmy."

The color drained from her face. For a moment she was speechless. Then with tears streaming down her cheeks, she seized his hands. "Jimmy! Jimmy!" she exclaimed. "You've come home. Mama always said you'd come back some day. Sit down and tell me where you've been."

"My sister," Jim said softly. "I don't remember when I lived with you. I'm—I've lived with Indians."

John and Marie told the rest of the story as Emily gazed at Jim. Finally she said, "Jimmy, you're a handsome young man. I can't wait for Papa to see you."

"Where is Henry?" John asked.

"He and Josie and Hank are getting the land ready to plant winter wheat."

"Where is David?" Marie asked.

"Taking his nap," Emily replied slowly. "He sleeps a lot."

"He's going on three now."

Emily smiled at Jim. "David's our baby brother. He's about as old as you were when you—left."

"I expect he's talking now," Marie said.

Emily's blue eyes clouded. "No. He was slow walking, too."

John got up. "Jim, let's go out in the field to meet your father and the rest of the family."

From a distance they saw Henry walking beside a pair of oxen on the harrow. He guided them with the touch of a light whip and commands of "gee" and "haw." Josephine, dressed in men's clothing, drove the team of horses as they pulled the roller across the soft soil.

"Big field," Jim remarked.

"Your father has a fine farm. He cleared much of it himself. Your sister, Josephine, has always worked outside with him, and young Hank is a help now, too. He's over there picking up stones."

"Hank? He's my brother?"

"He lives with your family. His parents are dead." Silently John observed the family resemblance between Jim and Hank.

They met Henry and Hank at the end of the field. "Hello!" Henry shouted removing his hat and wiping perspiration from his dusty forehead. "We ain't seen you in a coon's age."

"Been up at Arbor Croche." John paused noting the puzzled expression on Henry's face as he glanced at Jim. "Henry—"

"Huh?"

"Henry, I've brought you a surprise. This is your son Jimmy."

Henry staggered backward to lean against one of the oxen. "Jimmy! Where in hell have you been?"

Jim, his face flushed, stared silently at his dusty white man's shoes. His feet hurt.

"Jimmy! Answer me! Where have you been? Your mother died talking of you. Why didn't you come while she was alive?"

John broke in. "Henry, the boy was kidnapped. One of the Indian men on the boat stole him and Jim's always thought he was Indian until his Indian mother told him on her deathbed that he was Jim Parker."

"Humph! With blue eyes and fair skin, you thought you were Indian?"

Jim raised his eyes to his father's. He saw disapproval. His father was angry. Silently he stared into the forest, the friendly forest.

"Do you speak English?" Henry blustered.

"I don't have anything to say."

"After all these years you have nothing to say to your father who has worried and thought of you every day?"

John interceded. "You're both upset. You need time to get acquainted." He patted Hank on the shoulder. "Jim, this is Hank. He's a good worker."

Hank put his hand out. Silently their hands met. "I'll show you the farm," the boy offered. "It's nice."

Josephine stopped the horses nearby. She greeted John who said, "Josie, this is Jimmy."

"Jimmy!" She ran to him and seized his hands. "My little brother Jimmy! I'm so glad you found us. Now if Mama was here our family would be complete."

John explained, "He was kidnapped and brought up by Indians, Josie."

"Jimmy, we'll have a lot to talk about. My best friend was an Indian boy named Jake. I used to play at his camp when I was little. But he went away two years ago."

Jim's eyes showed interest. "Was he Chippewa?"

"Potawatomi. You tell me about your tribe and I'll tell you about Jake's. They're gone now—west of the Mississippi."

Jim nodded. "My family—my Indian family—ran away but we didn't go."

"Jake ran away too. If they didn't catch him he'll come back some day. He said he would."

Josie unhitched the horses from the roller. "I'm going to the house, Papa. Jim and I have lots to talk about." Silently Henry turned back to his work.

3 ———————————————— *1842*

LITTLE DAVID SAT WITH THE family at the breakfast table. Emily put a spoon in his hand. "Show Jimmy what a big boy you are. Show him how you feed yourself."

The child held the spoon staring blankly at Jim. "Eat your cornmeal mush," Emily urged. He gave no response. After a time Emily silently fed the boy.

Henry growled, "Something's wrong with him. He ain't bright. All the rest of my children were talking by the time they were his age. He doesn't talk or feed himself and he's still wearing didys."

Emily brushed back her blonde hair. "Maybe I've helped him do things too long. We'll work on it."

Henry's face was flushed. "Just my luck to have an idiot boy," he muttered. " 'Twasn't enough that he killed Susan, he's an idiot as well."

Josephine's eyes flashed. "It's not David's fault Mama died getting him born, and it's not his fault he is—slow. He's a sweet little boy."

Henry was working up to an explosion of temper. The family recognized the signals.

Marie said, "I've read that no two children are alike. Some take longer than others to learn to do things."

"We have to give Emily credit," John said. "She is like a mother to the boy. Just give him more time."

Henry shoved back his chair. "Time!" he bellowed. "Fred couldn't talk right until he was almost grown! Jim was gone and he doesn't seem like a Parker! David is an idiot! And if that isn't enough, Susan died and left me with nothing but problems!"

John said softly, "You have Hank."

Henry shot a warning glance at John as Hank said, "But I ain't a Parker."

John excused himself from the table. "Jim," he said, "Let's ride into Adrian and see Fred. Then you will have met the whole family."

The meeting between the brothers took place in Fred's office. As John shook hands with his nephew, Fred studied Jim's face.

"You look like a Parker," he said. "Are you one of our relatives?"

"I'm Jim."

"Little Jimmy?"

"Yes."

John beamed. "Your mother was right, Fred. He was kidnapped by one of the Indians on the steamship and brought up in a camp near Saginaw." Again the story was retold.

"How's Pa taking your return?"

Jim looked down. "He doesn't like me."

"What? For years he's been talking of you, always telling us you were his favorite child. He blamed me that you were lost. All my life I've been reminded that Mama and I didn't watch you well enough."

John said slowly, "Boys, your father is a strange man. I felt sorry for you, Fred, when you were growing up. Henry blows hot and cold and you never know when his mood will change. He doesn't even like himself." He spoke to Jim. "He was an orphan who was brought up by the Parkers. He's always been angry at the world that his mother abandoned him when he was a baby."

In a moment John continued. "He seems to vent his criticism and anger on the family—the ones he loves. Strangers are flattered by his polite manners and friendly ways. They would never believe how disagreeable he can be at home. He seems to take out his anger on his boys. He's a puzzling man. Right now, Fred, he's calling little David an idiot. Of course the boy does seem a little slow, but he's not an idiot."

Fred asked, "Jim, what do you plan to do?"

"I can't stay there with—Mr. Parker. I might go back with my Indian friends."

"Have you been to school?"

"No."

"Jim, I couldn't live at home either. I left when I was about your age and went to an academy in Tecumseh. Now we have a fine school just outside of Adrian, the Raisin Institute. It is run by Mr. and Mrs. Charles Haviland. Would you be interested in going there?"

"I don't have any money."

"I make contributions to the Institute. I'm sure you could go there. Mrs. Haviland has Negroes, Indians and whites attending. You'd live at the school and work on the farm growing food part of the time."

John said, "The Havilands are fine people. They're Quakers, Jim, and the school stresses academics, religion and good morals. They're strong anti-slavery people."

"Do they help slaves get to Canada?" Jim asked.

Fred smiled. "It's supposed to be a secret, but everyone in Adrian knows. We have many Quakers here. They're all anti-slavery, as our father is. He was brought up as a Quaker."

John got up. "Shall we ride out to the Institute and talk to Mrs. Haviland, Jim?"

"I can't read."

"You'd be reading in no time," Fred said. "And Mrs. Haviland thinks Pa is a fine man. She'd be glad to have his son at her Institute." He smiled smugly.

That evening at supper Henry exploded in anger when he heard Jim wouldn't be living at home. Pacing the floor, he ranted, "After all these years that you've been gone, you're not going to stay to help me? Fred ran off too. I don't know what I've done that my boys should turn out worthless! Josephine and Emily are good girls—but who knows, they'll likely turn on me too!" He looked at Hank. "But you'll stay with me, won't you?"

"Yeah, Pa," the boy replied. "I'll stay."

4 *1842 - 1843*

As the Thompsons made their way back to their home in Owosso through the late September sunshine, they traveled seldom used Indian trails. Marie wished to replenish her supply of medicinal herbs, for with winter approaching, the little settlement likely would be visited with numerous kinds of illness.

In muslin bags Marie gathered sassafras leaves to be used to make tea for boils, Indian tobacco for measles, boneset and willow for fevers and catnip for upset stomach. When she was home the leaves would be dried and stored.

Sickness was a dreaded thing and many of the early settlers were ill much of the time. Malaria, which they called "ague" or "ager" was common. Anyone who had lived a summer in Michigan was likely to be afflicted with repeated attacks of the disease. First they would be burning with fever, and next they would be shivering though the weather was warm. The people were not aware the disease was spread by mosquitoes.

Cholera visited the settlements nearly every summer. Sometimes entire families died of dehydration within two or three days.

Diphtheria, smallpox, typhoid and lung fever

(pneumonia) were diseases dreaded by every family. Doctors were few and poorly trained. Most of them used the herbal remedies of the local Indians.

John and Marie generally traveled in a northerly direction toward Owosso, stopping along the way to hold religious services wherever there was a need. Many of the areas now had churches and regular circuit riders or ministers. They passed through Webberville, went east to Fowlerville and Howell, north to Byron and in mid-October they reached their Owosso home.

Neighbors called to welcome them. Judge Elias Comstock and his wife; Charles Parkhill, the school teacher; Ebenezer Gould, attorney and owner of the store; and E. D. Gregory from the hardware were a few of the citizens who called at the Thompson home.

The little hamlet of Owosso consisted of fifty or sixty houses in the fall of 1842. No railroad had yet come to the area and almost no wagon roads. Indian trails or paths marked by blazed trees still were the only thoroughfares.

Throughout all of central lower Michigan the farmers complained that the summer and fall had been unproductive. Crops were a failure because of late frosts which killed corn, potatoes, vegetables and fruit. Droughts had resulted in small yields of wheat, oats, beans and barley, and late rains damaged the small amount of crops left at harvest time.

People in Owosso faced the winter with foreboding. A heavy fall of snow came in November. Drifts lay against the houses and in the streets. There were no breaks in the weather, no long thaws. Often more snow fell. Housewives rationed their pitiful store of food, knowing full well their families faced famine before another summer. Children were unable to attend school for they lacked shoes and clothing. Many entire families were without shoes. [1]

Early in the long winter food consisted of cornbread

and potatoes until the corn was gone and only a small supply of potatoes remained.

By February the people were desperate. Settlers congregated at the store of Ebenezer Gould. Judge Comstock, his face lined with worry, said, "I had two cows that would have died from starvation. We butchered them yesterday. They were just skin and bones, but we'll distribute the meat and bones to the people. They can make soup."

Ebenezer Gould surveyed the bare shelves of his store. "I still have some rice. The women can add that to the broth."

John Thompson said, "We can't sit here and let people starve. We have to organize a group to go outside for food."

Daniel Gould argued, "John, you know as well as anyone that we can't get through the drifts to go anywhere for supplies."

"We'd have to shovel but we might do it with a team and sleigh," John replied.

Storekeeper Ebenezer Gould said, "I don't have money to lay in flour, cornmeal and all the clothing people need."

"Maybe we could pool our resources and divide things up when we get back," John said.

"If anyone gets back," E. D. Gregory remarked.

"Where did you have in mind to go?" Charles Parkhill asked.

"Pontiac."

"That's sixty or seventy miles," Judge Comstock said, "And they may be out of food too."

"Surely the road is open from Pontiac to Detroit," John said.

"We have to do something," Ebenezer said. "I'm feeding my livestock straw from the ticks of our straw beds. Then I'll have to turn them out to shift for themselves. It's terrible. I've already turned my hogs out. Maybe they will find a few acorns." He grinned. "If 'twas summer they could clean out rattlesnakes around here. They eat 'em like they was corn."

David Fish agreed. "Our family is eating acorns. Mary boils them. But acorns are hard to find with the snow so deep it takes a lot of shoveling to get down to the ground."

"This winter reminds me of the one in York State in 1816 and 1817," John said. "We all were hungry then, too, but this year is worse."

" 'Tis strange we can't find deer and rabbits," Daniel Gould said.

"Deer stay in deep swamps in bad winters. They're far to the north and east," Judge Comstock replied. "I don't know why there aren't any rabbits."

David Fish said, "We've eaten a few muskrats, but I haven't had much luck trapping either. My wife sewed moccasins for the young ones from the hides."

John stood up. "Well—what are we going to do? I think we have to make a move—do something to help ourselves. I'm in favor of sending a couple men with teams and sleighs to Pontiac. Each family could put what money they have in the pool and perhaps by helping one another—and praying—we'll made it through the winter. I'll volunteer to go, only I'll have to borrow a team and sleigh."

Elias Comstock said, "I'll go and take a team."

"Do you think we can collect enough money?" Ebenezer Gould asked. "Are there still a few gold and silver coins in the settlement? We know the merchants in Pontiac won't take wildcat paper money."

Everyone nodded silently. Finally Elias Comstock said, "Let's think about it and meet here tomorrow to make a decision. Anyone who is in favor of the trip, bring whatever money you have, then we'll plan."

The next day they met and formed the Owosso Starvation Society. They decided to gamble their remaining gold and silver coins on the chance that John Thompson with

Ebenezer Gould's team, and Elias Comstock with his horses, would make the trip to Pontiac to bring back food. That evening, every person who was able gathered at the schoolhouse on the corner of Williams and Washington Streets for a prayer meeting. John talked hopefully of a successful trip and requested that Elias and he be remembered daily in the prayers of the settlement. [2]

That evening John and Marie had a long talk. Both of them spoke hopefully of a successful trip, but silently they pondered the chances for disaster. Could men and horses survive for days and nights in bitter cold with insufficient food and shelter?

Marie brought out a bag of gold coins which were from her first husband's estate. "If it seems there is too little money for supplies, use this to get what is needed."

"You gave more than your share this morning," John argued.

Firmly she responded, "Use it if you need it."

Armed with a tent, blankets, shovels, rifles, a bag of dried fish and venison, and a few precious loaves of bread, the two men left early in the morning. The day was pleasant with sunshine and a temperature in the low forties. They followed the path of least resistance, detouring around drifts when possible and shoveling when necessary. The delays while shoveling gave the horses needed rest periods. By late afternoon they stopped to make camp in a protected area at the foot of a hill.

Tender end twigs of branches were collected and piled before the horses. This tall hay was the only food they would have before reaching Pontiac. Snow would provide them with water. The faithful animals were blanketed beside the sleigh and left for the night.

John and Elias erected the tent over the box of one sleigh. After a supper of bread and dried meat which was washed down with water from snow melted over a campfire, they retired for the night.

Wolves howled nearby causing the horses to stamp and pull on their tethers. John chuckled at the recollection of Crazy Sal. Briefly he spoke of her and the unusual life she led. He concluded with, "The old woman has two shacks where she lives. She's old now and spends most of her time at the place near my brother-in-law's farm a few miles from Adrian."

"Does anyone know where she came from?" Elias asked.

"There are rumors that she and her husband were early settlers in Michigan and that he was a drunk and a gambler who beat her when he was in a drunken rage. We do know she hates men. Anyway the story around Adrian is that she finally ran him off when she held a gun on him and threatened to shoot him if he ever came back. Her threats must have impressed him for there never has been a man around her place since we've been in Michigan." John chuckled.

"If we were near Adrian I'd suspect those wolf howls came from Crazy Sal's throat—only she usually ends her wolf serenade with the snarl of a wildcat."

"She's harmless?"

"Yeah. My niece Josephine is about eighteen. She and Sal have always been good friends."

"Your brother-in-law's family—do you think they have food this winter?"

"I think they're all right. We were there last fall. Their wheat, corn and potato crops were poor, but they will have enough to get through the winter. Owosso was harder hit by last summer's late frosts. We are father north than Adrian."

The good weather held. Finally after five days the two men arrived in Pontiac. Tired and hungry, they rested for two days while they purchased and loaded their sleighs with supplies. Wheat and shelled corn were bought because they were less expensive than cornmeal and flour. The mill in Owosso would grind the grain. Because of the freezing weather no potatoes or apples were bought. Finally on the third morning after their arrival in Pontiac, the return journey was begun.

"We've been lucky with the weather," Elias said. "There hasn't been more snow so we shouldn't have to shovel."

" 'Tis good sleighing," John replied. "It thaws a little each afternoon, so even if we get wind the trail won't drift full again. Ya hoo! Owosso, here we come!" The horses jogged along on the homeward journey that day and the next.

On the morning of the third day there was no sunshine. The temperature was above freezing. Dark clouds hung to the northwest. Studying the sky, Elias said, "Could be we'll get rain soon."

"Yeah. We'd better hurry along as fast as the horses can go," John answered. "I can't wait to see people's faces when we unpack all this food."

By eleven o'clock rain was falling, and by mid-afternoon the wind came up and the rain changed to sleet. The horses' hooves slid on the slick, sleet-covered trail making it necessary to slow their pace. Though neither man mentioned it, both knew the disastrous consequences that might result if a horse broke a leg.

In late afternoon, wet and miserable, they made camp. The temperature had dropped and outer clothing was stiff and frozen. The wind alternately roared and moaned through the wilderness. It threatened to blow the tent away when they tried to put it over one of the food-laden sleighs. The air was filled with pellets of ice-frozen hail, hard as pebbles which the wind drove fiercely onto unprotected flesh. Their noses and cheeks were spotted red and white.

Finally in desperation they tied the tent to the sleigh and crawled beneath it for a few minutes protection. After a time Elias said, "I'll blanket the horses and tie them on the leeward side of the sleigh."

They crawled out to face the torturing blast of the storm. John tried to secure tender twigs for the horses but the wind-tossed branches were almost impossible to hold. Returning to the sleigh with an armful of twigs, he slipped. Unable to regain his balance, his ankle twisted and he fell. Above the roar of the wind he heard the telltale crack of a broken bone. He tried to rise but his leg crumpled beneath him.

In the dusky twilight Elias helped him to the protection of the tent-covered sleigh. "Are you in pain?" he asked.

"Only when I move, but soon it will wake up, I expect." He sighed. "I've really fixed things for us."

Elias said, "I'll take a horse and ride to Owosso for help."

"You can't go tonight. It'll be pitch dark soon and you couldn't see the trail unless—"

"Yeah. Unless the horse would know the way and he'd go home. I'll try it. We can't go very fast because it's slippery, but I'll be back with help as soon as I can—maybe sometime tomorrow."

After making John as comfortable as possible and covering him with many blankets, Elias tied three horses on long tethers and riding the fourth, he faced into the northwest pellet-filled wind.

Through the long night John suffered with excruciating pain each time he moved. He listened to the storm as it raged through the forest. Finally the rattle of sleet on the tent above was silenced, but the wind still roared in all its fury. Now and then a tree crashed to the ground. The wind seemed almost human as it threatened to tear the flapping tent from its fastenings.

Gradually the velocity of the wind lessened. The forest was silent except for the stamping of the horses' hooves. John slept fitfully. At last daylight came.

The next day seemed endless. Suffering with pain and cold, he wondered if his feet were frostbitten. He was hungry in spite of the discomfort. Finally, when he thought he might spend another night alone in misery, he heard shouts.

A few minutes later Charles Parkhill peeped beneath the tent. "John!" he shouted. "You'll soon be on your way home!"

"Thank God you're here," John whispered.

The Gould Brothers and Henry Smith had returned with Charles Parkhill who had some medical knowledge. While Charles did his best to make John more comfortable, he talked. "We'll wait to set this broken leg until after you're home," he said. "You'll need whisky to deaden the pain. As a Methodist preacher, will you object?"

John grinned. " 'Tis medicine, isn't it?"

"Yeah. 'Tis medicine."

Ebenezer Gould handed John a cup of hot snow water and a piece of bread. "Owosso will never forget, John, what you and Elias did for us during this hard winter. You've saved our lives," he said sincerely.

References

[1,2]Adele Ball, *Early History of Owosso* (Michigan Historical Society, 1944).

Chapter Twenty
1846 — 1847

UNDERGROUND RAILROAD ACTIVITIES

1846

1

Jɪᴍ Pᴀʀᴋᴇʀ's ᴇʏᴇs ꜰᴏʟʟᴏᴡᴇᴅ ᴛʜᴇ figure of his Indian bride, Owasco. Since they were twelve years old they had planned to marry. He had been a student but a short time at Haviland's Raisin Institute in Adrian when he returned to the campsite of feeble old Chief Ogemawkeketo north of Owosso. He found Owasco waiting for him. Somewhat reluctantly she left her parents to live at the Raisin Institute with the Haviland family and about a dozen Negro, Indian and white students. Besides their academic work, students were expected to work a few hours each day on the Haviland farm or in the house to pay for their food, lodging and education.

When Charles Haviland, the husband, died in 1845 during a smallpox epidemic, Jim Parker, then age seventeen, was put in charge of the farm work. Now at twenty-one he had completed his education and was the "right hand man" of Laura Haviland. His bride, Owasco, had become knowledgeable in cooking and baking during her more than four years at the Institute. She also had completed her education and was given the responsibility of overseeing the kitchen. The young couple were paid a moderate salary. They lived in a small comfortable tenant house on the Haviland property.

Energetic Quakeress Laura Haviland, in her late thirties, was a woman of many talents. Besides raising a large family of children, she taught at the institute, spoke frequently at anti-slavery meetings and at prisons, was active in temperance work and was a leader in Adrian's Quaker Society. Known to citizens of Adrian as "Aunt Laura," her energy seemed endless. She also contributed articles on education to newspapers and was a leader in helping slaves escape to freedom by way of the Underground Railroad. The route she used most often was called the "Quaker Route" and it led northward from Kentucky through Ohio. It began at Cincinnati, Ohio, went to Toledo, then to Adrian, Ypsilanti and Detroit. Slaves escaping by way of the Underground Railroad were usually passed on by night to the next station, a distance of ten or fifteen miles.[1]

Henry Parker had aged in the past five years. Though he still bitterly denounced his sons, Fred and Jim, he had a fair relationship with Hank, who at seventeen was doing most of the farm work with Josephine's help.

One day after the noon meal Emily sat at the table helping eight-year-old David with his arithmetic. "I'm tired of adding," he complained. "I do the problems over and over but they're always wrong."

Emily patted his shoulder. "I'll help you. Your teacher said you need help."

David sighed. "It's no use. I can't get them right."

"We'll work together. Watch my fingers. How many on this hand?"

The boy counted. "One, two, three, four, five."

"That's right. Now count the fingers on the other hand."

"One, two, three, four, five."

"How do we write five plus five?"

"I don't know."

"Like this. See, it says five plus five."

"Yeah."

"Now count how many five plus five are." She held up both hands.

"One, two, three, four, five, six, seven, eight, nine. Five plus five are nine!"

Henry sprang from his rocker. "Susan, it's no use! The boy is stupid!" He paced the floor.

"Papa," Emily's voice was soft. "I'm not Susan. I'm your daughter Emily."

"Don't confuse me! You're ashamed to admit you have an idiot son, Susan!"

Sobbing, David grabbed his cap and rushed outside. Emily argued, "David tries. He can't help it if it takes him longer to learn than someone else." She paused. "And I'm *not* Susan. Your wife Susan was my mother. She has been dead for eight years. She died when you were gone and David was born. Don't you remember?"

Henry slammed a straight chair down on the floor. "Don't you tell me my mind ain't right! I remember better than you!" He ran a shaking hand through his gray-streaked hair. "I remember when I come home to an idiot baby!"

Emily sighed and went outside to comfort David who leaned against the wagon, his eyes tear-filled. They sat quietly on a log beside the woodpile. He stood up to kiss her. "I love you, Emily," he sobbed.

She hugged him. "I love you too, little brother." She pointed. "Someone's coming."

A buggy pulled in. " 'Tis Mrs. Haviland," Emily said.

"Is Henry here?" the slender woman inquired.

"Yes—but—he's not himself." She whispered, " 'Tis his memory."

"Hm-m-m. I have some merchandise."

"How many?"

"Three."

Emily turned. "David, would you feed the chickens some corn?" When the boy was gone, she continued. "My father's not in any shape to make a delivery. He is so confused. But I know Josephine or Hank would make the delivery. Where is it to go?"

"Ed Arnold's place. They're watching the Institute so I daren't send your brother Jim."

"Where's the merchandise now?"

"At Crazy Sal's. They haven't found her place yet. They are watching the roads. It would be wise to go through the woods along the river after dark."

"I'll get Hank and Josie," Emily said running toward the barn.

A few minutes later they stood beside the wagon while Laura gave directions. When she finished, she asked, "You realize this is a dangerous assignment? If you're caught 'twill mean jail."

The young people nodded. Josephine hitched up her trousers. "I should be the one to go. Hank is needed here on the farm—if anything happens. I can be away better than he can."

"You know the way?"

"To Ed's? Sure. I've gone with Papa before."

Henry stormed out of the house. "What's going on?" he roared.

Josie said calmly, "We're talking with Aunt Laura."

His face flushed. "I heard you plotting! You think I'm not right in the head. I'll show you—all of you! I'll take them to Ed's tonight. Laura, you know how many I've transported." His voice suddenly was plaintive.

Mrs. Haviland smiled. "You've been faithful and you've taken risks. But it's time to pass the responsibility to younger people, Henry."

"Everybody thinks there's something wrong with me! I'll prove that I know what I'm doing. I'll take the—the merchandise to Ed's tonight!"

Mrs. Haviland picked up the reins. "Well—let's make this your last trip as a conductor. Where will you pick them up?"

"Er—er—Crazy Sal's! I ain't stupid!"

"Where will you take them?"

"Ed Martin's."

"No! Henry, no! They're watching Ed Martin! Don't go there! Go to Ed Arnold's! Walk along the river. No wagon or buggy, Henry. Walk!"

"Oh, I can do it. You'll see." Silently he returned to the house.

Josephine whispered, "I wish we could stop him but he's—bullheaded."

Mrs. Haviland nodded. "We'll pray things go right."

The night was dark. About ten o'clock, Henry dressed in a black coat and hat left the house. His step was firm. As he opened the door he said, "You'll see. I'm still not feeble-minded."

Reluctantly the family went to bed. A sense of foreboding permeated the house though no one voiced their concern.

Next morning at five o'clock Josie peeped into her father's room. The bed had not been slept in. Calling Hank, she ran to the barn. The team and the surrey were gone. She rushed back to the house.

"He's gone, Hank! He didn't follow directions! He took the surrey!"

"He must have been caught or he'd be home." The young man's voice quivered. "What should we do?"

"I'm going to see Fred and Jim. You stay here and do the milking. Tell Emily where I am."

Hank glanced at her. "You going in those clothes?"

"I forgot. Ladies don't wear men's clothes." She ran into the house soon to return dressed more appropriately. Five minutes later her horse was trotting toward Adrian.

Though it was early in the forenoon when Josie arrived at Adrian, the street was filled with people standing about in groups. She hurried into the newspaper office. It was empty. She rushed outside. Where was Fred?

A stranger, a man wearing the uniform with the star of an officer, approached her. "Officer," she said, "What has happened?"

"Caught one of your northern conductors with three of our niggers," the man replied in a voice heavy with the Southern accent.

"Oh. Who was it?"

"Old feller named Henry Parker."

"Where is he?"

"In the jail where he belongs. Northern people better learn they can't steal our niggers 'thout paying a price."

Josie bit her lip. "Where are the Negroes?"

"Locked up. I'm takin' 'em back to their owner. They'll pay for this with a few dozen lashes."

She turned away. Her stomach churned. She had to find Fred. Perhaps he was at the jail.

She found her brothers talking to the jailer. She hurried to join them. "How is he?" she asked.

The man shook his head. "Confused—or—or crazy. You folks never should have let him out last night." He whispered. "Your father drove right smack-dab through Adrian with his three Negroes straight to Ed Martin's place. The town's been swarming with slave hunters lately. 'Course they nabbed them."

"How's he taking jail?" Fred asked.

"Hasn't said a word since they brought him in. Think you can raise bail?"

"How much?"

"Thousand dollars. And there's likely to be a sentence of six months to a year."

Jim said, "I have two hundred."

Fred added, "He must have some money in the bank and I have a few hundred. I think we can make it." He hesitated. "Josie, he wouldn't want to see Jim or me. Why don't you let him know we're here?"

Five minutes later she returned. "He won't talk to me. He just stares at the floor." She smiled a twisted smile. "When Papa doesn't bellow at a situation like this, he's not himself."

Addison J. Comstock advanced to meet the Parkers. "Sorry to hear about Henry," he said softly. "If you have trouble raising bail, we'll all chip in."

"Thanks," Fred murmured.

"Comstock studied Jim. "Are you the boy from near Owosso?"

"Yes sir."

"Know my cousin Judge Elias Comstock?"

"Yes sir. He's a fine man."

A sudden commotion with a man's voice shouting, "Call Dr. Winter! Call Dr. Winter!" broke up the conversation.

An attendant called, "It's Mr. Parker!"

Fred, Josephine and Jim rushed to their father who was lying on the floor of the cell. They were bending over him as Dr. Winter hurried in and seized Henry's wrist.

He straightened. "No pulse. He's gone."

They were speechless with the suddenness of Henry's death. Always so active and verbal it seemed out of character for their father to meet death without a murmur of protest.

Three days later Henry Parker was buried from his home. Eulogized by his Quaker friends Addison J. Comstock and Laura Haviland, Henry would have gloried in the praise heaped upon him. Faithful husband and father, outstanding citizen, friend of the downtrodden—on and on the eulogy continued while deep in their hearts only family members knew the true character of Henry Oliver Parker.

2 ——————————— *1847*

Laura Haviland and Josephine discussed the slavery problem as they drove to Marshall for an abolitionist meeting. It was January and sleigh bells jingled with each step of Laura's sleek bay horse. The cutter slid smoothly over the snow-covered road. Winter birds, chickadees, cardinals and nuthatches hopped about chirping merrily as they searched for seeds.

With their boot clad feet on newspaper-wrapped heated soapstones in the bottom of the cutter, and a buffalo robe covering their laps, the women were comfortable in the still winter air.

Laura spoke in her usual spirited manner. "The Underground Railroad is costing southern slave owners thousands of dollars every year. They're complaining that the Ordinance of 1787 is not enforced." [2]

Josephine smiled. "Too bad. Michigan has been a free state since 1837."

Laura slapped a rein against her horse's side. "But under the Fugitive Slave Act of 1793 there always is the danger to Negroes living here that runaway slaves could be legally arrested, either by their owners or agents of the law.

Then they're taken back to their masters in the south."

Josephine said, "Free Negroes should be safe."

"They live in constant fear of being kidnapped by some white person who wants to collect the bounty offered by slaveowners. Sometimes even free Negroes are caught and forced into slavery."

"I understand there's quite a settlement of Negroes in Marshall."

"About forty. Some are freeborn and some runaway slaves."

"Is it against the law for white people to marry Negroes?"

Laura answered, "Congress likely will revise the statutes soon so that no white person can inter-marry with a Negro."

"Indians and whites marry. Jim and Owasco seem happy."

"They're a fine young couple," Laura said warmly. "They are a real help to me in operating the Raisin Institute."

"You're doing a great amount of good in the world, Aunt Laura. The Institute is educating anyone who has a need. And in the South, it's against the law to teach a Negro to read. Then your work in the anti-slavery movement —the Underground—has helped many Negroes to freedom."

"Quakers have been opposed to slavery for several centuries, Josie. We believe there is a higher law that governs man than those on the nation's statute books. Moses said, "Thou shalt not deliver unto his master the servant which is escaped from his master unto thee. He shall dwell with thee, even among you, in that place which he shall choose in one of thy gates, where it liketh him best: thou shalt not oppress him. Deuteronomy 23:15-16."

"I'm glad you asked me to go to Marshall with you,

Aunt Laura. I've always wanted to hear Sojourner Truth speak."

"So have I. Many of our Abolitionist leaders are of the Quaker faith—Lucretia Coffin Mott, John Greenleaf Whittier, Mary Ann Shadd and Susan B. Anthony, to name a few."

"Have you met Fredrick Douglass? I've read about him. He's a fugitive slave, I believe."

"That's true. I hope to meet him some day. He's a skillful Abolitionist speaker who they say is a master of wit, argument, sarcasm and pathos. He urges Negroes to work toward gaining the vote and pursuing vocational education." [3]

They were silent for a time. The sleigh bells jingled merrily. Finally Josie said, "You're doing so much good in the world. I feel—well—useless."

"Are you interested in being more active in the slavery issue?"

"You mean the Underground?"

"Perhaps."

"I've heard you sometimes go south and bring back slaves by yourself."

Laura laughed. "Sh-h-h. It's supposed to be a secret. If you're interested, on some trip I'll include you. But you must not forget the danger. You'll be a lawbreaker subject to fine and imprisonment."

"I know. I like adventure. Papa always said I should have been a boy."

Late that afternoon the women checked in at the hotel before visiting the Adam Crosswhite family on the edge of Marshall. Laura explained that Adam, a mulatto fugitive slave and his wife and their five children lived in a little home he had purchased on the edge of the village. Adam, his wife and the four children all were escaped slaves. Only the youngest child had been born in Marshall. [4]

Josie said, "Then that child is free born."

"Yes. I always visit them when I'm in Marshall. They are well-liked here." She knocked at the door.

Mr. and Mrs. Crosswhite welcomed them warmly. The children ranging in age from two to ten stood silently in the background.

After they were seated Laura asked, "How are things going?"

Adam shook his head. "We're always lookin' to be arrested and took back to Kentucky, Miz Haviland."

"You've been here several years. 'Tis likely your owner has given up. He likely thinks you're in Canada."

"I wish 'twas so," Adam said softly, "but somethin' strange is goin' on. There's a young white man from Kentucky in town. He says he's lookin' for a place to start a law practice. But today three other fellers come. My wife an' me are afeared they're lookin' for us, that Massa Giltner sent them here."

"Why do you think that?"

Mrs. Crosswhite smoothed her plaid apron across her ample thighs. "They walked past three times today an' they talked with the chilluns."

Adam ran his hands through his gray-streaked hair. "I talked with our neighbors. They said if them men come lookin' for us, I should fire my gun as a signal an' they'd come runnin'. White folks is been good to us."

Laura nodded. "We hope nothing comes of it. 'Tis likely all right." She paused. "Are you going to hear Sojourner Truth tonight?"

Adam shook his head. "While them men are in town I have to stay with my family."

"I understand. Our hopes and prayers are with you." Laura and Josephine shook hands with the Crosswhites and departed.

That evening the little hall was packed with people wishing to hear the message of Abolitionist Sojourner

Truth. The Negro woman, tall, thin and with a serious facial expression, gave a brief summary of her life. She was born a slave named Isabella in Ulster County, New York, in 1790. She was freed under state law in 1827 after which she moved to New York City. After a moving religious experience, she took her new name, Sojourner Truth, and traveled in Ohio, Michigan and Indiana urging abolition. [5]

Josephine was moved by the Negro woman's lecture. Stories of families torn apart at slave auctions, of vicious beatings and of many forms of cruelty made a deep impression on her mind. Silently she vowed to devote her life to helping erase the cancerous growth of slavery from the United States.

Soberly Laura and Josephine returned to the hotel where they retired. About four o'clock they were wakened by a nearby shot followed by a bell being rung by a Negro on horseback.

"Crosswhites!" Laura exclaimed. "We must go!"

Dressing hurriedly the women joined a throng of whites and Negroes who were running toward the Crosswhite home where they gathered in the yard. The southern sheriff and slave hunters pounded on the door.

The sheriff shouted, "Adam Crosswhite, you're under arrest! Open the door!" The house remained dark and quiet. "Open the door or I'll break it down!" Still there was no response.

The sheriff and one of the slave hunters slammed their shoulders against the door splintering it from its hinges.

One of the slave hunters held a pistol. "Come out, Crosswhite, or your family will be shot!"

An angry roar rose from the two hundred neighbors in the yard. "Leave them folks alone!" someone shouted.

"You're against the law! You broke into their house!" another yelled.

Several burly men mounted the steps and faced the

Kentucky sheriff and slave hunters. The spokesman said, "Get off this porch or we'll throw you off!"

One of the southern men said, "According to the Constitution of the United States and the Fugitive Slave Act of 1793, Adam Crosswhite, his wife and their four older children must be taken back to Kentucky to Mr. Giltner, their legal owner."

Adam Crosswhite stood in the doorway. "My youngest child is freeborn!"

"You can leave that one behind."

By this time the local officers from Marshall arrived and the Kentuckians were arrested for breaking into a house and threatening the Crosswhite family with a revolver. They were to be held in the jail until court the following morning.

When they were gone the neighbors waited in the Crosswhite yard to plan. "We gotta get Adam and his family out of here tonight," a bearded man declared.

Laura Haviland shouted, "Load the family into a wagon and take them to Jackson where they can catch a train for Detroit and from there they'll be taken to Canada!"

"Yeah!" the crowd shouted.

"When's the train leave Jackson tomorrow?" Adam asked.

"About eight in the morning," someone replied. "You'll be long gone before the Kentuckians are out of court!"

An hour later the Crosswhites climbed into a wagon driven by a citizen of Marshall. "Thank you, good neighbors, and God bless you," Adam said as they pulled into the narrow street and headed toward Jackson.

As Laura and Josephine traveled back to Adrian the following day, they discussed the Crosswhite case. Josie sighed. "Seven more Negroes have escaped to freedom. All's well that ends well."

References

[1]*Early Adrian* (American Association of University Women).

[2, 4]Ferris E. Lewis, *Michigan Yesterday and Today* (Hillsdale Publishing Co., 1956).

[3]*National Geographic* (July, 1984), p. 13.

[5]*World Book Encyclopedia*, T Book (*See* "Truth, Sojourner").

Chapter Twenty-One
1854 — 1856

JOY AND MISFORTUNE

1 ———————————————— 1854

WITH DIFFICULTY, JOHN THOMP-
son swung into his saddle. The years had not been kind to
the Indian missionary. His white hair hung below his battered old hat and his shoulders slumped.

Marie, her back straight and her eyesight keen, was
aware of John's infirmities. For a time they rode silently
heading southwest away from Owosso. Finally she said,
"Neither of us are—well—getting any younger. Maybe we
should give up horseback riding and buy a buggy. 'Twould
be easier for both of us."

He was so slow to answer that Marie thought he hadn't
heard her. Finally he replied, "I'm old. The Indians no
longer need me. Circuit riders are replaced by regular ministers. I've outlived my usefulness. This trip to see Chief
Okemos near Lansing, and young Simon Pokagon at Hartford, will be my last."

"Perhaps you need a rest. Maybe by a year from now you'll feel differently—especially if the rheumatism is better. You have spent too many long cold hours on the trail."

He smiled. She noticed lines in his face she hadn't seen before. "I'm not complaining," he commented. "I've had you as a helpmate for many years. I've been blessed."

Marie laughed. "We've both been blessed in having a happy marriage and good companionship." She hesitated. "There's only one regret in my life. I'm sorry I couldn't give you a child."

John nodded. "We'd both have loved a child but God knows best. Our life would have been a poor one for a child."

They rode by fields of corn, oats, wheat, barley and rye. Most of the log cabin homes had been replaced by clapboard houses. Schoolhouses and country churches were present in every community. They passed children fishing in the Looking Glass River.

"Any luck?" John shouted.

A boy held up a string of a dozen small sunfish. "They're bitin' good!" His sister pushed back her sunbonnet to reveal golden curls. Both children waved as the horses' hooves clopped over the plank bridge.

They neared Lansing located on the Grand River. It had been the capital of the state since 1847 when it was moved from Detroit. At that time the site of Lansing was a wilderness with no railroads within many miles. Now the new town was growing due to lumber mills, the Lansing—Detroit Plank Road and new businesses.

Reaching the plank road, John and Marie stopped at a toll gate to pay the penny per mile charged for single horses. They rode the short distance to the camp of Chief Okemos on the Red Cedar River. The old chief sat in front of his wigwam with a bright blanket about his shoulders.

Barking dogs and dirty children rushed to meet the visitors. The wrinkled old chief, a short heavy-set Indian, blinked in the sunlight.

John called, "Chief Okemos, we're the Thompsons. We stopped to see how you are."

The poker-faced old man stared at them with shrewd, dim eyes. He said, "Need tobac."

"Chief, you know we don't have tobacco. I haven't seen you since you visited the school in Owosso. Those children still are talking about that visit. They've studied about the battles you were in. They are proud to remember they saw you, the famous chief of the Chippewas."[1]

The old Indian straightened his shoulders and some of the lines seemed to leave his face. There was not a hint of a smile on his countenance. He looked beyond John and Marie. His face was calm as he shoved back a large red handkerchief to disclose a long deep scar over his right eye. Only one button remained near the top of his ragged blue coat. He rearranged the red blanket about his shoulders.

Marie said, "Chief, is there something we can do for you?" The dogs continued barking.

"Need clothes."

Marie dug into a saddle bag and pulled out a shirt. "For you," she said.

Chief Okemos silently accepted the garment. "Need coat," he begged.[2]

John said, " 'Tis summer. You won't be cold. We'd like to pray with you before we go."

"Don't need pray. Need food. No more fish. No more deer. Indians hungry."

John put out his hand. "We're sorry. What you say is true. I wish we could do more for you and your people."

Okemos ignored the extended hand and turned toward his wigwam as they silently rode away.

The next morning they headed their horses toward Battle Creek to the southwest. Farmers were at work cultivating corn and beans. Rarely, now, did they see oxen at work for most of them had been replaced by horses. About halfway, they stayed a night at Eaton Rapids. The next night they stayed at a hotel in Battle Creek near the Michigan Central Railroad depot.

The next morning John dressed before Marie was awake. He planned a long walk before breakfast to ease the pain in his rheumatic joints. His eye caught sight of a flyer in the hotel lobby. The two-inch black heading screamed for attention.

ORPHAN TRAIN

Orphaned children, as many as thirty thousand, are sleeping in doorways, cardboard boxes and on barges in the Hudson River. They survive by begging, stealing and prostitution. Generally they are the children of the thousands of immigrants who daily pour into the New York harbor. Many of the parents die leaving behind these orphaned children.

I am Charles Loring Bruce, a minister who founded the Children's Aid Society. It has been suggested that we relocate the orphan children. A large group from the age of 18 months to 14 years will be on the train arriving in Battle Creek on July 6 at 10:00 A.M.

Come see the "Children Without Homes." Meet them at the Railroad Station. Open your heart and give one or more of these children a home and family.

There are rules: We will accept only Christian homes where they will be reared as a member of the family with the same schooling, clothing and training as the family's children. When old enough they are to work for their room and board, and at the age of 18 they are at liberty to make their own arrangements. You, as foster parents, will report yearly by letter to the Children's Aid Society on the child's behavior.

Representatives of the Aid Society are on board the Orphan Train. They will talk with you and record the children you select.

God bless you for opening your heart to these unfortunate children.

CHARLES LORING BRUCE
CHILDREN'S AID SOCIETY [3]

Thoughtfully John limped out into the July sunshine. A plan was forming in his mind. He'd talk with Marie.

Two hours later they stood at the station with a dozen other families awaiting the arrival of the train. Half an hour later it came roaring into the station. The locomotive belched great puffs of black smoke as it rumbled along the rails and stopped beside the water tower. People choked as the half-burned carbon-laden smoke drifted back mingled with the odor of hot grease and steam.

"The children," a woman said. "They're at the windows."

Sad-eyed little faces were pressed against dirty coach windows. Behind them older children stood, some with hopeful expressions, others their eyes dull with misery.

Marie sucked in her breath. "This is terrible," she gasped.

A man with a horn stood on the steps of a passenger car. He bellowed, "The children will remain on the train until you make your selections. Each child is tagged with his name and birthdate. When you've made your selection bring the child to the woman with the red tag on her coat beside the depot. She will answer questions and record your choice of children and your address.

"You need not hurry. The train will remain here for two hours. Please be generous in accepting these homeless ones into your family."

People filed into the silent passenger coach. There were no smiles, no children's laughter—only sad, wan, hopeful faces peering up at the adults. They were not crying. It was as though they were drained of emotion—almost. Each child wore a handwritten ticket attached to his clothing. Some children were so young Marie wondered if anyone would know who they were if the ticket became lost.

John studied the scene. He could see family resemblances between some of the children. Somehow it reminded him of slave auctions in the south. Like the slaves, these children would be parted from brothers and sisters. They likely would never meet again. Their plight was heart-wrenching.

Marie had paused to speak with a fair-haired boy who held a small girl on his lap. She smiled as she looked at his name tag. "You are Andrew Anderson, and this is your sister Anne?"

"Yes, mam. I'm ten and Anne is three."

"Anne and Andrew Anderson. What pretty names."

"Thank you, mam."

John asked, "Are you from England, Son?"

"Yes sir. We've been in New York since March."

"Both your parents are dead?"

"Yes sir. Smallpox. They caught it on the ship. Me and Anne had it, but we got better."

The little girl pointed to her forehead, "Scars," she said. Suddenly she held her arms up to Marie who choked back tears as she picked the child up. "You'll be my mama?" the little girl lisped.

"I'd love to," she whispered.

Andrew's eyes clouded. "She's a good little girl," he said softly.

John asked, "You've been taking care of her?"

"Yes sir."

"Where did you live?"

"We found a big wooden box under a pile of junk. We lived in it. It didn't leak much when it rained."

John continued questioning. "What did you eat?"

"We went behind hotels and if we got there early enough in the morning we found bread and other food they'd thrown out—sometimes."

Anne said, "And sometimes we cooked rats."

Andrew sputtered, "You shouldn't tell that."

John looked questioningly at Marie over Anne's head. She nodded.

"Andrew and Anne Anderson, we are John and Marie Thompson. We would like you to be our son and daughter," John announced.

Andrew choked back tears and stared out the window. Finally he turned, smiling. "Thank you. Thank you. I thought you'd take Anne but not me."

John put his arm about the boy. "We want both of you. A boy for me and a girl for Marie. Come on, let's get rid of these tags. We know who you are!"

Jubilantly they left the train to report to the Aid Society representative about their choices.

As they stood in line Andrew watched the faces in the train windows. "I'm sad for the ones that weren't picked," he said.

John replied, "The train will stop many times between here and Dysart, Iowa. That's where 'tis going, it says on your ticket. They'll all likely be chosen by the time it gets there."

When they were properly recorded with the Children's Aid Society, it was twelve o'clock and time for a noonday meal. Andrew and Anne ate surprising quantities of meat, potatoes and bread. John and Marie were like children at Christmas.

Marie patted each child's head. "You've made us so happy. We've always wanted children. I only wish your parents knew you were well."

Andrew nodded. "Before she died Mama said, 'God will take care of you.' He has."

John inquired, "Did you attend church in England?"

"Yes. We're Methodists."

John chuckled. "You've joined the right family. I'm a Methodist minister and Indian missionary."

"Really? Will we see real Indians?"

"We're on our way to an Indian camp. That's how we happened to be here this morning."

" 'Twas God's will," Marie murmured.

An hour later they started west toward Kalamazoo. Anne rode in front of Marie and Andrew sat behind John, his arms about John's waist.

"What a change a few hours can make," Marie breathed, "in all our lives. Now we're a family."

"Can we call you Mama and Papa?" Andrew asked.

Marie's voice caught. She wiped her eyes. "Of course you can, Son." John patted the boys hands that were clasped at his waist.

"Ever rode horseback before?" John asked.

"No, but I like it."

"Your legs will be sore, but soon you'll be used to it."

The next day at noon they sighted Pokagon's village near Hartford. Andrew was excited and a little fearful. "Will they—scalp us?" he asked.

John laughed. "They haven't scalped people in many

years."

"We heard in England that Indians were savages that shot arrows at people and then scalped them."

"No. No. Marie and I have been around Indians for years. See, we have our scalps."

Andrew giggled. John continued. "Marie's mother was an Indian, so Marie is half Indian, and she's never scalped anyone yet, have you Marie?"

Andrew whooped. Anne looked puzzled. She couldn't remember hearing her brother laugh so heartily. When Andrew caught his breath, he asked, "Will we see an Indian chief?"

"We'll see young Simon Pokagon. He's about twenty-five years old and an educated young man. His father, old Leopold Pokagon was a great chief. He died several years ago and young Simon is the tribe's leader." John continued, "They're of the Potawatomi tribe, and I might add, they're devout Roman Catholics."

Andrew said, "I never knew any Roman Catholics."

"Their religion differs a little from ours, but it doesn't matter. We're all going to Heaven if we live good lives."

Marie noted the neatness of the camp. Simon's ideas must be catching on. Children and dogs ran to meet them as they dismounted. Andrew limped, his muscles sore from riding.

A boy ran up to speak to him. "Your leg hurts?"

"A little. I never rode horseback before."

The Indian boy regarded him silently as though he was a being from another planet.

"Young fellow," John said, "Is Simon here?"

"Down there." The boy pointed to a bark shack a short distance away. Squaws, cooking over their campfires, watched.

Silently Marie compared Pokagon's attractive camp with the untidy one of Chief Okemos. But Pokagon was

young and he had attended school for several years. Okemos was old and unable to change his ways.

Anne held tightly to Marie's hand as they made their
way toward Pokagon's home. He met them at the door, a
slender young male dressed in white man's clothing.

"Come in," he said cordially. "You've brought guests."

John smiled, "These are our adopted children, Andrew
and Anne. Now we're a real family."

"That's as it should be. Someone to carry on your
name."

"You've not taken a squaw?" Marie asked.

"Not yet. I have time."

Simon went to the door and called to two children.
"Show Andrew and Anne our camp," he said. "Andrew
might like to hunt with your bow and arrow, Tom, and
Molly, show Anne your corn husk dolls."

When the children were gone the adults sat at Simon's
book-covered table to visit. "You've made great changes in
the camp, Simon, since I was here," John began.

"Some. We change slowly. Arthur J. Blackbird and I get
together to compare our progress. He says he sees improvement in his camp. The people bathe and their clothes
are washed more often—just like here. But they'd slip back
if we didn't keep after them. And the whiskey. It's a constant battle to keep it out of camp."

"Seems like you have about as many wigwams as when
we were here last."

"Indian population is decreasing, John. I read that the
Federal government estimates there may be six thousand
Indians in Michigan by 1860. Of course, we don't know how
many there were in 1830 before many tribes were moved
west. My father fought like a tiger for us to stay here. He
won out."

"How did he do it?"

"He got an exemption in the Treaty of 1833 that allowed our band to remain on the land which he had purchased from Cass County. There were 250 of us then. Later he got this land near Hartford and we made our homes here. This is where I was born. Someday I'm going to write a book about our band." [4, 5]

Marie commented, "It needs to be done. Though I'm half white I plainly see that the white man's success has been at the sacrifice of the Indian's homes. We were once a happy race."

Simon nodded. "Once our wigwams stood wherever we wished. There our young men and maidens, old men and their squaws, met around our council fires. But now the eagle's eye can find no trace of them. Here was the center of our hunting grounds; stretching far eastward, and to the great salt Gulf southward, and to the lofty Rocky Mountain chain westward, and all about and beyond the Great Lakes northward, roamed herds of buffalo while moose, deer and elk were found from ocean to ocean; pigeons, ducks and geese moved in great clouds through the air, while fish swarmed our streams. All were provided by the Great Spirit for our use. We destroyed none except for food and dress. We had plenty and were contented and happy."

Marie nodded agreement as Simon continued. "But alas! The pale faces came to our shores and many times they were needy and hungry. We nursed and fed them—fed the ravens that soon were to pluck out our eyes and the eyes of our children. Locust-like they came from the Old World and swarmed all over our coasts.

"The cyclone of civilization spread westward. Forests were swept away; streams dried up, and all our fathers once loved to gaze upon was destroyed, defaced or marred, except the sun, moon and starry skies above, which the Great Spirit hung beyond their reach.

"They say of us that we are treacherous, vindictive and cruel; in answer to the charge we declare to all the world that before the white man came among us we were kind, outspoken and forgiving. Our real character has been misunderstood because we resented the breaking of treaties made with the United States, as we honestly understood them." Simon sighed. He went on.

"We shall never be happy here anymore. We look into the faces of our little ones and into the faces of our young men and maidens, but alas! Instead of smiles of joy, we find looks of sadness." Simon stopped speaking and stared at the floor. [6]

John stood up. "You have summed up the situation beautifully, Simon. Chief Okemos said the same thing in a different way a few days ago. I agree with you in all you said."

Marie commented, "Be sure to write your book. You put words together so they sound like poetry."

The next day the Thompsons began the journey back to their Owosso home. When they arrived after being gone several weeks they found anti-slavery feelings were running high. Congress had passed the Kansas-Nebraska Bill, which repealed that part of the Missouri Compromise that had prohibited slavery north of the southern boundary of Missouri, except in Missouri itself. This bill opened the vast western area to slavery until the time when states carved from it were admitted to the Union; at that time each state would decide whether or not they wanted slavery. Passages of the Kansas-Nebraska Act brought violent protests throughout the North and Owosso was no exception. [7]

Many meetings were held and out of these meetings, the Republican Party was born. The *Owosso American* carried articles about the new political party. A call was sent out for a meeting to be held at Jackson on July 6, 1854. Fifteen hundred people appeared. The crowd was so great that no building in Jackson could accommodate it. As a result the speaker's stand was erected outside "under the oaks" near the corner of Franklin and Second Streets, and there the meeting was held. A platform was drawn up and adopted, and candidates for state offices in the fall election were nominated.

The Republican slate was headed by Kinsley S. Bingham who was nominated for governor. At the November election the entire Republican ticket emerged victorious. [8]

John and his friends were elated. They declared the victory was a turning point in Michigan poiltics for several reasons. Pros and cons were discussed.

John delcared, "Michigan will remain overwhelmingly Republican for many years."

"Why are you so sure?" Charles Parkhill asked.

"Because the Republican Party regards the anti-slavery movement as a crusade for righteousness. And the temperance and women's rights movements are disgusted with the Democrats' failure to pass favorable legislation."

"Yeah," Elias Comstock commented. "The Protestant churches, except for the Lutheran, are strongly Republican and many of the party leaders are Protestant ministers." And so the discussion continued.

In the 1850s railroad construction in Michigan continued. Besides the Michigan Central which ran from Detroit to Jackson, Battle Creek and Kalamazoo and then southwest to Chicago, the Michigan Southern ran from Toledo, through Adrian and eventually to Chicago. Both lines carried heavy traffic. A Chicago newspaper reported on June 29, 1854 that two thousand passengers had arrived on four trains of the Michigan Southern in a single day. [9]

The Ramshorn Railroad between Owosso and Lansing was built in 1858 and had about thirty miles of track. Many humorous names were given this railroad, one of them being "Almighty Long And Tremendous Bad Railroad," but the name which clung to it longest was Ramshorn Railroad. [10]

1856

2

Two years later in 1856 John and Marie no longer rode the trails but spent their days in Owosso with Andrew and Anne. The boy, who looked to John as his model, now did the heavy work about the home. He cut and split wood, gardened under Marie's direction and ran errands. Both children did well in school. Marie often said, "Every day I thank God for our children."

John walked with a cane. He was in constant pain from rheumatism in his back and legs. However, few days passed that he did not make his painful way the short distance to downtown Owosso.

The fall of 1856 was long remembered in the village of nine hundred inhabitants. Weeks of unusually dry weather left forests and grass lands tinder dry. Corn stood ripe and ready to cut. Pumpkins and winter squash showed bright orange and green in the corn rows. Apple tree branches hung heavy with fruit. Potato hills bulged with large potatoes waiting to be dug. Heads of cabbage and rows of carrots and onions in gardens were ready to be harvested.

Day after day of beautiful October sunshine worsened the drought. Rye and winter wheat which had been planted in September was showing green above the ground, but it was growing hardly at all. Lawns were as brown and parched as they sometimes are in August. Pasture in the fields was non-existent and cattle, horses and sheep grazed in the shady woods.

Everywhere in the village the conversation revolved around the unusual weather. Farmers worked to hand cut and shock their corn and to harvest the fruit and vegetables. Over and over they said, "This weather will break, and when it does we'll have a downpour. Better get everything in that we can."

Then it happened. Children coming home from school noticed smoke rising above the trees outside of town. Andrew and Anne mentioned the fact to John who hobbled outside to look.

"I don't like it," he said. "With everything tinder dry a fire would run through the woods faster than a horse could gallop." He shaded his eyes against the western sun. "Andrew," he said, "Run over to Comstock's and see what Elias thinks should be done."

A few minutes later they boy sped back. Panting, he exclaimed, "They're all going to beat the fire out. They're taking shovels, brooms, blankets—anything to beat the fire out. Some of the folks already are gone." He caught his breath, gazing to the southwest. "It's spreading! Papa, I'm going to help!" He ran to get a shovel.

Marie and Anne met him as he dashed into the street. "Be careful!" Marie warned.

John shouted, "Watch that you don't get trapped!" But Andrew already was gone.

Women, children and old men stood staring to the southwest. The streets were deserted for every able-bodied man and boy and some of the younger women and girls were fighting the fire.

A breeze began to blow from the west. "I pray it brings rain," Marie breathed. Instead the wind carried great clouds of smoke over the drought-stricken village.

Anne coughed. John said, "We may as well go into the house. 'Twill be easier to breathe there with the doors closed."

Inside they watched from the window. "Mama!" Anne shouted. "I see fire above the trees! Are we all going to burn up? Is the world burning up?"

Marie held the frightened child. "We'll be all right. See?

We can breathe better in here."

But Marie had doubts. Outside the smoke was so dense she couldn't see the house across the street. She worried about Andrew. He was only a child who didn't realize how easily one could become trapped in a forest fire. And this now was a full-fledged forest fire.

Though they couldn't see them through the dense smoke, John, Marie and Anne could hear animals in the streets. Cattle bawling, horses neighing and hogs squealing —all of them terror-stricken as their hooves beat an irregular tattoo on the hard-packed earthen streets, while they ran blindly to escape the wildfire behind them in the huge forest outside the village.

The smoke blotted out the evening sun, but blazing trees showed an angry red below the heavy black cloud of smoke.

Anne asked, "Papa, will the fire come here?"

"They will keep it away from the village," John said confidently.

"How?"

"They'll pound it out with shovels, brooms and blankets. They won't let it get into town."

"But it's hard to breathe," Anne gasped.

Marie soaked three towels at the kitchen sink. They each breathed through the damp towel. "That's better," the little girl said. "I wish Andrew had a towel."

At last it was night. They waited. Nine o'clock, ten o'clock. The blazing forest fire like an evil demon, crept on —and on. John went outside to the well for a pail of water. Gasping, he came inside and slammed the door.

"There's a dead animal lying beside the well," he said. " 'Tis big—either a cow or horse."

Anne drank from the family water dipper. She made a face. "It tastes like smoke!" she exclaimed.

Marie tasted the water. "Well—'tis wet."

Finally Andrew staggered through the front door. Even in the dim candle-lighted room they saw his exhaustion. He rushed to the water pail where he drank dippers-full of the smoky-tasting water.

Anne gave him her towel. "Breathe through this," she urged.

After a time he relaxed. John asked, "How is it out there?"

"Bad. They're keeping the fire out of town, but the woods all are burning. They say we may be surrounded with fire unless rain comes soon."

Marie fixed a ham sandwich which Andrew refused. "I'm not hungry, Mama. I'm going to rest a little while, then I'm going back to help."

"Better lie down, Son, while you can," John said.

"Yeah. Just a little while. There's dead animals in the street," he said, "and others are running around like they're crazy. I walked close to the fences to keep from being trampled."

An hour later after the family knelt in prayer, Andrew returned to fight the fire.

For more than a week the village of Owosso battled to keep from destruction. Business places and the schools were closed. Sick people suffered and some of the elderly died. The streets were filled with dead animals.

Even the food tasted smoky—apples, potatoes and all things edible were affected. It was a dismal time for the village of Owosso. But finally the prayed-for rains came and the weary firefighters returned to their smoke-blackened homes, thankful that they still had homes to return to. [11]

References

[1, 10, 11]Adele Ball, *Early History of Owosso* (Michigan Historical Society, 1944).

[2]Bernice M. Chappel, *Bittersweet Trail* (Great Lakes Books, 1984).

[3]Dorothea Petrie, *Orphan Train.*

[4, 7, 8, 9]Willis F. Dunbar, *Michigan* (William B. Eerdmans and Co., 1965).

[5, 6]*Detroit Magazine* (Chronicles), *Detroit Free Press,* November 3, 1985.

Chapter Twenty-Two
1857 — 1860

THE APPROACHING STORM

1 _____ **1857**

JOSEPHINE MADE HER WAY DOWN the winding forest path toward Crazy Sal's cabin. She glanced over her shoulder at the darkening western sky. The forest was still. No birds chirped. No insects sang. No leaves rustled.

The air had been hot all day but now in late afternoon it was heavy. It hung over the trees and pressed on Josephine's shoulders. She felt a vague uneasiness. Again she glanced over her shoulder. Through the trees she saw the clouds in the west piling on one another to form a ridge of mammoth white columns rearing high against the darkening sky. She quickened her pace. Crazy Sal's cabin was still some distance away.

The piercing whiteness of the western clouds soon changed to reveal their darker nature. They covered the late afternoon sun. A sudden gust of wind stirred the tree branches and sent dry leaves scurrying toward the east. Another glance over her shoulder told Josephine the storm was fast approaching. She ran down the path as thunder rumbled nearby.

The first drops of rain were huge. Leaves shuddered under their weight before rebounding to dump their load of water. At last, there was Crazy Sal's cabin. Josephine dashed inside without knocking.

"Crazy Sal!" she called. " 'Tis Josie!"

There was no answer. She found a match and candle. There was food on the table—Sal's supper. Why didn't she come in out of the storm?

The rhythm of the raindrops accelerated until the sound was like a roll of drums. Lightning stabbed the earth. Josephine jumped at the crack of thunder. The window panes rattled in their rickety frames. The next bolt raised the hair on the back of Josephine's neck. The rain now became a torrent which found its way through the old roof to drip, drip, drip on Sal's table and floor. The rising wind tossed tree branches about wildly. In the distance a tree crashed to the ground.

Where was Crazy Sal? Josie was uncomfortable. She should look for the old woman. Peering from the window she could see only a few feet beyond the cabin. Hailstones thumped and pounded on the roof. They bounced white against the ground and splashed in the puddles.

Gradually the storm began to pass. The sky lightened. Josie threw open the door and cool fresh air rushed inside. She breathed deeply as she stepped outside.

"Sal!" she shouted. "Crazy Sal!" There was only the gentle sound of water dripping on the ground from wet leaves. Picking her way through the damp forest Josie followed the path to Crazy Sal's garden. From a distance she noticed something, some sort of black bundle in the potato patch. She ran to investigate.

It was Crazy Sal stretched on her back between the hills of potatoes. She had her hoe beside her. Her eyes were half-open and stared at the sky. There was something final about the position. Josie knew at the first glance that Crazy Sal was dead.

The old woman wore her black dress. Her body lay like a hummock on the ground as though she already was part of the soil. Beside her was a rusty basin which held a few rain washed potatoes. Her hands were still on the handle of the hoe. They seemed only sinews and bones and the fingers stuck out like thin twigs. Poor Sal, she had been thin and scraggly for years. She seemed as small as a child. Her mouth was open, a toothless hole. The old caved-in face was brown but the whites of her eyes shone from the downpour of rain and her scraggly gray hair lay wet across her forehead. She seemed mainly a pile of old clothing, a heap of bundled up rags.

Josie bent to pick up the old body. She wasn't heavy —no heavier than a child. She carried Sal to her cabin and placed her on the bed.

Thoughts of the many years she had known Sal rushed through her mind. Twenty-seven years ago when she had first met her, Crazy Sal had seemed old. She recalled the old woman's wolf howls, her dislike for men, her strange superstitions and folk remedies for sickness. Cobwebs to stop bleeding! Josephine shuddered as she remembered her mother's death and Sal's determination to stop the hemorrhage by using cobwebs.

And Crazy Sal believed she could cast spells on people. She declared she had cast a spell on Henry Parker for something that he had done when they first came to Michigan, and that was the reason for his dual personality. Though Josie questioned her, Crazy Sal would only say, "I saved his life in a blizzard. That gives me the right to cast a spell on him to make him pay for his sins."

But Josephine knew what Sal had been talking about. After Henry's death Fred spoke with the family, including Hank. They were told of the affair between Henry and Nancy Farmer the winter of 1830-1831, of her leaving Michigan and of Hank's being brought to the Parker home after his mother's death. Fred had concluded by saying, "It's only right that Hank, and all of us, know he is our brother."

Josephine shook her head to clear her senses. There were things to do. Aunt Laura Haviland would be bringing slaves here to the shack later that evening. Crazy Sal's body would have to remain until the Negroes were transported to the next station.

Josephine decided against leaving a note—too dangerous. Aunt Laura would know what to do if they arrived early. She hurried home through the twilight.

While seventeen-year-old David was helping Hank with the evening chores, Josephine told Emily of Crazy Sal's death. She ended by saying, "We'll bury her tomorrow. We're the only people who ever went to see her."

"She was a strange woman," Emily said. "I've wondered what happened to make her that way."

"I think she was always crazy but we'll never know." Josephine went upstairs. When she returned fifteen minutes later, she spoke in a gruff voice. "How do I look?"

Emily eyed her critically. "In Hank's clothes no one would guess you were a woman. You even walk like a man."

"I've practiced. I didn't like cutting my hair, but since I have the switch, I can change from a man's hair style to a woman's in a jiffy."

"Being a conductor is dangerous business," Emily said. "You're more brave than I am."

"Pooh. Aunt Laura Haviland is the brave one. She goes into Kentucky sometimes to bring out slaves. The South has offered three thousand dollars for her capture, dead or alive."[1]

Emily agreed. "She's a brave lady. But I don't think she's well. She has a terrible cough. You think it's consumption?"

Josie shrugged. "She says she's had the cough for years and that it doesn't get worse." She pulled on one of Hank's hats. "I'm going now. Don't look for me until you see me. We'll walk through the fields and woods to the next station." She went out into the darkness.

2　　　　　　　*1859*

As THE FEELING AGAINST SLAVERY continued to rise in the North, certain names appeared repeatedly in the newspapers. Fred continued working as a reporter for the *Adrian Gazette* which now was known as the *Adrian Times*. He occasionally covered stories outside his area.

On August 27, 1856 he reported on the address by Abraham Lincoln at a meeting of the new Republican Party at Kalamazoo. The party was growing rapidly because of the strong anti-slavery feeling in Michigan.[2]

The people of the state liked what they knew of Lincoln. A man from a pioneer family, self-educated, who had volunteered for service in the Black Hawk War and been promptly elected captain, who was known for his honesty and friendliness, and his great physical strength and sportsmanship in wrestling matches, Lincoln quickly won the approval of Michigan people. They relished his humility and chuckled about his part in the Black Hawk War. He recalled that he served a total of ninety days and saw no fighting, but that he "had a good many bloody struggles with the mosquitoes."

The people of Michigan approved of Lincoln's long anti-slavery position. Since 1837 in the Illinois General Assembly where he first made a public statement, his convictions remained the same. At that time he said, "The institution of slavery is founded on both injustice and bad policy." Twenty-three years later he was nominated for president by the Republican Party. [3]

Fred's anti-slavery articles were influential in the Adrian area. Several times he had written about the radical activities of Abolitionist John Brown who had hated slavery from his youth. For years he helped slaves escape to Canada. In the East he organized a league among Negroes for their protection against slave catchers. [4]

John Brown's ruling passion was the abolition of slavery. The father of twenty children, he did various types of work and had several business ventures. He was unsuccessful as a business man. After living in Massachusetts and New York he moved to Kansas in 1855. There he led an expedition to Potawatomi Creek against a group of pro-slavery men who had burned the nearby town of Lawrence. At this encounter, his men brutally murdered five pro-slavery settlers.

Fred reported many of John Brown's activities. The man was a single-minded abolitionist who brooded about the evils of slavery. He became increasingly obsessed with the idea that God had chosen him to liberate the slaves by force. Fred told graphically of accounts he had gleaned from Chicago and Detroit newspapers. On December 20, 1858, John Brown and a group of his followers had entered the state of Missouri and rescued a slave family that was about to be sold, together with other slaves to a total number of fourteen. A plantation owner was killed. Immediately three thousand dollars was offered for Brown's capture.

During the winter of 1858-1859, John Brown and his followers brought the group of fourteen slaves on one of the longest trips of the Underground Railroad. Part of the journey was made in a freight car of the Chicago and Rock Island Railroad. The group arrived in Detroit on March 10, 1859, and two days later they were ferried across the Detroit River to Windsor, Ontario. [5]

Upon learning of Brown's arrival in Detroit, Fred went by stagecoach. He wished to hear Frederick Douglass, an escaped mulatto and a well known Negro abolitionist who also was in Detroit to lecture. A large group of reporters and anti-slavery people including John Brown were in the audience.

Frederick Douglass was born Frederick Agustus Washington Bailey, a slave in Maryland. He told of his life. At the age of eight he was sent to Baltimore to work for one of his master's relatives. There he was helped by his master's wife to educate himself.

In 1838 at the age of twenty-one he fled from his master and changed his name to Frederick Douglass. He held numerous jobs, among them collecting rubbish and digging cellars. In 1841 he spoke before the Massachusetts Antislavery Society who were so impressed that they hired him to lecture about his experiences as a slave. Over the years he continued lecturing. His home in Rochester, New York, was a station on the Underground Railroad. [6]

Armed with extensive notes, Fred attended an anti-slavery meeting in Detroit after Douglass' lecture. John Brown was at the house on the corner of St. Antoine and Congress Streeets. It was there that a raid on the South at Harper's Ferry was discussed.

Fred was impressed with Brown's fiery impulsive nature, but he felt the man was so radical that he bordered on being an outlaw. However he received sympathy and aid.

Somewhat confused, Fred returned to Adrian the following day. Seven months later on October 16, 1859, Brown and eighteen followers captured the arsenal at Harper's Ferry in western Virginia, but they failed to escape.

The next day, Brown with his dead, wounded and a few prisoners, was bottled up by the local militia. Colonel Robert E. Lee forced the fort open on October 18 and delivered Brown to the state for trial. He and several followers were convicted on charges of treason and hanged on December 2.[7]

1860

3

Emily and Josephine bustled about the kitchen preparing a Christmas feast for the Parker family. This would be the first time they had all been together in some time. Beside the original family members there now were new wives and children. There was hilarity and horseplay causing Jimmy's and Owasco's two-year-old twin boys, Dan and Sam, to view the gathering with trepidation.

Hank, who sat beside his wife-to-be, Sarah Ellis, was fending off jokes about approaching matrimony. Fred, a bachelor at age forty-three, was the leader in the banter.

"Sarah told me about your marriage proposal, Hank," Fred said. "She had already refused you several times, but to let you down easy, she said, 'I'll always have a soft spot in my heart for you.' Then you said, 'Well, let's get married!' And Sarah replied, 'I said a soft spot in my heart, not in my head.' "

Sarah, a tall willowy brunette, joined in the joke. "He did ask me more than once."

"You'll be sorry you married him," Fred continued. "He'll make you work in the fields like he does Josephine. Just put your foot down and refuse, Sarah."

Hank grinned. "For an old bachelor you're pretty good at giving women advice. You're jealous of my good luck in finding Sarah."

Fred laughed. "I'd make a poor husband. Reporters' hours are uncertain. That doesn't make for a good marriage."

Jimmy entered the conversation. "Owasco and I planned to marry from the time we were children. We grew up together in our tribe. But Josephine, how about you? Aren't you going to marry?"

"Nope."

"What you waiting for?" Fred asked. "You've had plenty of chances."

Josephine replaced a loose hairpin in her switch. She grinned. "Know who I'm waiting for?"

"Who?" several voices asked at once.

"Jake."

"Come on," Fred objected humorously. "Jake's been gone for twenty years! He's found himself a squaw long before this."

Josephine shrugged. "We did have fun growing up together—wandering in the woods and fishing and climbing trees. 'Twas a nice childhood." She paused, then continued in a serious vein. "And now I have work to do helping Aunt Laura Haviland."

For a time no one spoke. Then Josephine continued, "Emily deserves a vote of thanks from this family."

Emily flushed. "I've never done anything but keep house."

Hank replied, "You've held the Parkers together. You've been a mother to us since Mama died, and David has never known another mother. You've brought him up."

He patted David's shoulder. "And you've done a good job, Emily. He's my right-hand man on the farm, aren't you David?"

The blonde, blue-eyed twenty year old smiled shyly. "Yeah, Hank."

The twins, Dan and Sam, ran to the window. "Out doors," Dan said, pointing.

"Wait until after dinner," Emily suggested. "We're going to have a good Christmas dinner soon."

"What do you hear from Uncle John's family?" Fred asked Emily.

"The orphan children are growing up. Andrew's sixteen and Anne is nine. I invited them to come to spend a few days with us but Uncle John hardly gets around at all anymore, his rheumatism is so bad. Aunt Marie is all right. 'Twas a lucky day for all of them when they found one another on the Orphan Train. Uncle John and Aunt Marie adore those children."

After dinner while the women did the dishes, the brothers discussed politics. David listened, but his facial expression revealed his lack of understanding.

Hank asked, "What do you think Lincoln's chances are of holding the Union together?"

"Poor," Fred answered. "He's a good man but his statement that 'a house divided against itself cannot endure permanently, half slave and half free' doesn't sound promising for the Union."

"Yeah," Hank agreed. "We have eighteen free states and fifteen slave states. There are three sections of the country and each one has a different type of economy; in the Northeast, it's industry and finance; the South relies on farming—crops like tobacco, cotton and sugar; the West also relies on farming but they sell their crops to the Northeast, while the South exports to Europe."[8]

Jimmy, the usually quiet brother, said, "We're like a

three horse team with each horse trying to go in a different direction. I don't know what might happen. South Carolina already has seceded from the Union, and other states are threatening."

Fred remarked, "Things don't look good. Harriet Beecher Stowe's novel, *Uncle Tom's Cabin* has had a strong anti-slavery effect in the North. Feelings are running high in both the North and the South." He lowered his voice. "What do you think of Josie's activity in the Underground Railroad?"

" 'Tis dangerous," Hank replied softly, "but she's adventurous and she and Aunt Laura Haviland are quite a pair. You should see Josie when she's dressed like a man. She takes long strides and swaggers around with a big cigar stuck in her mouth." He chuckled.

David spoke softly, "I hope they don't get caught. What would they do with them if they did?"

Fred shook his head. "There's a three thousand dollar reward out for Laura. The south has a three thousand dollar reward out for Frederick Douglass, too, and many others who are helping Negroes escape."

"Yeah," David said. "But what would they do with Josie if they caught her?"

" 'Tis hard to say. A long jail term and a big fine—at the very least." Fred spoke softly but forcefully as he looked into David's eyes. "We must not speak to anyone outside the family of what Josie is doing. Understand?" David nodded.

Later that afternoon a few Christmas gifts were distributed. Hand made aprons, knit mittens, socks and sweaters and two handmade sleds for the twins were given out as the Parker house rang with shouts of merriment.

Little did they know this would be the last time the entire family would be together for a long time.

References ————————————————

[1, 5]Ferris E. Lewis, *Michigan Yesterday and Today* (Hillsdale Educational Publishers, 1956).

[2]*Early Adrian* (American Association of University Women).

[3, 8]*World Book Encyclopedia,* L Book *(See* "Lincoln, Abraham").

[4, 7]*World Book Encyclopedia,* B Book *(See* "Brown, John").

[6]*World Book Encyclopedia,* D Book *(See* "Douglass, Frederick").

Chapter Twenty-Three
1861

DANGEROUS ASSIGNMENTS

1

LAURA HAVILAND AND JOSEPHINE huddled in Crazy Sal's old cabin. Though they were alone, they spoke in whispers. Laura, dressed in her dark Quaker clothing with a white bonnet, took a folded paper from her pocket. "Read this," she breathed.

It was a clipping from a Cincinnati newspaper and it began as all such did:

> *Ran away from subscriber on Monday, April 1, my man servant Sam, and my woman servant Jessie. Both are about twenty-five years old.*
>
> *Sam is six feet tall, bright gingerbread color and has a dour look. When spoken to he replies in a surly manner. Brand S on both legs. Recently cobbed for disrespect.*

> *Sam is believed to be travelling with his wife Jessie who is dark chestnut color, medium height. Large scar on right arm. Soft-spoken speech.*
>
> *I will give the following reward for them if taken out of the state and lodged where I can get them again, or if taken in Kentucky: $500 for the two or $250 for either alone.*
>
> *Thomas Perry*

Josie passed the clipping back to Laura. "You have a plan?" she whispered.

" 'Tis too late for Sam and Jessie. The marshall in Dayton jailed the runaway couple."

"Are they still in jail?"

"No. The owner's agents picked them up. Started back to Kentucky with them. Chained to the axle of his buggy."

"Not Jessie!"

"Josie," Laura said softly, "Southern gentlemen take slave women into their beds but they don't sit with them on the front seats of their buggies."

"But chained. Didn't they have to run to keep up?"

Laura nodded. "When last seen they were running."

"How'd they come to get caught?"

"They were hiding out in a big woods and had run out of food. Jessie was half sick so Sam tried to steal something. He was caught, didn't have any free papers, so he was put in jail."

"How'd they get Jessie?"

"Sam told them where she was."

Josie was shocked. "Why?"

"He had some persuasion. Besides Jessie was going to starve to death if she didn't freeze first lying out there in the cold rain."

"What a shame they were caught."

"There are stations in Dayton but they didn't know where they were."

Josephine sighed. "It makes me sick to think what happened when the owner got them back."

Laura shook her head. "It's not nice to think of Sam and Jessie having their backs laid open by a whip." She paused. "And I've had reports of turpentine being poured into wounds after a whipping."

Josie shuddered. After a long pause she asked, "What does cobbed mean?"

"It means Sam had been beaten with a club."

Josephine sighed. "Laura, I want to do more to help those people."

The older woman nodded. The cabin was hushed as she hesitated. A cardinal whistled in a nearby pine. Finally she said in a soft whisper, "I have information that a family, a man, his wife and child will be on the *Mississippi Miss* packet boat due to arrive in Cincinnati on April 6. They'll be nailed inside two wooden boxes marked as furniture and addressed to Mr. Benjamin Baxter."

"He's from Tecumseh."

"That's right. But he's sick with lung fever. He can't make the trip to pick up the merchandise and get it transferred to the train to Toledo."

"How long will those people be nailed inside the boxes?"

"Two or three days. They'll each have a little bread and a flask of water."

"How old is the child?"

"A few months. It will be given laudanum to keep it quiet." She hesitated. "Since Ben can't go, I need a man to go with me to Cincinnati. I thought about you."

Without a seconds hesitation, Josie replied, "I'll do it."

"We'll be disguised as husband and wife, Mr. and Mrs.

Joe Parks. We'll be picking up two crates of family heirloom furniture at Cincinnati where we'll have it transferred to the freight car of the train to Toledo. We'll ride the train. When we get there we'll be met by a conductor named Frank. He will have a wagon and will take the crate to a nearby station. Our job will be done then."

"Sounds like a good plan."

"I hope so. There's no room for error in this business. You should borrow Hank's best suit. We must look like a prosperous couple."

"Will you wear Quaker clothes?"

"Heaven forbid! I'll be the moneyed Mrs. Joe Parks from Toledo!" she smiled.

"What are the names of the family?" Josie asked.

"We only know their first names. Tom and Rose, and the baby is a boy. They are a young married couple—in the only way slaves can be married in the South. They live together."

"Do you know anything about them?"

"Only that Rose is very light, almost white. She is the daughter of the slaveowner who has recently remarried. His new wife refuses to have Rose on the property so she and her baby were to have been sold at the next auction. It was then they decided to try to escape."

"They must have had help," Josie commented.

Laura nodded. "I have Quaker Friends in Newport, Indiana. 'Tis on the Ohio-Indiana border. Levi and Catherine Coffin have helped hundreds of slaves escape. Levi grew up in North Carolina and as a child he saw a man chained, whipped and driven to market. He realized how he would feel if his father was abducted. After he and Catherine married they moved north and started a crossroads store at Newport. They sleep many escaping Negroes at their station. Levi was responsible for shipping Tom and Rose and the baby as furniture on the *Mississippi Miss.*"[1]

Josie commented, "He has an Underground Railroad station and he's also a conductor. I thought that was risky."

"It is. That's the reason I don't take escaping Negroes to the Raisin Institute. I'm only a conductor, though southern agents have searched the Institute several times. It also is the reason I don't want your brother Jim and Owasco involved. They keep things running smoothly at the Institute and I feel comfortable knowing they are in charge."

Josie stood up. "When do we start for Cincinnati?"

"Tomorrow. We'll drive to Toledo, two ladies on a shopping trip. You take Hank's clothes in a grip. We'll put my horse in the livery stable at Toledo until we return. You'll change to Hank's clothing before we board the train for Cincinnati. And don't tell anyone where we're going —just tell your family you will be away for a few days. I'll come by to pick you up early tomorrow morning."

The friends left Crazy Sal's cabin separately, half an hour apart. As Josie walked home her mind was filled with thoughts of the first of many dangerous assignments in which she would take part in the near future.

2 ——————————— *1861*

Laura and Josie had taken a room in a hotel near the docks on the Ohio River. The *Mississippi Miss* was late. Their thoughts were of the little family who were imprisoned in hot crates on the deck of the steamboat. By midday the steamer still had not arrived.

Periodically, Josephine dressed in Hank's clothes, with a huge black cigar between her teeth, swaggered along the waterfront. Timothy, the liveryman conductor, lived within sight of the docks. He would be waiting when the *Missis-*

sippi Miss docked, to transport the crates to the train depot.

Josephine gnawed on her cigar. The train was due to leave at three o'clock. If the boxes were not on board, Tom, Rose and the baby would have to remain in the crates until the middle of the night when the next Toledo train arrived. Finally at half-past one the steamboat came into sight.

Liverymen suddenly appeared with their drays and wagons. Josephine went through the motions of bargaining with Timothy for a suitable charge for his services. Loudly she exclaimed in a gutteral voice, "I'll give you a dollar and not another cent! 'Tis only two crates of furniture, Man!"

Timothy appeared ready to move on when he turned. "You drive a hard bargain, Sir—but I'll do it though 'tis worth more. I'm to look for crates addressed to what person?"

"Benjamin Baxter. I'll help you find them."

When the steamboat docked there was great confusion. Livery men with crates and passengers carrying luggage filled the gangplank. Josephine followed Timothy who quickly located the crates.

"Here!" she exclaimed, shifting her cigar to the corner of her mouth. "Don't drop those crates! I don't want the furniture marred. Let me help you!" Together they loaded the boxes onto Timothy's cart.

"My wife and I will meet you at the depot," Josephine said as she turned toward the hotel where Laura waited. Fifteen minutes later they found Timothy standing beside the train at the station.

At last the crates were loaded in the baggage section and Mr. and Mrs. Joe Parks took seats in the passenger car. A few short blasts from the locomotive whistle, the driving wheels slipped, grabbed and slipped again while the engine of the locomotive pounded. A few more blasts of the whistle and the train of cars gained momentum until it was rolling smoothly around a curve and out of town. A sudden breeze whipped through an open window and a cloud of cinder-laden smoke engulfed the passengers.

"Mercy!" Laura gasped. "Joe! Shut the window!"

Josephine silently obliged as Laura grumbled about the discomforts of traveling. She finally ended with, "A lady might better stay home than to go through such trials. Joe, look at my new traveling dress—it's covered with cinders and smoke."

"Yes, dear," Josie murmured. "I'm sorry."

They sat back listening to the clickety-clack of the wheels. There were many empty seats. Some of the men soon were sleeping, their heads against the high-backed seats. The whistle had a mournful sound.

Later as Laura and Josie ate the box lunch packed for them at the Cincinnati hotel, each one thought of the little family in the baggage car. Already they had been imprisoned in the crates for more than thirty-six hours. And the baby—how long could a small infant safely be sedated with laudanum? Impatiently they waited, each silently wondering what they would find when the crates were opened.

The train made numerous stops. Josie's heart lurched as she visualized a sleepy employee putting the boxes off at the wrong station and at their arrival in Toledo—what would they do if the boxes were gone? They'd have no idea where the crates had been left.

She shook her head. She had been dreaming. Of course the family was safe back there in their boxes. Finally morning came and the train screeched and roared to a stop in Toledo.

"Joe," Laura fretted, "don't forget your coat. And hand me my shawl. I have to cover up my soiled dress."

They got out and walked along the side of the train to the baggage car. The doors were open. A wagon and driver waited. Josie spoke softly to the man. "Frank, will you deliver our furniture for us?"

The man tipped his hat. "Yes sir. What is the address?"

"Four forty-five Washington Street." The driver nodded agreement. Josie jumped into the freight car. "Let me help you. My wife is very fidgety about how we handle this furniture."

When the crates were loaded Frank whispered, "Hire the driver with the white horse to take you to the Washington Street address."

Half an hour later the crates were unloaded in Frank's kitchen. His wife had coffee brewing and the table was set.

"We'll eat soon's we get them out," the woman said to Laura.

Already Frank and Josie were prying the crates open with claw hammers. As soon as a board was off a black face peered out. "Just leave me. Get Rose and the baby out."

They began work on the second crate. A minute or two later they peered inside. The worried face of a nearly-white woman blinked in the bright light. "Take my baby," she whispered. "I'm afeard he's dead."

Laura seized the child. The tiny body was cold and stiff. She bit her lip. "The little one didn't make it," she said softly. "We're so sorry."

Tears streamed down Rose's cheeks as they helped her from the crate. Tom and his wife wept in each others arms.

"He didn't have a chance," Rose sobbed. "The smoke—he couldn't breathe. I knew he was choking and I held my hand over his mouth so no one would hear. Oh God, maybe I smothered him."

Frank asked, "They smoked the *Mississippi Miss?*"

Tom nodded. "All the baggage. I almost couldn't stand it. I was afeard Rose and the baby both would be dead from the smoke."

Rose clasped her dead baby and rocked him in her arms. There wasn't a dry eye in the kitchen. Frank's wife brought a rocker. "Sit here," she said. "I wish we could do something."

After a time, plans were completed. Frank and his wife would bury the baby in their back yard at night after he delivered Tom and Rose to the next station on their way to Canada.

Josie changed from Hank's clothes to her own. She and Laura went to the livery stable and soon were on the road to Adrian. Their mission was completed.

3 ———————————————— *1861*

WAR! APRIL 12, 1861. FRED glanced at the three-inch black headlines of the *Detroit Free Press*. It had happened. Confederate troops had attacked Fort Sumpter. The North and South were at war. He felt a terrible depression. Already seven states had seceded from the Union; South Carolina, Mississippi, Florida, Alabama, Georgia, Louisiana and Texas. Jefferson Davis was president of the Confederacy.

Three days later newspaper headlines screamed, LINCOLN ISSUES A CALL FOR TROOPS. The story said that hopefully the insurrection would be over in a few weeks for the North thought the South couldn't hold out long. Johnny Reb would soon find he was no match for the Yanks, the article boasted, and that it should all be over by the middle of July.

But by the middle of summer people in the North were disappointed that the fighting was becoming more intensive. They began to see the war stretching on into the future. Johnny Reb in his gray uniform and Billy Yank in blue, fought well, but both remained civilians at heart with civilians' dislike of military rules and regulations. However, each side fought valiantly for their beliefs. At first the North was fighting to save the Union, and freedom for slaves became an issue at a later time.

The South, with Jefferson Davis as President of the Confederacy, did not have the powerful central government of the North with Lincoln as President. Still, the South was determined to be independent of the North.

Fred was dissatisfied with his work as an Adrian reporter. At forty-four years of age he was too old for active service in the army, but he felt he could be in the thick of things as a news correspondent. A few days later he bade the family goodbye and the next day he was headed for the Northern front.

Other than Fred's absence, life continued much as before for the Parkers. Hank and his wife Sarah had built a house a few rods from the old homestead. Hank and David worked the Parker farm and Jim and Owasco continued as managers of the Haviland land and Institute. Emily remained the efficient housekeeper and Josephine was active as a conductor in the Underground Railroad.

Laura Haviland often was gone for days at a time escorting slaves to freedom. Josephine took over Laura's responsibility in the Underground Railroad when the older woman was in the South. She enjoyed the thrill of danger and upon returning from each successful trip, she felt a surge of confidence and elation. She continued using Crazy Sal's cabin as a temporary hideout for escapees. Hank had purchased one hundred acres of the woodlot where the tumble-down shack was located, and because Josephine went there only at night with the slaves, they had not been discovered by southern agents who often appeared in Adrian.

It was a sultry hot afternoon in haying season when Amos Davis from west of Blissfield drove in at the Parkers.

Josie went outside to talk to him. He mopped his head with a red bandanna and replaced his tattered straw hat.

"Josie," he began. "I have a shipment to deliver to you tonight."

"How many?"

"Six. They're at my place now."

"Hm-m-m."

"Can you handle that many?"

"I'll handle them."

"Where you want me to leave them.?"

"I'll meet you on this side of the river near the bridge. There's woods there and it's dark with trees on both sides. You know where I mean?"

"I know. I'll try to be there around eleven."

"We'll use the screech owl signal," Josie said. "Three screeches and I'll know you're there. If I answer with three screeches, it means we'll make the exchange. If I don't answer, stay hidden."

As he drove away Josie noticed how Amos was aging. Though the Parkers had never been close friends with the Davis family, she recalled that only a few years earlier he had been a vigorous physical man. Today he appeared frail.

They must plan fast, Josie thought as Amos drove away. She ran to the barn where Hank and David were unloading hay. She told them of the plans.

"I'm worried about taking them to Crazy Sal's cabin. We're using it too often. Someone's going to catch on."

"Put 'em in a load of hay," David said.

"They'd smother," Hank explained.

"Yeah," Josie said slowly, "But we could build a box big enough for six people to sit inside and then bury it in a load of hay near the top where air could get through the cracks. Did you say there is sale for clover hay, Hank?"

"Yep. Many of the farmers have gone to growing hops and they're short of good hay. Addison Comstock mentioned to me last week that he'll have to buy hay."

"Good. We'll deliver him a load of clover tomorrow." Josie thought a moment. "After the box is ready you could take it to the hayfield near the river. Bury it in the load of hay so only the top is exposed. Then leave the loaded wagon there all night."

A hissing rattling sound came from a pile of hay on the barn floor. "Rattler!" Hank exclaimed as he seized a shovel. "Stand back!"

David with a pitchfork sifted the hay until the flat head with the darting red forked tongue of the rattlesnake appeared. Two sharp blows with the edge of the shovel and the snake writhed as it continued shaking the rattles in its death throes.

Hank tossed the dead snake into the barnyard. "How many does that make, David?"

"Ten. There's a lot of them this year."

By half past nine Josie was dressed in David's clothing. She walked along the Raisin River to the place she was to meet Amos Davis and the escapees. Concealing herself in a thicket, she waited.

Crickets chirped merrily in the warm night air. A cowbell tinkled in the woods nearby. A dog barked. Bullfrogs croaked in the river. Josie smiled as she recalled that in childhood she and Jake believed the bullfrogs said *Better go round! Better go round!*

She waited. A horse and buggy crossed the bridge. The clop, clop of the horse's hooves meant he was trotting. Few people were out this late on a dark night. Perhaps some young man had been courting. She settled down to wait for the signal. She knew every inch of the river from the bridge to far beyond the Parker farm. She and Jake had explored it many times. Where was Jake? Perhaps he had gone west to try to find his tribe. But why hadn't he written to her? She had taught him to read and write—he could at least have let her know where he was.

A pebble fell from the bridge causing a splash in the water. Something had moved on the bridge to knock it off. An animal? She listened. There was only the summer night sounds. Time passed slowly. Surely it must be eleven o'clock.

At last the plaintive call of the screech owl drifted through the night air. Every muscle tense, she listened. There was the second call, and a few seconds later, the third. This was it. They were here. Three times she answered the mournful cry of the screech owl before she silently emerged from the thicket. Shadowy figures were crossing the bridge toward her. She reached out. "Take hold of hands," she whispered. "Hang on."

Suddenly a heavy voice shouted, "Halt! In the name of the law, halt!"

Amos Davis yelled, "Run!"

"Halt! You niggers, halt!" the southern agent shouted.

Josie grasped a hand and pulling the escapees behind her, she disappeared into the thicket beside the river. They could hear shouting and commotion on the bridge, but the Negroes followed her lead. It was very dark but Josie kept her sense of direction. There it was, the old dugout in the bank that she and Jake had shored up with boards. She pushed the Negroes inside, counting. They were all there. She crawled in last. A bullfrog croaked *Better go round!*

Crowded together, they scarcely breathed as Amos and the agent fought on the bridge. The sounds of fists striking flesh and of grunts and groans reached the listeners. There was a splash followed by silence.

For hours they sat without moving. Where was the agent? Was he waiting nearby to pounce on them when they emerged? Josie wondered about Amos. He was so frail. She hoped he had escaped.

Finally she crawled outside. She must get the people to

the hay wagon and inside the box while it still was dark. She listened. Reaching inside, she took a hand. "Come," she whispered.

They walked slowly, planting their feet cautiously. With every step they expected to be challenged by the southern agent. Finally they reached the hayfield. There under a tree near the river was the shadowy outline of a loaded hay wagon.

Josie whispered the plans to the six slaves. She ended by saying, "There's food and water inside the box. Stay hidden. You'll be taken to the next station." After they were inside the box she put the cover on and lightly spread hay over it.

Climbing down from the wagon Josie hurried to the house. She hadn't seen one of the faces of the people she had hidden. She didn't know how many were women. It didn't matter.

Emily met her at the door. Quickly Josie related the night's events. Emily breathed, "Get rid of those clothes and into your nightgown."

By seven o'clock they were at the breakfast table. David finished his coffee and was leaving to join Hank who was harnessing the team. He shaded his eyes against the early morning sun. "There's somebody coming," he said.

A horse and buggy turned in. A large man held the reins. "This the Parker place?" he asked.

Josie's heart pounded. That voice—it was the southern agent who had been at the bridge!

"This is the Parker place," David answered. Hank was driving the team toward the house.

"Something we can do for you?" he asked.

The man got down from the buggy. "I'd like to search your buildings."

"What for?"

"Six slaves escaped near here last night. Maybe they're in your house or barn."

Hank laughed. "I doubt it. Do you have a search warrant?"

The red-faced man sneered. " 'Course I do. I know you nigger lovers."

"What's that supposed to mean?"

"It means I know you northerners would hide our property so we'd never find them niggers without a search warrant." He handed a paper to Hank who scanned it quickly.

"All right. Looks like things are in order. Go ahead."

"I'll search the barn too."

"Take your time. My brother and I have to get to the hayfield. Looks like rain and we have clover to get up." He turned to David and winked as they started for the field.

The agent searched the house thoroughly. Glumly he went toward the barn. Josie called, "Better be careful out there! That new hay is full of rattlesnakes!"

A few minutes later the man drove away without returning to the house. After a short time Hank, with the load of hay, started for the Comstock farm. Emily and Josie breathed a sigh of relief.

"Addison has a hidden room under his barn," Josephine said. "He'll keep them there until it's safe to go to the next station—might be several days before the agent leaves town."

In a moment she continued. "It's 1861. When we came here in 1830, Addison Comstock and Amos Davis were young men. Now they're old. Their hair is white and their bodies frail, but still they're carrying on the fight against slavery."

Emily smiled. "We're older, too."

"I'm worried about Amos. I didn't dare go back to the bridge when that agent was here but we could go now. Will you go with me?"

Josie hitched the horse to the buggy and they drove to-

ward the bridge. While Emily held the reins, Josie went
down the bank. At first everything seemed normal, but a
sound from behind startled her.

Amos lay under the bridge, his white hair matted with
blood, his face bruised and purple and with both eyes
swollen shut.

"Amos! 'Tis Josie. We'll take you home! What has he
done to you?" She raised the old man to a sitting position.
"Can you walk if I steady you?"

"I—I think so." With help he struggled to his feet. Together Emily and Josie got the injured man into the buggy.
A short time later they delivered him into his wife's care.

4 ——————————— *1861*

H ANK SAT ATOP OF THE HIGH LOAD
of clover hay. The July sun was warm on his back. He
clucked to the horses. "Get up, Major! Get up, Molly! We
got to shag right along to get this load delivered." As they
passed neighboring farmers he waved or shouted a greeting.
When there were woods on both sides he leaned over the
crate. "All right in there?" he whispered.

"We's all right," a whispered voice replied.

Passing down Adrian's main street Hank recognized the
horse and buggy of the agent who had searched the Parker
buildings. He came out of the jail and hesitated as he saw
Hank who waved. "Any luck?" he called.

The man turned his back without replying and untied
his horse from the hitching post.

Hank was worried. The agent was smart in tricks used
on the Underground Railroad. Was he suspicious? He drove
on. Glancing back, he saw the horse and buggy close be-

hind. Hank appeared nonchalant as he whistled a tune. It must be unbearably hot inside the crate. Outside of town the agent still followed.

The sun was high at noon. Addison Comstock might be in the house for dinner. Hank hoped he'd know how to handle the situation. He drove in at the Comstock place.

Addison came to the door. "You're just in time, Hank. Dinner's still on the table. Will you have a bite?"

Hank climbed down. "I think I will. Where should I put the team and hay?"

"I'll put them on the barn floor. Just go in while dinner is hot." He turned as though he was surprised at the sight of the agent behind Hank's wagon.

"Mr. Adams! I thought you'd left Adrian!"

"Nope. I want to look around your place again. Search warrant's still good."

"Go ahead. "You've been here before. Want to start with the house or the barn?"

"I'll do both of them."

Addison pushed back his white hair. "There's plenty of victuals. Set up and eat with Hank first."

"Thanks." He and Hank went inside together.

Addison led the team into the barn where he climbed up the front standard to the top of the load. Quickly he lifted the box top and the six slaves, four men and two women, emerged. He motioned to them to climb down. Grabbing a pitchfork, he moved a pile of hay to reveal a trap door.

"Get inside!" he ordered. They disappeared into the dark hole. A minute later the door was closed and loose hay again covered it.

Though he was old Addison moved quickly to the top of the load where he tossed the crate and its cover on top of the hay-covered door. He stopped to wipe perspiration from his face. Then he proceeded at a leisurely pace to pitch clover hay into the near empty mow.

Hank and Agent Adams came toward the barn. "You've finished dinner so soon?" Comstock asked.

"Thought I'd watch you unload. Never can tell what you might find in a load of hay," Adams replied.

"That's right," Hank said as he observed the empty crate on the floor. "Watch out for rattlesnakes, Addison. The hay's full of them this year."

The agent's eyes took in the scene at a glance. "What's that crate for?"

Hank laughed. "You're a suspicious man, Mr. Adams. As long as I was coming here with the hay I planned to pick up a sow I bargained for a few weeks ago." He turned to look up at Comstock. "Still want to sell her?"

"Yeah, we'll get her in the crate soon's the hay's unloaded."

Hank climbed up with a pitchfork to help Comstock. Adams strolled about poking into every nook and cranny. Finally he climbed into the haymow as Hank yelled, "Watch out! There's a rattler in that last forkful!"

The agent scrambled back to the barn floor. Hank winked at Comstock as their eyes met. "I've never seen as many snakes as there are around here this year, have you Addison?"

"They're thick. Did you hear about Butler's hired man?"

"No."

"One bit him on the leg. Before he could get to the house his leg was swollen and purple. Mrs. Butler cut the leg open above the bite and tried to suck out the venom, but it already was in his blood. He got sick to his stomach and was too weak to stand. His heart pounded so they could see his chest throb."

Adams asked, "Did he die?"

"No, but it was nip and tuck for a few days."

The agent stood close to the door. At last he said, "I'll go have a look at the house while I'm here."

Addison nodded. "You know the place. My wife is in the garden, but help yourself."

Ten minutes later Agent Adams drove away. While Hank continued unloading hay and watching the road, Addison pried open the trap door. "Are you all right?" he whispered.

"We is fine," a gruff voice from below answered softly.

"I'll get food and water, then when it's safe we'll move you to the next station." He closed the door and stuffed hay over it.

Hank said softly, "Guess I'd better take a sow back with me. If Adams saw me go through town with an empty crate, he'd be back in a hurry."

"Yeah. We fooled 'em again, Hank." The old man started for the house.

References ————————————————————

[1]*National Geographic Magazine* (July, 1984), p. 17.

Chapter Twenty-Four
1862 — 1866

THE WHEELS OF WAR

1862

1 ————————————————————

F<small>RED</small> <small>ARRIVED IN</small> W<small>ASHINGTON</small>
the morning of July 21, 1861. Federal and Confederate
troops were reported in battle positions near Manassas
about twenty-eight miles to the west in Virginia. Washington was in a state of elated anticipation. Many prominent
citizens were driving in carriages to an observation point
about six miles from where the troops were positioned.
They expected to see the defeat of the Confederate troops.
It was to be a gala day.

Picnic baskets were packed and excited ladies who accompanied their male escorts giggled as they climbed into
carriages and drove in a long procession toward the west.
First they passed through the hamlet of Centreville; three
miles southwest trickled the waters of Bull Run, and several miles beyond the stream sat Manassas Junction.

On his rented horse Fred carried only his reporter's

pad, a gallon of water and a few ham sandwiches. As he passed the merrymakers he marveled at their gaiety. Most of them must have relatives or friends among the Union troops. There were young people, middle-aged couples and even a few gray-haired ladies and gentlemen in the procession.

The day was humid, sultry and hot. In passing buggies and carriages, Fred noticed ladies in cool-looking dresses and bonnets daintily waving lacy fans. He thought of the soldiers a short distance away in hot uniforms who were waiting for the battle to begin. Didn't these people realize that war was no picnic?

They congregated near the little town of Centreville. The holidaying throng crowded streets and clogged the road. Soon in the distance they could hear the rumble of cannon and the faint firecracker roll of musket fire, but they were too far away to see the flashes. They leisurely ate their lunch and cheered when riders dashed back from the front with good news. A Union victory seemed near.

Fred continued on toward the front. As he drew closer the cacophony of battle became a continual discordant din. Smoke and flashes were combined with the roar of cannon and the cracking fire of hundreds of muskets. Finally, there they were—the blue-uniformed men facing those in gray. From his vantage point he saw man after man go down, but still the Union line held.

A fresh Rebel brigade threw itself at the Federal right flank with bloodcurdling screams. It crumbled. The Rebel General Beauregard and General Stonewall Jackson renewed the attack along the entire line. The Yanks began falling back. Under the pounding of artillery fire a dispiriting sense of failure seemed to engulf the men in blue.

Seizing their advantage the Rebel cavalry, sabers held high, screamed as they rushed on. The Northern retreat turned into a rout. The Union General Irwin McDowell ordered his troops to regroup at Centreville, though Fred was not aware of this fact until later.

Panic-stricken, the men in blue crashed through Centreville and the civilian picnickers plunged into the crush. They raced in headlong flight for Washington. An afternoon shower pelted rain on a hurly-burly of careening carriages, army supply wagons and exhausted, wounded, staggering men. Panic filled the mind of every Union soldier and sympathizer. Surely Beauregard now would invade Washington!

Riding as fast as he could through and around the fear-stricken horde, Fred raced to his Washington hotel where he dashed off a story on the crushing defeat at Bull Run. Rushing to the telegraph office through the fog and rain, he sent his message to Michigan newspapers.

After a few hours rest, Fred returned to the battlefield. People from Manassas, Centreville, Washington and all around came looking for the bodies of their sons and husbands. Some had searched all night by lantern light. As he walked over the battlefield he saw sights that would be repeated thousands of times before the terrible struggle ended.

There was a weeping father and mother carrying the bloody body of a young son, one leg missing and with his blue uniform in tatters. There were gray-uniformed corpses mingled with those in blue. Many of these men would not be claimed for not only at Bull Run, but at any other battlefield, men died unidentified. Before future battles many soldiers printed their names on handkerchiefs which they pinned to their uniforms. Still, hundreds never were identified.

After an emotionally exhausting day, Fred returned to Washington. The wounded had been removed to hospitals and only unidentified dead lay in the hot sun awaiting burial.

Fred telegraphed a report of his day on the now quiet battlefield. His impression was that the North was humiliated by the defeat at Bull Run but they now knew the real war was ahead and their resolve was strengthened. The South was elated by their victory and likely were filled with overconfidence.

Fred decided a visit to Washington hospitals might produce a story. He found hotels, clubs, warehouses and other public buildings were converted into hospitals under the supervision of Dorothea L. Dix, a New England writer and social reformer. As Superintendent of the United States Army Nurses, Miss Dix had unlimited power. She sent out an appeal for women volunteers, and for enormous amounts of medical supplies.[1]

Sanitary conditions in Washington were not conducive to healthful living. New soldiers were pouring in by the tens of thousands and Miss Dix was responsible to a large degree for their health.

During his short stay in the city Fred noted that refuse from the government slaughter house spewed into a canal; few houses had drainage and slops were emptied in the streets; unsanitary privies mingled their stench with that of manure piles. Flies swarmed over food in the shops and on hotel tables.

At the East Street Infirmary, Fred met Miss Dix, a stern-appearing, dark-haired woman in her mid-fifties. Her plain black dress had a touch of white at the neck. Reluctantly she agreed to a short interview.

"Miss Dix," Fred began, "What do you consider to be your greatest need as Superintendent of Nurses?"

Her dark eyes clouded. "Clean hospitals, clean food, more nurses, more surgical dressings and supplies—the list is endless."

"What are the qualifications for nurses?"

"I have sent out a press release published in newspapers

throughout the North stating the requirements. Women should be thirty years of age to serve in government hospitals. Nurses are required to be plain-looking women. Their dresses must be brown or black, with no bows, no curls, no jewelry and no hoop skirts." A fleeting smile crossed her face. "Some of the women say they feel undressed without curls, jewels and hoop skirts. Especially hoop skirts!"

"Do the women need special training to apply?"

"Such a stipulation would be useless, Mr. Parker. There are practically no trained nurses in the country. Only the crisis of war would induce most women to become nurses. They have cared for husbands and sons for ailments from measles to smallpox, so now many of them feel called to follow their relatives and friends to military camps—and even to gory fields of battle."

Fred stopped writing. "I have a thirty-six year old unmarried sister who might be interested in nursing. Where would she apply?"

Miss Dix replied quickly. "Tell her to report at once to my house, corner of Fourteenth Street and New York Avenue here in Washington." She hesitated. "Tell her also that she will be paid forty cents a day and rations, clothing and medical attention all are included."

Fred got up and held out his hand. "Thank you, Miss Dix. You're performing an important service to the country. May I take a brief walk through the hospital?"

She nodded. " 'Tis not pretty, the things you'll see." They shook hands and she left quickly.

Hospital conditions were appalling. Some wounded men waiting for attention still lay in mud-stained uniforms. Flies buzzed about lighting on men's faces and on the bloody uniforms and open wounds. Groans came from unfortunate victims waiting for attention. The sweet smell of ether permeated the room where several amputees quietly slept on not knowing the shock they would receive when they wakened.

A surgeon in a bloody uniform passed through to select the next urgent case. He chose a young man whose arm was shattered at the elbow.

"Please don't cut it off," the young soldier begged.

The doctor shook his head. "We'll do what we can, Son," he said kindly.

Two or three dark clad nurses circulated through the big room as they cared for the suffering men. Fred realized the terrible need. The stench in the place was nauseating. Unwashed bodies, festering wounds, and many of the men were ill with dysentery which left them without bowel control. There was no way the few nurses could keep up with the work.

Feeling ill, Fred walked from the place. He couldn't publish a story about the horrors of the hospitals—not with northern families knowing their husbands and sons were confined in one of these places.

Later that night he poured out the abhorrent conditions he had observed in a letter to Josie. He was sure she would respond.

2   *1862*

THE WHEELS OF WAR GROUND ON. Abraham Lincoln's patience was sorely tried by General McClellan's inactivity. Seven months after the fiasco at Bull Run, McClellan still hadn't moved.

In April the battle known as Bloody Shiloh took place. Ulysses Grant with an army of more than forty thousand men met the southern army and forced them to retreat. Losses on both sides were heavy, but thirteen thousand

Union soldiers were lost. General Grant recalled the carnage more than twenty years later. He wrote, "I saw an open field, in our possession on the second day, over which the Confederates had made repeated charges the day before, so covered with dead that it would have been possible to walk across the clearing, in any direction, stepping on dead bodies, without a foot touching the ground." A total of twenty three thousand Rebel and Yankee men were lost in the battle of Shiloh as Rebels strove unsuccessfully to stem the Union's western invasion of the Confederacy. [2]

April 6 and 7, 1862, the days on which the battle of Shiloh was fought, were unseasonably hot. Many of the wounded and dying soldiers, thirsting for water, crawled to a small pond, staining it red as they drank. From that time it bore the name of "Bloody Pond."

Three separate desperate battles were fought at Antietam. The bloodletting lasted until dark. "The lanterns of the ambulance corps on both sides were soon flickering like fireflies on a southern river," writes Douglas Southall Freeman, "but they did not reach all corners of the field or penetrate the shadows in the woods and under the rocks where dead stiffened and the wounded cried out in vain for water." [3]

Again McClellan hesitated to press his advantage. Lee, knowing his shattered forces could not face another attack, took his army of Northern Virginia unmolested, as he recrossed the Potomac for home. McClellan made little effort to bother his retreating foe.

The North now held the advantage. On September 22, 1862, Lincoln issued the preliminary Emancipation Proclamation which was a warning to the South that on January 1, 1863, "all slaves within any state or district in rebellion against the United States shall be then, thenceforward, and forever free."

Mid-December, 1862, found citizens of both the North

and South weary of war. Soldiers of the North ate better than the Confederates. Billy Yank's staples included bread, meat, dried vegetables and coffee; Johnny Reb ate mostly cornbread and salted or pickled beef and pork. He had no coffee because of the Northern blockade.

However the Federal men complained loudly about their cracker ration, a flour and water biscuit about three inches square and one-half inch thick, which they called "hardtack." They said it broke their teeth and turned their stomach; it was usually filled with weevils. Dunking a biscuit in coffee brought the weevils to the surface where they were skimmed off. Some men preferred to eat hardtack in the dark. Ten crackers made up the daily bread ration in the field. The biscuits, smashed fine by a rifle butt, thickened stews and soups.

Pay for Union infantry privates was sixteen dollars a month; their Southern counterparts received eighteen dollars. The Yanks were more comfortably dressed for winter than the Rebels who often were cold and sometimes shoeless.

In one of his reports from the battle front Fred related this human interest story: "After the battle of Fredricksburg, Sergeant Richard Kirkland of the 2nd South Carolina could no longer stand the pitiful cries for water. Expecting a Yankee sharpshooters bullet, he bravely walked into that no-man's land. But no bullet came. He gave water to the nearest Federal, and the next. Time after time he returned for water for an hour and a half. He did not stop until he had attended every wounded man on his part of the front."[4]

The Northern General Burnside was defeated at Fredricksburg, and Lee chose not to attack. The Federals drew back and winter took command. Now it was clear to the Union and Confederacy alike, there would be more. Much more.

3 _____ *1863*

It was a wintry day in early 1863 when the shivering Federal and Confederate soldiers stared at one another across the Rappahannock. A Union band serenaded the South with Northern tunes. The Rebels on picket duty shouted for their own songs. Immediately the band struck up the lilting music of "Dixie," "Maryland, My Maryland," and "The Bonnie Blue Flag." A cheer rose from the Confederate men. Then, after a moment of silence, the band sent forth the sad notes of "Home, Sweet Home." Men on both sides of the river shouted in joy and tears filled many veterans' eyes. Love of home and misery had momentarily united the estranged Americans. [5]

Scurvy cut soldiers down the winter of 1863. For a time Federal soldiers ate nothing but salt pork and hardtack. Confederates also fared poorly. General Lee wrote, "Their ration consists of one-fourth pound of bacon, 18 ounces of flour, 10 pounds of rice to each 100 men about every third day, with some few peas and dried fruit when it can be obtained."

The specter of death by freezing hung over both camps. Some wounded Northern boys died in unheated hospital tents. Many Southerners slept without blankets. Both armies existed by living in holes scraped from the ground with rough log huts thrown up over them.

At home in both the North and the South, soldiers' wives worked desperately to feed and clothe their families as they prayed against word of death, which often arrived.

Now towns and cities took back their sons who had been used in battle and discarded—the empty-sleeved ones, the hobbling and legless. The South felt hunger pangs as inflation soared. Everything in the food and clothing lines became either prohibitive in price or non-existent in supply.

Enterprising Confederate women sewed coverings for their feet from pieces of carpeting already cut up for soldiers blankets. Hats were plaited from dried and bleached palmetto, with chicken feathers decorating them. Dresses were fashioned from window drapery.

But bad as it was, it would grow worse. Both presidents, Lincoln and Davis, became whipping boys for politicians. After twenty months of war, the Confederacy had won only a tenuous stalemate. Davis, who was blind in one eye and constantly pained by facial neuralgia and serious digestion problems, did his duty as he saw it.

In 1863 the North had little to show for its war effort but misery and disappointment. Press, politicians and ordinary citizens poured venom on the hapless Lincoln. Many people were fed up with the war and blamed the president's choice of generals, harped on the way he conducted operations and ranted against the mounting inflation.

Another deplorable situation was the condition of the hospitals. Superintendent of Nurses and appointee of the United States Sanitary Commission, Dorothea Dix worked untiringly to secure nurses, medical supplies and clean hospitals. Disliked by surgeons of the Medical Bureau who resented the "unnecessary intrusion of petticoats prying and poking about and exceeding their authority," Miss Dix continued fighting for reforms as she prepared hospitals for the wounded sure to come, whether from victory or defeat. [6]

At first word of an impending battle, Miss Dix dispatched nurses to the area where a makeshift hospital was set up so that army surgeons could extract bullets and make amputations.

Later the wounded, exhausted, bleeding troops were

transported to regular hospitals, if there was room. Many times the wounded were left lying in the gutters and nurses were sent to attend to them there.

Early in the war no one had thought to prepare for the wounded. It had been assumed that each regiment would care for its men with its own surgeons and equipment. But this did not work for the regiments were hopelessly intermingled, and the hospital tents were far in the rear. There was no ambulance corps and a shortage of everything from tents to cooking equipment, food and uniforms.

After Josephine Parker received her brother Fred's letter informing her of the deplorable hospital conditions and the need for nurses, she spoke with Laura Haviland. Together they decided that since the Emancipation Proclamation had freed the slaves and their work in the Underground Railroad had ended, they should volunteer as nurses. A short time later they were in Washington housed in Ebbitt House on the second floor of the rambling old hotel on F Street near Willard's. Cots were set up for nurses and crowded into spaces left over from stacks and bundles of hospital supplies.

Josephine threw herself into the work with her usual enthusiasm. Along with most of the nurses she studied from cover to cover the little book written by Dorothea Dix titled *Hints On Nursing.* Like all nurses, Josie was sent to hospitals where, at the time, the need was greatest. This might be an emergency tent in a battle zone, a village or city hospital. She dressed wounds, bathed and fed men too ill to help themselves, changed beds, listened to feverish ramblings and hallucinations, comforted the dying and wrote letters for the homesick, ill, wounded young men. At times she was pressed into assisting the surgeon with amputations in battleground tents or in a private home which had been commandeered for an emergency hospital.

Josie's nursing duties also included caring for soldiers ill with contagious diseases such as typhoid fever, diphtheria, smallpox, dysentery and consumption. She worked sixteen- and eighteen-hour days on many occasions until finally she could fall into bed for a few hours of restless sleep.

In her exhaustion the names of battles became a blur, the men an endless confusion of humanity with every ill imaginable. Chanscellorsville, Vicksburg, Chickamauga, and Chattanooga became names which meant hundreds of suffering, wounded, dying men—and always there was the shortage of supplies—ether, medication, bandages, bedding and blankets. Some of the field hospital tents had no stoves. Josie knew many men died in winter of exposure who might have recovered in more favorable circumstances, just as many died of infection and blood poisoning who might have survived with proper sanitary conditions and medica- tion.

Soon Josie went mechanically from bed to bed doing what she could to comfort the suffering soldiers. Eventu- ally they all looked alike to her—pale, drawn, suffering faces, and bodies writhing in agony. She tried to concen- trate on the wounds instead of the faces.

In Alexandria one day she said cheerfully, "Let's see what we have here. Hm-m-m." She inspected and removed the muddy bandage from a bloody gangrenous thigh wound. "When did this happen?"

The soldier gasped. She continued probing. The man had a fever. "I'll be as careful as I can. We have to clean the wound. When did it happen?" She continued probing.

"Josie!" the man exclaimed. "My God, 'tis Josie!"

Startled, she stared at the gaunt dark face, the black hair and eyes. "Jake!" Her voice caught. "Jake! I can't be- lieve it! Where have you been all these years?"

"Twenty-three years since I've seen you," he said softly.

She seized his hand. "Why didn't you write to let me know where you were? I've wondered."

"I thought you likely were married—that you'd forgotten about me."

Tears streamed down her face. "No. No, I'm not married." She hesitated. "Are you?"

He silently shook his head. She squeezed his hand. "We have to take care of your leg. I'll get bandages and we'll clean it. I'll be right back."

Later as she cleaned the hot, festering wound, they talked of their childhood. "Remember how we liked to climb trees?" Josie asked.

Jake flinched as she probed deeply. "Yeah, I remember. You'd climb higher than I wanted to, but I did it to keep up with you."

She smiled. There had been so little to smile about since she had been nursing. "Papa always said I was a dare devil." After a moment she told him briefly of her Underground Railroad activities and of Laura Haviland.

Jake said, "I remember the Havilands. But working for the Underground—that was dangerous."

She nodded. "Jake, where have you been since you left Adrian?"

He rubbed his feverish forehead. "I don't know anything about my people or the tribe. I guess they're somewhere west of the Mississippi. I've been in Ohio. I worked as a hired man there." He flinched as she continued cleaning the wound. "Does it look bad?" he asked.

"Well—I've seen worse, and I've seen better."

"Think they'll have to amputate?"

She didn't answer for a time. Finally she said, "I'll have the surgeon look at it." She bandaged the thigh and took his hand. "I have to go now. I'll see you as often as I can. I'll ask the surgeon to see you soon."

As she looked into his dark eyes she recalled that Indians seldom smile. "I'm glad I found you," he said softly. That was all he said, but knowing Jake, it was enough. He felt as she did—happy they were together again.

The next morning Jake's right leg was amputated between the hip and knee. Stoically he accepted the surgeon's decision, and stoically he faced the future; Indian-like, there were no complaints.

Josie professed a cheerfulness she did not feel. "Soon you'll be around on crutches," she promised, "and when your stump heals, you'll get along fine with a wooden leg." When he didn't answer she said, "Jake, you'll soon be able to leave the hospital. Then I want you to promise me you'll go to our old home at Adrian. Emily still is there and we have a brother, Daniel, who is twenty-two. He lives with Emily. Mama died when Daniel was born," she explained. "I want you to go there to live. After the war, when I'm home, we'll—make plans."

His solemn dark eyes met hers. "You'd best forget me."

"Don't say that, Jake! I've waited twenty-three years to find you again! Promise you'll go to Adrian. I'll write the family to tell them you're coming."

"I'll think about it." He stared at the spot under the sheet where his right leg ended.

Josie rambled on. "Remember, I told you how we lost our little brother Jimmy in Detroit in 1830?" He nodded. "He was kidnapped and brought up by a Michigan Indian tribe. He works for Laura Haviland and he's married to his Indian sweetheart, Owasco. He's as much Indian as you are."

"I'd like to meet him."

"You will when you get to Adrian. I'll write Emily to expect you when you're released. You can take the train to Toledo and right on to Adrian."

Reluctantly he agreed he'd wait at Adrian until she returned. "But," he added, "we won't make plans for—for anything until the war is over."

Quickly she bent and kissed him on the forehead. Loud

derisive hoots came from several of the soldiers. "Bear, how do you do it?" one called. Another shouted, "Nurse! My leg's off too!" Still another laughed, "It's always the dark, silent fellows the nurses like!"

"You're all wrong," Josie joked. "I like his unusual last name. Bear. I'll bet you've never known another man named Bear. Jake Bear. 'Tis a nice name."

Josie's face was flushed as she went to the next ward. Here she attended to the men ill with scurvy and dysentery caused by inadequate army diet. She knew Miss Dix often went to the Sanitary Commission to beg for healthful foods to supplement the soldiers diets—vegetables, jellies, jams, dried fruits—to prevent the spread of scurvy. She also had seen Miss Dix's reaction to carelessness, inefficency and drunkeness on the part of doctors on duty. The woman expressed her displeasure with caustic energy which endeared her to patients but caused surgeons and other officers to view her visits with dismay. She was protective of her army of nurses.

Josephine recalled the day Miss Dix had sent her to the hospital near a recent battleground. She had been warned that the surgeon in charge disliked Miss Dix. "Proceed with your work," she had said, "and take no notice of opposition he gives you."

As she arrived at the old brick hospital, ambulances were unloading victims. Josephine edged her way in through a double line of stretchers, one with wounded going in, the other with dead being carried out.

From the start it was obvious the surgeon would oppose her. "Follow us," he said gruffly. Obediently she accompanied him and his assistant through the dirty wards so filled with cots there was scarcely room to move between them. The smell of blood and pus was overpowering in the August heat. Many of the men had been lying for days, their wounds not dressed. Josie was given the repulsive task of

changing dressings. There were no instructions but if she
failed to do what was expected, she was sharply criticized.
She was given no place to sleep. Sometimes a nurse would
let her use her room, and she would drag in a straw-filled
tick and place it on the floor. She overheard the surgeon
remark, "We'll make it so hot for that Dix woman's nurse
that she won't stay long. We don't need them snooping
around here."

After some weeks Dorothea Dix came to inspect the
hospital. She smiled warmly at Josie. "You must bear it a
while longer, my child." She stayed. It was a torturing experience but her stubbornness and loyalty to Miss Dix won
the day for finally the inefficient nurses in the hospital
were replaced by those of Miss Dix's selection.

Josephine, tense from the activities of the day, tried to
relax on her cot but her mind went back to her duty at the
Union Hotel in Georgetown which now was used as a hospital. Within a few days of her arrival there, the ambulances started bringing victims from the terrible Northern
defeat at Fredricksburg in December of 1862. Ambulances
brought gaunt, pale men, mud to their knees, bloody gangrenous wounds with bandages untouched for days. She had
rushed from cases of pneumonia, typhoid and diphtheria to
those of amputations and pus-filled sores. She recalled a letter she had written to Emily at the time: "I'm up at six,
dress by gaslight, hurry through my ward and throw open
the windows. The men grumble and shudder, but the air is
bad, and no one pays attention to requests for better venti-
lation, so I do what I can. Poke up the fire, get extra blankets and joke with the men, but I continue opening doors
and windows as if my life depended on it. And mine does,
and others too, for this place is a pestilence box—cold,
damp, dirty and full of putrid odors. There's no competent
person in charge, and a jumble of indifferent nurses, surgeons and attendants complicate the chaos even more.

"After this introduction to the day, Emily, I go to breakfast with little appetite for fried beef, salty butter, husky bread and dishwater coffee." [7]

Josie tossed restlessly on her straw tick. She must sleep. She was hungry but rats had eaten the cheese she'd bought and there were weevils in the crackers. Jake—her heart ached for him. Silent, stoic in the Indian way, she knew how deeply he resented the amputation. But he would have died without it. There still might be a life together for them after the war, if she could instill some hope in his mind. At last she slept.

Two days later she bade Jake goodbye as she left for Gettysburg. Dorothea Dix was sending all her available nurses. She cooperated with Secretary Stanton in an endeavor to keep unauthorized volunteers out of the battle area. Josie saw the frail woman standing in the broiling July heat at the Baltimore station trying to keep unauthorized women from boarding the train to the front. Only those with passes from the Sanitary or Christian Commissions were permitted to go to the battle area for crowds would create pandemonium in an already hopelessly confused situation.

On July 1, 2, and 3 of 1863 the terrible battle of Gettysburg was fought. Lee, confident from the recent Confederate victory at Chancellorsville, decided in June to invade the North. The Army of the Potomac was now in command of General George G. Meade.

For the first three days of July, a Northern army of ninety thousand men met a Southern army of seventy-five thousand in the greatest battle ever fought in the Western Hemisphere. After two days of seesaw attacks and counterattacks, Lee decided to aim directly at the center of the Union line. After a fierce artillery duel, he ordered fifteen thousand men under General George E. Pickett to charge the Union lines. The fifteen thousand men, marching in perfect formation, swept across an open field and up the slopes ignoring the murderous enemy fire. Only a fraction of the Confederate troops reached the crest of the ridge where for twenty dreadful minutes they held their ground. Then they yielded to superior Union strength and fell back.

At last the slaughter ended—a total of forty thousand dead and wounded. In the broiling July sun, seventeen thousand five hundred Union men lay mingled with twenty five thousand five hundred of their Confederate brothers. Lee withdrew his battered army to Virginia. The Northern victory marked the turning point in the war, for never again did Lee have the strength for a major offensive. [8]

And once again the army nurses faced the hopeless task of caring for the wounded in hastily thrown together temporary hospitals in barns, homes and churches.

But there was still more to come.

1864 - 1865

4

FARMERS ALL OVER THE NORTH worked from daylight to dark during the war years to wrest every possible bushel of grain from the land. Prices were good though inflation never reached the level that it had in the South where the *Free Press* reported that while the six-week siege raged for control of Vicksburg, Mississippi, the starving city saw wheat sell for one hundred dollars per bushel and rats appeared for sale in food stores. [9]

As Hank and Daniel stacked their sheaves of wheat, Hank said, "Farming's getting easier. We have our new reaper and the threshing machine will be along in a few days. It's better than when our father had to cradle and flail the grain by hand. Now a few men do in hours the work that used to take days. The war, terrible as it is, has brought prosperity to farmers."

"Yeah."

"I've got my farm, the old Martin place, almost paid for." Hank brushed a sweat bee from his face. He removed his straw hat and mopped his forehead. "It's none of my business, but I've wondered if you're saving your money. You've made quite a bit working for me and from your share of the income from Pa's farm. Are you saving it?"

"Yeah. Emily helps me at the bank."

"Good old Emily. Soon now, Jake Bear, Josie's Indian friend will be here to live with you and Emily. Think you'll like him?"

"I don't know any Indians."

"You know Owasco—and Jim's more Indian than white."

"I like them—and the twins." The mentally handicapped young man smiled. "We play games together."

"You'll like Jake. I remember him." He threw another bundle from the wagon to Daniel. "Someday this damned war will be over. It's already been more than three and one-half years. And now Sherman's trying to trap Johnston so we can capture Atlanta. The paper says our men are on the outskirts of the city. 'Twould help Lincoln to be reelected if Sherman could take Atlanta before the November election."

"Yeah."

"Daniel, did you know Grant's initials, 'U. S.,' stand for 'Unconditional Surrender'?"

The young man laughed. "That's funny."

"And did you know we have a regiment of colored Michigan soldiers in the war?" Hank asked.

"Do they fight good?"

"According to Fred's reports they do. Their regiment took part in an expedition through eastern Florida where they built a fort. The colored Michigan 102nd have been in several skirmishes to disable the Savannah and Charleston Railroad. Finally they met the enemy in force and a battle was fought. They fought with determination and according to reports, though many men were severely wounded and blood was flowing from their wounds, they refused to go to the rear. Now the white regiments who have fought beside them hold them in high regard." [10, 11]

And so the wheels of war relentlessly ground on. President Jefferson Davis in the South lacked Lincoln's mental and physical vigor. He also lacked Lincoln's skill in managing men. The economy of the South was strained almost to the breaking point by the demands of the total war. As the North tightened the blockade, imports dwindled. Southern factories were unable to produce needed resources. Inflation raged and weakened the people's will to fight, but they stubbornly refused to surrender.

In both the North and South, songs showed the spirit of the people. Northerners hummed "The Battle Hymn of the Republic," "Tenting On the Old Camp Ground," and "When Johnny Comes Marching Home." In Michigan everyone sang the popular "Michigan, My Michigan," while citizens of the South marched to war to the stirring music of "Dixie" and "The Bonnie Blue Flag."

Finally on November 15 Sherman's troops left Atlanta in flames, and his sixty thousand men set out for Savannah. As they marched across Georgia virtually unopposed, they destroyed civilian property and laid waste to anything that might help the South to continue fighting.

In their Owosso home John and Marie Thompson and their thirteen-year-old adopted daughter, Anne Anderson, gathered around the kerosene lamp-lighted table to read a newspaper. Silently they read accounts of the rape of Georgia by Sherman and his men. There were stories of stripped houses, barns and fields, of ruined crops, of railroad tracks torn up and the ties burned. Sherman boldly estimated that his men destroyed one hundred million dollars worth of property in Georgia. He hoped the horrible destruction would break the will of the South and bring them to their knees, and thus bring about an end to the war.

Anne put the paper down. "I'm not going to read any more of this. It scares me." Her voice caught. "Maybe Andrew is there where these awful things are happening."

Marie patted the child's hand. "We hope he's not." She hesitated. "We've not heard from him in so long, maybe he's been captured. At least, then he'd be safe."

John cleared his throat, started to speak, but thought better of it. He had heard reports of the terrible conditions of the prisons. Starvation, epidemics, men dying like flies. He had heard that seven of every ten deaths were due to sickness and disease in this war. If Andrew was a prisoner he well might starve to death in a southern prison. If the civilians were starving their prisoners must be in a deplorable condition.

Marie rubbed her forehead. "Maybe we'll get a letter soon. But I don't understand why the North needs to destroy the cities and the crops and farm buildings. Why, they burn everything they can't use. So the Southern people are the enemy, but I know how we'd feel if our animals were taken and our buildings burned." She sighed. "I pray it will end soon."

John added, "They're defeated but they won't admit it. The South reminds me of a chicken with its head cut off. They flop and jump and jerk, but it doesn't do any good because they have no head to direct them. The South is in its death dance now—jerking and flopping around with no real head."

Anne said, "Maybe we'll hear from Andrew soon. Or maybe Aunt Josephine or Uncle Fred will run across him somewhere."

John struggled to his feet and stood with the aid of his crutches. "One day this war will end and we'll have a hilarious family reunion," he said cheerfully. Neither Anne or Marie replied.

The long winter of 1864-1865 passed. In their reports Fred and other news correspondents predicted an early end to the war. On April 2 Confederate troops gave up Petersburg and Richmond. Then on April 9, 1865, word came over the wires that Lee had surrendered to Grant at the Appomattox Court House in Virginia.

People in the North were jubilant. The war was over, the South was conquered and soon their loved ones would return. Victory celebrations were held in every community.

Then on April 14 a new disaster struck the country. President Lincoln was assassinated at Ford's Theater in Washington by an actor, John Wilkes Booth. Families pored over copies of the latest newspapers. The word fell like a thunderbolt on citizens of the North where cities and towns wore a funeral aspect for the solemn black garb of mourning draped nearly every building.

In Northern homes the assassination of the president was the main topic of conversation. Jim Parker discussed the tragedy with Owasco. "Remember last fall the *Free Press* called Lincoln the most miserable, civil, military and financial failure the world had ever seen? And they said his reelection would bring untold misery to every family in the land?"

Owasco's eyes were sad. "I remember. But now he's dead, he's praised for his goodness. It's too bad he didn't know while he was living how much he was loved."

The twins ran in from outside. "It's summer!" Dan shouted. "Can we go barefooted?"

Owasco shook her head. "Two days ago we had snow. The ground is cold. Wait a few weeks."

Sam stamped his foot. "We want to go barefooted now!"

"You heard your mother. Go outside and play," Jim said.

Both boys frowned as they stamped outside. Owasco smiled. "Indian children never act that way. That must be their Grandfather Parker's disposition showing."

Jim's face was serious. "We'll have to be strict to keep them in line. You're right, they have Henry Parker blood." He hesitated, then said slowly, "Fred, Emily and Josephine say I was his favorite before—before I was taken away. They say he mourned for me all the years I was gone. But when I came back he didn't have one word of welcome for me. His first words were, 'Where in hell have you been?' And he was mad! He never spoke a kind word to me after I was back." Jim paused. "I don't want our boys to be like him."

"Your father was a strange man," Owasco said. "What is it white folks say—he blows hot or cold?"

"I can't understand it. He seemed to get along with the girls, but his sons—none of us pleased him. Fred, Daniel and I were disappointments to him. Hank is his son too, but he liked him. And poor Daniel, I wonder how many times he was told by our father that he was stupid?"

Owasco murmured, "Poor Daniel."

5 _____ *1866*

O<small>NCE AGAIN THE</small> U<small>NITED</small> S<small>TATES</small> was at peace, but the effects of the Civil War would be felt for years to come. About one million men were killed or wounded. Deaths, including those from disease, totaled more than five hundred twenty-nine thousand. [12]

Because most of the fighting occurred in the South,

they suffered the worst damage. Many Southern cities and towns were destroyed and farmlands and fine old homes lay in ruins. Railroads had been destroyed and trade and industry almost stopped. The economy of the South completely collapsed.

But many people felt the most important result of the war was the heritage of hate that was left on both sides. Many Southerners grew bitter in defeat and some Northerners were revengeful.

On July 4, 1866, the Parker relatives met for a reunion at the old homestead near Adrian. While the women chatted as they worked in the kitchen, the men sat under the shade trees in the yard drinking beer and cold tea.

Fred leaned against an ancient oak. The wind gently ruffled the leaves. "This is peaceful," he sighed. "All the wanderlust has gone out of me."

"You'll stay in Adrian?" Hank asked.

He nodded. "I'm buying the *Gazette,* and in my spare time I have ideas for several books buzzing about in my mind."

Hank chuckled. "We half expected you'd come home from the war with a Southern bride."

Fred shook his head. "I'm near fifty years old and set in my ways. No woman would put up with me—and I'm like Pa was—I don't change easily." He glanced at his uncle, John Thompson. "You weren't young when you married Aunt Marie."

John sat on a straight chair, his crutches beside him. His hair was snow white and his face lined with wrinkles. "I'm seventy-three years old, but the best years of my life have been since Marie and I have been together and we found Andrew and Anne on the Orphan Train. God has been good to me."

"You did a lot of good, too, Uncle John," Jim commented. "I remember when I was small and you'd visit our camp. You praised me because I was a good shot with the bow and arrow and I could run faster than the other boys. I could never understand why my Indian parents and the other braves were uneasy when you were with us. Of course they were afraid you'd figure out I was the lost Jimmy Parker. When we'd talk with other tribes they often spoke of your visiting and praying with them."

" 'Twas an interesting life. There's still work to be done with the Indians, Jim. Our government has treated them poorly," John said.

Andrew's face showed concern. "While I was in the prison at Andersonville I had plenty of time to think. I decided I want to be a minister and carry on your work with the Indians. Maybe I can have influence in bettering conditions for them as well as preaching the gospel. Of course I'll have several years of study before I'm ready to start."

A rare smile flashed across Jim's face. "I almost envy you the opportunity to work with my people." He hesitated, embarrassed. "Though I'm of Parker blood, I still feel I'm an Indian," he explained. "But Owasco and I will stay with Mrs. Haviland. She needs us to keep things going at the Raisin Institute."

Fred commented, "She's a busy lady. She must be close to sixty years old."

Jim nodded. "She's working on the temperance thing now. She wouldn't approve of this." He held up his mug of beer. "She's started a women's temperance group called the 'Women's Christian Temperance Union,' WCTU for short."

Hank added, "And someone said she's soon starting a Girls' Training School here in Adrian, and the Boys' Vocational Home in Lansing already is operating. Then she's into prison reform, I understand."

"There's plenty to be done to improve the prisons," Andrew commented drily.

Jake Bear had been silent while the others talked. His

back against a tree, his peg leg extended before him, he studied the changing cloud patterns in the sky.

"Jake," Andrew began, "What do you think of my plan to work with the Indians?"

"It's good," he replied.

"I'll need all the help I can get. I'll come to you and Jim and Owasco and my parents many times with questions, I'm sure."

Hank said, "Jake, I understand you and Josie are talking of buying the old homestead."

"We'd like to, if we can settle on a price with all of you. Josie would be happy here, and this also was my home," he motioned, "down the road there, when I was young." He glanced at Daniel. "And if we buy the place, we'd like Daniel to be our hired man."

The mentally retarded young man smiled. "I'd like that. I never worked anywhere but here."

Jim's five-year-old twins came tearing down the steps. "Aunt Emily says we'll soon be ready to eat! There's lots of good things!" Sam shouted.

"Chicken and ham and cherry pie and cake—and lots more!" Dan yelled.

"Nice boys you have, Jim," Fred said seriously.

Jim nodded. "But they've got Henry Parker blood. They are hard to handle sometimes. We have to keep a tight rein on them."

Hank said, "Sarah's in the family way."

"Congratulations!" Fred exclaimed. "The family is growing."

Fourteen family members gathered around the picnic table under the trees. John said grace after which they sang, "Blest Be the Tie that Binds." After a leisurely meal the women cleared the table and washed dishes as they chatted.

"It's good to have all of you home," Emily said brushing

back a gray-streaked lock of hair. "During the war I often thought what Grandma Parker used to say back in New York about slavery. She'd say, 'If we sow the wind, we'll reap the whirlwind.' "

Josephine nodded. "I remember that, too. I didn't know what she meant, but it sounded funny to me. Remember Emily, how she always said 'thee, thou and thy'?"

"Sow the wind and reap the whirlwind. That's from the Bible, Book of Hosea, I believe," Marie added. "I've often heard John use that expression. Our country surely proved that quotation is true in the awful war we went through."

Owasco said, "I don't like to think of all those young men who were killed. Josephine, you're a strong woman to have been able to see the terrible sights you saw, and to live and work in the hospitals all those months."

Josephine answered, "It was hard, but if I hadn't gone, I wouldn't have found Jake. We understand one another. If we hadn't found each other, neither of us would have married. Now if we can have a child or two, life will be complete." She paused. "That is if the family will agree to sell us the farm."

Emily put an arm about Josephine's shoulders. "I think we all would like that. And I know Mama would be happy about it, if she knew, and Papa too, in his strange way."

They were silent, each one satisfied with their life.

References

[1, 6, 7]Dorothy Clark Wilson, *Stranger and Traveler* (Little, Brown & Co., 1975).

[2, 3, 4, 5]Robert Paul Jordan, "The Civil War" *(National Geographic,* 1969).

[9, 11, 12]*World Book Encyclopedia,* C Book *(See* "Civil War").

[8]Bernice M. Chappel, *Bittersweet Trail* (Great Lakes Books, 1984).

[10]Jno. Robertson, *Michigan in the War* (Lansing, W. S. George & Co., 1882), pp. 488-491.

Appendix

Historical Characters Mentioned in 'REAP THE WHIRLWIND'

Anthony, Susan B.
Ball, Daniel
Baughman, John
Baw-Beese (Chief)
Beauregard, Pierre (General)
Bingham, Kinsley S.
Brown, Cornelia & Joseph
Brown, John
Blackbird, Arthur J.
Blackbird (Chief)
Blackbird, Margaret
Blackburn (Family)
Black Hawk (Chief)
Blanchard, Stillman
Bolieu, Henry & Angelique
Bowerman, Tom
Brainard (Family)
Burnside, Ambrose (General)
Cadmus (Family)
Cass, Lewis
Chandler, Margaret

Clay, Henry
Coffin, Catherine & Levi
Collier, Rufus
Comstock, Addison
Comstock, Elias
Crooks, Henry
Crosswhite, Adam (Family)
Davis, Jefferson
Dix, Dorothea L.
Douglass, Frederick
Fish, David
Fletcher, Daniel
Freeman, Douglas Southall
French, Isaac
Goodrich, Ira
Gould, Daniel
Gould, Ebenezer
Grant, Ulysses
Gregory, E. D.
Griswold, John
Hall, Simon

Other Books By
BERNICE M. CHAPPEL

IN THE PALM OF THE MITTEN

This book is full of delightful Michigan nostalgia, written by a lifetime Michiganian. Experience the joys and sorrows of the Klein family in this autobiographical saga of the years before 1924 in Michigan's rural Livingston County.

Experience family reunions, rural school education, sickness and health, life and death. History through the charm of nostalgia! 'The good old days' spring to life in this exciting tale of the early 1900's.

285 pages, 40 photographs

ISBN: 0-9606400-0-2 (Paperback) $7.95

BITTERSWEET TRAIL

Bittersweet Trail provides genuine entertainment as you travel back in time 150 years and history comes alive. This book depicts a four-generation saga of an American family in the 1800's. From the felling of forest trees in 1836 the reader will travel through this account of the settlement of Michigan's remote areas to the latter years of the 19th century.

471 pages, 20 photographs

ISBN: 0-9606400-1-0 (Hardbound) $12.95
0-9606400-2-9 (Paperback) $9.95

LURE OF THE ARCTIC

Lure of the Arctic is an authentic story of past and present Eskimo life. It provides action, adventure and suspense in a narrative of Canada's Northwest Territories. If you are a reader who loves the outdoors and has a hankering for adventure and suspense, Lure of the Arctic will transport you to the beautiful but unforgiving region of the Mackenzie River Delta area in Canada's Northwest Territories.

267 pages, 1 map and 37 illustrations

ISBN: 9611596-2-6 (Paperback) $10.95

Satisfaction Guaranteed. You may return books within 10 days for a full refund if not entirely pleased. Send order to:

Wilderness Adventure Books
320 Garden Lane, Box 968
Fowlerville, Michigan 48836

Wilderness Adventure Books
320 Garden Lane P. O. Box 968
Fowlerville, MI 48836

Please send me:

_____ copies of **REAP THE WHIRLWIND**   at $10.95 US $ _____
_____ copies of **LURE OF THE ARCTIC**   at $10.95 US $ _____
_____ copies of **BITTERSWEET TRAIL**   at $9.95 US $ _____
_____ copies of **PALM OF THE MITTEN**   at $7.95 US $ _____

Postage will be paid by publisher. Send check or money order — no cash or C.O.D.

Autographed □ Yes   □ No

Mr./Mrs./Ms. _____

Street _____

City _____ State/Province _____ ZIP _____